SILVER TOWN WOLF: HOME for the HOLIDAYS

TERRY SPEAR

sourcebooks
casablanca

Published by Sourcebooks Casablanca, an imprint of Sourcebooks
P.O. Box 4410, Naperville, Illinois 60567-4410
(630) 961-3900
sourcebooks.com

Printed and bound in the United States of America.
OPM 10 9 8 7 6 5 4 3 2 1

Howling Good Holiday Reads

"An enchanting tale of kismet—werewolf style!"
— *Fresh Fiction* for *Dreaming of a White Wolf Christmas*

"The best of holiday romances...a howling good time."
— *Long and Short Reviews* for *A Silver Wolf Christmas*

"There is nothing like a marvelously captivating paranormal romance by Terry Spear to get you in the holiday spirit."
— *Tome Tender* for *A Highland Wolf Christmas*

"A holiday treat—romance that sizzles and entertains."
— *Fresh Fiction* for *A Highland Wolf Christmas*

"A witty, passionate paranormal romance that will lift your spirits... Ms. Spear is an amazingly gifted storyteller."
— *Romance Junkies* for *A Highland Wolf Christmas*

"Edge-of-your-seat action... Spear's wonderful gifts as a writer [are] on clear display."
— *RT Book Reviews* for *A SEAL Wolf Christmas* 4 stars

"Delectable...a 'Recommended Read' for Christmas and all year long!"
— *Romance Junkies* for *A SEAL Wolf Christmas*

"Sensuous, heartwarming romance, enhanced by an adorable wolf pup and wintertime fun."
— *Library Journal* for *A Very Jaguar Christmas*

Also by Terry Spear

Mary Riley Pettigrew made my day when she said this to me on Facebook: "You're going to laugh…but you can't write them fast enough for me… I LOVE your books!" She doesn't know how much that means to me while I'm working on another book. Thanks, Mary! I dedicate this book to you!

Chapter 1

"I HAVE TO CHANGE CLOTHES," MEGHAN MACTIRE SAID to her sisters, Laurel and Ellie. She was feeling a little anxious about the date she was going on with Sheriff Peter Jorgenson tonight, since she needed to tell him about her psychic ability to speak with and see ghosts.

Running their Victorian inn in wolf-run Silver Town, Colorado, had been keeping the triplet sister busy during the holiday season. And now it was just ten days until Christmas. Meghan had hoped she and the sheriff could go to her home for an intimate dinner and watch Christmas movies, like they'd been doing whenever they could get the free time. But tonight he wanted to take her out to the Silver Town Tavern. The food and atmosphere were great there, and it was private membership, so only wolves were allowed. Still, it wasn't as relaxing after a hectic day. Especially when everyone in the pack was wondering if Peter and she were mating. If not, other bachelor males in the pack were waiting in the wings. Some were sure to see her and Peter at the tavern and would be keeping an eye on their relationship.

"Do you think he's going to ask you tonight if you want to mate him?" Laurel asked. Her sisters had been dying to know when Peter would pop the question. They were both mated to Silver brothers and couldn't wait until Meghan was mated as well.

"I don't know. I'll let you in on it if it happens, you

know." Meghan had been dating Peter for over a year now, not really typical but everyone was different. Sam and Silva, owners of a tea shop and the tavern, had dated for years before they finally tied the knot. Peter didn't seem to be in a rush to ask Meghan to mate him, and *she* needed to discuss some issues with him that could affect how he viewed her.

Besides her ghost abilities, she had sent a wolf to prison before she moved to Silver Town, something one of their kind was never to do, and she hated to tell Peter. Even if he could live with what she'd done, she didn't want anyone else in the pack to know. Would he be willing to keep her dark secret? Or would it bother him that he had to?

She could imagine the news getting out to the rest of the pack, and she knew some would no longer see her the same way. She wished that night had never happened, but it had. And there was nothing she could do to take it back.

She'd been so hurt the last time she'd mentioned it to a wolf boyfriend that she never wanted to discuss it with anyone again. The ex-boyfriend and her sisters were the only ones who knew. But she had to tell Peter before long. Tomorrow night. She couldn't do it at the tavern. She had to talk to him privately about it before he asked her if she wanted to mate him, and she thought he might ask soon. She kept thinking something might be holding him back too, some dark secret of his own. Unless she was projecting her own mistake on him.

Meghan managed a smile for her sisters before she became too melancholy thinking about the notion. She pulled on her coat and headed for the back door of the inn.

"Have fun," Laurel and Ellie both said.

"Thanks!" Meghan hurried outside to reach her

Victorian house through the snow-covered garden. Just in case Peter proposed, she planned to wear a red satin dress, hoping she didn't look too overdressed, as if she was expecting something to happen. But it *was* Christmastime, and she was going to dress up since she didn't normally.

When she arrived home, she went upstairs to her bedroom and pulled the dress out of the closet. Maybe it would be a little much. Too dressy. Too shiny. Too sexy. Maybe she should just wear a green sweater and her MacTire plaid skirt and boots.

She brought them out and laid them next to the red dress on the canopied Victorian replica bed. She stripped out of her slacks and sweater and considered both outfits. It was cold out. Really cold out. And snowy.

She eyed the red dress. She'd never worn it for Peter. Hopefully, it wouldn't be the wrong choice. She pulled off her bra and put on the red strapless one she'd purchased to wear with the dress. Then she pulled on the dress and struggled to reach the zipper on the low, low back. *Darn it.* She couldn't reach it, no matter how hard she tried. She'd only worn the dress once—to a Christmas party two years ago when she and her sisters still lived in St. Augustine, Florida—and she'd forgotten she needed help with the zipper.

Before Peter arrived, she called Laurel. "Hey, I can't get my zipper zipped. Can either you or Ellie come over and zip it up for me?"

"Ohmigod, you're wearing *the* red dress. I'll be right over. Unless you want Peter to zip it up for you."

"*Right.* Hurry, before he gets here." Meghan hated to ask. She knew Laurel would tell Ellie that Meghan was wearing *the* dress, created to hook a guy for sure. Yes, it was an eye-catcher, but she'd never caught a wolf's attention while wearing it.

She brought out her red high heels before Laurel arrived. If Peter proposed, she wanted to be dressed for the occasion, though she reminded herself they still had to talk before she could say yes.

Deputy CJ Silver watched as Peter hurried to get his Stetson and the dark-brown suede coat lined with sherpa fleece that kept him warm on cold, snowy days like today. He was eager to pick Meghan up for the date.

"I think it's a great idea to take Meghan to the tavern for dinner, but you really gotta tell her about your late wife, Peter," CJ warned.

"I will. The time just hasn't been right."

CJ snorted. "It will never be right." He raised an eyebrow. "You're not proposing to her tonight, are you?"

Peter wanted to. With all his heart, he wanted to mate Meghan. He'd just been waiting for the right time to tell her he'd already had a mate.

"Her sisters keep asking her when you're going to pop the big question. You've been dating Meghan for over a year already. The other bachelors are getting anxious."

Peter smiled. "It'll happen before long. I'm going to tell her. Not tonight. I wanted to take her out for dinner. She's always cooking for us, so I wanted to treat her to something special for the Christmas holiday. Tomorrow, we'll have dinner at her place and I'll tell her then."

CJ's brows rose.

"Okay, don't go telling anyone else, but I plan to propose to her after we go caroling with the group. I've arranged to take her on a sleigh ride. I don't want to ruin the surprise for her, and you know how word spreads in the pack. Besides, if she's angry about what I have to tell her, things might be called off or delayed a bit until we can work them out."

CJ smiled. "I understand. I don't think you'll have a problem with her, but in any case, mum's the word."

"Thanks, CJ. I appreciate it." Peter said good night and headed out into the blowing snow. He'd thought of talking to Meghan about his late wife while they had a nightcap after he drove her home from dinner, but he didn't want to ruin a lovely night. He would have to play it by ear. He'd decided he would tell her, no matter what, tomorrow night.

He arrived to pick Meghan up at her house, figuring she'd be dressed in slacks, or maybe a skirt, and a sweater. But when he saw her in the red dress, her hair curled about her shoulders, hell, he didn't want to leave the house. Not with her shoulders bared and the satiny fabric fitting smoothly over all her lovely curves. She sure filled the dress out in all the right places. A pair of high-heeled shoes made her legs look shapelier too. He wanted to ask Meghan if they could skip going out and just eat at her place. He had expected her to look as beautiful as usual, but more warm and cuddly, not hot and sexy.

"If it's a little too dressy, I can wear a sweater and a plaid skirt," she said, appearing a little self-conscious.

He was probably making her feel that way because his tongue was hanging out and he was taking in all her hotness without saying a word. He was stunned and intrigued. "Hot damn, Meghan, you are a feast for sore eyes." He was torn between showing her off at the tavern and keeping her to himself in the privacy of her home.

She smiled brilliantly at him, and he pulled her in for a kiss. He meant it to be soft to begin with, but a barely soft kiss went straight to passionate and then ravenous, lips pressing, tongues exploring, bodies pressed together in hot delight. "God, you feel good."

"You like the dress?"

"Hell, yeah. And I love the body it's hugging. The dress and the lady are...*hot*."

Meghan chuckled and wrapped her arms around his neck while he slid his hands down her satiny dress, realizing just how low the back was cut, and reached down to her buttocks and cupped them.

"You won't be too cold?" he asked.

"You'll keep me warm."

He smiled. *She* was making *him* hot. As much as he wanted to stay here and hug her and kiss her, and a hell of a lot more, they had dinner reservations and he didn't want to hold up the table. He sighed. "I guess I'm going to show you off tonight." He helped her on with her winter coat, then escorted her outside to his car, holding her tight to make sure she didn't slip on the icy sidewalk in her sexy heels.

A few minutes later, they arrived at the tavern. Peter escorted her inside, and everyone seated there turned to look, naturally.

Wolves were wary and had to keep humans out, so it was an instinctive reaction. But as soon as he removed her coat and handed it to Silva to hang up, the bachelor males whistled their approval. *Bunch of wolves*. They didn't do it in a disrespectful way, but in a way that said he was one lucky guy.

Silva and Meghan smiled, but Meghan's cheeks blushed beautifully. Peter shrugged out of his coat, and Silva took it too.

Peter led Meghan to their table and sat her so her naked back was to the wall. He sat close to her so they could talk in the noisy tavern while everyone was drinking, eating, and conversing. Orchestral Christmas music played overhead, courtesy of Silva. A poinsettia and a cinnamon-scented candle sat in the center of their table, the golden flame flickering.

Silva brought them white Christmas margaritas with green limes and a cherry adding a bit of Christmas color to the white drinks Peter had preordered. "Peter said they're your favorite," Silva said to Meghan.

"For Christmas, yes. Thanks, Peter," Meghan said to him.

"I'm surprised he let you out of the house wearing that dress," Silva said.

Peter hoped Meghan didn't take Silva's comment wrong. Though he'd been thinking the same thing.

"Oh, he wouldn't have dared," Meghan said, smiling. "I heard you have a steak special. With crumbled blue cheese? That's what I want. Baked potato, the works, and a small salad with blue cheese dressing. I've thought of nothing else all day."

"I'll have the same," Peter said, having acquired the taste once he'd tried it a while back after Meghan ordered it. She'd been good for him as far as trying out new things.

"You've got it," Silva said.

When Silva had gone to the kitchen to give the new cook the order, Meghan said to Peter, "Thanks so much for taking me out to dinner tonight. You know me. I'm usually just as happy going home for the night and fixing us something to eat. But this is truly special."

"It was about time I took you out for dinner. It's been a while."

"Well, this is really lovely, Peter. Thank you." She sipped her drink and sat back in her chair, relaxing finally, and he was glad to see it.

Especially after the way he'd reacted to seeing her in *the* dress. "I was afraid I'd screwed things up when I was so..."

"Speechless when you saw me dressed *too*..."

"Dressed *perfectly* for tonight."

"You didn't screw things up." She lifted her margarita off the table again. "If you'd acted like I *wasn't* wearing anything special, I would have been disappointed. With the way your tongue was hanging out, I was worried it might be a little too dressy. But it's Christmas, and as long as you can handle it..." She gave him a teasing smile.

Peter chuckled and took a swig of his ice water to cool down. "I certainly won't have any trouble 'handling' it, but the *other* wolves... *That's* another story."

She laughed.

He loved hearing her laugh and was glad he'd brought her here for dinner and she was all his.

After a lovely dinner and the usual conversation about the crazy happenings at work, they finally headed back to her place. Peter sure wished they were ready to mate and he was peeling her out of that dress to expose all the curves the fabric was caressing.

When Peter took her home after dinner, Meghan asked him in, wanting to enjoy even more of the night with him. "Do you want a drink?" She always asked, and he always said yes. She appreciated that he didn't just expect the night to end this way, as if they were already mated and this was the status quo. Instead, he'd wait on her porch, looking eager for the invite.

"Sure, a beer would be good if you have one." He shut the door behind them and locked it, then she retrieved her phone out of her coat pocket. He helped her out of her coat and hung it up for her in her coat closet before he removed his coat and set it on the coatrack by the front door.

"I'll get the beer for you." She slipped off her shoes, setting them under a side table in the living room so no one would trip over them, then went into the kitchen and placed her cell phone on the phone charger on the island. She opened the fridge and grabbed the beer, but heard Peter walk into the kitchen to join her.

Turning, she smiled and handed him the beer just as her cell phone rang. Thinking the call was from one of her sisters, she looked at the caller ID, and her jaw dropped. *Bill Weaver.* Her *ex*-boyfriend. The guy who had a heated fight with her when she told him she'd sent a wolf to prison. Why in the world was he calling her now?

He'd better not believe he could get into her good graces and they could date again. Maybe he thought she was still living in St. Augustine. But his call sure put a damper on things tonight. All she could think of was Rollins—putting him in prison and finally telling Bill about it.

She ignored the phone and got herself a glass of ice water.

"Out-of-area call?" Peter asked.

She smiled and took his hand and led him into the living room, not about to tell him about Bill or make up a story. She'd barely made it to the sofa when her phone rang again. Trying to hide her annoyance, she set her glass of water on the coaster on the table. "Be right back." She'd kept her tone lighthearted to mask her irritation.

She strode to the kitchen and checked her phone. Bill was calling again. *Damn him.* She turned the phone off, then rejoined Peter in the living room.

Peter was still standing, unopened beer in hand. "Is it a crank caller?"

"No." She was used to Peter wearing his sheriff's hat and being ready to take anyone to task who was causing trouble, so she should have known he would be ready to take care of someone who was bothering her. "Can you unzip my dress?"

Peter's brows rose and his mouth curved up slightly, a spark of interest lit in his darkened amber eyes.

She smiled. "I had to call Laurel to zip me up. That's the trouble with this dress. If you leave before I take it off, I'll have to sleep in it or have her come over and help me out of it. I just want to throw something on that's more comfortable to relax in."

"No trouble at all." He quickly set his beer on the table. He rubbed his hands together as if he were eager to undress her.

She smiled.

His smile was on the wolfish side. "My hands are cold." He carefully unzipped her dress while she held on to the bodice so the dress wouldn't slip down.

He pulled her hair aside and then shifted his hands to her shoulders, caressing, his mouth nuzzling her neck. She loved his gentleness and thought she ought to wear strapless dresses around him more often. He moved his hands around to cup her breasts still covered by the satiny fabric, his mouth pressing kisses against her neck and shoulders.

Then he slid his hands down her hips. "Hmm, Meghan."

He turned her around and slipped the dress down her body and over her hips. She quickly rested her hands on his shoulders to keep her balance and stepped out of the dress. He carefully set it over a chair as if he was afraid to wrinkle the garment. Then he turned to look at her underwear—strapless bra, lace panties, lace garter belt, all in red, and stockings.

"Man, oh, man." Peter breathed out.

She smiled at him. He pulled her into his arms, his hands combing through her hair, his mouth capturing hers. They locked lips, their bodies rubbing hotly against each other, sharing their pheromones, working up the urge to mate. They couldn't have consummated sex, or they'd be mated wolves. *Forever*. So they had been careful not to go too far, but she wanted him in her bed tonight. She wasn't sure he wanted to go that far, but then again, he seemed ready and willing.

"I need to slip into something more…comfortable," she said.

"Do you need my help?"

"Yeah." Not really, but *she* was ready to take this further. She grabbed his hand and headed for the stairs. Once they reached her bedroom, he didn't hesitate to take charge.

He took hold of her shoulders, then caressed the swell

of her breasts with his mouth. He unfastened the bra and tossed it on the bed. She savored the feel of his mouth and warm breath on her flesh.

She briefly thought of how she should tell Peter about Rollins, the man she'd put in prison, but she didn't want to ruin this for them now. When had she become such a coward? Since she didn't want to lose him, that's when.

Peter slid his hands down her sides, past her garter belt. He began unfastening her stockings, kissing her legs as he went while she combed her fingers through his hair. He stripped off her stockings and garter, but before he could pull off her panties, she began undressing him.

It wasn't as though they hadn't seen each other tons of times while stripping to shift. But the setting and the reason they were undressing put a whole other spin on the situation.

Meghan pulled his plaid shirt out of his jeans and unbuttoned it, then opened it so she could run her palms over his sculpted abs, his smooth skin, and his hard nipples. Right before she kissed and licked and gently nibbled on them.

Peter's heartbeat had ratcheted up several notches. His breathing was ragged, his hands stilled in her hair. She loved that she could do that to him.

He hurried to unbutton his sleeves and then yanked off his shirt and dropped it on the floor. He pulled her in for another close encounter of the sexy kind, his naked chest pressed against hers, their tongues tangling. He slipped his hands under her bikini waistband and cupped her buttocks.

She moaned, feeling his now-warm hands cupping her naked flesh. His erection was swelling beneath his jeans, and she stepped back to unfasten his belt. He quickly sat down on the bed to remove his boots and socks, and then dispensed with his jeans. Loving the way his black boxer briefs hugged his rigid cock, she ran her hand over it, smiling when she made it jump.

She figured he wouldn't go any further if she didn't initiate things, waiting for it to be her call, so she pulled down his boxer briefs, freeing his rigid cock surrounded by dark, curly hair. He quickly slid her panties down her legs before she changed her mind. Which made her smile. She was *not* changing her mind.

Then they climbed into her curtained bed and were kissing all over again. She knew she was being reckless in not waiting until she'd told him what she'd done, but a part of her hoped he wouldn't be able to give her up if he could feel the sexual draw between them, not to mention all the rest that they enjoyed with each other—the times when they relaxed and visited, the wolf runs they had, even the skiing. She loved how he could take to task the wolves who were doing wrong, and yet be just as sweet as could be when it came to helping others. She couldn't think of anything she didn't like about him.

He slipped his hand between her legs and began to stroke her, gently at first, but she covered his hand with hers and pressed his fingers harder against her swollen and sensitive clit so he was touching her in a way that made a difference, fast, pushing her toward the heavens. She felt like a bird in flight headed for the moon, her breathing labored, her heart beating hard. He kissed her mouth, licking her lips and touching his tongue to hers.

She swept her hands down his back, feeling the tension in his muscles as he worked her to the top. She felt the end coming, his strokes harder, faster, as she moaned with pleasure. And then she couldn't hold on to the rush of orgasm as it hit her all at once, her body thrumming with ecstasy in the aftermath.

Taking a moment to catch her breath, Meghan smiled up at him with what she was sure was a totally satiated look and then took charge of him. He was ready as she pushed him onto his back and began to stroke his cock, up and down, kissing his mouth as he ran his hand through her hair cascading over his chest.

She kept stroking and kissing him, thinking she'd be the one to make him come next, but he moved onto his side so he could reach between her legs and began trying to coax another climax out of her. He was her dream lover. Now she wished more than ever that she'd told him the truth about Rollins. She couldn't help but think about it, because she wanted to pull Peter on top of her right now and tell him to do it. To mate her, because she loved everything about him. To push his cock into her and to shatter her into a million pieces, only this time inside her.

Thinking about it, she'd slowed her stroke on his cock, and he placed his hand on hers to make her go faster. She smiled and obliged. But he was stroking her slowly, slipping his fingers between her feminine lips, then stroking her again. Their bodies tensed as if he was ready to come, like she was. And then the climax stole her thoughts and she cried out, feeling the orgasm ripple through every inch of her being, and he groaned with release.

For a few seconds, they just lay there, feeling the moment, and then he pulled her into his arms and kissed the top of her head, just holding her close against his hot body, not saying anything.

Why hadn't he just asked her to mate him? She knew why she was reluctant. But why was he?

She thought maybe he might even stay the night, but then again, he couldn't without everyone in town thinking they'd mated if they saw his car parked at her place all night.

Her landline rang, and she turned her head sharply to look at it. She couldn't see the caller ID from the angle the phone was sitting. She could hardly jump out of bed and look, but if it was Bill and he'd found her home phone number...

The unanswered call went to voicemail. *Oh my God, no!* If it was Bill, no telling what he'd say, or how Peter would view it. Talk about an ice-cold wet blanket thrown on their little party!

Meghan quickly got out of bed and disconnected the phone from the outlet before the caller could ring her any further. How suspicious did that look? That some unknown male, she assumed Bill, was calling her this late at night—and she didn't want to answer it? Not when Peter was here. Naked in her bed.

She. Could. Kill. Bill.

She didn't even know what to do next. She knew as soon as she turned around, Peter would be wondering what the hell was going on, watching every move she made, seeing her every action and reaction. He'd already seen enough. *Damn it.*

Peter had propped his arms behind his head, his eyes studying her. "Not a crank caller, I take it."

Okay, fine, she would tell Peter the whole story while he lay gloriously naked in her bed. She opened her mouth to explain, but he got out of bed.

"It's not like we're mated wolves," he said, pulling on his boxer briefs.

What? Peter couldn't think she was seeing anyone else. He'd smell the wolf on her, for one thing. But she never saw anyone outside the pack and not in a dating situation. He had to know that. Unless he guessed Bill was an out-of-town interest. She closed her gaping mouth and threw on a pair of pajamas.

Peter finished dressing. "I guess I'd better leave before the pack gets the notion we are mated." He smiled at her, but the smile didn't reach his eyes. She knew he was upset about the caller, but she was upset with Peter for thinking the worst of her. Even though he might still think that once he learned her secret.

They went downstairs, and he grabbed his coat. She picked up her dress and heels, furious with Bill and disappointed with how the night had ended with Peter.

Peter paused, then joined her and kissed her mouth lightly. "See you tomorrow for the snow sculpting?"

She'd forgotten all about it. She was surprised he still wanted to do it with her. "Uh, yeah." She managed a small smile for him.

"Be sure to turn your phone back on in case you get an important call."

She frowned at him.

"From me. You know."

"Sure." Once Peter was gone, she'd give Bill a piece of her mind! She walked Peter to the door and let him out. "See you tomorrow."

He nodded, then walked through the crunchy snow to his car. She shut and locked her door and leaned against it. It had been the best night of her life, and the worst.

Chapter 2

PETER WAS TRYING NOT TO MAKE ANYTHING OF THE caller who was bugging Meghan, but he wanted to end the guy's miserable life! At least he assumed the caller was a male or Meghan would have told him who it was or taken the call. Yet Peter couldn't believe he'd gone so far with her before he'd told her what he needed to. He didn't really believe she was seeing anyone, not with the way she was always available to see him. Certainly, he had never smelled any guy on her. He should have handled that so much differently. Shown he trusted her. At least they were still on for tomorrow, if she didn't cancel on him after the way they had ended things tonight.

He couldn't go home to bed and sleep. He couldn't stop thinking about it, so he drove straight to his deputy and best friend CJ's house. He had to talk to him about this and get it off his chest. He knew CJ would tell his mate, Laurel, what Peter had said, but he couldn't stew about this all night. He needed to talk to someone.

Their home was close by, so he drove over there, parked, and called CJ to let him know he needed to talk, hoping the deputy wasn't in the middle of anything important with his mate. "Hey, CJ, can we talk?"

"Yeah, sure. Is everything okay between you and Meghan?" CJ sounded concerned, and Peter assumed he thought Peter had told Meghan about his late wife and things hadn't gone well.

"No. But it's not about that. I'm…at your house now. Can we talk?"

"Uh, yeah, sure. I'll just throw on some clothes and meet you at the door."

"Thanks, CJ. I owe you one."

"Hell, you were my sounding board when I was dating Laurel whenever I needed one. See you in a second."

Peter was glad CJ could spare the time to talk with him. A few minutes later, they were sitting in the living room, each drinking a beer, which reminded Peter that he never drank the one Meghan had gotten for him.

"Laurel's going to sleep," CJ said.

"I hope I didn't interrupt anything."

CJ smiled. "Your timing was spot-on."

Peter was thankful for that.

"If it's not about your late wife, what *is* it about?" CJ asked.

"Meghan had some caller tonight. She wouldn't answer her cell phone and turned it off when he called the second time. Then when…well, later, a caller, most likely the same one, tried to reach her through her landline. She wouldn't answer the phone, and she unplugged it when he left voicemail."

"I'm assuming you didn't handle it right."

"I didn't. I was irritated that the guy was calling her, if it was a guy, and that she wouldn't tell me what it was about. Hell, what was I to think?"

"That some guy is harassing her?" CJ asked, brows arched.

Peter let out his breath and took another swig of beer. "I asked if it was a crank caller, and she said...no. She didn't explain who it was, though."

"So you assumed the worse. She's seeing some other guy...but you know it's not true. She couldn't without you knowing about it."

Peter set his can of beer down on the coffee table and ran his hands through his hair, exasperated with himself. "I asked her if she was still going with me to create the snow-wolf sculptures tomorrow, and she said yes."

"Okay, so what's the problem?"

"I still didn't handle it right, damn it. She knows I wasn't happy about the caller."

"Which shows you care about her."

"Like hell it does. I should have brushed it off, taken her into my arms and kissed her good night, and acted like nothing was the matter."

"You didn't kiss her good night?" CJ sounded worried now.

"Hell. Yeah, I kissed her good night, but not like I should have. Like I really meant it and felt all the emotion I was pouring into it." Unlike before that.

CJ sighed. "Listen, you'll get together tomorrow, you'll clear the air, and everything will be fine. I take it you didn't tell her about your late mate."

"Things got a little out of hand and...I couldn't. Not then."

CJ laughed. "I heard about the red dress. Well, more than heard about it. Some of the guys eating at the tavern shared the photo of you two. That's some dress. I could see why you couldn't resist her. You know she wouldn't have worn it for you if she was thinking about seeing some other wolf." CJ frowned. "Was it someone in the pack? I'd say we'll just arrest his sorry ass and—"

"No one from the pack. I'm sure of it."

"Hmm, maybe an old boyfriend. Okay, she wouldn't take his calls, so that tells you something."

"Hell, yeah, I was there!"

CJ chuckled and shook his head. "What if the roles were reversed and you got a call from an old girlfriend you're no longer seeing and she's dying to get with you to…well, renew the relationship? About that time, you're kissing away on Meghan. What would you do? Answer the call? Ruin the moment with Meghan? Turn off your phone and deal with it once you and Meghan had said good night and you were alone?"

"Yeah, I guess you're right."

"Of course I'm right. And damn it, Peter, tell her about your late wife and get it over with." Then CJ smiled. "You feel any better?"

"No, but I'm headed home, and I'll give Meghan a call and apologize."

"That's the spirit." Peter and CJ rose from their seats, and CJ slapped him on the back. "Call me if you have any further issues tonight."

"Thanks." CJ was right. If the roles had been reversed, Peter would have waited to deal with it.

Then they said good night and Peter headed home, but as soon as he was in the car, he called Meghan, hoping she'd turned her cell phone back on and plugged in her landline.

She answered the call on the first ring, and he thought

that was a good sign—unless she was going to break up with him. If so, he would do everything he could to change her mind and make it up to her.

"Hey, miss me already?" she asked, sounding sexy and sultry, and all he could think of was her wearing that beautiful red dress, and then out of it and wearing all that red lace, and then naked in his arms in bed.

"Hell, yeah. I just wanted to make sure you turned your phone back on, just in case someone important called you."

"Like you."

"Yeah, me. Listen, um, can we have dinner tomorrow night at your place?" He was going to tell her everything tomorrow night. No waffling this time.

"Uh, yeah, sure. I just wanted to say I really had a lovely time, Peter. Thanks for dinner and…for all the rest."

He chuckled. "Yeah, honey, it was good. Real good. You're welcome. See you in the morning." He fully intended to stop by her house and see if she'd like to go for a wolf run first thing in the morning. She seemed so upbeat that he realized he'd had nothing to worry about. At least he didn't think so. But he was going to prove to her beyond a doubt that he was the only one for her.

Meghan was about to drift off to sleep when she got a call, and she wanted to scream at the caller when she realized it was her sister Laurel. "Yeah, Laurel?"

"Hey, what's up with you and Peter?"

"What?" How in the world would her sister know anything about what was going on between her and Peter?

"CJ had to talk to Peter about something that was eating Peter after seeing you."

Meghan let out her breath in frustration. "Nothing. Well, I mean, Bill, of all people, called several times."

"Bill...?"

"Bill Weaver! Can you believe it? Anyway, it put a damper on the last bit of our evening, but we're good. I guess if CJ and Peter talked about it, he came around."

"Okay, good. I was worried, and CJ wouldn't tell me anything about what they discussed, but I had to know you were all right."

"Thanks, Laurel. Yeah, we're good. Night."

"Night."

Meghan must have finally fallen asleep when her landline rang and she sat upright in bed, disoriented, thinking someone was ringing the doorbell. She glanced at the caller ID. Bill. The sun hadn't even risen yet.

She grabbed the phone, but before she could give him an earful, he said, "Hey, Meghan. God, I'm glad I got ahold of you. I need to talk to you about something really important."

"About what?" She didn't think it could be about anything more than him wanting to see her again, and that wasn't happening.

"I have to talk to you in person. I'm at Wolff's Timberline Ski Lodge."

"What?" She'd kill him. "You can tell me what you have to say over the phone."

"I have to see you. For breakfast, first thing?"

"No. I don't know when. I've got important stuff to do. And just so you know, I'm dating someone. We're serious, so I'm not getting back together with you."

"I'll call you later. I do want to tell you how sorry I am about how I was with you...before. I want to have a go of it, and I'll call you back."

"Bill, no. It's over between us."

"Later, Meghan." He hung up on her, and she was thinking she was going to have to change her number.

Damn Bill Weaver! Why did he have to show up in Silver Town, Colorado, now, of all times!

Unable to sleep any longer, Meghan climbed out of bed and rubbed her eyes, then pulled aside the gray-blue curtains surrounding her canopied bed. She'd often fantasized about having Peter naked in that bed, sliding around on the cool cotton sheets, rubbing her body with his hot nakedness, with the curtains drawn shut to keep the cool air out. Though she imagined she and Peter would be getting things pretty steamed up before long, she couldn't believe they'd actually ended up in her bed, doing just about everything she'd fantasized about—except for the consummation part.

Hopefully, Bill wouldn't mess everything up between her and Peter.

She quickly shifted into her gray wolf. At least she didn't have to pause to apply makeup or fix her hair or get dressed. She was good to go once she shifted.

She raced down the stairs past the nine-foot blue-, gold-, and silver-decorated Christmas tree, hitting the large blue-and-beige Turkish rug beneath it with her paws and making little gold bells jingle on the tree. Which made her think of an angel, or several in this case, getting their wings, courtesy of *It's a Wonderful Life.*

She hurried out through the wolf door to take a run, trying to work out the frustration she felt over her ex-boyfriend repeatedly calling her and now renting a room near town, of all things. She left before sunrise, running alone, which she never did. A couple feet of snow covered yards and the woods, but the streets and sidewalks had been cleared.

Christmas lights sparkled through the trees as she ran. That's something she'd love to do with Peter...see all the homes decorated with Christmas lights one of these nights.

She always ran as a wolf with her sisters when they could get away at this hour. Of late, they preferred staying in bed with their mates. Not that Meghan blamed them. If she was mated, she would feel the same way. And if Bill hadn't called her early this morning to say he wanted to talk to her pronto, she probably would have just slept in a little later.

The snow-chilled air swept across her nose, the rest of her covered in a double coat of thick, warm fur that kept the cold from reaching her skin. The moon was nearly full, offering a hazy light on the misty morning. Branches were sagging from the weight of the snow, with more predicted for later in the day. She could smell the cold freshness of the air and the scents of a rabbit and a deer that had run through the area recently.

Despite trying to enjoy the sounds and smells as she ran through the forested land the Silver wolves maintained to provide an escape on the wild side close to town, Meghan couldn't quit thinking about the reason she was out running. *Bill.*

Brushing against Colorado blue spruces, she collected snow on her thick winter top coat, which protected her soft ur.dercoat of gray fur and her skin from the cold and wet. She leaped through the snowdrifts, loving the cold, unlike when she'd arrived here a little over a year ago.

She began to see other wolves out for a run in the woods before their workday commenced, and guilt washed over her. She didn't want anyone to know what she'd done before she had arrived in Silver Town. She'd never planned to tell another soul, though her sisters had been supportive. Bill was another story. One mention of it, and he'd been history. Now he was a wild card who could turn her whole world upside down in a heartbeat.

She saw a few more wolves she knew running at this early hour: Tom Silver with his mate, Elizabeth, who both woofed at her in greeting; Jake and his mate, Alicia, and also their friends Sam and Silva; male ski instructor twins Kemp and Radcliff Grey; and then a few wolves Meghan didn't recognize. Everyone was out right before dawn broke, and seeing the wolves in pairs, Meghan felt guilty she hadn't bothered to ask her sisters to go with her. They lived in different areas, and though she usually loved to be with them, she preferred being alone for now.

A large male wolf she didn't recognize caught her eye—mostly black with gray fur under his chin and on his belly. He was a long distance off, but he was observing her. Something about him made Meghan feel…uneasy. Maybe because he didn't greet her with a nod of his head or a small bark, but was staring at her in a menacing manner. Then he turned and disappeared into the woods. He could be any of the wolf guests visiting the wolf-run town and ski resort, so she wasn't sure what about him had spooked her so.

She hoped to reach home well before her sisters arrived at the inn so they wouldn't know she had run without them. Then she saw Peter loping toward her, looking eager to meet up with her. What was he doing out this way and at this hour as a wolf? Sure, he worked at the sheriff's office nearby, but usually he was in uniform, not wearing his wolf coat at this time of day. Still, he'd been less and less predictable lately where she was concerned, and she thought it was because he wanted to make sure they were all right with each other.

She waited for him to join her, and when he did, he affectionately nuzzled her cheek and rubbed his body against hers in a way that said he wanted to move their courtship right along. Which again made her think of hot nights she could spend with him in the middle of winter in her curtained bed. She felt like royalty when she slept in it, and she couldn't imagine a better way to have fun than to have her very own wolf prince sharing the sheets.

She responded with the same kind of affection to show she wanted it, too, though she felt awkward about it because of Bill being in town. Then again, maybe that's why Peter had shown up at this time of day to run with her. He already knew about Bill.

In that case, the news would be all through the pack before she was ready to deal with Bill and tell him to go home.

Peter licked her nose, she nipped gently at his ear, and he woofed at her in fun. She sighed, her breath a frosty mist, and then nudged him to continue on home.

He ran beside her the rest of the way to her place. He still hadn't played with her as a wolf, as if he were afraid he would be too rough on her or annoy her. Instead, he loved watching her play with her sisters, looking as though he'd love to join in but just couldn't make himself do it. He should. If he did, all three of them would pounce on him in fun.

If she hadn't needed to get to work, she would have tried tackling him when he'd approached her this time, since there were no other wolves that she could see. She'd love to know how he'd respond. Playing was just as important as any other aspect of a *lupus garou*'s nature. Especially if they were considering mating each other. She couldn't imagine not playing with her mate, which would help teach their offspring how to play and play-fight. Peter and his brother, Bjornolf, must have play-fought when they were younger. Then again, they didn't have any sisters, which might explain Peter's reluctance to play with her.

Forget waiting. One thing Peter had to know about her by now was that she could be predictable at times and totally unpredictable at others. She figured now was as good a time as any other. She swept around and tackled him, totally blindsiding him, and he fell into a bank of snow, looking surprised for an instant.

Chapter 3

PETER WAS GLAD HE'D BEEN ABLE TO CATCH UP WITH Meghan to run with her as a wolf. He'd dropped by her house first to see if she wanted to run with him, and it had taken him some time to track her down. She'd run three miles from her home and was heading back before he finally saw her. He hadn't liked that she'd been alone in the woods and was relieved he had located her. Even though the property was privately owned by the pack and *No Hunting* and *No Trespassing* signs were posted all over, a human hunter might ignore the signs and shoot a wolf for the fun of it.

He also was glad Meghan didn't seem upset with him this morning. He'd been worried she might have rethought things last night, which was why he had wanted so badly to see her first thing. He didn't want to admit he would like to tap her phone to see who was calling her.

No matter what, Peter couldn't stop thinking about those calls. When he told Meghan about his late wife tonight, maybe she'd feel free to tell him who the guy was. Peter needed to cool it until then.

They'd been running together toward home when he saw her suddenly turn, but he hadn't expected her to tackle him. Being unprepared, he fell against a bank of windswept snow and woofed with delight. He meant to get up and tackle her in return, but she pinned him against the snow, tenaciously nipping at him with glee. He bit back at her in play, redoubling his efforts to scramble free. And then they chased each other in the snow, her lying down, waiting for him to come after her, and then him charging forward. She wrestled him, growling and barking with sheer excitement. God, how he loved her. He didn't remember a time when he'd had so much fun play-fighting.

She dashed off, and he raced after her. And then she lay down, waiting for him again. She was still, her eyes on him, and then he ran forward. She tackled him, both standing on their hind legs, their teeth clashing playfully, and then she ran off toward home, and he dashed to join her.

Now this he could get used to on a daily basis.

Meghan was glad they had played as wolves, though she was still surprised he'd met up with her. When she and Peter emerged from the woods, she saw her sisters' cars parked in the paved lot next to her home behind the Silver Town Inn. She nuzzled Peter in parting, and he responded with a lick to her muzzle. She smiled and licked him back, wishing they could spend the whole day and night together, and that Bill hadn't shown up in her life.

She sighed and ran through the wolf door. The home had been her sisters' and hers when they bought it and the inn as a package deal, but her sisters had ceded the deed over to her once they were mated and living with their mates. Meghan loved the gingerbread-trimmed house and hoped Peter, or whoever she ended up with as a mate, would want to live here.

She raced through the house and up the stairs, then

shifted in her bedroom. She now had the master bedroom instead of Laurel, and she loved having her own bathroom. As soon as Meghan was dressed, she headed out of the house and through the snow-covered garden to reach the inn. The fountain had been turned off for the winter and icicles dripped off the basin, shimmering in the orange and yellow rays of the sunrise. Christmas lights sparkled on her house, the gazebo in the garden, and the inn, making it look like a winter wonderland.

When she entered the inn, Meghan grabbed supplies from a closet and began dusting the sills on the back windows and then washed the windows, avoiding her sisters. She knew if they so much as looked at her, they'd realize something was wrong. She didn't want to tell them that Bill was actually here in Silver Town.

Each of the sisters was assigned daily chores to keep up with managing the inn. Ellie, the youngest, was manning the front desk for now. Laurel was vacuuming, but she shut off the vacuum as soon as she heard Meghan in the sitting room.

"Meghan?" Laurel called out.

"Yes, I'm here. Are all the guests gone?" Meghan asked as she moved to the lobby and dusted the piano and coffee tables.

"Yes. What's going on with you?" Laurel asked her. "You and Peter are supposed to be doing your share of building the snow castle this morning."

Ellie finished making another reservation and turned her attention to Meghan.

Meghan glanced at the grandfather clock. She had time. "He's not picking me up for another hour or so."

"Don't tell me nothing's wrong with you. I know you better than that. You dusted the windowsills and washed the sitting-room windows yesterday. And you went running as a wolf first thing this morning without asking either of us to accompany you. You never do that unless something's bothering you," Laurel said. "Peter was looking for you, appearing somewhat unsettled when he didn't find you home. I told him you might have gone running. So he went after you. We thought maybe you needed some wolf time alone with him before you went to help create snow wolves at the snow castle."

Meghan could never get anything past her sisters, but she didn't explain what was going on either.

"Have you had a disagreement with Peter?" Ellie prompted. Then the reception-desk phone rang, and she booked another reservation.

"She got a call from Bill last night when she was home with Peter," Laurel said, since Meghan hadn't told Ellie what was going on.

"Ohmigod, how awful. I can't imagine what I would have done if something like that had happened when I was dating Brett," Ellie said. "What did you do?"

"I didn't answer it and turned off my cell phone, figuring that was the end of it after he called twice."

"Oh, no, there's more?" Ellie asked, her eyes widening.

"He called my landline after that."

"Totally awkward," Laurel said.

"I unplugged the phone, but not until after Bill left a voicemail and the light was flashing on my phone."

"You told Peter he was an ex-boyfriend, right?" Ellie said.

"No. If I told him that, I'd have to tell him about Rollins. I plan to. Tonight. It just wasn't the right time to talk about it."

Her sisters' eyes widened. Then Ellie and Laurel smiled.

"The landline in your *bedroom*?" Laurel asked.

Meghan knew her sisters would learn soon enough that her ex-boyfriend was staying at the lodge. She'd wanted to surreptitiously send him packing without anyone in the pack being the wiser. In a bigger human-run town, it might have worked. In the small wolf-run town? The word was sure to get out. She was certain Peter wouldn't like it one bit and would have Bill Weaver arrested for any infraction of the law, no matter how minor, just for thinking of getting back together with her.

Ellie asked, "Well?"

"Well, what?" Meghan had forgotten she'd dusted everything yesterday. Whenever something was troubling her, she either ran as a wolf or did chores. Or…both. She hoped she could take care of Bill before Peter learned the ex-boyfriend was in their territory, if he hadn't already.

"Something more is bothering you," Laurel said. "Spill."

The *or* was silent, but Meghan knew her sisters would enlist everybody's help in learning what was troubling her if she didn't tell them.

She began to dust the piano again. "I didn't want Peter or anyone else to know."

Her sisters' eyes grew wide in surprise.

"Bill Weaver is here, wanting me back. He's staying at Wolff's Timberline Ski Lodge."

"Are you kidding? Does he want you to return to St. Augustine with him?" Laurel asked, sounding shocked and a little worried.

The sisters had never been separated for very long and they never wanted that to happen, as close as they were to each other.

Meghan shook her head. "I don't know. Maybe he wants to move here."

Ellie laughed. "That's not happening—no matter what important skill sets Bill might have or how likable he can be—if Peter has any say in it."

Meghan rolled her eyes. "Peter and I *aren't* a sure thing."

Her sisters looked like they didn't believe her. Well, she and Peter might be a sure thing, but they weren't there yet.

Thankfully, the inn guests—all wolves who knew to book well in advance for the holidays—were all out sightseeing or hitting the slopes, so the sisters were free to talk about anything they needed to discuss.

The fragrances of cinnamon spice and evergreen garlands and wreaths scented the air, perfect for the Christmas season. The ten-foot-tall living Christmas tree, courtesy of the Silver brothers and cousins, was decorated with Victorian lace bows, strings of berries, and twinkling white lights. A special angel took center stage on the fireplace mantel among the collection of German nutcrackers. The angel was a gift from a lady whose husband had died. Meghan and her sisters had been able to help his spirit find peace after telling the lady he loved her one last time. Each of the sisters had the gift of being able to see ghosts and help them on their way, most of the time.

This was Meghan's favorite time of year, when everything was sparkly, twinkly, and festive. At least this year she'd gotten a lot more used to the snow and loved having a white Christmas. She and her sisters grew up in Florida and had been restoring Victorian hotels mostly in the southern states, so she hadn't been prepared for the winter in Colorado last year.

Laurel finished mopping the floor. "No one knows about your past but us. And we're not sharing. If you and Peter are the least bit serious, you have to let him know."

"If they were in his bedroom while the light was going off on her landline, they are getting serious," Ellie said.

Laurel was their oldest sister by ten minutes, and Meghan was the middle child. Which meant she was the "lost" child caught in between, and she'd had to prove she was just as important as her big sister and baby sister growing up. But she'd screwed up big time when she'd witnessed a male wolf's attempt to murder a human woman, though her options to rectify it had been limited, and none of them had been good.

"Peter's got some secrets too." Meghan began dusting around the banister. She didn't need to dust it again. She just needed to have something to do with her hands. She didn't know why she was so nervous about Bill showing up in town. There shouldn't be a problem, unless the Silver pack made a big issue of him being there or tried to force him to leave and he fought them about it.

She didn't want him ruining things for her. She couldn't believe he'd even consider trying to change her mind after all this time and after all the ugly things he'd said to her. He'd been right—Rollins could have exposed the wolf kind for what they were—but still, she couldn't ignore how or what Bill had said in his tirade after hearing what she'd done.

She'd never revealed to her sisters that she had told Bill about her past. She'd hesitated to tell him, fearing he would end the relationship once he'd learned what she'd done, which he had. She had told her sisters that he and she just weren't mate material. And that was true too. She'd never felt drawn to him the way she was to Peter.

"Oh?" Laurel returned the mop and empty bucket to the closet.

"What kind of secrets does Peter have?" Ellie tidied up the reception desk.

Meghan began dusting their grandfather's clock. "I have no idea."

Ellie scoffed. "You said he has secrets, so you have to know something."

"You know how when Mom and Dad were up to something, they'd quit talking when any of us entered the room? I've seen Peter speaking with some of the Silver guys, and they all clam up when I approach."

"So that they can greet you." Laurel leaned against the check-in counter.

"Well, yeah, they greet me, but it's as if they don't want me to overhear what they're talking about."

"Maybe it's a criminal case Peter's working on," Laurel said.

"If he can talk to any of the Silvers about a case, what difference would it make if he talked about it in front of me?"

"True. Maybe it's about an old girlfriend," Ellie said.

"I've considered that."

"If it is, don't worry about it. Old girlfriends aren't important." Laurel started making a pot of tea in the kitchen.

Meghan joined her. "Just like my old boyfriends aren't important." She suspected Peter wouldn't think so if he saw Bill in the flesh. If she and Peter were mated wolves, it would be different because wolves mated for life. But with them becoming more serious, she didn't think Peter would be happy about Bill saying he wanted to get together with her.

"So what did Bill say?" Laurel asked.

Meghan brought out a tray of cranberry scones and put them on the kitchen table. "He said he had to talk to me. That it was important. He sounded anxious. I told him it was over between us. I don't want him getting the idea that I'm interested in dating him again. I mean, he could have just called me and not come all the way out here to see me personally."

"And? What else did he say?" Ellie poked her head into the kitchen and saw the scones sitting on the table. "Oh, more fresh scones. I thought the guests ate the last ones."

"They did. I made new ones," Laurel said.

"You're the best," Ellie said. "Hey, you'll need to pick up the ingredients for the gingerbread house contest too. We didn't have time to participate last year, but I have all kinds of plans."

Meghan agreed. Laurel made the best baked goods.

"Bill said he'd like to work things out, but he had to talk privately with me," Meghan said while placing Santa napkins on the table. She sat down at the table.

"About what?" Laurel poured hot Christmas tea in reindeer mugs for each of them.

Meghan blew on her tea, her sisters giving her the look that said she'd been taught better, but the black tea infused with cinnamon and cloves was calling to her, and she was too impatient to wait. She took a sip, glad it had cooled enough and she hadn't scalded her mouth and tongue. If she was going to be questioned to death, she needed some fortification.

"I don't know. Really. If I did, I'd tell you."

Laurel was eyeing her with suspicion. Meghan knew Laurel suspected she hadn't told them everything. Laurel and Ellie sat down at the table.

"You know, you are too much like Mom." Meghan let her breath out in a huff. She could never get away with anything when their mom was alive, and her sisters were just as wary. "I told Bill. Okay? When I was dating him, I told him everything about Rollins."

Ellie's and Laurel's eyes widened.

Ellie's face turned stormy in an instant. She slapped the table with her hand. "That's why the two of you broke up, isn't it? I knew it!"

Meghan steeled her jaw. "Yeah. But it's still only my fault. I'm the one who sent the wolf to prison."

Laurel frowned. "If Bill had been the one for you, he would have seen your point of view in the matter. You didn't have a choice! There were no male wolves in the vicinity and no pack in the territory. No one else could have taken Rollins down. You had to deal with him the best way you could think of. He would have killed the woman if you hadn't intervened. You couldn't have stopped him any other way. If you'd tried using your own might, he could very well have killed *you*! You were lucky the police were just around the corner, or he might have killed both of you anyway, once he saw you calling the police."

"I could have become a wolf. I would have had the advantage then. I should have shifted instead of calling the police. We're just damned lucky he's a royal and doesn't have to shift during the full moon while he's incarcerated."

"Like I said, the police were just around the corner.

What if the woman or the police, or both of them, had seen you shift? It was just a bad situation all the way around. Either one of us would have done the same thing in your place," Laurel said.

"No, not you, Laurel. You would have shifted and killed him." Meghan knew that for certain. Laurel had done so in a similar situation.

"I don't know what I would have done, given the circumstances." Ellie tucked her red hair behind her ear. "Laurel's right. No way is perfectly good. The woman was unconscious when Laurel attacked and killed the man who had injured her. Laurel didn't have witnesses that way. What if the woman hadn't been unconscious? That would have been an entirely different story. Just like the woman you saved, who hadn't been. So it's not the same situation."

"You can't tell me what I did was right. It's been drummed into us since we were little that it's too dangerous for wolves to go to prison. Too many variables exist. Even if they're royals, they could still get angry enough to shift and take out someone who is hassling them." Meghan had given a lot of thought to how she would react to being bullied in such an environment. Turning wolf would definitely be something she'd want to do.

Most of the time, Meghan was glad the *lupus garous weren't* out of the closet. But sometimes, like then, she wished they were. Then, she wouldn't have had any trouble with wolves over what she'd done.

"All right, well, we said we wouldn't talk about that anymore. Since you've discussed what happened with Bill, it sounds to me as if he has amended how he feels about what you did," Laurel said.

"He wants to date you again. You can't talk about that over the phone. Betcha that's what it is. He's come to his senses about the issues between the two of you." Ellie took another bite out of her scone.

"But you told him you were dating Peter?" Laurel asked, her brows raised.

"Yes. Well, I didn't tell him Peter's name. I didn't figure that was any of Bill's business. But I told him I'm dating a wolf. That's not a secret. I'm sure if Bill talked to anyone about… Oh…my…God, I hope he didn't mention me to the ski lodge's staff, or any visitors up at the lodge. I can just imagine that news getting around the pack like a bad case of the flu." Now Meghan felt even worse about this mess. Why in the world did Bill have to turn up here? He hadn't talked to her, not once in the year and a half they'd lived here. Was that why Peter had met up with her as a wolf this morning? Because he'd learned Bill was there to see her, and to make sure she didn't want to start dating the old boyfriend?

Laurel rose from her seat and gave Meghan a hug. "Everything will be just fine. But you might want to give Peter a heads-up first."

"I haven't told Peter about putting the wolf in prison either."

Laurel sighed. "I told you if you were dating him seriously, and you have been, you'd need to tell him. He'll understand."

"And if he doesn't? If he reacts the same way Bill did? What if Peter tells the other pack members and they all react the same way toward me? Most of the wolves love us. All of us. But that could change in a heartbeat once they learn what I did."

Ellie joined them and leaned down to give Meghan a hug too. "You've got to tell Peter. We've finally set down roots here. Nowhere else. Laurel and I are married to Silver brothers in the pack. CJ's one of Peter's best friends. Brett will understand. Most would, I'm sure. Peter wouldn't risk upsetting you over it."

"Right," Laurel said. "Our mates wouldn't dare do anything but come to your defense."

Meghan managed a small smile. She loved her sisters. They always stuck together, no matter what.

"I always thought we'd meet up with some wolves at the next city while renovating a new Victorian hotel. But it never happened, not until we landed in Silver Town to learn about our aunt's disappearance. We definitely hadn't planned to stay here for any length of time," Meghan said.

"But then some of us hit the mother lode," Ellie said.

Laurel agreed. "Talk about Silver Town having a real silver lining. Even if Peter's not the one for you, the bachelors will be getting in line in hope you'll choose one of them over him. You better believe if you ever give Peter the boot, you'll have dates galore. For now, no one will chance asking you out while the sheriff and you are an item."

Even though that should have cheered Meghan, getting to know a new wolf was like starting all over again. Each trying to present their best image, hiding their secrets. The wolves who had lived here forever all knew one another so well that they already understood each other's foibles and strengths and probably knew all their secrets. Not Meghan. It was new territory.

Peter was anxious to spend the morning helping build the snow wolves with Meghan, but as soon as he arrived at the inn to pick her up, he sensed something wasn't right. Not with the way the sisters were looking at him differently, both frowning as if he'd done something wrong.

Meghan was hurrying to put on her gloves and scarf.

"Is everything okay?"

"Yeah, yeah." She gave him a smile, but it was strained.

Peter thought about how she'd acted earlier as a wolf and realized she'd seemed a little preoccupied then too—at least before she tackled him. Then she was all play. "Are you ready?"

He hoped she'd tell him what was bothering her, if something was. Though the phone calls she'd had certainly came to mind.

They said goodbye to her sisters, and he drove Meghan to Silver Town Square where the pack was building the snow castle, complete with a slide, as a fun pack-building effort for Christmas. He wanted to take her to the Christmas celebration the pack put on too.

When they arrived, six men and three women were already working on one of the walls. "Hey, Meghan, Peter," everyone said, pausing to greet them.

They greeted them back, and then Peter began helping Meghan build the first wolf.

He'd really been looking forward to taking part in creating the wolves with Meghan as his partner. It helped to see how compatible they could be in team efforts. Mates needed to be able to work and play well together. Not that they wouldn't have differences of opinion, like all couples did, but they still had to be compatible. He and Meghan had signed up to build two of the snow wolves guarding the castle. Others had built the towers, the slide, and several families of wolves running or playing.

"I was glad we could sign up to create a wolf couple," Peter said. "I've had to deal with so many car accidents due to the last snowstorm that this is a nice break." He was thoroughly enjoying being out in the snow with Meghan. She was concentrating hard on starting the sculpture's legs, and he loved how eager she was to do this with him.

"Oh, I agree. This is so much fun. But how awful to have all the car accidents! My sisters and their mates worked on the snow slide because they wanted to be the first ones to slide down it."

Peter laughed. He could imagine CJ and Brett getting as much enjoyment out of that as their mates.

"Are you going to help us make a gingerbread house?" Meghan asked.

He'd thought she'd never ask. He hadn't wanted to invite himself if this was just her sisters and their mates participating. He piled up more snow to make another wolf's leg. "I'm game. I've never made one before, but that should be fun. Maybe I could put it on my résumé if I ever need a new job. Course, it depends on how well I do."

She chuckled. "You never know until you try. We'll have fun doing it."

Peter was glad to take part.

He felt good doing something with her that was fun, even though he was still wearing his sheriff's uniform. She was quiet for a while, and then she took the snow she'd gathered but didn't press it against the wolf as he'd expected her to. Instead, she balled it up and threw it at him.

The snowball splattered on his shoulder, and Peter laughed. He sure hadn't expected a snowball fight—though after the way she'd tackled him on the wolf run, he knew how unpredictable she could be—and he was quick to retaliate.

Chapter 4

MEGHAN AND PETER HAD NEVER PLAYED WITH EACH other before, except for her tackling him as a wolf this morning, and she thought he wasn't used to playing with a she-wolf. To get her mind off Bill and enjoy the time she had with Peter, she'd decided that last bit of snow she'd gathered would make for a great snowball. To her delight, Peter had followed suit, whipping up snowballs while she was throwing hers as fast as she could.

He was laughing, and she'd never seen him this animated. Others had paused to watch them and were laughing too. When she knocked Peter's cowboy hat off, he came around the snow wolf and tackled her in the snow. She laughed and he kissed her. At least they were below the castle's snow slide where they had a bit of privacy. His cold mouth pressed against hers and quickly warmed her up, and she swore with the way his hot body pressed against hers, they were going to melt the snow all the way to the dormant grass in the town square.

She wrapped her arms around his neck and held him tight. God, she hoped Bill being here didn't ruin things.

Peter sighed. "I wish I could take off the rest of the day and just spend it with you."

She agreed and tongued his mouth before he kissed her deeply. Then he reluctantly moved off her and helped her up. But she wasn't done playing. As far as she was concerned, the big snow wolf they were working on was the male. And she added the parts to prove it. When Peter looked down to see what she was doing, he laughed out loud.

They spent three hours on the two wolves, and then Peter took Meghan back to the inn. They'd had fun, and she was glad they'd been able to get away for a few hours to do it.

"Are you sure the male snow wolf was anatomically correct?" he asked her, pulling into the parking area behind the inn.

She ran her hand over his leg, making him smile at her. "I was modeling him after you."

He raised his brows a little and chuckled. "Okay, then you had it right."

She sighed. She'd had such a good time that she didn't want to even think of the business with Bill, but she needed to call him first thing after Peter dropped her off.

"As long as we don't have any real trouble tonight, I'd still like to get together with you for dinner," Peter said, escorting her to the inn.

"I'd like that." If she wasn't still dealing with Bill.

After having such a good time with Meghan, Peter found his day going downhill fast. Due to the recent snowstorm, he'd had to take care of more fender benders, which landed three people at the medical clinic with broken bones, and another storm was on the way. Then while he was trying to get paperwork done on the accidents, Kemp and Radcliff Grey, twin brothers who were ski instructors at the ski resort, dropped by to hassle him before they had to report for work. Peter glanced at his calendar. Yep, it was Tuesday. They went into work a little later on Tuesdays, so that's usually when they bugged him about Meghan and her single status.

"You know, if you don't mate Meghan soon," Kemp said, "the rest of us bachelors are going to be old and gray before you ever make the move."

"Yeah, if you're not interested in mating her, give us a chance to court her," his brother said.

Peter shook his head. "Every week you drop by to hassle me about this, and every week I tell you to look for your own she-wolf—somewhere else." He was certain the pack members who had been building the snow castle exhibit today would spread the word about how much fun he and Meghan were having, and that would help show they were headed for a mating.

"What if some old beau of Meghan's drops in from someplace else?" Radcliff asked.

"Yeah, and they take up where they left off," Kemp said. "If you'd give one of *us* a chance—"

"Preferably me," Radcliff said.

"—I'd date her, and she'd *know I* was interested in mating her."

"Yeah, before some other yahoo who has a past with her rekindles the flame."

Peter eyed the brothers speculatively for a moment, wondering again about the calls Meghan had received last night, but then dismissed their concern. They were always coming up with different reasons for why he should give Meghan up so they could date her. She had never said anything to him about any old boyfriend.

He got a call from his deputy, CJ, and figured there'd been

yet another vehicle accident. Trevor Osgood, another deputy, was still directing traffic for the last incident. "Yeah, CJ?"

"See ya, Sheriff," the brothers said, smiling and waving as they headed out of the sheriff's office. They were good-natured men, blond, amber-eyed, sporting Viking heritage, and Peter always took their joking for what it was—though he knew if he ever said he and Meghan were no longer seeing each other, the twins would ask her to go out with them in an instant.

Peter figured they'd catch some she-wolf's attention someday, if they had the chance.

"Hey, we've got some real trouble," CJ said, his voice tight with concern.

Now what? At least Peter had lucked out in seeing Meghan running as a wolf first thing this morning. That had been the highlight of his day until they were building the snow wolves together. He'd been so busy with work for the last few days, he hadn't had a chance to see her except for dinner last night. He hoped he wouldn't have to call off dinner with her tonight. "Yeah, CJ, what do you have?"

"A man was attacked in one of the Timberline Ski Lodge's rooms around approximately six this morning."

"What?" Now that was news Peter hadn't expected. He was on his feet in an instant and heading for the door.

That's all they needed—for their guests in town to get mugged.

"He's a wolf, thirty-two, and he's suffered a head injury. He's being taken care of at the clinic. The maid found him semiconscious when she went to clean the room at nine this morning. I'm still at the crime scene. His name is Bill Weaver, and his home address is St. Augustine, Florida."

"St. Augustine?" That was where Meghan and her sisters were from, and the calls she'd had last night came to mind for Peter with a vengeance. "I'll be right over." They didn't have murders or attempted murders in the wolf-run town very often, and they were usually wolf-related, though humans did visit the area and occasionally get themselves into trouble. Anytime they had out-of-town wolves causing issues, the whole pack was made aware of it.

"Yeah, but here's the real kicker. Meghan's name is in his cell phone contact list. I was looking for a family member to notify. I didn't find one. A handwritten note listing the Silver Town Inn and its phone number was sitting on the desk in Weaver's room."

"Meghan MacTire?" Peter caught himself before he called her *my* Meghan as he got into his car and drove to the clinic.

He and Meghan had been dating for over a year, but she'd been reluctant to go very far with their relationship until now. He thought it had something to do with her ability to see ghosts. He didn't see them, but he was open-minded about the whole issue. When CJ had courted Meghan's sister Laurel, she'd had the same concern about CJ believing in her psychic ability. The same with Brett and Ellie. Despite Peter telling Meghan that he didn't have problems with her talent, she'd been holding back from their relationship. Until now. Her sisters weren't giving him any hints as to why either. Maybe they really were clueless too.

"Yeah." CJ clearly hated to be the bearer of bad news.

Meghan and her two sisters had a business renovating Victorian hotels and had lived in different parts of the country before finally settling down in Silver Town. Being with a pack had convinced them to stay. As much as Peter cared for Meghan, he vowed to work out whatever issues she was having with him about agreeing to a mating. He and the other pack members loved the women's hint of an Irish accent. Their parents had been born and raised in Ireland, and though the sisters had been born in the States, they had picked up their parents' accent. He could listen to Meghan all day, feeling as though she transported him to the green isle of Ireland.

"I've talked to the owners of the lodge, the brothers Blake and Landon Wolff, about this," CJ said. "Their sisters, Roxie and Kayla, still haven't moved here from Vermont. I believe they're hoping to be here before Christmas, but it might not be until after New Year's. The brothers are perturbed something like this could have happened at their ski lodge and want us to go over their security procedures to give them advice."

"Okay, good job. We can do that." Peter couldn't help wondering if the stranger in town might have something to do with Meghan not wanting to settle down and the calls she'd received last night. Hell, had that been what the Grey brothers were referring to? Just how many other pack members knew about this guy? Maybe he wasn't an old boyfriend from where she'd previously lived. Maybe they'd just assumed he was. Then again, maybe he was, and he'd been looking to take Meghan back to St. Augustine with him.

Hell. "I'll let Darien and Lelandi know about the attack on the wolf at the ski lodge. And CJ?" Peter said.

"Yeah, Peter?"

"Don't share the information about the wolf having Meghan's phone number on his contact list with *anyone* until I can speak with her about it."

"Absolutely. Though I can't say whether he's spoken to anyone at the ski lodge about knowing Meghan. I didn't think to ask the Wolff brothers, but if they knew of it, I'm sure they wouldn't have shared it with me, knowing how you'd feel about it. And just for your information, Meghan's sisters aren't listed in his contacts. Just her number."

That's what Peter was afraid of. Bill Weaver was Meghan's former boyfriend and was interested in renewing his friendship, maybe even joining the pack. *If* Peter's educated guess was correct.

As to the wolf joining their pack? He'd only do it over Peter's dead body.

"I'm calling Bill to arrange for us to meet up," Meghan told her sisters as they cleaned up after having roasted pumpkin soup and ham sandwiches for lunch.

"You better not meet with him at his hotel room, or there will be all kinds of rumors spreading," Laurel warned. "I wouldn't go with him to your home either."

Meghan shook her head. "I don't want to meet him in public, or the same thing will happen."

"Have him come to the inn. You can speak to him in our office. We'll be here to chaperone the two of you and defend you if anyone thinks you have a new—or old—out-of-town boyfriend," Laurel said.

Ellie agreed, but then she said, "On the other hand, it could stir things up a bit. Sometimes that can be a good thing." She winked at Meghan.

"Are you kidding? Peter would arrest Bill on the

spot—for anything! I was thinking the inn's office would be the best place to meet too." Meghan sometimes felt like she was in a fishbowl in the pack. She assumed that once she mated someone, the interest in her love life would vanish. And that would certainly be welcome.

She had to punch in Bill's number, having removed it from her contact list when they'd broken up, and waited to hear him answer the call.

"Hello? Meghan?" Peter said, sounding really surprised to see her phone number pop up on Bill's caller ID.

Meghan nearly dropped the phone, just as shocked to hear Peter's voice. She wanted desperately to pretend she hadn't called Bill. Why in the world was Peter answering Bill's phone? This was *so* not good.

"Yeah, Peter, where's Bill?" Her voice was way too shaky. Her sisters' jaws dropped.

So much for keeping this whole situation under wraps as much as possible. But now Meghan was worried something bad had happened to Bill, since the sheriff was answering his phone. Which reminded her that Bill had sounded concerned about something last night when he'd called her. Had Peter known all about Bill and arrested him on something minor to keep him away from her?

"Someone attacked him in his room at the Wolff's Timberline Ski Lodge. Dr. Weber's seeing Bill at the clinic now," Peter said.

"What?" She felt a total disconnect from the conversation. "How… What… I—I don't understand."

"We don't know the details yet." Peter sounded sympathetic.

"I'll head over to the clinic now." She hung up on Peter.

She should have said something more, but she was so worried about Bill that she wasn't thinking straight. She explained what had happened to Bill to her sisters.

Laurel grabbed her car keys. "I'll drive you over there."

"No. I'll be fine." Meghan thought it was better if she just dealt with this alone.

"You didn't tell Peter anything," Ellie said as Meghan grabbed her purse and headed for the back door of the inn.

"I'll talk to him later. I need to run." Meghan did feel badly about that, but she didn't want to discuss this right away with Peter. Not when Bill had been hurt.

"Wish him well for us," Laurel said.

"I will." Both her sisters had liked Bill. He *was* a likable guy. But the issue of her turning a wolf over to the police had been a sticking point with him.

She drove the short distance to the clinic and was only halfway surprised to find Peter there, awaiting her arrival. Was he afraid she was dumping him for an old boyfriend? No way.

The office manager at the clinic, Carmela Hoffman, a red wolf and distant cousin to their pack leader Lelandi, greeted Meghan before Peter had a chance to say anything to her.

Peter immediately joined Meghan and gave her a small hug that was as warm as ever, but when he was in uniform and in public, he was usually more reserved and reluctant to show a lot of affection. Except when they'd been building the snow wolves, and that had been a welcome change in their relationship.

She imagined this business was making Peter feel a little unsettled.

He kissed her lightly on the cheek. "I'm sorry about your friend."

"He's an *ex*-boyfriend," Meghan told him right off, emphasizing the *ex* so Peter would know she had not invited Bill to visit her in Silver Town. She was glad Peter wasn't standoffish and putting some distance between them. "How bad is he?"

"He has a concussion. Whoever attacked him tried to kill him. His assailant must have thought he had finished him off. Doc is running some more tests on him. Was Bill in Silver Town to see you?"

She suspected Peter knew Bill was here for that purpose, but he was being careful how he handled discussing the matter with her. She appreciated him not jumping to conclusions or at least not acting as though he were.

"Yeah. He's an ex-boyfriend from when we lived in St. Augustine. We broke it off way before my sisters and I moved here."

"He wouldn't be coming here to see you unless he was thinking of making a go of it with you again." *Now* Peter sounded concerned.

"He did mention it."

Peter let out his breath. "He was the caller last night. He—"

Before he could say anything more, Meghan placed her hand on his chest. He immediately placed his hand over hers and squeezed lightly. "I'm *not* interested in him. I told him last night we weren't getting back together. It would never happen."

Peter didn't look reassured. She understood his concern. She'd obviously felt something for Bill, since she'd dated him. But that truly was the past. She shrugged and gave Peter a slight smile of encouragement. "He doesn't move me like you do."

Peter still wore his serious sheriff expression.

She sighed. "I need to see him."

"Right. And I need to speak with him."

She frowned.

He tipped his head. "About his assailant."

"You and I need to talk." It was past time, and if Peter couldn't handle what she had to say, then he wasn't the one for her. Besides, he'd want to know why she and Bill had a falling-out, and it was time to tell him the reason. "This evening. After you get off work."

"All right. Dinner at your place still?" he asked.

"Yeah." They needed to speak in private. She'd never expected to have to talk to Bill at the medical clinic, though.

The nurse joined them in the lobby. "Mr. Weaver's asking for you," Nurse Matthew said to Meghan.

"How's he doing?" she asked as she followed Matthew back to Bill's room.

"He's feeling some dizziness and nausea. His assailant bashed him in the head with a heavy object. We don't know what it was. He might have some short-term memory loss. Maybe long-term. We just don't know yet. We've had skiers with bad concussions who walked right out of here. No memory loss at all. Others might be all right for a couple of days and then collapse. Head injuries are still unpredictable, despite us being wolves and healing in half the time humans can. You never know how a patient will react. He seems to be doing all right for now. Answering questions coherently, remembering some details, not others. But he's in bed naked."

Meghan raised her eyebrows at Matthew.

He shrugged. "We keep helping him into his hospital gown, and he keeps shifting periodically, which is a sign the head injury is affecting him."

That wasn't good news. "All right. Thanks, Matthew." Meghan couldn't help feeling bad about what Bill had gone through—and all because he'd wanted to see her. She couldn't imagine why someone had done that to him. He was really easygoing, except about her putting a wolf in jail. Some random mugger? Someone with a vendetta against him? She knew Peter and everyone he could solicit would be searching for the assailant. She hoped it wasn't a pack member who knew Bill was trying to see her.

Meghan walked into Bill's room. His normally tan skin was pale and his blond hair longer than she remembered. The blankets were resting at his navel, showing his naked chest, and he had a bandage around his head. His eyes were closed, but as soon as he smelled her scent, they opened. Soggy blue eyes stared at her. He cast her a small, tired smile.

"Bill, I'm so sorry. What happened?" She approached him but noticed Peter's shadow spilling into the room. She glanced back to see the sheriff filling the doorway. *Possessive wolf.*

"A man in a black ski mask attacked me. He was waiting in the room for me when I came in after getting a bite to eat in the lodge's restaurant early this morning. But I recognized his scent. *Rollins.* The bastard. I have to warn you that he's out, even though I hadn't thought he'd be out this soon. And he may be coming for you. I didn't think he'd come after me too."

"Hell. Why?" Peter entered the room in investigative mode, taking notes.

She hated that Bill had brought it up first, that this was the way Peter had to learn of her mistake. She couldn't believe the attempted murderer was in the area and could be planning to hurt her, too, or that he had attacked Bill. This was so not good.

"Ralph Rollins?" she asked, as if there was any other that she knew of. She couldn't believe he was out of prison already, but if it was him, she was glad she was with the Silver Town pack. Rollins should have been grateful she had helped send him to prison, rather than having him put down by one of their wolf kind. If he was coming after her, she was worried that he might also try to eliminate her sisters in revenge. They had both been observers at the trial, and he'd cast them some vicious looks, they'd informed her.

"Yeah. Sorry. After you told me what you had done, I stewed about it for a long damn time. Too long. You and your sisters had already sold your hotel and moved from St. Augustine. I didn't know where you had moved until recently. I had gone to see Rollins in prison."

Dread washed over her as she saw Peter turn to study her. He looked astounded to hear the news.

"A wolf? In a human prison?" Peter asked Bill.

"Yeah. After Meghan told me she had turned him in to the police, we ended things between us."

Meghan felt her blood chill as soon as Bill mentioned it. Peter turned to observe her again, his lips parted in a look of surprise. She really had meant to talk to Peter about it tonight. Privately. In person. She should have told him before this.

"Why did he come after you?" she asked Bill, not understanding why Rollins would.

"When I went to see him in prison, I told him he was lucky to still be alive. That if male wolves had been in the area at the time, they would have eliminated him for attempting to murder that woman. By being incarcerated, he'd been given a reprieve. I wanted him to know he had lucked out. Because of it, I hoped he wouldn't come after you once he was released from prison.

"I told him if he caused any more problems, I planned to eliminate him myself. I had fully intended to terminate him anyway, worried he wouldn't stop brutalizing women and might possibly go after you. Hell, he could easily have gotten caught again but ended up with a longer sentence, or life, and not been able to hold his form in prison. Last I heard, he wasn't due to be released for another six weeks." To Peter, Bill said, "I didn't know Meghan when all this happened in St. Augustine. I was new to the area, or I would have taken care of him then."

That's not what Bill had told her! He'd been furious with her. He must have changed his mind when he saw Rollins in prison.

"I had to tell you how sorry I was that I broke up with you, and I understand you did the only thing you could have under the circumstances. I'm here now to protect you."

Peter gave him an evil glower. "*I'm* here to protect Meghan."

Did that mean Peter was okay with her turning a wolf in to the police? She couldn't believe how all this had landed in his lap. She felt terrible that she hadn't revealed the truth to him as soon as they began dating.

"Sure, as sheriff. It's expected of you," Bill said as if she wasn't already dating someone. "But I'll be staying at Meghan's house."

Of all the gall! "*Peter* and I are dating," she told Bill. She'd already told him she was seeing a wolf, but not who or what his occupation was. And no way in hell was Bill ever entering her home. Staying with her? No. Way.

Bill's eyes widened. Then he narrowed his eyes. "You can't take care of her 24/7."

"I can, and I will. Between pack members and me, we'll have her covered." Peter folded his arms across his chest.

"My sisters need protection too," Meghan said, anxious about them. "I wouldn't put it past Rollins to go after them. At the trial, two other women came forth to say he'd beaten them and they'd been hospitalized. So he has no qualms about hurting women."

"And your sisters." Peter immediately got on his phone. "Hey, CJ, we have a situation with this mugger, and it involves Meghan and her sisters." He explained more but didn't leave the room, as if she was already in his protective custody. Then Peter called their pack leaders to get more men involved in searching for Rollins and protecting the ladies.

Meghan gave Laurel a call after that, but CJ had already talked to her, and two men in the pack were on their way to watch over Laurel and Ellie.

"Peter knows about Rollins and is okay with it?" Laurel asked Meghan.

"I'm not sure. I'll get back with you on that later." Meghan knew Peter was going to be busy with trying to ensure she and her sisters were protected and searching for Rollins. When Peter had a moment to reflect, then what?

She couldn't talk to her sister about it with Bill and Peter listening either.

She figured she and Peter would talk about it over dinner tonight. Then again, maybe not, if he was leading the force looking for Rollins. At least because of Rollins's prison sentence, they had a mug shot of him—his hair dark brown, his face bearded, his eyes slate-blue. She and Bill knew his scent. She guessed anyone who had been to the crime scene would. None of them knew what he looked like as a wolf, though.

"We'll put a guard on your room at all times," Peter said to Bill. "Dr. Weber said you won't be leaving here anytime soon."

Meghan guessed Bill's injury was worse than she had imagined. She'd thought—from the way he had talked about protecting her and his lack of memory loss—that he was about ready to leave the clinic. He did look wiped out, though, and not having any control over his shifting could be a real problem.

The nurse poked his head in the doorway. "Dr. Weber says Mr. Weaver needs to rest."

Bill looked as though he wanted Meghan to stay, but they wouldn't be alone. Peter wasn't leaving until she did. And she had no reason to stay. She needed to return to the inn to finish doing her work.

She finally wished Bill well. "I'll check in on you later."

"I want us to get together again. I'll even move here, or wherever you and your sisters end up." Bill looked sincere and hopeful.

"Ellie and Laurel married pack members here. We're staying." *And you're not*, Meghan wanted to add. "I've moved on, Bill. Like I said, I'm dating Peter." Though if Peter wasn't happy about the talk she had with him tonight, she might be seeing someone new...later. But she'd never get back together with Bill.

Before she left the room, Bill startled her by throwing aside his covers as if he wanted to show off how well built he was. Peter looked like he was getting ready to punch him when Bill suddenly shifted into his brown wolf form and sat on the bed growling softly, as if annoyed with his lack of control.

Peter looked like he was fighting a smile and said to Bill, "One of my men will be here in a bit. I'll stay at the clinic until he arrives."

That was the great thing about the pack members. Many were already deputized for any emergency and knew how to fire weapons and had martial arts training. Some would be running as wolves to pick up Rollins's scent at the ski lodge and then chase him down if he was running as a wolf.

Peter followed Meghan out of the room. "So what was that all about? This Rollins character?"

One wolf patient and one human were waiting to see the doctor. Minx, a nineteen-year-old gray wolf, had a cast on her arm from a skiing accident earlier in the season, and someone Meghan didn't know was coughing up a storm nearby. Probably a human on vacation in the area. Meghan didn't want to discuss Rollins around anyone else. She figured the news would spread among the pack members eventually, but she didn't want to let them in on it right now. Though she supposed they would need to know why the wolf was after her. *If* he was. Maybe he'd only been after Bill and had followed him here. But she figured that was wishful thinking on her part.

"In the break room?" She'd thought Peter was going to go after Rollins or watch Bill, not question her. She guessed he might think she had more to share about Rollins that could make it easier to find and capture him. And kill him.

"Yeah."

Meghan led the way, and once they were in the break room, Peter shut the door.

She made a cup of tea for herself. Peter just watched her.

When she sat down at the table, he finally sat kitty-corner from her. "I witnessed Rollins beating a woman nearly to death in an alley in St. Augustine near where we were renovating a Victorian hotel. A grocery store was located near there, and I often walked down the street to it when we needed something. I'd never had any trouble before. It was at night, about six blocks away, and no one was on the street at the time.

"I was about to walk past a dark alley between two buildings when I heard a struggle. At first, I thought Rollins was a random mugger, beating a woman, but then she cried out, 'No, Rollins,' and I realized she knew the man. It was personal. I had no weapon on me and no way to stop him without tearing off my clothes and shifting. The woman was conscious, barely. I whipped out my phone and called the police."

"After you knew he was a wolf?"

She hesitated to answer. She knew Peter wouldn't approve of what she'd done.

"Okay, after." Peter was good at his job. He wouldn't need her to tell him everything. Her hesitation told him all he needed to know.

"Yes. I called the police, and Rollins swung around to

see me on my cell phone. I could have moved out of the view of the alley, but he would have heard me anyway, and…and I couldn't let him beat her to death. I had to stop him."

"At the risk of losing your own life," Peter said, frowning.

Good. Peter didn't seem to be too upset that she'd called the police on Rollins.

"I had to do something. He had to be stopped. I didn't think I could get away with stripping and shifting and killing him without the victim and others seeing. No pack was in the area, so there was no one else I could call on. I even had the notion of paying someone to eliminate him in prison."

Peter raised a brow.

"I was afraid I'd get caught. I wouldn't have known how to go about finding someone who could contact a prisoner and do such a thing."

"Good thing for you."

"Yeah. I'm sure I would have been facing attempted murder-for-hire charges of my own. I'm sorry, Peter. I never thought the bastard would get out of prison this soon, or that he'd come after me. I didn't know Bill had seen him in prison, threatening him even. Bill dumped me after I told him what I had done."

"You said no other wolves were in the area."

"At the time I had the issue with Rollins, no. Bill moved into the area three years after Rollins was sent to prison. I wanted to come clean with him, but I assumed he'd be upset with me. I hadn't expected him to end our relationship. I planned to tell you, but…"

"You were afraid the same thing would happen with me." Peter reached over and squeezed Meghan's hand. "No way in hell. You did what you thought you had to at the time. If you had to do it over again?"

"I would have shifted. But that's only because I now know no one else walked by the alleyway while Rollins was beating the woman. She might have thought she was hallucinating if she'd seen a wolf shift. But if anyone else had seen me?"

"You were right to have done what you did. We can't all be perfect. Leaving a witness alive who had seen you shift could have been just as dangerous for our kind as Rollins shifting in prison. Normally, we'd say to eliminate the witness, but I know you couldn't have done it. Some of our kind wouldn't have had any qualms."

"What about you?"

He let out his breath. "She was already the victim of a brutal attack." He shook his head. "I honestly don't know what I would have done in your place. I've never been put in that position. You might have turned the woman, but that has plenty of complications. Seems to me, the simplest choice is the one we face now. The deed was done. We have only one goal: take down Rollins for good." Peter caressed her hand. "Now, what are we going to do about Bill?"

"Make sure he remains protected and heals? He'll have to stay here until we take Rollins out, since there are no wolves to protect him in St. Augustine. At least there weren't while we were living there."

"After that?"

She smiled. "I'm not interested in him, Sheriff Peter Jorgenson. So don't worry about Bill's comment. He ended the relationship over this business in the first place. There's no going back for either of us. There was never enough of a draw between us. I'm sure that's why it was so easy for him to end things."

"That's all I wanted to hear. If I had to step back…"

"You'd better not," she said in an authoritative manner.

Peter smiled and pulled her from the break-room chair into his arms. "Good. I don't want anything to come between us."

"Like secrets?"

"You should have told me, Meghan. I would have understood. We'll talk more tonight. Over dinner, okay?"

About *his* secrets? Maybe she'd been feeling so guilty about her own that she had believed his secretive behavior with the Silvers was something he didn't want to share with her.

"Okay. I need to get back to the inn and help out." She just hoped they'd catch this bastard and end him quickly before he hurt anyone else.

Peter couldn't believe all this business with Bill and Rollins had to do with Meghan. Turning a wolf in to the police was bad news. But he was sorry Meghan hadn't felt she could talk to him privately about this earlier.

Peter called Trevor. "Hey, I need you over at the inn watching over the ladies." He explained the situation. "Just call any of our deputized men to take care of the traffic issues. Thanks."

Just then, CJ arrived at the clinic's staff break room. "Hey, Meghan, Peter. I'll take first watch here. We've got other men coming—our resident retired Special Forces officer Michael Hoffman, for one—but I know you'll want to escort Meghan back to the inn and start the search for Rollins. I'll help with that as soon as I'm relieved here. Jake said he'll be watching over your sisters."

"Good show. Trevor's on his way over there too. Are you ready to leave, Meghan?" Peter asked.

"Yeah, let's go."

Peter knew not everyone would be in agreement with what Meghan had done. But she was a petite woman, not a muscular man, and couldn't have taken Rollins out at the crime scene and stopped him permanently. Not unless she'd been a wolf. Even Bill, who was well muscled, hadn't been able to fight back sufficiently to stop his attacker from knocking him out at the lodge.

Peter had to eliminate this bastard before he could hurt anyone else—and make sure Bill left town for good.

Chapter 5

WHEN PETER ESCORTED MEGHAN TO THE INN, HER SIS-ters hurried outside to greet her. Jake and Trevor followed them out in protective mode.

"Oh…my…God, Meghan," Laurel said, giving her a big hug.

Ellie quickly followed suit.

"I'm off to try to learn what I can about Rollins's where-abouts," Peter said.

Everyone said goodbye, but Meghan kissed him, hug-ging him as if she wanted things to go further with him, which she did. She didn't want any of this to come between them. He kissed her back as if he'd forgotten about their audience or that he was wearing a uniform, even though part of that uniform was jeans that hugged his muscles and made her want to run her hands over them. Every time they kissed, her blood pumped with heated desire. She felt his erection pressing against his jeans and her. He'd never kissed her in front of her sisters like this. She really didn't want to let him go.

His tongue tangled with hers briefly, and then he reluc-tantly pulled away, kissing her forehead and whispering in her ear, "Tonight."

For a moment, she was lost in the feel of him. He gave her a roguish wink, showing a side she rarely saw of him, and she wondered if they'd end up in bed together tonight.

If they did, hopefully, they'd end the night in a better way. She decided right then and there she wanted to see a lot more of that side of him. She smiled, watching him get in his vehicle and drive off, and turned to speak to her sisters, both of whom were smiling at her. Jake and Trevor were taking in the whole situation too. She just hoped neither would tell the pack leaders that it looked as though Meghan and Peter were finally becoming mated wolves.

"I can't believe that bastard followed us here," Laurel said.

"*Me*, not you." Meghan adored her sisters. They were like the Three Musketeers, female versions, always there for each other. "Or maybe Rollins was just after Bill for threatening him and doesn't realize I live here."

"Bill threatened him?" Laurel asked as they all moved inside the inn and congregated in the lobby.

"Yeah, at the prison."

"Great. What if Rollins learns Bill had come here to see you? Then Rollins could take care of both of you at the same time." Laurel frowned. "How is Bill?"

Meghan figured Trevor and Jake already had gotten the word from Jake's cousin CJ and that's why they weren't drilling her for information too.

Ellie got another call on the reservation line and hurried back to the front desk.

"Rollins hit him really hard. The doctor wants Bill to stay in the clinic for several more days, but he'll be well guarded the whole time. I hope the woman Rollins attacked is safe and that he didn't go after her again." A woman never knew the trouble she could be in if she picked the wrong kind of boyfriend and then tried to leave him. "Or even the other two women who testified against him."

"I was going to say Peter needs to call and ask the St. Augustine police to do a health and welfare check on the three women, but since the bastard's here and we need to take him down personally, it would be best if we check on that later. We don't want the police there getting involved in our wolf affairs. How are you feeling about all this?" Laurel asked.

Ellie was still manning the registration desk and looking like she wanted to end the calls so she could talk about this too. She usually chatted away with whoever called to reserve a room, but instead she was quickly making the reservation and ending the call.

"It's a shock. It's all so hard to believe," Meghan said. "I'm not even entirely sure why Bill wanted to speak to me. He wouldn't say over the phone, and at the time, he didn't know Rollins was already out."

"Because he wanted to see you in person to tell you how stupid he was for dumping you," Ellie said. "And he couldn't do that over the phone."

"Right, I agree with Ellie. But Bill could have put you in danger by not warning you sooner that he'd talked to Rollins in prison. That could have set Rollins off. Your testimony helped to put him in prison. He has to resent being locked up like that," Laurel said. "You knew there was always the possibility he might come after you once you'd called the police on him and, along with three former girlfriends, testified in court against him, which helped in putting him away. CJ wants you to stay with us at our home. Or we could stay at your house, but Rollins may already know you own it and be watching it."

"Peter's coming over for dinner later so we can talk at my house. I told him about everything."

"And his secret?" Laurel asked. She glanced at Jake and Trevor.

The brothers cast each other a knowing look. Meghan swore they knew Peter had a secret he wasn't sharing with her.

"I'm going to take a look around your home," Trevor said to Meghan.

"All right." Meghan handed him the set of keys to her house.

"I'll walk around the inn grounds," Jake said.

When the guys left, Meghan said, "Maybe Peter doesn't have a secret and him ending the conversation so abruptly was just because it was guy talk. But Trevor and Jake seemed to want to leave here in a hurry, as if they didn't want us to question them about it. I want to talk to Peter about my ability to commune with ghosts, to make sure he understands about that. At least he knows about Rollins now."

"That's a good idea. It was so important for me to know CJ didn't think I was just imagining things," Laurel said.

Ellie hung up the phone again. She was already making reservations through the summer next year. "The same with Brett and me."

Laurel asked, "So how long has the kissing like *that* been going on between you and Peter?"

"In public and when Peter's wearing his uniform? Never," Meghan said, amused her sister would bring it up now. Though if Laurel hadn't, Ellie was sure to have.

"Except for the scene at the square today," Ellie said.

"Oh yeah, that. What about in private?" Laurel asked.

Meghan felt her cheeks warm several degrees. Her sisters smiled.

"Duly noted," Laurel said. "You've been holding out on us."

"Well, we wondered when you had to pull the plug on your bedroom phone," Ellie said. "Oh, wait, you were wearing the red dress! Unless Laurel ran over to your house late last night to unzip the dress, bet you had to ask Peter to unzip it and that led to...more."

Meghan didn't confirm. "The business with Rollins was just dropped on poor Peter all at once. Who knows how he'll handle the paranormal issues."

"Unless he's hiding how he feels about them, I don't think you have any worries there," Laurel said.

"Yeah, and if kissing you like that in front of us and Trevor and Jake is any indication, it seems your actions with Rollins don't bother him. Plus, having Bill pop into the area may have pushed Peter to get this show on the road," Ellie said.

"It's not a show," Meghan said.

Laurel and Ellie smiled again. "It was for us," Laurel said. "A really enjoyable show."

Her sisters laughed. Meghan smiled, then frowned. "But he's never seen me in action when I'm trying to deal with lost souls. He might not be able to handle it." Meghan had watched a show where a psychic helped police solve criminal cases and her husband was totally supportive of her ability—talking to her about her cases, offering suggestions, always giving her emotional support—even though he couldn't sense ghosts at all. Of course, it was only a TV show, not real life. Even so, that's what Meghan hoped for. A mate who would be understanding, even if he didn't have her abilities.

She could think of nothing worse than having a mate

who thought she just had a wild imagination. What if she had kids who had the same ability as she had? Would he want to stifle their abilities? Be afraid others would judge them badly? She swore if she and Peter didn't work out, she'd be totally up front with the next guy she dated. First date, she'd say…well, she wouldn't know what to say. The only way to know for certain how a possible mate would view her abilities was to have to deal with an apparition in front of him, she imagined. She suspected if she came out and asked a bachelor what he thought of her ability to see ghosts, he'd say it was fine with him. But only because there was a shortage of she-wolves in the pack. Would he truly be supportive of her after the mating? Or wish he'd found someone who was more…normal?

She realized her sisters had been talking to each other while she was thinking this over and were both looking at her as if they figured she hadn't been listening to the conversation they'd been having.

"You and Peter will be fine." Ellie placed her hands over her heart and looked heavenward. "After what we saw of the…*kiss*."

Laurel agreed. "Yeah, I think things are moving right along for the two of you. After you and Peter have dinner at your place, he can bring you over to my house."

"All right." Meghan knew if she said she'd stay at her own home, more men would have to safeguard her around the clock, but if she stayed with one of her sisters, her mate could be Meghan's protection. Normally, she'd prefer to stay home and not feel like she was interrupting anything between CJ and her sister, but with the idea of facing Rollins alone? She wanted some male wolf muscle.

If she had to call the police this time? No problem. They were all wolves.

She and her sisters suddenly heard their resident ghost, Chrissy, sobbing in the basement. They all turned to look in the direction of the hall that led to the stairs. They had additional guest rooms down there, so they were glad all their guests were out enjoying the area and not in their rooms hearing the ghostly sounds. If they were able to.

"Chrissy," Meghan said. "*Now* what's wrong?"

Meghan and her sisters didn't know how to help the ghostly Victorian-era maid find closure and move on. She'd grown up here as a young girl and was working as a maid before she died of a fever, just as her mother had worked as a maid here earlier. Her mother had apparently died before that and her spirit must have left well before Meghan and her sisters bought the place. Meghan and her sisters had tried everything they could think of to help Chrissy move on, but none of the methods that had worked on many of their ghostly exorcisms had succeeded for her. Chrissy had sworn up and down that she was happy here. But from time to time during the holidays this year, she'd had crying fits and no one could learn what the matter was.

"Since you left to see Bill at the clinic, she's been sobbing off and on. Ellie and I took turns trying to console her. Nothing has helped, and she can't seem to tell us what's bothering her," Laurel said.

"She needs to find peace." They had enough troubles with an attempted murderer lurking around Silver Town, if Rollins was still in the area, without having the added problem of a wailing ghost in their basement. Because all three sisters could hear and see ghosts, sometimes they forgot that not all people were as sensitive to such sightings. Still, they worried about how their guests would view this if they could see and hear the ghost. Certainly, her wailing wouldn't be conducive to a pleasant stay.

"I'll see her." Meghan headed for the stairs to the basement. She'd even tried to convince Chrissy to move to her home behind the inn so if Chrissy continued to have meltdowns, she could do so in the privacy of the house. *Not* in the inn filled with guests. Though Meghan wasn't sure she could "move" Chrissy. Some ghosts were attached to a place. Others to objects. Some to people. Chrissy appeared bound to the inn.

Thankfully, Chrissy had stopped sobbing before Meghan arrived at the bottom of the stairs. When she reached the room that had been Chrissy's while she worked as a maid, Meghan could see the woman as plain as day, dusting the furniture with a feather duster. Her long, blue dress touched the top of her short, laced-up boots, her white apron trimmed with lace. Her blond hair was pulled back in a bun, and she wore a traditional maid's cap. "Chrissy, what's wrong?"

Chrissy turned to face her, tears streaking her face, her eyes red from crying.

"We can hear you all the way upstairs. We're worried about you."

"It's going to be Christmas soon," Chrissy said, suddenly vanishing and then reappearing next to Meghan.

Even though Meghan was used to the way ghosts moved about, appearing and disappearing at will, Chrissy's sudden movement startled her. Chrissy looked hopeful that Meghan might be able to do something about her being upset.

"You mentioned Christmas."

Chrissy nodded.

"Lots of Christmases have passed and—"

"Not since you and your sisters arrived. The inn was vacant forever and in ruins. No Christmases. No celebrations. No lights. No…no presents."

"You weren't this distraught last Christmas." Meghan knew something more had to be bothering her.

"Your sisters have found mates."

Meghan frowned. They'd wondered if Chrissy was a wolf like them, but they'd never asked. What benefit could come of it? It could upset her more. They couldn't smell her scent, except for violets sometimes. But not her actual human scent. Or wolf, if she had been one.

Meghan finally asked, "Are you a wolf too?"

Chrissy's eyes widened. She nodded. "Now *you're* going to mate soon. And then I'll be the only one without one."

Meghan's mouth gaped. Chrissy wanted a mate? Ohmigod, how in the world could they find a ghostly mate for her? That would take one Christmas miracle.

"Was there anyone you were sweet on?" This could be a total nightmare. If he was a wolf, he could still be alive. Wolves could live hundreds of years. If he was human, he would be dead, but could Meghan even find him, no matter what he was?

Chrissy nodded.

Meghan felt chills run up her spine. What if the two of them became ghostly mated wolves and… Well, she didn't even want to think of what could go on between them and the disturbances they could cause.

"You're in trouble," Chrissy said matter-of-factly, and

Meghan realized she'd been eavesdropping on her and her sisters.

That was the thing about ghosts of *lupus garous*. With their enhanced hearing as wolves, they could easily eavesdrop.

"Yeah. I made a mistake a while back," Meghan said, thinking that maybe if she shared what was troubling her with Chrissy, the ghostly maid would continue to share with Meghan what was going on with her. "I sent a man to prison for attempting to murder his ex-girlfriend. He's a wolf. Now he's come here to Silver Town to kill me, I'm afraid."

Chrissy put her hands against her chest in alarm, the duster resting against her clean white apron. "Oh my. You must ask Alvin if he can protect you, though I haven't seen him in so long, I don't know what's become of him." Her eyes misted with fresh tears.

"He's your beau? Alvin?"

"Alvin Browning Mainstreet. He works in the silver mine."

That had been shut down. A whole bunch of miners had worked there. Some had died. Meghan brightened. What if Alvin had died and his spirit was still hanging around the old mine? Not that she hoped he had died. But what if he was still living and had mated someone else? Ugh.

Meghan didn't recognize the name offhand. Maybe some of the old-timers would.

"Was he your beau?" Meghan asked again.

Chrissy nodded. "I keep hoping he'll come see me. I thought he was going to propose to me for Christmas. But that was so long ago. Maybe he's got a new girl. I just…I just want to know. It's nearly Christmas, and...and I don't have anyone to share it with."

"Okay, I'll see what I can learn about him. Why didn't you tell any of us about him before?"

Chrissy pursed her lips. "How would you feel if Peter found another girl and he didn't mate you?" She sighed. "I guess...I didn't want to know if Alvin is seeing someone else. Not until you and Peter..."

"We're not mated wolves yet."

"I know, but if you don't mate him, Peter will die."

Meghan smiled.

"I'm serious. When his wife died, Peter was inconsolable."

"Wife?" Meghan hadn't meant to sound so shocked, but man, was she!

Chrissy bit her lip, her eyes wide. "He...he didn't tell you yet?"

Meghan cleared her throat. "Uh, no, but I'm sure he is going to tonight over dinner." She couldn't believe he hadn't told her about his mate! Was that the secret? Was he still carrying a torch for her? Some wolves never mated again after they had lost their mate. He had to have lost her, or he wouldn't be courting Meghan now, if Chrissy knew what she was talking about. Meghan wanted to ask how Chrissy knew about it, but she wanted to hear the story straight from Peter. Was he afraid she'd think badly of him because he'd already been mated? Some wolves would feel guilty if they found another wolf to love and worry that others would feel they were being disloyal to the memory of their first wolf mate.

"I'm sorry," Chrissy said, looking forlorn all over again.

"You have nothing to be sorry for." Meghan wanted to give Chrissy a hug and comfort her. She felt terrible seeing the maid so upset and being unable to give her a human hug. "I'll see what I can learn about Alvin. Just…talk to us if you're feeling down, okay?" What if Meghan found him and she couldn't get the two of them together? She could see being a ghost courier—taking messages back and forth between the ghosts to make them happy. Forever.

"All right." Chrissy gave her a winsome smile and began dusting the dresser again. Too bad her efforts were in vain. Yes, she could move objects, throw them, write on a fogged-up mirror, and more, but actually picking up dust with her ghostly duster? That didn't seem to be doable.

Which meant Meghan had to dust over any place that Chrissy had already cleaned, hoping the sensitive spirit didn't catch her at it. The last time Chrissy had, she'd been scared to death Meghan or her sisters would fire her for not cleaning the inn properly. As if they could fire her.

Chrissy faded into thin air, and Meghan figured she was done talking. At least Chrissy wasn't crying any longer. For *now*.

Meghan walked up the stairs and joined her sisters in the lobby. "Have any guests returned yet?" She didn't think so since she hadn't heard anyone's voices other than her sisters' muted ones.

Ellie shook her head. "You got Chrissy to stop crying."

"For the moment." Meghan asked them if they knew an Alvin Browning Mainstreet.

"Nope, but you can always ask my mate if he has any-thing in the archives at the newspaper office," Ellie said.

"That's a great idea," Meghan said. "I'll just run over to the newspaper office and—"

Her sisters shook their heads.

Meghan frowned, then realized why they were saying no to the plan. "I will kill Rollins myself this time." She was so angry, realizing just how much she hated confinement when she was eager to solve Chrissy's dilemma.

"Who *is* he?" Laurel asked.

"Chrissy's old beau. A silver miner."

"No," both Ellie and Laurel said at the same time.

"You don't think you can bring his ghost here if he's a ghost and still earthbound, do you?" Laurel asked.

"I don't know if I can or if I should. What if I somehow managed it and they became mated wolves?"

"She's a wolf?" Ellie asked.

"Yeah. And then we could be hearing their mating moans and whatever else we might witness."

Ellie smiled. Laurel shook her head.

Though she didn't make an appearance, Chrissy's voice could be heard in the distance. "We'll shut the door." Chrissy definitely had a wolf's hearing.

The sisters shared looks that said they didn't think that would help, but then they all smiled.

"All right, I'll call Brett and ask if he's got any information on Alvin," Meghan said, tapping in Brett's number. She hated making any calls Chrissy might overhear. "Hey, Brett, Chrissy's a bit melancholy over the holidays, and she said she had a beau named Alvin Browning Mainstreet and he was a silver miner. I'd go over to the newspaper office to check it out, but I need around-the-clock-protection, and so do your mate and Laurel."

"I'm looking it up now. Okay, I have an obituary for Alvin, died in a mining accident...well, six months after Chrissy died, apparently. He had no next of kin."

"Was he a wolf?"

"I can't tell from this. All I know is that some of the miners were wolves and some were humans. I don't remember him."

"Chrissy would know. And if she figures he's still alive, he must be a wolf." Meghan half expected Chrissy to pop up and tell her what Alvin was. "Was he at the main shaft?"

"Uh, yeah, but you've got to be careful around the mine. Not to mention you can't go unescorted anyway."

"Do you want to use it for a news story and go with me?" Meghan was hopeful he would.

"You mean a ghost story? Hotel ghost in love with miner ghost in a story of star-crossed lovers." Brett chuckled.

"More in the vein of two people in love who were never able to share mated love? Married bliss. And yes, they'd be star-crossed lovers. I'll find out what I can from Chrissy, and then if I can..." Meghan paused. She didn't want to say Alvin was dead without telling Chrissy in person first. "Well, you know."

"Don't worry. Whether there's a story in it or not, I'll help you."

"Thanks, Brett. You're a great brother-in-law."

"Thanks. I'm only too glad to help. But you need to okay any field trips with Peter first. The story about Rollins is my first priority, and I'm trying to get the word out to all our people to be on the lookout for him."

Meghan's heart sank. She didn't want everyone to know why Rollins was here.

When she didn't say anything, Brett said, "Hey, if you're worried about how our people feel, most everyone's behind you on this. You did what you had to do. Some would have just let him kill the woman instead of turning him in to the police. Would that have been a better solution? Not for the woman he had been attacking. And while he was free, he could have continued his rampage. He could very well have landed himself in prison later. So it worked out for the best. Now he's in our territory, or at least we hope so, and we can handle him. Let him take on men more his size."

"He could have killed Bill."

"Bill wasn't prepared. We *will* be. When did you want to go?"

"Now."

Brett chuckled. "You're just like Ellie when she wants to get something done. All right. Let me clear out my inbox, which will take about an hour. I'll pick you up. Just call Peter first and get the okay, will ya?"

"Yeah, sure." Meghan hoped Peter would be fine with it. Not only did she want to help Chrissy, but they really needed the peace and quiet around the inn.

As soon as Meghan got ahold of Peter and explained where she and Brett were headed, Peter was silent for so long, she was afraid the line had been disconnected.

"Peter, are you still there?"

"We have a manhunt going on right now."

"I know that." She tried not to sound annoyed about it, but she wasn't going to put her life on hold when Chrissy could cause a real stir at the inn as soon as their guests returned for the night. "I shouldn't be bothering you with this now, but I thought you'd want to know if I left the inn. See you tonight." This was *exactly* what she was afraid of.

She wanted to learn about Peter's mate, but that would have to be tonight at dinner. She didn't mention it to her sisters in case Chrissy was wrong. Meghan knew if she did, they'd be hounding their mates for details, and she'd prefer to speak about this privately with Peter.

She ended the call, not about to hear why Peter didn't think she should do what she had to do.

Chapter 6

PETER UNDERSTOOD MEGHAN'S CONCERN ABOUT THE ghost causing trouble for her guests, at least in theory. He'd dropped by to check on Bill again at the clinic. CJ and Michael Hoffman were still guarding him, but Bill was sleeping as a wolf. It was a good thing all their medical staff were wolves. Peter had planned to ask Bill more questions about Rollins and let him know he had no chance of getting back together with Meghan. Now, Peter was staring at his silent phone after Meghan had hung up so abruptly on him. He quickly punched Meghan's contact number again.

Peter had never seen or heard Chrissy or any other ghosts. Which Meghan said meant he wasn't as sensitive to psychic phenomena. What with the ongoing manhunt, Peter preferred that she stay at the inn with her sisters and their guards. But if Meghan wasn't going to, he wanted to be the one safeguarding her. Not that Brett couldn't do a good job, but Peter would feel better about it if they were both there with her.

He knew she was peeved with him, or she wouldn't have ended the call so brusquely. "Hey, Meghan, I'll meet you over at the Silver Town Mine."

CJ was eyeing him, probably wondering what was up now.

"You don't have to stop what you're doing to protect me. I'll be with Brett, and we will be perfectly fine," Meghan said, sounding annoyed.

"Listen, if you're going to be out there like bait, I'll be there. See you in a few minutes." Peter wasn't about to be deterred from protecting her. If nothing else, he wanted to prove he wasn't trying to make light of her situation.

"Thanks." Meghan sounded relieved Peter wasn't upset with her.

He was glad because he sure as hell didn't want Bill worming his way back into her good graces, just because Peter hadn't handled this ghostly matter well. They ended the call, and he knew that was something else they needed to discuss tonight. Peter had given the issue of this ghost business she was involved in a lot of thought. As it was for CJ with Laurel and Brett with Ellie, it was hard for Peter to believe in something he couldn't see or hear. CJ and Brett had witnessed some paranormal happenings, and Peter suspected if he was exposed to this business long enough, he might too. He was determined to prove to Meghan that what she had to deal with was just as important to him as it was to her. So like CJ and his brother, Peter had been reading a lot of books concerning paranormal phenomena.

Peter let CJ know he was headed out to the Silver Town Mine because of the ghostly issues.

CJ snorted. "You?"

"Meghan and your brother Brett are going there in search of a miner's ghost."

"The sisters must be having trouble with Chrissy again. Don't tell me he's a relative of hers or...a boyfriend?"

"Yep, he was Chrissy's beau." Peter shrugged. "I have no idea what Meghan intends to do about it, but I want to make sure she remains safe. I'll let you know when I'm back to the business of hunting Rollins down."

"Good luck with the ghost." CJ sounded amused that Peter was having to juggle his time between real sheriff business and paranormal mysteries, just like CJ did as Laurel's mate.

When Peter arrived at the Silver Town Mine, he found Meghan and Brett already there. Peter wasn't sure if he wished he could see what she did or not. He could imagine how disturbing it would be to see something no one else could. And worse, to have to do something about it. Arresting people or eliminating rogue wolves he had no problem with. Dealing with a ghostly entity? He wasn't sure how well he could handle it.

Meghan was peering into the mine shaft where there had been a couple of deadly mine accidents in the nineteenth and twentieth centuries.

"See anyone?" Peter asked her.

She turned and frowned at him. "No. I've been calling out to anyone who might be down there, but no one's responded. I need to go to the area where they died. If any ghosts are hanging around down there, they're going to be stuck, just like the men who died there were."

"Even though we removed the bodies?" Peter asked.

"Yeah. If they felt the hopelessness of being unable to leave the mine, the horror that they couldn't rejoin their loved ones, the trauma of their injuries, and the lack of oxygen making them suffocate, their spirits could be trapped there forever."

It started to snow, and their breaths were frosty in the cold air. "You don't want to wait on this?" Peter didn't think she would, but he was hoping she'd return to the inn and he could get back to helping track Rollins down.

"Chrissy could be a real problem for us. For whatever reason, this Christmas has hit her harder than last year."

"All right. Let's do this." Peter would do anything he could to not only safeguard Meghan but also help her. No amount of talking would prove he could back her on this as much as actually doing so for real.

"I'll go down first and make sure it's safe enough," Brett said, returning to his car. "I just need to take some climbing gear, helmets, and lanterns in case they're needed."

"You were prepared," Peter said.

"Being married to Ellie makes me prepared. I never know what to expect when it comes to dealing with spirits. Or with trying to find fresh stories for the newspaper."

Brett had never shared that he helped with spirits. Peter wondered just how involved he'd been in this stuff.

"I'll go down with you," Peter said to Meghan. "Brett, if you would, stay topside and watch out for trouble. If we have any problems, I'll let you know. If you have any trouble, same thing."

"Okay, sure thing." Brett handed the climbing equipment over to Peter.

A workable ladder led down into the mine shaft, but it had been a while since anyone had used it, that they knew of. Kids might have been playing down there, though it was forbidden. But kids loved to explore and create their own adventures, so it was possible. Even some adults might have done so.

Fitted with climbing gear and a headlamp on his helmet, Peter gave Meghan a hug, then began the descent into the blackness, wondering what *he* might find down there.

———————————

Meghan couldn't have been more appreciative of Peter for coming with her into the mine. She would have understood if he'd stayed up above to watch out for Rollins and call in support if Brett and she got into trouble, but she was really glad Peter wanted to be there for her. And she was glad he wasn't dismissing her concern.

"I'm at the bottom of the first level. Do you want to come down?" Peter asked her. "The ladder is safe."

"Yeah, sure, heading down now." Meghan put on the extra helmet with a headlamp. She had never considered seeing if ghosts were stuck in the mine until Chrissy mentioned wanting to see Alvin. Meghan and her sisters hadn't been in Silver Town that long, and they'd been so busy renovating their inn after years of disuse that there hadn't been much time for exploring.

She could see a lantern sitting on the rocky floor where Peter was waiting for her, the light on his headlamp shining brightly. The ladder was in really good shape, for which she was grateful.

As soon as she stepped onto the floor of the mine, Peter wrapped his arms around her and gave her a hug. It was cold down here, but without the wind chill. She loved when he hugged her. And then kissed her. Hmm, this was rather a romantic spot for the two wolves.

"Hey, are you two all right down there?" Brett hollered down.

"Uh, yeah, we're going into the tunnel now," Peter said as if he'd forgotten his duty.

Meghan liked when Peter wanted to hug her when normally he was so mission-oriented. *Do it right, and finish it quickly* was his motto. "Where did the miners die?" she asked Peter.

"Next level down. There was a massive cave-in. We tried to move enough rocks to make a hole through the cave-in area to get the men out, but only two made it out alive. The other ten suffocated. We never cleared the debris to work on that part of the mine again."

"I'm so sorry."

"Yeah. It was awful. We had another accident much later, and not long after that, geologists declared the silver veins were no longer profitable, so the Silver pack leaders closed the mine."

"If we'd thought of it, my sisters and I could have come down here to help these men find peace."

"I'd never considered it either," Peter said.

They came around a bend in the tunnel and saw a sleeping bag and cans of food—some open and used up, others still sealed, and bottled water for a campout, sitting next to a wall covered in wet moss. New equipment, nothing that had been sitting here for eons.

Peter immediately got on his radio. "Can you hear me, Brett?" All he got was static back. "I can't get a signal this deep in," he told Meghan.

"I don't smell anyone's scent on it."

Peter picked up the black backpack and then dumped out the contents on the sleeping bag. A can of hunter's concealment spray caught their attention. "I doubt it's a coincidence that Rollins is in the area and this is a fresh stash. Why would anyone wear hunter's spray unless he's a rogue wolf who's up to no good? I'm surprised he didn't use it earlier when he attacked Bill. That is, if it's his. Most likely, this stuff belongs to Rollins and he's been camping out here. From the number of cans of food he's eaten, I'd say he's been here for at least three or four days. I need to let Brett know and get some men over here to help search the tunnels."

"Whoever it was will smell we've been here. I doubt he'll return," Meghan said.

"Probably true."

"I'll stay here, if you want to warn Brett and let the others know Rollins most likely has been camping out here."

Peter studied her for a moment. He clearly didn't like the idea of leaving her down here alone.

"He's not here." She thought she might be able to get ahold of the ghost while Peter was gone.

"What if Rollins is still here, heard us coming, and is hiding from us deeper in the tunnels?" Peter asked.

That sent a chill up her spine. "Okay, I'm coming with you." No way did she want to encounter the wolf alone after he had nearly killed Bill.

When they reached the ladder, Peter used his radio again and this time got ahold of Brett. "Hey, we found camping gear and supplies, probably Rollins's stuff."

"Hell, good thing Meghan had a mission and that you agreed to come with us," Brett said to Peter.

"Yeah, he might be off prowling the woods or something, or he might be deeper in the silver mine. We're coming up until we can get more men to help us make sure he's not here."

"All right. See you in a few."

"Ladies first," Peter said to Meghan.

She so wanted to go find the ghosts, but she didn't want to run into Rollins and risk becoming a ghost down here herself. Her sisters would be furious with her!

Meghan began the climb up, hoping to make it out of the

mine in record time so they could get some men here and she could do what she vowed to do—help Chrissy.

Once she was up top, Peter didn't take long to join them. Then he was on his phone to his deputies, asking several of them to join him at the silver mine. "Any luck finding any sign of Rollins anywhere else? Are there any unaccounted-for vehicles parked in isolated areas?" he asked his men. "Okay, well, he's not from here, so he'd need to make his way here somehow. Maybe he hitchhiked, but I still figure he's got a vehicle somewhere. See you soon."

That was one thing about the wolves who had lived here all their lives. They knew every bit of the Silver Town wolves' territory, unlike her and her sisters, who were so new.

Meghan called Laurel to give her the news.

"Rollins has been hiding out at the silver mine? I hope they can catch him. You're not going back into it, are you?"

Meghan turned off her headlamp. "Yeah, I have to. For Chrissy's sake, if only to let her know I found Alvin or not."

"All right, but be careful."

"I will be. There will be a ton of us down there, so I'll be safe. I'll tell you when I know something."

"Good luck," Laurel said.

They waited until ten men arrived to check out the mine. Meghan wanted to go with them, or behind them, and look for any ghosts that might be down there. That way, she'd have plenty of protection, and she might still be able to make some headway on Alvin's whereabouts today.

Chapter 7

"I KNOW YOU. YOU'RE NOT GOING TO WANT TO WAIT TO GO back down into the mine." Peter wished Meghan would return home with an armed guard of wolves. He didn't like that she'd be in the mine if Rollins was running around down there. He was surprised the bastard would actually be in the mine. It would be easy to get lost without knowing his way around, and it wasn't the safest place to camp out. But Rollins probably figured no one else would think to search for him down there.

"You're right. With all these men looking for him, it will be the safest time for me to find the spirits that might have been left behind."

Despite his misgivings, Peter gave in. He didn't usually. He couldn't in the line of work he was in if it meant keeping order and protecting people. He just didn't want to get into any issues with her over it. He realized when it came to relationships with women he cared for, he really didn't like conflict and avoided it if at all possible. "All right. We'll go down together. Brett and a couple more men will stay up top to watch for any signs of Rollins if he should return and that was his gear down below." This time, Peter let her climb down first, since the other men were already down there, deciding which teams would go where.

When she reached the bottom, Meghan called out that she was safely down and Peter followed.

Once he joined her, they went together to search through the first of the tunnels, the men having split off into groups of three and headed down three different ones. CJ joined Peter and Meghan in the mine after having left Ranger Michael at the clinic to guard Bill. Peter knew Michael wasn't there just to safeguard Bill but also his mate, Carmela, the office manager at the clinic.

CJ hung back a little. Peter wondered if CJ might be able to see ghosts down here too.

"What are you going to do if you see any miners' ghosts?" CJ asked Meghan.

"If I can talk to them, I will. I don't have anything with me that I could use to exorcise them, though sometimes just getting to the root of why they're stuck where they are works to release them. Using psychology can make all the difference. If Lelandi ever has some slow time from her practice, she could help us with what to ask the ghosts."

Peter shook his head. "I doubt it. She doesn't have time except for her patients, the kids, and helping Darien lead the pack."

"You never know. She might find she has a real calling for it."

"If you ever need help, I'm sure she'd give you some advice." Peter couldn't see Lelandi entering the mine of her own accord. He recalled when she'd been kidnapped and forced to hide in the caves, and Darien had come to her rescue. She was terrified of enclosed spaces. Not everyone knew that, and Peter had no intention of telling anyone who hadn't witnessed it.

CJ continued to follow behind them as they made their way to the first of the cave-ins, and Peter appreciated he was there too. They had to crawl through the hole the pack members had made to rescue the only survivors of the earlier mine accident. When they reached the other side, they heard voices in the tunnel. It was just three of the men who were searching for Rollins, not ghosts.

Peter glanced back at CJ to see if he was sensing anything. He smiled and shook his head.

And then Meghan slowed her pace way down and Peter glanced at her. She was looking straight at something, and he wondered if she'd found Alvin. He was hoping she had and could resolve this situation. After that, he'd take her directly back to the inn.

───────────

Deeper into the mine, Meghan saw two men sitting on some timber, watching them approach, with lanterns and pickaxes sitting nearby. They were wearing old jeans and suspenders, wool plaid shirts, and boots, their clothes and bearded faces covered in dust. One was wearing a torn piece of bloodstained cloth around his head.

They looked perfectly real and not like spectral beings. She assumed they were two of the miners' ghosts. "Are either of you Alvin?" she asked, forgetting that most likely neither Peter nor CJ could see the spirits. Maybe CJ could.

They glanced at her and then in the direction she was looking.

"I am." The fairer man with the bandage wrapped around his head frowned. "You can see us? And hear us?"

"Alvin?" Meghan's heart raced, and she hoped this was Chrissy's former boyfriend.

"Yes, ma'am."

"I'm Meghan. My sisters and I have renovated the Silver Town Inn. Chrissy was working there."

Alvin's jaw dropped. "She died." He said the words as if he expected Meghan to say he was mistaken. "I went to her funeral."

"Yes. But like you are trapped in the mine, she's trapped at the inn. She wants to…hear from you." Meghan caught herself before she said "see" him. She was excited to see Alvin and sorry that the men's spirits were stuck down here.

"You're the first person who's seen us," the darker-bearded man said. "The first. I'm Oliver Fraser." Oliver's arm was in a makeshift sling, and he favored it as if his arm still hurt.

"I'm sorry this happened to both of you." To Alvin, she said, "If I can, I'd like to help you somehow connect with Chrissy. Then maybe you'll find your final resting place."

Oliver snorted. "We ain't leaving this place, sister. We've tried. We don't know for how long, but we've tried every day now. The two of us got stuck here. The others left, but later there was another cave-in. Fifteen more men died. They visited with us, and we got to catch up on what was going on in the wolf pack. Though a couple of them weren't wolves." He smiled a little evilly. "They finally believed we could shift."

"Do you? Shift?" Sometimes Meghan and her sisters saw ghostly wolves, but mostly the ghosts they saw were in human form or strictly human.

"Had to. We would've never proved to them we're *lupus garous* otherwise. Besides, running as a wolf is in our blood. We scared them to pieces, but we would never have convinced them if we hadn't. Then they all left." Oliver let out his breath with frustration. "We'll never get out of here."

"I'd do anything to see Chrissy again," Alvin said, getting back on point.

"What would you like to tell Chrissy?" Meghan asked him.

"I want to tell her how sorry I am that I wasn't there for her at the very end. That I hadn't mated her beforehand. I love her, and I never felt that way about anyone else. I was going to ask her to mate me on Christmas Eve. I...I wish I had mated her. I will never stop loving her. It would be my fondest wish if I could see her again."

"If you have something you were going to give her, maybe for Christmas, I can tell her what it was." Meghan had no idea how she could get them together, but maybe she and her sisters could come up with some kind of plan.

"I bought Chrissy a silver locket with a small sapphire," Alvin told her. "She'd been admiring it at a shop. I had the shopkeeper put it on layaway for me afterward, and I was paying on it every month. Chrissy had the prettiest blue dress, and it was the same color. She wore the dress when I took her to the tavern for dinner one night."

"I'll tell her you planned to give the locket to her for Christmas."

He gave a sad kind of smile. "She died before I could give it to her. She wore it and her blue dress when they placed her in the coffin."

"I'm so sorry," Meghan said. It was so difficult seeing ghosts who could still feel angst for losing their loved ones. It was like being stuck in a rabbit's hole.

"My parents were already gone when the accident happened," Alvin said. "Tell Chrissy I want to join her. To be with her however I can."

"I will," Meghan said.

"We wondered why all of you were down here wandering around. We hoped you'd come to help us out, but there's been no help for us in the past. We even saw Scrapper," Alvin said.

"Damn his soul," Oliver said. "He came through here a while ago, and Alvin and me said a few choice words to him, but he walked right past us without saying a word."

Alvin said, "We did, on account of he set the blast that sealed us in."

Meghan frowned. "On purpose? Or by accident?"

"He did it on purpose. I tried to stop him, but I couldn't," Alvin said.

Meghan was shocked to learn the mining accident might not have been accidental. No one in the pack had ever called it anything but an accident, as far as she knew. She was certain there'd be hard feelings if they learned someone had sabotaged the mine and killed the men.

"So Scrapper is down here with the two of you?" If he was and he had collapsed the mine on purpose, it would serve him right to have died and be stuck here.

"No, ma'am. He made it out. I ran toward Scrapper to stop him, but the kid threw a wrench at me and it struck me in the head. I collapsed. Before I could shake off the injury, Scrapper set off the explosion. We'd hoped he'd perished too. We had no way of knowing. Though neither of us has seen him down here in all this time, stuck like us. Unless the Lord above took him in. I can't imagine why he would have, though."

Meghan asked Peter and CJ if they knew a man named Scrapper who'd been a pack member. What if he was still a member of the pack, and no one had ever known he wasn't just a survivor but a murderer?

"I don't know anyone named Scrapper," Peter said.

CJ didn't either.

"His real name was Ralph Rollins, if that helps," Oliver said.

Meghan's heart raced, and she felt a little light-headed. "Ohmigod. He's the one we're looking for. Did he come through here recently?"

"Don't rightly know," Oliver said.

Meghan turned to Peter. "Do you have a picture handy of Rollins's mug shot?"

"Yeah, here." Peter pulled out his phone, found the picture, and handed her the phone.

She offered it to the two ghosts to view.

The men stared at the phone. "That's some kind of a new contraption. But yeah, that's him. I mean, when we first seen him come through here, we weren't sure. He's aged a lot, and he's wearing a heavy beard. He was sixteen and barely had any whiskers last time we seen him. He'd been grumbling under his breath about having to return here. Hell, pardon my language, miss, but he should have died here like the rest of us," Alvin said.

Oliver agreed with him.

"They identified Rollins. He came this way," Meghan told Peter, her heart pounding. "And he was from your pack."

"Hell, I don't remember this guy at all." Peter looked at the mug shot again.

CJ looked at it too. "Couldn't say that I do either."

"He lived out a way and had a stepfather who abused his mother and died mysteriously. Some say it was a human hunting accident. Some say his wife finally had enough of his beatings and shot and killed him," Oliver said.

Meghan told Peter and CJ what Oliver had shared with her. "Maybe that's why Rollins is abusive to women, because his stepfather had abused his mother and that's all Rollins knew."

"Hell," both Peter and CJ said at the same time.

"No one really knew the kid that well. He had a chip on his shoulder as big as the state of Alaska, kept picking fights as if he wanted to prove he could fight like his stepdad. It's one thing to fight men like us, another to fight a woman. Anyway, I lived in a cabin a mile beyond his, so I knew the situation. I told him if he wanted to fight someone, he should take on his old man and end it. He needed to protect his ma," Oliver said. "No one would have faulted him for it."

"What did Rollins say to that?" Meghan asked.

"He said she deserved all the beatings she got. Scrapper was an ornery bugger. I'll give him that. He was only sixteen, but he was a hard worker or the boss would have canned his…um, fired him."

How awful. She was glad at least the stepdad had been stopped.

"I don't remember any Rollins family," Peter said.

"I don't either," CJ agreed. He was looking on his phone for something.

"They didn't get involved in any pack functions. They kept to themselves," Oliver said. "His biological father was a drinker, and he froze to death out in the wilderness one night when he'd drunk too much and was checking his traps, so the story goes. None of them had been with the pack earlier on. She and the boy moved into the area after his father had died, and then she picked up the new wolf, a drifter, when Scrapper was around ten. The stepfather was just as abusive as her first mate. He was a hunter and trapper too. Seemed she couldn't find a decent wolf to be with."

That was so sad. Maybe Rollins would have turned out all right if he hadn't lived through all that he had. "You didn't report it to the pack leaders?" Meghan asked. That was some of the importance of a pack, to take care of rogue wolves.

"The old man threatened to kill me and mine if I said anything to anyone about it, the first time I saw his wife all bruised and battered. He said she'd fallen down when she was collecting wood, clumsy as an ox. The next thing I knew, he was dead," Oliver said. "So there was nothing to be done about it."

Alvin nodded.

Meghan frowned. "So Ralph Rollins—Scrapper, the son—took off and left the area after the mine collapse."

Oliver shrugged. "I haven't been out of the mine since the explosion. He could've been living in the area all this time while we'd been stuck down here, for all we know."

"Okay." She explained everything to Peter and CJ.

"I can't believe one of our own did this. The pack will be furious over it. I can't get reception on my cell phone, or I'd let Darien know," Peter said.

"Yeah, I was just trying to call out, but mine isn't working either," CJ said.

"When did Rollins come this way, and has he passed back through here?" Meghan asked.

"Not sure," Oliver said, scratching his head. "We don't sit here all the time. We keep looking for a way out. If we could have, we would… Well, I guess we couldn't do much about it, but I'd sure like to send him down one of them shafts."

She was surprised Rollins would want to come back to the territory for fear someone else might recognize him. Then again, if no one knew he'd caused the cave-in, he wouldn't have anything to worry about.

"Wouldn't his name have been included as one of the men who made it out?" Meghan asked Peter and CJ.

"Yeah. Which makes me suspect he was thought to have died. Maybe they didn't find his body, and the two men who were rescued didn't know he'd made it out," Peter said.

"Why would he do something like that?" Meghan asked the ghosts.

"We learned he was being physically abusive to his ma. We figured we'd take care of him. We thought maybe he'd overheard us talking about it," Oliver said.

"Take care of him, how?"

"Send him down a mine shaft. Only, he got the best of us instead. I know we should have told our pack leaders about it, but we take care of one of our own. The miners do, I mean," Oliver said.

"Okay." Meghan told Peter and CJ what Rollins's motive had been for killing the other miners.

Both men shook their heads.

Then she said to the ghosts, "We'll do everything in our power—my sisters and I, that is—to help you leave this place."

The men glanced at each other, but when they faced her, they wore haunted expressions, proving their skepticism.

Peter was concentrating on the area Meghan was addressing when she reached over and squeezed his hand, hoping he wasn't feeling left out by what she could do. She wondered if CJ was seeing or hearing any of this, but he didn't appear to see the men either. He had more ability than anyone else she'd met in Silver Town, though rumors had surfaced that CJ's cousin Tom had seen Chrissy too.

But this business about Rollins being a former pack member? She was certain the whole pack would rally together to take him down now that they'd learned he was a rogue who'd taken their own pack members' lives. At least she hoped they would.

"Yeah. Scrapper, damn his soul. He came this way. Don't know how long ago. Time means nothing to us down here. I couldn't believe it when I saw him, right as rain, except for the bloody claw marks on his cheek. It had to have happened recently, or they would have disappeared by now," Oliver said.

"Claw marks? Wolf or human?" she asked.

"I figured a woman clawed him good. Wouldn't put it past him to be beating up another woman, and she got a few claw marks in."

Meghan worried one of the women who had testified against him at trial had been fighting for her life against Rollins. Or maybe someone else he'd picked up once he was released from prison. Too bad the ghosts couldn't take care of Rollins themselves. Especially since they had good reason to end his miserable life.

Alvin raised his fingers to the bloody spot on his forehead. "He done that to me. Scrapper. If only I'd been quicker, I could've stopped him. Some of the ghosts blame me for the cave-in, but it wasn't me spouting off about killing him for what he was doing to his ma. Not that I didn't agree with the others, but they should have been quieter about it and just done it. We all figured, after we were stuck down here, that he had overheard some of the talk. If Wendell, another of the men who had been down here that fateful day, had shoved him down a shaft when he had the chance, like he was supposed to, none of us would have died down here. We'd be up there." He pointed to the ceiling of the mine. "Living among the rest of you."

"And Scrapper, the pissant that he was," Oliver said, "would have been roaming the tunnels instead of us with no one able to hear or see him, except for you. That would have been a good end for a bad wolf." Oliver frowned. "Is that why all these men are down here? Looking for *him*?" He seemed to be upset that they weren't there to save him and the other lost soul.

"I came to look for Alvin. I didn't know Rollins had been down here. Rollins attempted to murder a woman, and I called the police on him. Now he wants to kill me for it."

Alvin's blue eyes narrowed. "He's still a rogue wolf then. I'm not surprised. If I could, I'd send him down one of the shafts without hesitation. See how he likes being dead."

She nodded. "He will be…dead, one way or another, as soon as we can catch up to him, before he hurts any more people."

"I…I miss my family. Can you let them know I miss them?" Oliver asked.

This was the really hard part. Telling family members who didn't believe in ghosts that their departed loved ones wanted to have a word with them. His family might not even be alive.

"What are their names?"

"Clementine and Jessup Fraser. My dad was supposed to work in the mine that fateful day, but he was sick. I'm glad. I would've hated it if my mom had lost both of us at the same time. I never did see Dad working down here after that." Oliver frowned. "I hope they're not gone."

"Clementine and Jessup Fraser?" Meghan asked CJ and Peter.

"They live out of town," Peter said. "Are you speaking to their son?" He sounded amazed to learn of it.

"Yes." She turned her attention to Oliver. "I'll speak with them as soon as I can." She wanted to resolve Alvin and Chrissy's issue first, if she could.

"Can you bring them down here to see me?" Oliver asked.

"I'll try. They might not be able to see you, but I can share what you wish to speak with them about. They might not believe that I can see you or that I can hear you."

Oliver nodded. "No one sees me. Except for Alvin. And you."

"I'll bring them, if they'll come."

"I want to see them. It's been my fondest wish, besides getting out of here."

That could be the key to releasing his spirit! Bringing his family here to say their goodbyes. If she could convince them to come.

At times like these, she felt really good about her gift. She shared what she and Oliver had discussed with Peter and CJ, and then she told the ghosts she'd return.

Afterward, she, Peter, and CJ began to make their way out through the cave-in rubble.

Peter asked, "Do you want me to take you to the inn now?"

"Yeah, thanks. If I can get this resolved with Chrissy, I want to see the Frasers afterward."

"All right. Oliver's parents are wolves, naturally, or they wouldn't still be alive. They may not believe you," Peter said.

"We get that all the time. I have to do it for Oliver's sake, and hopefully his parents will consent to meet with him. It gets really emotional sometimes. They buried him a long time ago. It's like dredging up the hurt all over again. But it could be the key to setting him free. Did you want to call off dinner?"

Peter frowned at her. "No way in hell."

CJ chuckled.

Meghan smiled. "Good."

Chapter 8

PETER COULDN'T BELIEVE ROLLINS HAD BEEN ONE OF their own. The miners should have told the pack leaders about the abuse at home. They would have taken care of Rollins's stepdad so he wouldn't have hurt anyone any further, and maybe Rollins would have turned out all right. Maybe not, though. But they would have dealt with him before it escalated to the murder of so many men.

Peter got on his radio to warn the other men in the tunnels about what they had discovered before they left the mine. "Rollins has been down here. And he's one of ours—a miner who apparently set the explosion causing the cave-in during the first incident. On purpose, not by accident."

"Hell, you're not serious," Tom said.

"Yeah, I know. Unbelievable. It's bad enough that those men had to die down here, but to think it was deliberate? Everyone in the pack will be furious, but I'll discuss more of it later."

"You found him?" Tom sounded surprised Peter would know all this if he hadn't located Rollins and learned it from him.

Peter glanced up at Meghan as she was climbing out of the mine. "Uh, no. None of us have located him. Let's just say Meghan has some insight into the matter."

"She's seen some of the ghosts."

"Yes, a couple of the miners. They saw Rollins headed this way, but they don't know if he left or not."

"We'll keep searching."

"All right. Just be on the lookout in case he's still running around down here and could be armed and dangerous."

"I wish I had Meghan's…insight," Tom said.

Peter let out his breath. "Yeah, I'll keep in touch. Out here." He guessed if her ability could help solve criminal cases, that was a good thing. He still had a hard time really envisioning she could speak to and see ghosts. He joined Meghan outside the mine.

"What did Tom say?" Meghan asked.

Peter suspected she wasn't as interested in hearing if Tom had found any evidence Rollins was down here as she was in knowing what Tom thought about her abilities. He was Darien's youngest triplet brother and somewhat sensitive to sightings.

CJ joined them after that.

"Tom said he wished he had your talent. It could make our job much easier." Peter paused before he added, "I feel the same way."

"I wouldn't bet on it. Sometimes ignorance is bliss. I feel bad for the spirits who are stuck where they died and can't find their final resting place."

"I guess you're right." It was bad enough seeing people die, but to have to witness their spirits left behind? Then again, if someone had been murdered, the spirit could tell him right then and there who did it. Couldn't it? Maybe not if they hadn't known the person. Peter was drawing sketches of criminals to try to locate them, and he thought how bizarre that would be, to draw the face of an assailant from the recollection of a ghost. But next time he had a murder case he was working, he wouldn't hesitate to see if Meghan could help him with it.

Meghan still couldn't believe how patient Peter had been with her when she was certain he was anxious to go after Rollins and make sure the bastard couldn't attack her like he had attacked Bill.

When they arrived at the inn, she wasn't sure whether Peter was going to drop her off so he could get back to his work or continue helping her.

He kissed her before he escorted her inside the inn, no holds barred. He pressed her back against his car and held her face in his hands, his warm mouth sweeping across hers, his tongue licking the seam, and then she parted her lips to accept his intimate touch.

She wrapped her arms around his buttocks and pulled him tight. She couldn't feel his arousal because of their coats, but she had the sudden urge to tease him just a little. She opened his coat and hers and then pulled his heated body against hers, rubbing and loving the hot and hard feel of him. His hands slipped up her sweater, and he caressed her breasts. She moaned, enjoying the feel of his warm hands against her breasts.

"You're so beautiful, Meghan." His breath was frosty mist in the cold air.

She smiled up at him and then kissed him again, their tongues tangling and lips sliding against each other. "So. Are. You."

He cleared his rough throat and kissed her cold nose. "Your sisters are most likely watching us."

"And whoever's here still guarding them, making sure we're not the bad guy."

Peter chuckled. "Hopefully, no one is shooting videos this time."

"Not my sisters, and the guys wouldn't dare do it either."

Peter wrapped his arm around Meghan's shoulders and walked her to the entrance of the inn. As soon as he opened the door, both her sisters quickly moved away from the windows, but not before she caught them at it. Not that she was surprised. Wolves were innately curious creatures when it came to wolf relationships and particularly because she was their sister. They were dying to know if Peter and she were ever going to become mated wolves. Of the three sisters, she could be the most impulsive, but at other times, she was extremely cautious. Especially where relationships were concerned. She'd even been slow to warm up to Bill. After she had dated him for six months, she'd finally told him about Rollins, and that had been the end between them.

"How did it go with Alvin?" Laurel asked. "Did you see him?"

Trevor had stationed himself in the lobby, while Jake returned to the sitting area in the back of the inn to guard the women.

"Chrissy has been quiet, waiting for word from you about Alvin," Ellie said quietly.

"I did manage to speak with him," Meghan said.

Immediately, Chrissy appeared in the lobby. "He's alive?"

"He…he died in a mining accident six months after you

died," Meghan said. Then she relayed everything Alvin had shared with her.

As soon as Meghan mentioned the locket he'd gotten Chrissy for Christmas, Chrissy touched her throat. "I want to see it."

"It's…it's buried with you at the cemetery." Meghan was afraid Chrissy would burst into tears.

Instead, Chrissy folded her arms. "I never got to see it. I want to."

Meghan turned to Peter. "How difficult would it be to exhume Chrissy's body so she can see her Christmas locket? The ground's probably frozen."

Peter shook his head. "Alvin's parents paid for a tomb for both their remains, their son's, and a wife, should he have one. Alvin paid for Chrissy to be entombed there. I'll check with Darien and Lelandi, though."

Chrissy smiled.

Peter called it in to Darien and updated him on the situation with Rollins being their former pack member. "Okay, thanks, Darien." Peter said to Meghan, "Are you ready to go to the cemetery?"

"Yeah." She glanced at her sisters. "You're okay with me not staying here to help run the inn?"

"Are you kidding?" Laurel said. "We need this resolved."

"Okay." Meghan told them about the Frasers and wanting to run by there after she did this for Chrissy and Alvin, if it wasn't getting too late by then.

"Take all the time you need," Laurel said.

"Thanks." Meghan and Peter headed outside to his car.

"Because of you, we have a lead on where Rollins has been staying," Peter said, and after he got her door for her, he climbed into the driver's seat. He seemed glad she'd helped in that regard. "Besides taking this bastard down, I want to help in whatever way I can in assisting these men—and Chrissy—to find the peace they deserve."

Meghan was surprised Peter would get behind her on this. And she was glad. "How many died in the mine?"

"We've lost twenty-three men. Well, twenty-two. Scrapper was listed as one of the men killed in the first mine collapse. The two survivors said no one got out but them, according to a newspaper account back then, Brett said. They had missed one of the bodies, figuring he had fallen down a shaft."

"So his body was the only one not recovered."

"Correct. During the second tunnel collapse, the men were even deeper in the mine."

"How awful. Your offer to help means the world to me."

"I just wish I could really be a help to you and that you didn't have to repeat everything the ghosts said." Peter drove her to the cemetery where Darien was having men meet them.

She hoped this would finally work to release Chrissy from their world.

Three men were wearing their wolf coats while standing guard as others opened the coffin inside the tomb.

Inside the coffin were the skeletal remains and the locket Chrissy had worn in death. Meghan moved in closer to look. Peter wondered if Chrissy would suddenly appear for her here. This whole day had been pretty bizarre. Though he had to admit that was one thing that made Meghan so interesting. She was totally unpredictable.

He wasn't sure what she hoped to do. He'd asked Meghan, but she'd said they never knew until they investigated the situation further.

"We should take her locket with us," Meghan finally said as the snow continued to fall.

Peter felt as though he'd quickly been immersed in a class titled Ghostly Encounters 101.

"Can we take the locket with us?" Meghan asked Peter again.

"She has no other relatives who would object. If it helps her, I'd say go for it."

"Okay, we'll take it back to the inn right away and return it to her coffin when we're done," Meghan said.

Peter put the locket in a plastic baggie and then drove them back to the inn.

When they entered, the bagged locket in Meghan's hand, Laurel fetched one of Chrissy's empty Victorian boxes from the library where they'd kept it for decoration, and they carefully placed the locket inside. Peter hoped this wouldn't backfire when Chrissy saw the shape the locket was in.

Laurel opened her mouth and said, "Chrissy—" Before she could say anything further, Ellie stopped her.

"Some of our guests have returned."

"Upstairs?" Meghan asked.

"Yes."

"We'll see if she'll meet with us downstairs," Laurel said.

Both she and Meghan went downstairs with the box, and Peter followed behind them, hoping this would help send Chrissy to her final resting place once and for all.

Chapter 9

NORMALLY, MEGHAN WOULD HAVE BEEN MANNING THE front desk by now if it hadn't been for all this ghost business.

Meghan called out to Chrissy as Laurel set the box on the bed in Chrissy's old room. When there was no sign of Chrissy, Meghan thought she wasn't going to make an appearance. Suddenly, Chrissy was standing next to the bed, staring into the box, her hands clasped together, tears filling her eyes. "It's the most beautiful locket I've ever owned. Tell Alvin thank you. I remember it from the shop." She pointed to her dresser. "I have Alvin's gift in there."

Meghan's heart sank. The furniture from the basement rooms had been in storage, and when the sisters purchased the inn, Darien had given the furniture to them. The dressers were empty for their guests' use. She didn't know what had become of Chrissy's things.

"The drawers are empty," Meghan finally said.

"Oh, I know. It's behind it. Or underneath. I can't remember."

Meghan was about to get on her hands and knees, but Peter asked what she needed.

"Chrissy says she might have put something underneath the dresser."

Peter got down on his hands and knees and reached under the dresser. He felt around and then tugged at something, finally freeing a large envelope, and handed it to Meghan.

Feeling elated, Meghan glanced at Chrissy.

"Yes, yes, that's it."

"Do you want me to open it?" Meghan asked, being respectful of Chrissy's wishes.

Getting to his feet, Peter said, "Yes."

The ladies all laughed.

"Yes," Chrissy said.

Meghan opened the envelope and pulled out a men's handkerchief, a beautifully hand-embroidered wolf in the woods and Alvin's initials on one corner.

"It's beautiful," Laurel said.

"It is," Meghan agreed. "Did you want me to give the gift to Alvin?"

"With his card," Chrissy said. "I guess I put it behind the dresser."

Laurel and Meghan began to pull the dresser away from the wall, but Peter hurried to put his back into it.

A handmade Christmas card in an envelope was taped to the back of the chest.

To my love, Alvin, Merry Christmas, Chrissy.

A hand-drawn Christmas tree and doves decorated the card.

"You did this artwork?" Meghan asked. "It's beautiful."

"Thank you. Yes. He loved my artwork. And my embroidery. I had made his mother pillowcases with the same wolf and forest embroidered on them. He loved it so much he kept them after she died. I wanted to make something for him that he could carry close to his heart."

"He will love the card and gift," Meghan said, Laurel agreeing. But Meghan knew she couldn't really give them to him. And what would she do with them afterward? She sighed. Then she had a thought. They could bury them with his body, just like the locket would be buried again with Chrissy's. She hoped Darien would be agreeable to having his men open another coffin, but she had to share the gifts with Alvin first.

"Will you give it to him? Now? Please?" Chrissy begged. Her eyes were full of tears again. "He loves me. I love him. He's shared his Christmas gift for me. I want him to have my Christmas gift for him."

No way did Meghan want to return to the mine again right now, and she figured no one else would want to accompany her there either, again. "Yes, I will. Tomorrow. It's getting late."

"What about your locket?" Laurel asked.

"You said I am wearing it? Then that's where it belongs."

"Do you want me to run you by the cemetery?" Peter asked.

Meghan was glad Peter seemed to realize how important this was to them. She said, "Yes. I'll return to the mine tomorrow." What if she couldn't see Alvin right away? She could pretend she saw him and tell Chrissy he loved the gift and card, but unless Meghan was protecting a ghost's feelings, she didn't lie to them.

They went upstairs and joined Ellie and Trevor in the lobby. Meghan told Ellie what Chrissy wanted. "Is it okay with you if I leave again?" Meghan asked Ellie, since she was supposed to be manning the desk now.

"Yeah, go ahead. You've started the dialogue with Alvin and the other miner and Chrissy. Laurel and I will help when we can." Ellie glanced at Laurel as if she should have asked her first.

She was the oldest sister, by ten minutes, and they were used to her making a lot of the decisions, though she always wanted their input.

Laurel agreed. "That's the way we do this. They seem to be willing to talk to you, and as long as that works, that's what we need to do."

"I told them we'd all help," Meghan said.

"And we will, when you need us."

Meghan knew her sisters were glad they didn't have to take this on right away.

When Peter returned Meghan to the inn, he got a call from his deputy Trevor, telling him they might have found some fur left by a wolf that had no scent. "Okay, I'll join you," Peter told him. Then he said to Meghan, "Dinner tonight, if I don't get held up with the business with the rogue wolf?"

"I'd like that."

If it got too late, he'd have to cancel. He kissed her and then took off for old Bastion's place. The wolf had no family. When he died, no one in the pack had wanted the old farmhouse because repairs or renovations would be too costly, and so it had sat as a weathered old building, looking the worse for wear every year that went by. It reminded Peter of his own old homestead and how the pack needed to knock down the old buildings that hadn't been used in years. The pack always reclaimed the land when the taxes weren't paid.

Peter soon reached the old place and met up with some of their men, searching for any other signs of a wolf they couldn't identify by scent. Using flashlights, the men who didn't shift moved in a line to look for any clues. Peter and another couple of men stripped and shifted to cover more territory and kept their noses to the ground, trying to find a trace of Rollins's scent. And then he found it. Some of the hunter's concealer must have rubbed off on the wolf's feet, and Peter could smell a hint of him. The scent glands between Rollins's toes had given him away.

His heart thundering with excitement at the prospect of the hunt, Peter barked to let the others in the vicinity know that he'd found something. He could have howled, but his wolf's voice would have carried too far. Even his bark could be heard a distance from here. If the wolf was nearby, he would be aware they'd caught on to him. Still, Peter needed to ensure he had backup before he proceeded.

He continued to move in the direction the wolf had taken and heard the river nearby. Disheartened that Rollins could be washing away his scent in the water, Peter hoped the wolf would leave another trail they could follow once he left the river.

Several of the men joined him at a run, and then they headed for the river. The wolves swam across while the *lupus garous* who hadn't shifted split up and continued searching alongside the river, downstream and upstream. Peter hadn't gone far when he smelled that the wolf had taken a dump. Wolf scat sat in a pile near some rocks, and the wolf had kicked snow back with his hind feet to cover it, but then he had headed back into the river.

They searched for hours and finally gave up. Wolves could trot five miles per hour, searching for food for thirty miles a day, but with methodically looking for clues, they didn't go that far. They must have gone ten miles in either direction alongside the river when Peter called off the search.

It was late when he got home and called Meghan. He was afraid he'd woken her. "Hey, sorry about not getting together with you tonight."

"No problem. Trevor kept me posted as to what you all were doing. I'm just glad everyone is safe. I can't believe Rollins would leave wolf scat anywhere you might be searching for him."

Peter chuckled. "When you've got to go, you've got to go. Can I pick you up tomorrow to return to the mine to look for Alvin?"

"Yes, thank you, Peter."

"I'll bring cinnamon rolls from Silva's tea shop."

"Okay, I'll see you tomorrow."

"Sweet dreams." Peter knew that if he didn't go to sleep thinking about Rollins, he'd be dreaming about being with Meghan in her big bed, the bed curtains shutting out the rest of the world.

———————————

The next morning, Meghan met with Peter at the inn where he'd brought her and her sisters cinnamon rolls.

"I can't believe Rollins is risking his life by hanging around here," Laurel said, fixing them cups of hot peppermint mocha.

Ellie shook her head. "Some people are so filled with vengeance, they can't let go, even if it means their own self-destruction."

"I agree. No sign of Chrissy?" Peter asked.

"Not this morning," Meghan said, worried that the maid was upset that Meghan hadn't gone to the mine last night to try to resolve this.

Peter got a text and said, "Brett and Tom are waiting for us at the mine. Are you ready to go?"

Meghan licked the cinnamon and sugar off her lips, Peter watching her and smiling a little, and she figured if her sisters weren't here, he would have licked it off her mouth himself.

They bundled up and drove over to the mine after that.

Brett and Tom were waiting for them next to the mine shaft, and Meghan was concerned that this might be a bust. She usually connected with ghosts on her own or with her sisters and didn't have to worry about wasting anyone else's time. She could imagine just how boring this could be for the men as they trekked back through the mine, one tunnel after another, seeing nothing but one another and their lights highlighting the rock walls, ceiling, and floor.

But near where she'd found the two men before, she saw Oliver's ghost leaning on a mining cart, and she brightened. "Hi, Oliver. I haven't spoken to your parents yet, but I intend to. Do you know where Alvin is?"

"Here," Alvin said, suddenly appearing.

"Oh, Alvin, Chrissy was delighted to see the locket you gave her. She wanted you to have these." At least with his gifts, they were nearly pristine, just a little yellowed at the edges. Meghan pulled the handkerchief and the card out and approached him. She let him see both before she opened the card so he could read the sentiment Chrissy had written.

Tears filled his eyes.

"She loves you and always has. She wants to be with you forever, Alvin. Your mate for…" Meghan almost made the mistake of saying *life*, but they were past that. "Your mate forever."

He reached out to take the items or to hold Meghan's hands; she wasn't certain which.

"Tell her we will do it. You'll make it happen." Then Alvin faded into oblivion.

Meghan stood there, wondering if that had done the trick. She would have been elated if it had worked, but she wasn't sure if it had. She said to Oliver, "I'll be back. I promise."

He inclined his head, and then she and her escort headed to the exit.

"Did Alvin leave?" Peter asked.

"Yeah, but I don't know if it was permanent or not. He was thrilled with the gifts, though. I'll call Laurel to see if she can get hold of Chrissy as soon as we leave the mine."

When they had climbed out of the mine, Meghan immediately called her sister with the news. "Hey, I spoke to Alvin, showed him Chrissy's gifts, and he said he loved her and that they'd be together forever. Can you see if you can relay the message to Chrissy?"

"The inn has guests right now. I'll do it as soon as I can though," Laurel said.

Great. Meghan relayed the information to her escort. "Okay, then the next thing we need to do is open up Alvin's coffin."

The men smiled.

Peter got on his phone to Darien. "Hey, Darien, can we open another coffin?"

Checking out Alvin's coffin was next on the agenda. Peter just hoped they wouldn't need to dig up Oliver's remains during the spring thaw. Yet, he reminded himself, if it helped the restless ghosts find peace, they had to do it. Luckily, Alvin didn't have any living family that would object to his coffin being opened. At the vault, men gathered around to open Alvin's coffin.

Tom and Brett opened it, and Meghan said a prayer over his remains, then set the handkerchief and card on top of them. She nodded to the men, and they sealed it up.

She waited. Everyone waited. Peter didn't think she'd ever agree to leave, but she wasn't speaking with anyone, and he suspected Alvin hadn't made a ghostly appearance. She suddenly wiped tears off her cheeks, and Peter took her into his arms. "We're done here, men, thanks. We need to keep looking for Rollins."

"Yes, sir," several of the men said.

Tom and Brett waited to hear what Peter was going to do next. "I'll take Meghan back to the inn."

"Thanks, Peter," she said, her teary eyes looking up at him.

Tom and Brett followed behind them in Brett's vehicle.

"You're all right at the inn with Trevor and Jake, right?" Peter asked.

"Perfectly."

When they arrived at the inn, Tom and Brett headed off to do whatever they needed to. Peter walked Meghan to the front of the inn, and Trevor opened the door for her.

"Success at the cemetery?" Trevor asked.

"Hopefully," Peter said. He asked Meghan, "What about seeing the Frasers?"

"I think tomorrow would be better, and I'll see you tonight." Meghan kissed him and then headed straight for the kitchen. "Chrissy," she said under her breath.

Trevor exchanged looks with Peter. Yes, Peter knew she was going to be a handful. And hopefully all his...*soon*. He suspected she wasn't comfortable about telling the Frasers their son's spirt was hanging around the mine, but Peter would be there when she saw them, just in case there was trouble.

"Chrissy's been trying to hold on until you returned," Laurel said to Meghan.

Chrissy's eyes were filled with tears, her hands clenched together. "Laurel told me you gave Alvin the presents."

"I did. He loved them, Chrissy. He loves you." Meghan fought the tears welling up in her eyes. They'd known Chrissy since they'd begun renovations on the inn. She was part of it, but she wasn't happy here any longer. She needed to be with Alvin and finally rest in peace.

Chrissy smiled. "He wants me to be his mate." Her form morphed into a ghostly wolf and back into her human form as if she couldn't hold her shape. Then she did it several more times, her form ghostlier each time.

"He does. And he treasures your gifts to him. He has them now. Chrissy, before you go, I just wanted to say you're the best maid we've ever had. We're so glad you'll be with Alvin." Meghan wanted to tell Chrissy they'd miss her, because they would, but she was afraid she might sabotage things.

Chrissy beamed. "Thank you. I know Alvin loves me. I'm leaving now."

"What about Alvin?" Meghan was still afraid he'd be in the mine when she returned there to help Oliver.

"He's waiting for me. I was only lingering here for your return. To say thank you. I'm going now."

"Have a good life with Alvin. You both deserve it."

Chrissy nodded, and then she shifted again into the wolf and howled as if to tell Alvin she was coming. They heard a ghostly howl in return. A male wolf. And then she was gone.

This time, Meghan could sense that Chrissy was really gone. The room became warmer; there was a whiff of violets, and then nothing.

"You did it," Laurel said, hugging her. "You did it for Chrissy and Alvin."

"They'll be together for Christmas, wherever they end up." Meghan hugged Laurel back and wiped her tears away. She was glad Chrissy had found her final resting place with the one she loved.

"I'm glad she won't be crying about Christmas in the inn any longer. She'll be happier now." Laurel was just as misty-eyed. "You didn't want to see the Frasers yet, I take it?"

"No. I'll do it tomorrow." Meghan fixed them a pot of tea. "You should have told me Chrissy was waiting at the inn."

"You were already on your way home. The star-crossed lovers finally are back together. But Ellie really needs a break from the front desk. Can you take over for a few hours? I know I said you could have the free time, but I've got to take care of some financial business. Be sure to ask Peter to come and help us make our gingerbread hotel tomorrow night."

"Oh, right." Meghan couldn't quit thinking about ghosts.

She needed to enjoy the holidays. But she had to help her sisters run the inn too. She carried two mugs of cranberry tea to the front counter. "Hey, Ellie, I've got this." She gave her sister a mug of hot tea and set her own down on the counter, then waited for any calls to come in.

"Thanks," Ellie said. "I'm taking a nap."

"Okay, good show." Meghan was busy most of the rest of the afternoon, taking a break for a bowl of chicken noodle soup and a spinach salad while Laurel took over, and then returning to the desk. Between reservations and general guest calls, she continued to stay busy.

But she couldn't wait to have dinner with Peter, hoping he would tell her about his late wife. She had to make sure he was all right about her sending a wolf to prison, and if he really was okay with her ghostly abilities.

Chapter 10

WRAPPING UP PAPERWORK AT THE SHERIFF'S OFFICE, both concerning the attack on Bill and the countless car accidents they'd had earlier, Peter was glad he didn't also have to write up anything on ghostly encounters. He was uneasy about telling Meghan tonight at dinner that he'd had a mate before, though. He couldn't remember a time when he'd ever been this anxious about anything.

He'd lost his mate many years ago, but some of the wolves in the pack frowned on him even considering taking another mate. Truly, he hadn't believed he'd do so either. Not until he'd met Meghan. She was a breath of fresh air, eager to help others in need, playful with her sisters, fun for Peter to be with, yet he'd been holding back. Afraid to tell her he'd already had a mate. Afraid she'd think less of him, like some did.

Still, most were supportive of him, thankfully. All the Silvers believed Peter and Meghan were right for each other. They felt Peter should have a second chance at finding love. He couldn't appreciate them more for it.

In the position he held as the sheriff of Silver Town, he'd earned the pack members' respect. After everything their former sheriff had pulled, Peter prided himself on doing the right thing. The mate issue was something born of being a *lupus garou*, not something most humans probably could fathom. He knew, even in the wild, some wolves found new mates after losing their own.

No one had informed Meghan that Peter had already had a mate, but it was way past time to discuss it with her. All his friends had told him countless times he needed to come clean with her. Either they'd work it out or they weren't meant to be together, he kept telling himself.

Every time he considered she might reject him over it, he felt physically sick. He just couldn't imagine seeing her in Silver Town courting some other wolf. Not when he was so stuck on her.

He thought again about Bill and had called Lelandi to ask her if she'd learned more about Bill's state of mind, since she was not only one of their pack leaders, but also the pack psychologist. She'd told him Bill seemed to believe if he could talk to Meghan, he could convince her how wrong he'd been before. Peter had hoped the guy had figured it was time for him to move on. *Damn it.*

Peter heard someone enter the sheriff's office and looked up from his computer monitor to see CJ sitting down at his computer. "Still no sign of Rollins in Silver Town or our surrounding territory," CJ said. He began checking online for any news concerning murders or attempted murders in St. Augustine. Peter had asked him to see if Rollins had gone after any of the three human women who had testified against him.

The scratch marks on Rollins's face that one of the miner's ghosts had noticed made Peter suspect the worst.

"I've alerted the leaders of the Green Valley wolf pack to keep a lookout for Rollins, in case he slips into their territory," Peter said. "Everyone in the pack has been made aware of the fact that Rollins was one of our own, in case there are any hard feelings about the notion that the wolf is only here because of Meghan."

"Good. Hopefully, Rollins won't give the pack any trouble over there…and we'll be able to terminate him without anyone else getting hurt. There have been a couple of armed robberies and several other crimes in the St. Augustine area, but I don't see anything concerning the women who testified against Rollins." CJ looked away from the monitor. "You know, Meghan will be fine when you tell her about your previous mate, Peter. Lena was a good woman, and you know she wouldn't have found fault in you taking another mate, especially as long as we live and how many years have passed since her untimely death."

Peter had already told all the Silvers that tonight was the night he was going to tell Meghan. "Maybe. But Meghan might be angry with me for not mentioning it to her before this."

"It's possible someone has already informed her or one of her sisters, and she's just waiting to hear what you have to say about it." CJ and Darien had been the most vocal about Peter telling Meghan the truth once he started dating her.

CJ's oldest quadruplet brother, Eric, had reassured Peter several times that his own mate had lost hers earlier on, and everything had worked out fine for them. Even when one of the pack members hadn't liked it.

"I should have told her when I first started dating her." But Peter hadn't known he'd fall hopelessly in love with Meghan.

"Well, you're mentioning it to her now. Look, she was afraid to tell you—or any of us, for that matter—that she sent a wolf to jail. How did you react to the news? You had her back. You sympathized with her. You still feel the same way about her, even after learning the news. And that was before we learned the bastard was one of our own and had murdered several of our men."

"This is different. We're born with the need to take a mate for life."

CJ sighed. "Tell her before someone else does. Like Bill, who informed you that Meghan sent a wolf to jail. What if he learns you had a mate and tells her before you have a chance? He might even do it in the hope he can get back with her."

Peter agreed with CJ there. "Okay, well, I need to run by the grocery store for a bottle of cabernet and a bouquet of roses." He'd already special-ordered a Victorian vase for the flowers.

Smiling, CJ shook his head.

The guys all gave Peter a hard time because he gave Meghan flowers for any occasion and had shown CJ and his brothers and cousins up after Brett did it the first time with Ellie. Peter was a quick study. Their mates had wondered why they never received flowers, forcing the Silver men to hurry to rectify the situation.

"She'll be fine. Oh, and by the way, can you drop Meghan off at my place after you have dinner with her? Or do you want me to pick her up at her place?"

Peter wanted to take Meghan home with him or stay with her at her place, but if he got called in the middle of the night about Rollins being sighted somewhere, he didn't want to leave her unprotected, or take her with him and put her in the line of fire. Besides, he wasn't sure how she'd view his previous mating. "Yeah, sure."

Hopefully, tonight's dinner wouldn't be a disaster.

Jake was watching out the front window while guarding Meghan at her home. She was busy roasting a chicken, potatoes, and carrots in the kitchen before Peter arrived. She hoped he really was all right with the ghost business and the situation with Rollins, and not just because he was trying to put on a good show in front of the pack members.

"Peter's here," Jake called out, though she'd heard his vehicle pull into the parking lot and the engine shut off. As soon as Jake went to answer the door, she washed her hands and removed her apron.

"Are you staying for dinner?" Peter asked Jake, though she was certain Peter hoped Jake was going home to his mate and kids so she and Peter could have a private dinner.

"Nah. Alicia's expecting me. You'll be taking Meghan to CJ's tonight, right?" Jake asked.

"Yeah. After dinner. Thanks for watching over Meghan."

"Sure thing."

"Thanks, Jake." She hated that Rollins had created such a mess for all of them, but she appreciated how everyone had pulled together even before they knew the wolf had been one of their own.

Jake left, and Peter locked the door. He had brought Meghan a beautiful Victorian vase of flowers—lilies and roses this time. The porcelain was decorated with a raised red porcelain bow, along with red pears, holly, and berries, making it perfect for displaying on their check-in counter at the inn. He was always so thoughtful, not just giving her generic vases of flowers, but always making sure they fit the inn's decor so the sisters could put them on display.

Peter pulled off his coat and hat and hung them on her coat-rack. He'd changed into his well-worn jeans and a soft blue-plaid-flannel shirt she would love to get her hands all over.

"I just adore this." She looked over the beautiful detail

on the vase, turning it this way and that, admiring the gold filigree along the base and top edges, and smelled the tea scent of the roses. "They're lovely. Thank you, Peter. I'll put it in a place of honor at the inn so everyone can enjoy it. Mostly me." She set the vase in the center of the table.

He smiled appreciably, knowing he had done something right. That's one of the things she loved about him. He really gave a lot of thought to what he was going to give her.

She gave him a hug and a kiss. Slowly, just a peck. But that wasn't enough, not for either of them. He slid his hands around her back and pulled her close, her anchor as he deepened the kiss. This was what she needed. The physical closeness, the intimacy between two wolves on the verge of…mating, hopefully, if things worked out between them like she hoped they would.

He groaned as he pressed his rigid cock against her belly, and she ran her hands over his flannel shirt, loving the feel of the soft fabric against his hard muscles. His hands shifted up her back, underneath her green cashmere sweater, and caressed her bare skin.

She was already getting wet, just thinking about taking this to the next level, their kisses deepening, their bodies rubbing against each other in a prelude to sex. But then Peter kissed her forehead and pulled his hands out from beneath her sweater, and she knew something was bothering him that he needed to share with her before they went much further.

She sighed and kissed his cheek, then pulled away to fetch the butter she'd forgotten to set on the table.

"I didn't think we'd ever be alone after all that's happened today." Peter's voice was ragged with lust.

"I agree. I'm sorry about Rollins coming here." Her own voice was a bit husky with need.

"We'll take care of him, if he's in the area. If not, my brother, Bjornolf, is a retired SEAL, and he and his wife, Anna, go after rogue wolves like Rollins." Peter lifted the carving knife and fork and began to cut up the chicken. "If Rollins isn't in our territory any longer, I'll ask Bjornolf if he can do this. Darien would okay the funds for it, though I'm sure Bjornolf would offer to do the job for free if it means keeping pack members safe."

"That sounds great." Meghan was relieved they could send someone else after Rollins if they didn't terminate him in Silver Town. She didn't think Rollins would ever quit his abusive behavior. And after he'd murdered the men in the mine, he needed to be terminated.

They took their seats and began serving the meal. Peter cleared his throat, and Meghan was afraid he was going to tell her how he felt about her concerning Rollins or the ghostly business.

Peter set his fork on his plate. "Okay, I need to talk to you about something important."

Maybe it wasn't about her. Maybe it was about the secret? He sounded so serious.

"Except for anyone who is fairly new to town, most everyone knows I had a wife back in Victorian times."

So Chrissy hadn't made a mistake. Meghan was surprised no one else had made the slip about it.

She was glad Peter had finally told her. "Um, okay, no, I didn't know about that. I mean, not from anybody who was living." She let out her breath. "Chrissy made the mistake of mentioning it. Not that I was totally convinced she knew what she was talking about. Sometimes ghosts get stories mixed up."

Peter's brows shot up. "Chrissy?"

"Yes. I didn't say anything to my sisters about it. If it was true, I wanted to learn that from you." She suspected he hadn't mentioned it before because, as with her and Rollins, it wasn't something he'd want to bring up unless he had to.

"Yeah, she wasn't like you. She was quiet, reserved, usually eager to please—"

Meghan smiled a little.

He chuckled. "I mean you're different in a good way. Not so quiet, but in this day and age, I love that. You have a mind of your own. You love renovating hotels and really getting into the nitty-gritty part of the business. You're good at time management, people management, getting things done, and still having fun with family and friends. I can't imagine all that you do to keep the inn running and still have time for anything else. You're much more outgoing, and I love that. Yet you have your quiet periods too."

He picked up his glass of wine. "I can't believe of all the people who knew and could have told you about my wife that it came down to one unhappy ghost who shared the secret with you. But yeah, my life just wouldn't be the same without you in it now."

"I'm good with it, Peter. Listen, after the icy response from Bill when I told him what I'd done regarding Rollins, I was so afraid you'd feel the same way. The thing of it was, I hadn't even told Bill about my paranormal abilities." Meghan let out her breath, wanting the truth more than anything. "How do you feel about the ghost business as it pertains to me?"

Peter shook his head. "It's fine with me. It just makes you more intriguing." He gave her a little smile. Then his smile faded and he was serious again. "Okay, so that's part of what I'd wanted to tell you—that I was mated. I've been wanting to tell you all this, but I was afraid of revealing it to you. But now it's even more than that. I'm afraid if I took you to the old homestead, you might even find Lena roaming around there. I had never given it any thought, believing I'd buried her many years ago and she was gone. Not from my heart, but she was no longer in our world. I never considered that her spirit would be caught up in our world, not until you found the miners' spirits stuck in the mine. You made me realize how real it all could be. Hell, what if you saw Lena caught between worlds like the others?"

"Ohmigod, Peter." Meghan didn't know how to feel about that. What if his deceased mate was still haunting their old home? What if Lena didn't want Peter to mate again? What if Meghan went to see her, and Lena attached herself to Meghan and tried to make her life a living hell? If Meghan went to see Lena, she could *really* be stirring up a hornet's nest. On the other hand, Meghan felt compelled to ensure Lena had found peace. At least to give Peter some peace of mind. He might not feel free to mate Meghan until she checked into it. Sometimes she felt her ghostly abilities were a calling. Other times, like now, a curse!

"I really never thought about it. Even if I had, I couldn't have done anything about it. The thing was, she died a violent death and that sometimes means the spirit is left behind. Right?" Peter asked, sounding worried.

"Yes." Meghan hated to admit it.

"All right, so ever since we went into the mine, I've been

thinking about it." He stiffened his back a little and continued talking. "I need to tell you, too, that I did something I shouldn't have done back then. The man who killed her was human, looking for money and jewelry when he visited our home. We were poor. And you know as wolves, we don't wear jewelry. I was a hunter at the time. There was nothing really at the home for him to steal."

"I'm so sorry, Peter." She truly was. Wolves mated for life for a reason. They were devoted to each other for all time. At least Lena's ghost, if it was earthbound, hadn't attached to Peter. "Thank you for telling me." Meghan knew it had to be difficult for him to discuss it or he would have told her a long time ago. "So you weren't a deputy sheriff then."

"No, not then. I tracked the man down in the forest where he'd wrecked a stolen carriage and was running on foot. He turned to fire a gun at me, and I ducked, the tree taking the round. The next time he shot at me, I was able to take aim and I shot him dead. I should have wounded him and turned him over to the sheriff. I should never have taken revenge like I did. He was human. He should have had a trial."

So *that's* why Peter had been so reluctant to tell her everything. His secret wasn't just that he'd had a mate. He'd tried to do exemplary work, wanting to be all that the sheriff, Sheridan Silver, hadn't been. And yet he'd had his own demons to face.

Meghan touched Peter's hand. "You did what I would have done, had I been able to. If I'd seen Rollins in the woods, you better believe I would have stripped, shifted, and killed him."

"*He* is a wolf. You would have been justified in ending his miserable life before he claimed any more victims."

Meghan sighed. "Okay, I see your point." Though she still felt the human had it coming to him. But if the regular police had learned of it? Peter could have been found guilty of murder.

"Anyway, the sheriff deputized me, backdating the paperwork, and said I had been after the man for stealing the carriage while in the line of duty, in case anyone looked into it. The murderer was armed with a gun and fired a couple of shots at me before I eliminated him. And he had shot and killed my wife. So it was justified, to an extent. Sheridan wanted it to look as if I didn't know the man had murdered my wife when I went after him."

"Sheridan seemed to have a good side and a bad side to him." She knew Sheridan had been in so much trouble for killing Darien's first mate. Then Sheridan had been involved in several other bad situations. He had been just as much a rogue as Rollins.

"I'm sure Sheridan did it because of all the shenanigans he'd pulled over the years. He liked to think he wasn't the *only* one who had done wrong. If he ever needed to hold it over my head, he could."

"Did he?"

"A time or two."

"So no one else knew what you had done."

"It would have been too much of a coincidence that I'd suddenly been deputized, that my mate had died, that I had chased down and killed her murderer, and that it had all been in the line of duty. Some probably suspected the truth. No one contradicted the sheriff. No one ever questioned me. And it's been so long ago now that I never talk about it and hadn't ever planned to, unless someone asked me or someone special came into my life, like you."

Meghan could imagine how much that had weighed on his conscience. Peter always seemed to do everything by the book when it came to obeying wolf and human laws. He seemed always to take the moral high ground, which she admired.

"I believe that everyone was glad the man had been eliminated for what he had done to my mate, no matter how it had come about. Still, I knew better. Yet at the time, I couldn't stop myself."

"Why didn't you tell me about your mate before this?" Meghan suspected Peter felt guilty about even thinking of having another mate. That it would make him appear disloyal to her memory. For wolves, that could be a big issue. Just like the triplets' mom wouldn't ever take another mate after she lost hers when Meghan and her sisters were little.

"It took me a long time to get over losing her. For over a year, I howled my distress for nights on end. I wasn't eating. Darien read me the riot act. And so did all the Silvers. Tom and CJ are my best friends, and they harangued me the worst. I left the pack for about nine months. Everything reminded me of her and of killing the man who had murdered her. But Sheridan sent out a search party of you know who—"

"The Silver brothers and cousins," Meghan guessed.

"Yeah, and a few other good-hearted souls who said they were putting me under arrest for dereliction of duty."

Meghan smiled. "In other words, quitting your deputy sheriff job wasn't going to be allowed." She and her sisters had never been part of a pack, so learning the ins and outs of the wolves and their dynamics had been a real education. She loved the pack and all they did for one another. Darien and Lelandi had even dropped the price of the inn and the

Victorian house so she and her sisters could afford to purchase them—all because they had renovated and managed hotels before and were three eligible she-wolves in a pack without enough of them.

"Right. I'd sworn an oath of upholding the office, and I was shirking my duty." He smiled a little, but then his smile faded. "I had a devil of a time coping for years. Everyone and everything reminded me of her. I wanted to isolate myself at the house we'd owned, but everyone kept dragging me to all the pack's social functions. And the place reminded me too much of her and all that had gone on there.

"I finally abandoned the old homestead. I still pay the taxes on it, but I never lived there again. Slowly, I began to recover after losing Lena, and when Sheridan was finally removed as sheriff for murdering Darien's first mate, I became sheriff. Hell, I knew I'd never find another she-wolf I was in the least bit interested in. I wasn't looking. I had no intention of ever courting another." He scoffed.

"Then here you are, all bushy-tailed, red-haired, beautiful green eyes, and well, hell, it was like I'd been given a second chance. I couldn't stop myself from seeing you. I didn't tell you about all this because I was afraid you would see me in a bad light. And there wasn't any sense of bringing it up until we were further along in our relationship."

"I completely understand. How long did you court Lena before you mated each other?"

"Three years."

Meghan closed her gaping mouth. No way could she last that long if she really treasured the wolf.

"I don't want to wait that long this time," Peter said. "Her parents had courted on and off for five years. So she thought three years was fast. Because of my work, I was gone a lot, and she was living at home with her parents, so we didn't see each other on a regular basis. Not like I see you. It would be months before I'd see her, and we were always chaperoned when we got together again."

Meghan smiled. "Unlike with us."

"Certainly not in this day and age." He sighed. "We'd been mated for only a year when she was murdered, so we hadn't had any children yet. We'd both wanted to wait and get to know each other as a couple first."

"Which is a good idea, if you can wait. Then you can have fun as a mated couple before you're doing everything as a family. My sisters are holding off for that reason too." They lived long lives, so they could afford to wait, and they mated for life, normally, so that was another reason to enjoy their early mated bliss without having to take care of wolf kids for a while. "I'm so sorry for what you went through, and for what happened to Lena."

"You really don't feel anything negative about me having had a mate already and then…all the rest? Especially with a mating in the plans?"

"Is that what you're trying to do? Propose to me?" She couldn't help but be amused at the offhand way he was leading up to it.

"I'm working up to it."

She chuckled. "You don't have to worry about me. I was glad Eric could convince his mate, Pepper Greycoat, to give him a chance after she'd lost her first one. They're perfect together." Then she frowned. "But you're all right about my paranormal abilities? And the situation with Rollins?"

"Hell, yeah. And if I don't get you to agree to be my mate

soon, I'm afraid other bachelor males will do something about it. I don't want to tarnish my reputation of being a good sheriff by throwing them in jail if they hit on you."

She laughed. "And Bill?"

"Bill better not even think about coming near you."

"You don't want to wait three years?"

"Hell no." Then Peter's brows lifted a little. "Do you?"

"No, but I don't think you're ready." That was the hardest thing for Meghan to say. She realized, after how good Peter had been about the Rollins and ghost situations, that he was the right one for her. She was certain that until this business about Lena possibly being a ghost was resolved one way or another, he could have real misgivings. Neither he nor she needed that kind of conflict in their lives. It sure wasn't something she could have anticipated either.

Peter glanced down at his food and poked at his chicken. "You're right." He looked up at her again. "After I saw the way you were talking with the miners' ghosts, I figured I couldn't settle down until I knew for sure if Lena was at peace or if she was roaming around the old homestead. If it wasn't that we promise our mate it's for life..."

That was what Meghan was afraid of, but she was glad Peter wasn't ignoring his feelings. She thought it was best they got this out of the way first. Hopefully, Lena would already be gone, and it wouldn't be an obstacle for them.

Chapter 11

ONCE HE'D SEEN MEGHAN COMMUNICATE WITH GHOSTS, Peter knew he couldn't mate her until they were certain Lena was at rest. Not only for his own peace of mind, but especially for Meghan's. After all, she was the one who could see her and be bothered by it most of all. What if his mate's spirit would speak to or hassle Meghan if they discovered she was still hanging around the homestead?

He hated putting Meghan in this position and even considered that one of her sisters might be the one to ask. He didn't want to slight Meghan in any way, though. He suspected she'd want to be involved.

"Okay, so I don't really want to ask this of you, and I could ask your sisters instead, but I want you to be completely honest with me. Will you see if Lena's at peace? Or would it be too upsetting for you, and should I ask Laurel or Ellie instead?"

"I'll do it, Peter. But I have to warn you there might be consequences." She ate a bite of her chicken leg.

"Like…?"

"Ghosts often are attached to something. In one case we worked, it was a ghost who had built a home for his lovely wife and daughter. We had looked at it as a possible Victorian bed-and-breakfast in Waco, Texas. His wife and daughter had died of cholera. He stayed in the home until he died of old age. As a ghost, he continues to live there.

Some are hard to exorcise. He's content there, and he's not moving. The heart and soul of him are wrapped up in that house. All the love he poured into it to make his wife and daughter happy is still there."

"So you're saying if Lena's spirit is still at the homestead, she might never want to leave."

"Right. My question to you then is can you live with her being there if we can't give her peace?"

Hell, he'd never expected to have to deal with anything like this. "Yes." But he suspected he'd never want to go to the old homestead again. He'd have to sell it. Then again, deep down, he must have considered she'd never left the place. That he didn't want anyone living in their home. That he didn't want anyone tearing it down and leaving her "homeless."

"Here's another scenario. Sometimes people will attach themselves to objects. And sometimes to…people. If she attached herself to you, I probably couldn't do anything about it. You wouldn't know she was with you, but I would."

Hell.

"I don't think we could make it together. It's also possible she'd attach herself to me. I'd definitely have to do something about that."

Peter was rethinking the whole business about making sure his late wife was at peace. "It's not necessary to go out there."

"Yes, it is. That will be between us forever, Peter. You might say it doesn't bother you, but we mate for life. You still have some deep sense of commitment to your mate. It's completely understandable. And it's something we need to resolve."

"What if one of your sisters goes there instead?" No way did Peter want his mate's ghost to attach to him or to Meghan. Hell, even CJ might be able to see her. Then he had an idea. Maybe he could ask CJ and Tom to see if they sensed her ghostly presence out there instead.

Meghan was right. He needed to resolve this first.

"I'll ask them," she finally said. And then she began eating the rest of her meal.

He was no longer hungry, and his wife's potential ghost had put a real damper on his libido. For an instant, he had the notion that if Meghan didn't have these ghostly abilities, they could have been mated wolves. But that's what made her Meghan, and he wouldn't want her any other way. That's what had made him fall in love with her.

They finished their meal mostly in silence, though she asked him if he'd want to come over and help her and her sisters and their mates create the gingerbread house for the contest tomorrow night. If it meant seeing more of Meghan, yes! He just hoped they didn't ask him to bake the ginger-bread. He could imagine what a mess that could be. The last time he'd tried to bake a cake for a party, it had been flatter than a pancake.

Then the next day, the pack Christmas party was being held. And the night after that, they planned to go Christmas caroling, like several of the wolves did to share the spirit of the holidays. He hoped she was still agreeable, but he would play it by ear.

Once they'd cleaned up after the meal, he thought that if Meghan had agreed to a mating, he would have been staying with her tonight at her place. Everything had changed—all because of the possibility of a ghostly mate still roaming about. When he kissed Meghan before he took her to Laurel and CJ's house, her kiss was very brief, loving, but he could feel her pulling away, as if she was afraid she'd be hurt if things with his wife's spirit couldn't be resolved. Yet he reminded himself Lena could already be gone.

He suspected Meghan believed his wife's spirit was still hanging around or didn't want to chance that it was.

When they arrived at CJ and Laurel's two-story home all decorated in Christmas lights, welcoming them, CJ opened the door to greet them.

"I don't want to let you go for anything, Meghan," Peter said, his voice heavy with concern.

CJ frowned at them.

"Um, we'll figure out something, Peter. Thanks…for everything. Night." She kissed him on the cheek and hurried into the house.

CJ raised his brows at Peter.

"We might have a problem," Peter said.

"What's going on now between the two of you?"

"Lena could still be hanging around the homestead."

CJ glanced at Meghan as she and Laurel went into the kitchen to visit.

"Okay."

Peter lowered his voice. "You don't think you and Tom might be able to run over there tomorrow sometime and see if she's there, do you?"

"Neither Tom nor I could see any of the ghosts in the mine, so probably not."

Peter nodded. "Okay, just a thought. Maybe Laurel or Ellie could."

"Not Meghan?"

"Hell, she said a spirit could attach herself to a person: me or Meghan even."

CJ's jaw dropped. "Hell, I don't want that happening to Laurel either."

"All right. Get some sleep. We still need to run Rollins down." Which should have been Peter's focus all along. But he was totally stuck on Meghan, and he knew when he went to sleep tonight, she would be all that was on his mind. And how they could resolve this other issue of Lena, if it was an issue.

Once Peter was gone, CJ joined Meghan and Laurel in the kitchen.

Laurel looked from her mate to Meghan and said, "Okay, someone spill. I know something's gone wrong between Peter and you. Did he finally tell you his secret? Or is this about you?"

"Peter had a mate."

"Oh," Laurel said.

"She died violently."

Laurel's eyes widened. Her sister knew just what that meant and could see the whole scenario all at once. "Oh."

"Yeah. You know he can't let go of her until he knows she's really gone."

"He didn't worry about it before," Laurel said, being her overprotective self when it came to her sisters.

"He's never been ghost sensitive. He never considered she might be hanging around the place. Then after he saw me speaking with the ghosts in the mine... Well, it all hit home for him. He began worrying she might be hanging around the old homestead."

"Oh."

"You know we have to do something about it."

"You can avoid the old homestead," Laurel said.

"It's not just that."

"Okay, you're right. Peter will always wonder, and you will too," Laurel agreed. "You could never let it be."

The triplet sisters always knew what the others were thinking and could finish each other's comments. "Yeah. We need to resolve this."

"But—" Laurel began.

"There could be real complications."

"Like what?" CJ asked, leaning against the kitchen counter.

Meghan explained what they could be.

CJ shook his head. "Yeah, Peter told me about that. I don't want Peter's deceased mate hanging around here bothering Laurel, should she go out to see if she's there. Same with Ellie. Or you. Or Peter."

"It has to be done. Someone has to do it," Meghan said. There was no getting around this. Not unless they all moved, and that wasn't happening. The ghost, if she was there, would have to leave.

CJ snapped his fingers. "Your ghost-hunter cousin. The only one who really has the ability. If Lena attaches herself to him, he doesn't live here and she'd be gone."

"Except when he's here looking for material for another ghost-hunting show or dropping by to say hi over the holidays. And then I'd see her, and she'd see me with Peter and... Well, it wouldn't be totally resolved," Meghan said.

"True," CJ conceded and let out his breath. "We have a long day ahead of us with the extra guard duty and hunting people down and all the Christmas activities. Are you ladies ready for bed?"

"Yeah, we'll think about this. We'll resolve it, Meghan. You and Peter are meant to be together."

But would Lena feel the same way?

Early the next morning, Peter was just getting out of the shower after a restless night, a towel wrapped around his body, when his cell phone rang.

"Hey, Peter," Tom said. "We found a Jeep parked in an old barn. The snow had been disturbed, catching the attention of some of our searchers. It looked like the driver had shoveled the area so he could drive the Jeep inside. Then he shoveled the snow back to try to cover up what he'd done. Snow has been falling intermittently for three days, so it's covered some of the tracks."

"Is it Rollins's Jeep?" Peter asked, hoping it was.

"No. It belongs to a Ted Haversack. He reported it stolen a week ago today."

"In St. Augustine?" Peter guessed.

"Yeah."

"Okay. Call the St. Augustine Police Department to let them know we have the car. Were there any scents in the car?"

"Human and a wolf's. Rollins's. And we found a half-used package of fruity gum."

"All right, good show. We've got his vehicle, and if the

camping gear in the mine was his, we've got that too. Warn everyone to be on the lookout for break-ins. He'll need supplies, and if he's running as a wolf, he'll have to get a change of clothes. He might try to steal another vehicle."

"Will do. We're impounding the Jeep as soon as we clear the road of snow again."

"Okay, thanks, great job." Peter was glad they'd found the Jeep, unless it made Rollins more desperate to break into other people's homes. Hopefully, no one would be hurt this time. Only him.

His doorbell rang, and Peter went to get it. He checked the peephole, wary that it might be Rollins, though Peter had no reason to believe he would come here. Instead, he found Meghan standing on his porch, her breath frosty in the cold air. "Hey, Tom, I've got to go. I'll call you in a little while."

Peter couldn't believe Meghan was here. CJ better have brought her over to his house and not let her come by herself with Rollins on the loose. Peter opened the door and saw CJ and Laurel in his car. Both waved, smiling, and Peter realized he was still wearing only a towel, and water droplets were dripping down his bare skin. He gave them a salute and let a smiling Meghan into the house, then shut and locked the door.

He pulled her into his arms. "I couldn't stop thinking of you last night. We have to resolve this, Meghan. I'm not giving you up for anything. I was serious about that."

She wrapped her arms around his body, her blue parka cold against his wet skin. "I was thinking the same thing. Come what may, I'm going over there first thing."

He frowned at her. "I thought you wanted to speak with

Oliver's parents. Jake and Trevor will continue to watch your sisters. I'm taking care of *you*."

She kissed his cheek, her hands roaming over his back in a sensual caress. "All right. We'll do that first."

Hell, he wanted to ask Meghan right now if she'd consider mating him and forget about anything else, but he was sure she wouldn't agree to it.

"Okay, I'll just put some clothes on."

"Yeah, good idea. It's cold out there." Meghan seemed to be in such good spirits. He knew that was one of the reasons why he loved her. Nothing brought her down for long.

He went into his bedroom, thinking she'd wait in the living room for him, but she followed him. She folded her arms and looked at his clothes all over the floor, the bed disheveled, as much as he tossed and turned last night, and four pairs of boots piled to one side on the floor. He couldn't find the matching one he wanted and had pulled out several before he discovered it and then took a shower. He wished he could have straightened up the place before she had seen it.

"I'm usually not this messy." Peter didn't want her to think he was this much of a slob. It depended on how rough the day and night were as far as his sheriff duties went, but usually he was a bit tidier.

"Me neither," she said.

He chuckled as he ditched his towel and pulled on his boxer briefs. "You are *always* neat."

"Not *always*. I have my moments."

"I bet if I went to your house right now…"

"You'd see my sheets and comforter were just as messy as yours. Well, not at my house; at Laurel's, since that's where I slept. I tossed and turned all night. Looks like you did as well. I was in too much of a rush to get them to drive me over here before you headed into work, so I didn't have time to straighten out the covers."

Still feeling guilty for the way the place looked, Peter pointed to the pile of boots. "I couldn't find the matching one to the pair I was going to wear today."

Meghan smiled. "You haven't eaten breakfast yet, have you?"

"No, but we can just grab something out."

"I've eaten. I'll fix you something. Eggs?"

"Uh…" He tucked his shirt into his jeans in a hurry.

"Don't tell me your kitchen is a mess."

"No, it's clean." At least the last he remembered, it was. He usually had lunch at the tavern to see what was going on with the pack, and usually CJ brought home-baked goods Laurel had made for breakfast. Dinners? Well, he'd been having those at Meghan's place whenever he could. He wasn't sure how old some of his food was. He hoped she didn't look and see.

"Do you want eggs?"

"I may not have any in the fridge."

The doorbell rang.

"I'll go get it." Meghan headed for the front door.

"No, wait, I'll get it." Peter hurried to pull on his other boot. He really didn't think Rollins would come to his house, but he wasn't going to risk it.

When he reached the door, he peeked out the peephole and saw CJ. Peter frowned and opened the door. Then he smiled.

CJ had a box of home-baked pastries for him. "I took

them to the office, but then I realized you were going straight to the mine." CJ smiled at Meghan. "And I bet he has nothing to eat in his fridge."

"We didn't get that far, but you could be right." Meghan motioned to the kitchen. "Did you want to join us and have some coffee while Peter eats?"

"No, I'm good. I already ate my share. See you later. I guess you'll be staying with us again tonight," CJ said to Meghan.

"Yeah, if Rollins is still on the loose," Meghan said.

CJ left so they could have their breakfast, and Peter fixed coffee while Meghan brought out a couple of plates. "I already had a scone, but I can't resist having another."

Peter smiled. "We can work it off later." He wondered how breakfasts would be if he was mated to Meghan. Would they eat at her house? Or continue to enjoy her sister's baked goods?

He sure hoped that his thinking about being with her for the long term meant it would come to pass. Lena had always been so sweet—too sweet, especially with an old boyfriend. If she was a ghost, Peter hoped she would be reasonable and leave this plane of existence for good without causing undue trouble.

But he was afraid that after the horror she'd suffered, she might not be the person he remembered at all.

Chapter 12

MEGHAN HAD TO ADMIT SEEING PETER DRESSED IN ONLY a towel had made her morning. She was certain he was just as concerned about Lena as she was, though she'd tried hard not to let on that she was anxious about it. Seeing him nearly naked had briefly taken her mind off Lena. Meghan wasn't giving him up to the ghost of his past mate either.

She had proposed they go straight to the homestead where she could see if Lena was still there. Meghan couldn't help wanting to resolve that situation pronto.

Yet she needed to assist Oliver, who had already asked for her aid. She glanced around at the messy state of Peter's bedroom. She tended to be a neatnik, so she didn't relish the idea of picking up after a mate who left a mess all the time. Being on his own, Peter wouldn't need to keep a showcase house. Her home was always neat because her sisters dropped in on her, and their mates too. Plus, she liked it that way.

She'd been amused he'd worried about how she'd viewed it, though. There was hope for him yet.

Sigh. First things first.

Meghan needed to check on Bill too. But she decided she'd just call him. She didn't want him getting any ideas she was still sweet on him.

"Do you want to go with me to the Frasers' place?" she asked Peter.

"Yeah, of course."

She was glad, but she hadn't wanted to presume.

After they ate, Peter drove her out into the country and finally pulled into the driveway of the Frasers' modest brick country home. The snow was piled up around the house, but the driveway had been cleared.

"Pack members come out to clear the driveways and sidewalks for our elderly," Peter said.

"And for us," Meghan said. "I love the pack."

She and her sisters so loved living with this pack. Everyone was so considerate. For the most part. There were contrary wolves, but most were the best kind of people.

She just hoped she wouldn't make an enemy of the Frasers over this.

Peter didn't know what to expect when the Frasers learned their son's spirit was trapped in the mine. He hoped they wouldn't be angry with Meghan. Not all the wolves in the pack had embraced the sisters' abilities, but they hadn't been really vocal about it, not wanting to offend the ones in the pack who were fine with it.

The last couple of days was the first time Peter had seen Meghan in action with ghosts. He hadn't known what would happen. He knew the pack leaders would agree to anything he wanted to do, so it wouldn't be a problem if he stayed with Meghan for hours or days on end, taking care of the issue of the ghosts, but he really hoped it wouldn't come to that. He was much more proactive, liking to get things done and feeling he had some impact on the mission. He needed to view it as a mission to protect Meghan: as long as she was safe, he was doing well.

Not to mention, she was the one who had broken this case wide open when they'd never known it was murder. Rollins was a serial killer now, and he had to be taken down at all costs.

Unless he had a death wish, Rollins was crazy to come back to Silver Town.

Peter straightened as he stood on the Frasers' front porch, Christmas lights twinkling all over the frame of the house and around its windows. He hated to confront the Frasers with this. They only had the one son, and Oliver's dad had been so heartbroken, he couldn't return to the mine to work. Not to mention his mate hadn't wanted to lose him too. Jessup had always regretted he couldn't have taken his son's place that fateful day.

Meghan was wringing her hands as Peter pushed the doorbell, but she quickly shoved her hands in her parka's pockets.

When a gray-haired woman answered the door, she narrowed her clear gray eyes at them. "We heard about this Rollins character. We told CJ we'd call if we saw any sign of him." She cast Meghan an annoyed look. "Rollins would never have been here causing trouble if someone hadn't sent him to prison in the first place when—"

"We're here about your son," Meghan said, interrupting her, but her voice was calm and professional.

The woman's irritated expression turned to shock. Peter didn't have the heart to tell her Rollins had murdered her son in cold blood. Maybe then she'd feel differently about it.

"I can see…spirits," Meghan said.

The woman's face drained of color, and Peter grabbed her arm before she passed out. "Can we come inside?"

Clementine continued to scowl at Meghan but nodded to Peter.

Peter hadn't expected Meghan to be so blunt, but he suspected that was because of Clementine being so antagonistic. Meghan was feeling defensive. He didn't blame her. Yet even so, she'd been businesslike and calm, not sounding annoyed.

He helped Clementine into the house. If he hadn't been afraid Clementine would collapse on them, he would have reached out to reassure Meghan he stood by her in this.

"Peter, I don't know why you brought this woman here. You're one of the most sensible people I know and not subject to whimsy and fantasy," Clementine scolded him. "No throwing snowballs in a snowball fight. No tackling a she-wolf in the snow." She gave Meghan another withering look.

"We're *lupus garous*," Meghan reminded her, though her cheeks were stained red at Clementine's mention of them frolicking in the snow. "*We* are the stuff of fantasy."

Clementine harrumphed as Peter helped her sit down on the couch.

Her husband suddenly walked into the living room with a beer bottle in his hand. "Peter, what brings you here? We heard about this Rollins issue already."

"Her," Clementine said, pointing an accusing finger at Meghan.

"I'm here about your son," Meghan said before Clementine mentioned Rollins again.

"You run the inn," Jessup said, frowning. "What has *that* to do with our son?"

"She's one of those self-professed ghost seers," Clementine said with a sneer. "You've heard all the rumors."

Jessup eyes rounded. "You've seen him?" Jessup sounded more open-minded about it, for which Peter was grateful.

Meghan seemed to relax a little too, pulling her hands out of her pockets and unclenching them.

Peter realized just how much it bothered him when other wolves didn't believe in her abilities.

"Can we go now to see him? Um, speak with him?" Jessup asked, sounding eager to make contact with his son.

"If it's all right with Peter," Meghan said, and he appreciated that she included him in the decision-making.

"Yeah, sure." Peter just hoped Oliver would be there when they arrived at the mine. Not having him there would ruin Meghan's chance at credibility with Clementine for sure.

"He was in one part of the mine, but when we arrive, we might not be able to... Well, I might not be able to see him. Ghosts aren't on any schedule, and making contact with them can be iffy. He might have moved off for the time being."

"Ha! First you say you can see him, and now you're waffling about it?" Clementine turned to her husband. "You can't be serious about seeing our son's ghost. He's gone. It took us years to move on, and now you're going to dig up all the old hurt again?"

"If there's a chance I can communicate with him through Meghan, I want to try. He was gone, honey, before we could tell him how much we loved him." Jessup said to Meghan, "If his spirit is in the mine, it's because he hasn't found a way to leave our world, isn't that true?"

"Yes. He wants to leave the mine, just like Alvin did," Meghan said.

"Alvin too?" Jessup sounded a bit choked up.

Peter suspected he hadn't imagined any of the deceased miners had left their spirits behind. Jessup had worked and socialized with the men, so he knew them personally.

"Uh, yeah, but Alvin has moved on."

"Because of Meghan's help," Peter explained.

"Oliver wants to see you both. To tell you he loves you. It's possible he will find resolution when he's able to see you one last time. But it's never a sure thing. He may be so glad to see you, he'll want to see *more* of you. There's no way for me to know." Meghan slipped her hands back into her pockets.

Clementine shook her head. "There's no way any of this is true. This is all a grand hoax."

"I wouldn't be here if it wasn't true. What good would it do either of us to make up a story about this?" Meghan asked. "I certainly have no stake in it."

"Why did you go into the mine in the first place?" Jessup asked.

"She was looking for where men had died so she could pretend to speak to them and 'prove' she has these abilities, because we've been saying all along it's all a bunch of hooey," Clementine said.

Meghan glanced at Peter as if she was asking his permission to tell the whole story. He inclined his head. The Frasers, and everyone else, would soon learn the truth about what Rollins had done. There was no reason to try to sugarcoat it.

After she explained everything, Jessup sat down on the couch beside his wife, his jaw dropped in horror, and Clementine's eyes filled with tears.

Meghan said, "I'm sorry to have to tell you all this, but

the whole pack is being told about it and needs to be on the lookout for *your* former pack member." She directed the comment to Clementine.

"All right. Well, if we can give him peace, I want to do this. Let's go," Jessup said, ignoring his wife's glower.

"You're as crazy as she is."

Peter thought Clementine might get up off the couch and stomp off, but she just continued to scowl at them and watched them go.

Peter figured the couple were bound to argue about this later. He was glad at least Jessup seemed eager to speak with his son if he could. Peter just hoped that Meghan could locate Oliver again.

As soon as Jessup got into his car, Peter and Meghan led the way in his vehicle.

"I'm sorry about getting a little testy with Clementine," Meghan apologized to Peter, sounding truly repentant.

"You were fine. Clementine might have issues with what you did to send Rollins to prison, but that's her problem. After all that we've learned about him, I'm sure everyone who hadn't supported your decision would now. As much as I hate that he might be here to kill you, at least he could still be in our territory, and everyone will be ready to eliminate the bastard.

"As to the business of ghosts, well, not everyone believes in them. Plus, it has to be a touchy subject since I'm sure she didn't imagine she'd have to resurrect the pain of losing Oliver all over again."

Meghan let out her breath. "I agree. Still, he has needs too. I just wanted to get her off the topic of Rollins. I'm usually a lot more sensitive to the feelings of someone who has lost a loved one. I didn't handle it well at all. I wasn't sure about telling them the rest, but I assumed they'd learn about it soon enough. When Jessup asked me why I was down there, I felt I really had no choice but to tell them everything."

"I agree, and I don't blame you. I thought they might already have learned about Rollins. Clementine has her ups and downs. She's the kind of wolf who has to think about something for a while. She might fight the notion you can communicate with her deceased son, but depending on what happens between you, Jessup, and Oliver, she might come around. As to the business with Rollins, you better believe if Clementine was wearing her wolf coat and she came upon him as a human, she'd kill him. No longer is it an issue of you 'bringing' him into our territory; he was part of the pack all along and deliberately murdered her son and needs to be eliminated."

"I still want to make it up to her somehow. I don't know her, except for seeing her at social functions. She's never been overtly friendly. I sort of blew it with making friends with her now."

"I believe that's because of you and your sisters' abilities to communicate with spirits."

"And we have Irish accents. And we weren't born and raised here."

Peter smiled. "Yeah. We need new blood in the pack, but a few of the older wolves like the status quo and don't like to see changes. But after another decade, she'll be more used to you."

Meghan laughed, and Peter was glad he could lighten the mood for her.

"And the frolicking in the snow?" she asked.

Peter laughed. "I don't think anyone's ever seen me playing with a she-wolf in public before."

She smiled and patted his leg. "As long as no one took a video of it and shared it with everyone in the pack."

"Have you checked your phone?"

She let out her breath. "No." She pulled out her phone and checked her emails. Sure enough, there was a video of her throwing a snowball at Peter and him grabbing some snow to ball it up and throw it at her. She was hoping the video hadn't caught everything, like his tackling her in the snow and kissing her like there was no tomorrow. But yep, there it all was in living color. She groaned, figuring her sisters had seen it already.

"Well?"

"It's all there."

Peter laughed. "Who uploaded it?"

"Six different people."

He laughed again. "The wolves like to be kept well informed of all kinds of happenings in the pack. Especially when it comes to courtship."

She sighed. "Next time we have a snowball fight? It's going to be somewhere nobody can see us."

He smiled.

When they arrived at the mine, Tom met with them up top. "There's been no sign of Rollins, but we've got six men down there still looking. CJ's in charge of them. Brett went back to the newspaper and is in the process of letting everyone know that Rollins, a.k.a. Scrapper, one of our former pack members, is back in the territory, as far as we know, and out for blood." Tom glanced at the car Jessup was getting out of. He raised his brows at Peter in silent question.

"Jessup came to see Oliver," Peter said quietly. "Meghan's already told him and Clementine why she's been down in the mine."

Tom glanced at Meghan. She nodded. Tom took a deep breath. "All right. Good luck with that."

"Thanks," she said. "Oh, I was thinking no one would know what Rollins looked like as a wolf. But many *would* know."

"A black wolf, yeah sure," Tom said.

"Black?" She frowned.

Peter rubbed her arm. "What?"

"I don't know. I saw a black wolf watching me before you caught up with me, all growly looking when we ran together in the snow. I didn't recognize him, but he wasn't all black. He had gray fur under his chin and belly."

Peter let out his breath. "Hell." He couldn't believe the wolf had gotten that close to her.

"But he wasn't all black," she said.

"Some black wolves gray as they age."

Then Jessup joined them, looking a little pale but determined to do this.

Peter gave Meghan a reassuring hug, and then she climbed into the mine shaft first. Jessup climbed in after that. Peter followed them down and hoped all would go well, but the way things were going today, he had his doubts.

Chapter 13

MEGHAN WORRIED SHE WOULDN'T BE ABLE TO FIND Oliver again and would upset Jessup. She could just imagine what Clementine would say to that. Meghan knew it had been a risk to offer to bring him down here to see his son, with the chance they might not find him. For Oliver's sake, and for his dad's, she'd wanted to try. Since ghosts didn't seem to relate to time, he might hang around or feel they had been gone for so long they weren't coming back. She wondered if a ghost's appearance in more human form took a lot of energy. Maybe when they'd used up their energy, they just vanished. The problem was that ghosts were downright unpredictable. Which was why scientific studies about them were so difficult to conduct. Way too many ghost-hunter shows were frauds, purely for entertainment, and gave real spirit seers a bad name.

This was the first time Meghan had ever shown this side of herself to Peter. He seemed to be taking the whole situation in stride, for which she was grateful. Most of the men she'd dated hadn't believed in her abilities. It wasn't essential that they did to have a loving relationship, but it really helped if her mate believed in her and understood her need to make the connections.

"He was back down this tunnel," Meghan told Jessup. She was glad Peter was behind her on this. Not once had he suggested it might be a mistake to try to contact Oliver so she could communicate between him and his father. She had to admit she was disappointed Oliver's mother hadn't come, but in a way, it was probably for the best. Especially if she'd come down here and then Meghan hadn't found Oliver.

When they finally arrived at the place where she'd seen Oliver, there was no sign of him. Her heart sank. She'd so hoped he would be right here where she'd left him, but she should have known that would most likely not be the case. Unless by some miracle he had already moved on.

She called out, "Oliver, I'm Meghan, and I've returned with your father, Jessup."

There was no response, no ghostly apparition, no sounds, just the cold tunnel air surrounding her.

Jessup waited anxiously, his gaze darting around the tunnel, looking for something he probably couldn't see. Though it was dark down there, between their headlamps and their superior wolf's night vision, they were able to see fine.

Peter was crouching nearby, looking at something on the tunnel floor.

"Do you see something?" she asked.

"A wrapper from a stick of gum. Same fruity gum that was found in the stolen vehicle." Peter used a baggie he had in his pocket to pick up the gum wrapper. "None of our men would litter down here, and it's a new wrapper."

Meghan felt a chill sweep across her skin. "Rollins has been down this tunnel too?"

"Or a human dumped trash down here. But I don't see anything else. Like bottles or cans or other food wrappers."

"Rollins's scent?"

"Nothing. No one else's. Nothing."

"Okay." Meghan started looking at the tunnel floor for any other evidence someone had been here. Then she called Oliver's name again. She'd asked Chrissy if she ever ignored her when the maid didn't want to visit with her or her sisters. Chrissy had looked embarrassed, her cheeks coloring a bit, but she'd quickly denied she had ever done that. Meghan figured Chrissy was afraid they'd fire her if they'd known the truth. Poor thing.

Meghan didn't think Oliver would ignore her, unless he'd changed his mind about wanting to see his parents.

But then she saw Oliver coming and she smiled, relieved. She relayed the information to Jessup and Peter.

"Son?" Jessup said.

Oliver tried to hug his dad, his eyes tearing up.

"He just gave you a hug," Meghan told Jessup.

Jessup's eyes filled with tears. "Son, you don't know how much we've missed you."

"Same here for me. Where's Mom?" Oliver asked his dad.

"She isn't ready to accept that I can speak with you," Meghan answered for his dad.

"Tell her I'm sorry I broke the window in the cabin that time I was tossing a ball when I was around ten years old. I told her a bear must have done it."

"I will." Meghan assumed he was trying to give her a clue about a family secret that would help convince his mother Meghan was really speaking to him. "What would you like to say to your dad?"

"Tell him I miss fishing with him in the Colorado River and hunting and running as wolves. He really scolded me once when I was about five while we were running together as wolves. I saw a family picnicking, and I wanted to play with the kids. The two boys were about my age, but they weren't *lupus garou*s. I'd never been around humans before, and Dad was afraid their dad might have a gun and shoot me."

"Oh, no." Meghan could see the whole scenario unfold before her eyes. Wolves and humans wouldn't mix well in a setting like that. She told Jessup everything his son had shared with her.

Jessup smiled. "Your mother told me about the bear breaking the window, Oliver. Both of us knew you had done it. There wasn't any smell of a bear in the area, for one thing. And the ball had splinters of glass on it."

Oliver laughed. "You both let on that you believed me the whole time. I guess I could never pull the wool over your eyes."

Meghan told Jessup what Oliver had said, and they talked back and forth while Meghan shared Oliver's comments with his dad. Both dad and son seemed to enjoy talking with each other again, catching up on everything that had happened over the years, and Meghan felt good about that.

Oliver said, "You know Mom wanted me to mate Gwendolyn, but we weren't suited to each other."

Meghan shared that with Jessup.

"She had ten children with a wolf from Green Valley," Jessup said.

Oliver smiled. "I'm glad she did well. Tell Mom I miss her blueberry pies, but not the pea soup. She probably remembers how much I hated it. I miss her storytelling and her smiles and hugs." But then he grew serious. "You know I didn't love Gwendolyn."

Oliver was staring hard at his dad. When Oliver didn't speak any further, Meghan told Jessup all that his son had said. Jessup's face reddened a bit at the mention of Gwendolyn, and Meghan suspected he had tried to push the issue. Jessup looked down at the ground as if he couldn't face the accusation.

"What happened?" Meghan asked, but Oliver just stared at his dad with irritation.

His dad knew what Oliver was referring to. She wasn't sure if dealing with the issue could help Oliver leave, but it might. She'd ask Jessup in private later.

"Tell Mom I carved a bird for her garden," Oliver finally said to his dad. "Tell my mom and dad I love them, and I want to leave the mine. I'm ready to move on. I don't want to be trapped down here for all time," Oliver said. "Alvin's gone now. I don't even have him to talk to."

"I'll do that," Meghan said, feeling bad about him missing his friend. She relayed what Oliver said to his father.

Oliver gave his dad another ghostly hug, then vanished.

"He's gone." Meghan felt drained. "He's told us what he wants. It's possible that if we can get Clementine to visit the mine and be with her son, he might be able to leave here for good."

"I'll tell her what Oliver said, but it doesn't mean she'll believe me. Or you."

"Which is understandable. It could be enough that she comes to see him. We just don't know. I apologize for being so blunt about Oliver wanting to speak to the two of you when I spoke to her earlier."

"It wouldn't have mattered how you approached the subject. She would have been just as disturbed by it. As to

Rollins, don't mind Clementine. We've had worse problems with local wolves. And Rollins was one of our own."

They began walking out of the tunnel toward the shaft that would take them out of the mine when something caught Peter's eye and he went to investigate.

"I'll head on out," Jessup said to Meghan and Peter. "I want to talk to Clementine right away to see if we can help our son."

"Do you know the way back all right?" Peter asked, sounding worried.

Jessup scoffed. "I worked down here for more than thirty years. I should think so." Then he said to Meghan, "Thank you. I'll be in touch."

"You're welcome."

"If you run into Rollins—" Peter said.

"He'll wish he hadn't tangled with me. He won't be hurting another soul." Jessup gave them a harsh look as if emphasizing his point, then continued on his way out of the mine.

Peter went over to one of the mining carts sitting half off its tracks and peered in. "I thought I saw something."

Meghan hurried to see what he might have found and saw an orange jumpsuit. "Ohmigod, a prison jumpsuit. Rollins wasn't released? He escaped? That's his scent."

"Hell," Peter said. "All we need is a human manhunt out this way searching for him." He bagged the jumpsuit, and then he took her hand and headed for the exit. When the tunnel widened a bit so they could walk side by side again, he wrapped his arm around her shoulders and gave her a squeeze. "I can't imagine what you have to go through dealing with the spirits like this. We're still on for dinner and gingerbread baking, though, correct?"

She slipped her arm around his waist. "Of course. I wouldn't miss it for the world. I guess this puts Rollins in a worse light, if that's possible."

"Yeah, it does. He could have listed Silver Town as his home of record."

"Just what we need." Meghan began to think about Oliver and his mother's refusal to visit him in the mine. "You know Clementine better than me. Do you think she'll change her mind about seeing her son?"

"I honestly don't know. Maybe she'll play along with this some if she wants to make Jessup feel better about it, even if she doesn't believe you're really in contact with her son. If she does go down there and Oliver's able to visit with her, will he be able to leave?"

"I sure hope that will do the trick. But we never know what will work. Every time we do this, it's by trial and error." Meghan didn't want to tell Peter she might have opened the proverbial can of worms if she couldn't send the ghost off to his final resting place and instead had to relay messages from him to his family forever or help his dad visit his son from time to time to keep their…spirits up.

"You'll do it." Peter sounded completely confident in her abilities.

Chapter 14

AS SOON AS THEY WERE TOPSIDE, PETER PULLED HIS CELL out to call Darien and alert him they had an escaped prisoner in their midst. He closed Meghan's door and then climbed into the car.

"Hell, that's all we need in town," Darien said. "I'll alert everyone that Rollins wasn't released early from prison as we first thought."

Then Peter got another call, this time from Dr. Weber. "I've got a call from Doc."

"I'll let you go then."

Peter worried Bill Weaver's condition had worsened. He wanted the guy to get well and get out of their territory and Meghan's life. "Yeah, Doc, what's up?"

"I just wanted to alert you that Bill left the clinic today. He apparently called one of the Wolff brothers to see if someone could drive his car to the clinic parking lot so when he got ready to leave, he could. I imagine because of the concern the Wolffs had that Bill was attacked at their lodge, they were willing to accommodate him and free up a parking space there at the same time."

"Hell."

"Yeah, I know. He should remain here for at least another day, maybe two. I called you right away when I learned of it."

"Thanks, Doc. You wouldn't have any idea where he went, would you?" Peter asked, heading to the inn.

"Your guess is as good as mine, though he's been asking my staff how close you are to Meghan. I get the impression he thinks he can woo her back if he can see her alone without you influencing her."

"You know what, Doc? He had his chance. He's not getting her back. Thanks for letting me know. I'll either run him down and return him to the clinic or take him into custody and you can visit him in jail—for his own safety."

Dr. Weber chuckled. "Works for me."

Peter was pissed off at Bill, not because he thought Bill could change Meghan's mind about courting him again, or that he could get himself killed because of his injury, but because if Bill went to see Meghan and Rollins knew it, Bill could put both Meghan and himself at real risk.

Peter's other choice of handling Bill was running him out of town, but Peter suspected Bill would still return to try to see Meghan. If Peter had been in his shoes, he would have done everything he could to get her back. Of course, Peter wouldn't have ever pulled the crap Bill had. Peter would have backed her on what she'd done.

Peter immediately got on his Bluetooth to alert his deputies and Darien that they had a missing patient from the clinic.

"Serves him right for being so foolhardy if Rollins learns Bill is no longer under protection and terminates him," CJ said.

Peter agreed with his deputy. "While we're trying to track down Rollins, keep an eye out for Bill, and arrest him on sight. Darien will alert the notification roster so if anyone sees Bill, they'll let us know or, if they're capable of it, arrest him and take him to the jail until one of us can arrive."

"You know Bill will be headed straight for wherever Meghan is," CJ said.

"Yeah, she's with me, but I'm taking her to the inn. The problem is that wherever Bill goes could put our people in danger if Rollins aims to take him out and hits someone else."

"I agree. The guy's a self-centered jerk. I'm headed over to the inn, even though I know we've got Jake and Trevor over there watching out for the sisters. If Bill shows up, I'll take him into custody."

"All right." They ended the call, and Peter said to Meghan, "Let any of us know if you see him if we don't catch him first. I worry that he'll attract Rollins's attention."

"I can't believe Bill. He's taken a long time to figure out he wants to see me again."

"He probably couldn't find another she-wolf who is as fascinating as you are. He really made a mistake in letting you go." Peter parked at the inn and opened her door. He walked her to the front door of the inn and said, "See you tonight." And he kissed her long and hard, holding her tight against him, never wanting to let her go. He finally ended their kiss and nuzzled his cheek against hers, and she smiled.

"See you before long."

It wouldn't be soon enough.

Meghan worked the front desk, alternating with Laurel and Ellie, the rest of the day. They were both as irritated as she was that Bill had left the clinic. She hoped he wouldn't show up here.

She was just finishing with a reservation, her sisters having already headed over to her house to prepare some of the ingredients that would be used in decorating the gingerbread hotel. Meghan was still manning the front desk, waiting for their night manager to arrive. They'd hired a couple of night managers for the inn so the sisters didn't have to man it all night. Now, Meghan was glad they'd hired men. She and her sisters would have worried if they'd had a female night manager working while Rollins was still creating havoc.

When Bryce Morrison arrived, she greeted him. "Got to run. All the guests have returned for the night. If you need anything from us, just call and we'll be right over."

"Enjoy making your gingerbread creation," Bryce said. "I guess I'll get to see it here tomorrow night." He moved behind the check-in counter with his laptop. He wrote horror stories for publication, but he reminded everyone he was a starving artist so he had to keep a day or, in his case, night job. It was the perfect job for him because most nights, it was dead quiet and he could write all night long. He told them the inn provided the perfect ambience, but he wished he could see what the sisters did so the stories could practically write themselves. Though he often interviewed them for true ghost stories they'd experienced. He'd been asking Meghan when she could give him the interesting details on the miners' ghosts, but she hadn't had time to spare when he'd been free.

"Have a quiet and productive night."

"Thanks."

CJ and Brett were already at Meghan's house helping their mates with whatever they needed done in the gingerbread-making department. Trevor, Meghan's protection, had gone outside to look around. It was such a short walk through the snow-covered gardens to her house that Meghan figured she'd see Trevor when she left the inn and didn't need an escort. But as soon as she stepped outside, someone hiding in the bushes grabbed her and covered her mouth with his hand before she could scream.

Her heart was racing, but she quickly smelled Bill's scent and felt a modicum of relief. Anger too. She quickly twisted free of him and glowered at him. "You ass!"

She was fuming that he'd practically scared her to death. She'd thought he was Rollins. "Trevor!" she yelled, intending for him to take Bill right back to the clinic and lock him in handcuffs there.

As soon as she yelled out, Bill grabbed her, covered her mouth again, and pinned her tight against his body. "Shh, be quiet," he whispered, trying to move her to the corridor of trees that led to the forested land. "You want to take down this bastard as much as I do. We can do it together. You and me. If we don't have half the damn pack protecting you, he'll come for you. And me. Then we'll kill him."

The head injury must have made Bill delusional!

Meghan struggled to free herself from Bill's iron grip. If Bill's physical strength was any indication, she didn't think he was suffering much from his injury any longer—except for the delusional part.

She stomped her boot on his, but he only tightened his hold on her. "Be still. We can do this."

He was crazy! They'd end up both getting themselves killed. Was he even armed? How did he think he was going to take Rollins out?

CJ and Brett burst through the front door of her home with guns pointed at Bill. Trevor came around the corner of the inn and slugged Bill in the side of the head. Bill let out a strangled cry and fell face first into the snow. Trevor quickly rolled Bill over onto his back and crouched down to secure his wrists while Brett kept his gun trained on Bill. He was out cold.

"Are you all right?" CJ asked Meghan, taking hold of her arm and leading her toward the house, but she stopped in her tracks, wanting to know what Trevor was going to do about Bill.

She wasn't in any danger now.

"I'm all right," she told CJ. "Better than Bill." She was worried about him, despite what he'd pulled with her. She was afraid he'd suffered another concussion and that this time he might not recover all the way.

"Serves him right." Trevor got on his phone. "Doc, we've found your escaped patient. We were going to put him in jail, but he'd taken Meghan hostage and I knocked him out. Suffice it to say, he's still out cold. We'll bring him to the clinic. We'll handcuff him to the bed and post a guard. Okay, see you soon." Trevor made another call after that.

"Hey, Peter, I know you're coming here to help out with the gingerbread house, but we've got Bill in custody. I'll haul him back to the clinic… Yeah. He needs Doc to look him over again. I'll guard him there, and you can hear all about what happened when you get here. Meghan's fine. She's headed to the house, and Brett and CJ are already here to watch over her and her sisters." Trevor smiled at her.

Bill was lucky Trevor didn't kill him for trying to take her away from here where neither of them would have had any protection. She hoped Bill would be all right, but she also hoped he wouldn't do anything stupid like this again. She could just imagine how Peter was feeling about this, as angry as she'd been with Bill.

Peter would be ready to kill him.

Chapter 15

FROM THE DARK TONE OF TREVOR'S VOICE, PETER KNEW Bill had manhandled Meghan, and he wanted to kill the bastard. He couldn't believe no one had caught Bill before he reached her and tried to take her hostage. But he was glad Bill was in custody now. The guy didn't have a lick of damn sense.

When Peter arrived at Meghan's house, the aroma of Irish beef stew and gingerbread captured his attention and reminded him why he was here—to enjoy the Christmas festivities with Meghan and her family. CJ had opened the door for him, gun in hand. "Hey, glad it's just you."

"Yeah, thanks, CJ." Before Peter could ask him how Meghan was doing, she was heading out of the kitchen to greet him, all smiles.

He hoped he wouldn't get any calls while he was helping with the gingerbread house because he really felt the need to be with her right now, despite that she was surrounded by family and would be safe enough. He had brought a poinsettia for Meghan and the ingredients for frosty winter cocktails of coconut cream, vanilla vodka, and crème de cacao, and he hoped that would make her feel better after what she'd been through.

CJ shut and locked the door, then left the two of them alone in the living room, the others conversing and laughing in the kitchen. "Jingle Bells" was playing in the background, "making spirits bright…"

Meghan gave Peter a long hug and a lingering kiss. She was trembling a little, and that made him angry about Bill all over again. Before he could say anything, she said, "The poinsettia is beautiful, Peter, and the ingredients for the drinks look yummy. Thanks so much." She took the poinsettia and set it on the dining room table, and he placed the drink ingredients in the kitchen.

Everyone said hi as they continued to work on gingerbread-house tasks. Peter nodded, not able to get into the Christmas spirit just yet.

He moved Meghan back to the living room out of sight of everyone. He was hurrying to shrug out of his coat, and he felt the sudden urge to help remove her clothes and the rest of his and take her straight up to her bedroom and her canopied bed. He wanted to close her bed curtains, shut out the rest of the world, and make love to her.

She dropped his coat on the back of a chair, and he pulled her into his arms and kissed her again. Dressed in a soft green sweater, blue jeans, and boots, she pressed her body against him in a way that said she was just as needy as he was. Their lips melded, pressing gently, harder, her lips parted, encouraging him to take his fill of her. He was randy with need, his cock stirring, their pheromones taking over, insisting they do something more about the way they felt toward each other in a carnal sense.

Hearing the laughter in the kitchen again, he sighed and kissed Meghan's forehead. "I should have been here to protect you, damn it." Even though it wasn't the same as the time he'd lost Lena, that old hurt returned.

"I'm all right, really, Peter." She smiled and held him tight.

"Okay, so what happened?" Peter didn't want to hear it secondhand from anyone else. He would know if she was trying to minimize what Bill had done to her when he heard it from her own lips. Even now, Peter couldn't let her go. He reveled in all her warmth and sweetness, the scent of her, a mixture of cinnamon and spice.

Meghan explained what Bill had done, and Peter was trying not to get any angrier than he already was. He couldn't believe the guy was such an idiot or would even think of putting her life in peril like that when supposedly he cared about her and wanted to get back together with her. Bill sure had a screwy way of doing it. Total moron.

Peter stroked Meghan's cheek and kissed her again. He could never lose her.

She finally pulled her lips away from his, but she wasn't putting any distance between them otherwise. "Peter, really, I'm all right. Come on. Let's go make the gingerbread creation. We'll have fun, just like we planned. I can't wait to try some of that drink concoction you brought."

Peter knew he had to let go of the anger he was feeling toward Bill or it could ruin things between him and Meghan. What would she think of him if he harbored angry feelings toward Bill or over any other situation he might be faced with? Peter wanted her to see that he could let go of the emotion. At least for a while. He certainly would have words with Bill when he had a chance to see him at the clinic.

"All right." Peter wrapped his arm around her waist, and they went to the kitchen where everyone was busily working on different aspects of the gingerbread masterpiece.

"I was just finishing up making the sugar glass for the windows of the inn," Laurel said.

Trying to set the other business aside, Peter truly was in awe. "I didn't know you could make glass out of sugar."

"Sure. You just combine water, granulated sugar, corn syrup, and cream of tartar, then mix, boil, and pour it onto a baking sheet, and let it cool for an hour." Laurel pointed at the large golden "pane" of sugar glass.

"I've never seen 'real glass' windows on a gingerbread house. That should help to make it a winner. Wait, not a house, but a hotel?" Peter had thought they were making a plain old gingerbread house. He had believed the guys wouldn't actually do much because they'd be in the way. But he would help if they needed him—as long as he didn't mess things up too badly.

"Yes, that's right. We're doing a whimsical version of the inn," Laurel said.

Ellie and Laurel were cutting out the windows from the sugar glass and Peter began to assist them. He wasn't sure how much help he could be, but this was fun.

Then Brett served everyone wine while Meghan brought out the ingredients to make the gingerbread hotel. While CJ was checking on the Irish stew he'd made, Meghan was mixing the dough for the gingerbread: butter, dark brown sugar, dark corn syrup, cinnamon, ground ginger, ground cloves, baking soda, flour, and water, then stirring it until it was well mixed. Then she set the dough in the fridge.

"It needs to chill until it's firm for about a half hour," Meghan explained while Peter watched the proceedings.

He was finally able to let go of the anger he felt toward Bill and get into the spirit of the gingerbread party, like he'd meant to all along.

"We're going to make a replica of the inn as much as

possible," Laurel said as CJ served the Irish stew and Peter set out the silverware and plates.

"The white picket fence and Christmas lights too?" Peter was looking at all kinds of candy, set in neat little areas on wax paper on the big island counter.

"Red-and-white candy canes topped with red Jaffas candy balls will be the fence for the replica, so not exactly like our white picket fence." Ellie pointed to the candy canes already cut to size. "And the Necco wafer candies will form the scalloped roof shingles on the hotel and the gazebo. But we'll put the actual miniature Christmas lights on the ginger-bread hotel once we move it to the inn's check-in counter."

"A gazebo too?" Peter had never seen anything so cre-ative before. Certainly, he would never have thought of it. Of course, in all the years Silver Town had been having the contest, he hadn't participated in it. This was the first year for Brett and CJ too.

"Yep, and a snowman and a wolf or two." Meghan wrapped aluminum foil around a baking sheet they would set the gingerbread hotel on.

"Yeah, Meghan's gotten really good at making wolves out of fondant," Ellie said with pride.

"Is that so?" Peter smiled at Meghan. There was a lot he still didn't know about her.

While they were waiting for the gingerbread to chill, they sat down to eat the stew.

"Perfection," Laurel said after taking her first bite.

"Hmm, just like the way Grandma made it back home," Meghan said. "Do you know how to cook it yet, Brett?"

"I suspect my lesson's coming up soon." Smiling, Brett toasted her with his drink.

"Sure thing. Everyone who marries into the MacTire family learns our family's recipe from the old country." Ellie leaned over and kissed Brett on the cheek.

Peter noticed everyone turning to smile at him. He cooked on the outdoor grill, but he often ate out otherwise. Not that he couldn't fix something to eat in a pinch. But he usually enjoyed being with others and participating in conversations at meals. Of course, of late, he'd mostly had dinner with Meghan. But yeah, if that was one of the tests of being a mate to one of the MacTire sisters, he was game.

"How many gingerbread houses have you made?" Peter asked the sisters. It wasn't just idle curiosity on his part. Money prizes were being offered in three categories: adult, youth, and professional. Two hundred dollars would go to the first-place winners, and a hundred for the runner-up in each category for originality, creativeness, overall appeal, and neatness. Each house had to be made of all edible materials, except for the Christmas lights for those who added them. Peter thought the sisters might stand a really good chance of winning this year.

"We've made about twenty gingerbread houses over the years. But we're not professional bakers, so we'd come under the adult category. Every time we renovated a hotel, if we were still there over Christmas, we would make a gingerbread hotel to put on display on the check-in counter. Things were kind of hectic last year, so we didn't make one here. But each one is unique with a special, personal touch. Everyone who visited the hotels loved them," Meghan said. "We've never won anything, if you're thinking you should team up with someone else who has a better chance at winning."

Peter laughed. "Hell no. Even if we don't win, the fun is in making it and doing it with friends."

The ladies smiled. The guys all raised their wineglasses to Peter in salute.

"But then again, we never entered the hotels in contests before," Laurel said. "We just did it as a fun Christmas activity and to share with our guests."

"I'd say we'll have a sporting chance," Brett said. "Not to put a damper on the conversation, but I just wondered if there was any more word on Rollins. I heard Bertha thought she might be missing a container of oatmeal and a package of brown sugar from her bed-and-breakfast. From what I understand, she doesn't keep an inventory list on hand, but she swore she had more in the cupboard or she would have shopped for extra."

"Her place is like the inn. People come in and out all the time," Laurel said. "Oh, damn, you know we meant to check our supplies at the inn but never got around to it. We don't keep formal inventory either. We don't serve breakfast there on a regular basis like Bertha does with her bed-and-breakfast, but we do try to make scones and other baked treats for the morning and evening, if we have time."

"I'll run over there and check to see if anything's missing while we're waiting for the gingerbread to bake and cool," Meghan said.

"I'll go with you." Not only did Peter want to spend some time alone with Meghan, but he didn't want her going anywhere unprotected. After what had happened with Bill, he suspected Rollins would make his next move. "As to Brett's question about Rollins, nothing new, except we now know he's an escaped convict, and that means we might have outside law enforcement checking us out."

"Possibly more trouble than we already have," Brett said, everyone agreeing.

After they ate dinner, Laurel pulled out the bowl of gingerbread dough. She rolled it out on a large cookie sheet while the rest of them were cutting out paper pattern pieces to the correct specifications. After they set the patterns on the dough, they began cutting out the pieces of the house, leaving them in place on the cookie sheet.

Ellie had already started the oven, and it dinged to let them know it was the right temperature. Laurel placed the sheet in the oven to cook it for fifteen minutes.

"Let's check out your pantry while the gingerbread cooks and then cools," Peter said.

Meghan agreed. He chased her through the snow in the garden to the inn to check the stock of food in the kitchen. She was trying to outdistance him, but with his longer stride and his eagerness to have her in his arms, he caught her halfway there. She stifled a squeal and laughed out loud as he swung her around, before he kissed her. He noticed both Brett and CJ peering out the window, making sure they were all right. He smiled at them, holding Meghan tight against his body, and she smiled up at him. It was too cold to linger long out here dressed the way they were without wearing coats, hats, and gloves, but he loved just being with her alone in the dark, all the Christmas lights reflecting off the white snow and icicles. Magical. Yet more than the snow and the Christmas lights, *Meghan* made the moment truly magical.

"I love you, honey," he said, declaring what he'd felt for her for a very long time.

She kissed him tenderly on the mouth, tears dribbling down her cheeks. "I love you right back."

He smiled a little. "I hope those are tears of joy. I better take you in before they freeze on your cheeks." He'd heard the hesitation in her voice, proclaiming her love for him. The unspoken "but." He kissed away her salty tears and hugged her tighter. "We'll get through this somehow." And he meant it.

"We will," she said sincerely.

He could have set her down on the ground and they could have walked the rest of the way hand in hand, but he scooped her legs up, then saw her sisters had joined their mates at the window. He smiled, shook his head at their audience, turned, and carried Meghan the rest of the way to the inn.

When they were at the back porch, he set her down and they knocked the snow off their boots, then went inside.

They greeted Bryce, who was typing away at his laptop at the check-in counter. He was a big, burly guy, their resident horror author, and he loved his night job working for the ladies. They couldn't have found a better man for the job.

"Getting some writing done?" Peter asked, his hand resting on Meghan's back.

"You bet."

"We're just here to make sure Rollins didn't steal any of our food," Meghan said.

Bryce frowned. "I sure as hell hope not, or it would be on me. I doubt he would have done it in the middle of the day."

"Hopefully, he's never been here," Meghan reassured Bryce, and then she and Peter went into the kitchen and began opening cabinets.

Since he didn't know what she would have in the cabinets, he started watching her instead.

"Everything looks like it's here." Then she looked in the pantry. "Oh. No. Except for the cans of soup we keep in case we have a bad snowstorm and people are cut off from going anywhere. We usually have about twenty cans in here. There are about half that number now." Meghan got on her phone. "Laurel, last time I looked, we had about twenty cans of soup. Unless you or Ellie moved the others or used them up when I didn't know about it, they've gone missing." She glanced at Peter. "They were there two days ago? I think that's about the last time I looked in the pantry too. Thanks. Yeah, about ten cans are gone. He probably left the rest to disguise the fact that he'd taken the others. I'll put it on the grocery list." Meghan wrote it on the list on the fridge. "Okay, we're headed back now."

"Hell," Peter said, waves of ice flooding through his system when he realized Rollins had actually been at the inn. "I can't believe Rollins was here. But when?"

"I can't either, but it might have been before we knew he was in town and had all the guys guarding us on a regular basis." She kissed Peter. "The inn is locked through the night, though guests can use their key cards to get in whenever they want."

"But *lupus garous* can use lockpicks to get in. He had to have done it in the middle of the night some time when you and your sisters were gone and your night manager was busy."

Bryce was frowning as they passed the check-in counter. "Hell, I'm so sorry. I'll pay for the missing food."

"No way, Bryce," Meghan said. "If the guy got in, he could have done it any time. I doubt he'll do it again now."

But Bryce still looked down about it.

"Put it in your story," Peter said. "Come on, Meghan, let's get back to the party."

"Yeah, I can add it to the story, but if he shows up here again, he's dead meat," Bryce said and sounded like he meant it.

"Hey, yeah, we all agree on that account," Peter said, angry they kept missing the bastard.

When they returned to the house, CJ was having a discussion with the others about Rollins and the stolen cans. "Hell, Laurel, you and your sisters could have been injured."

"Or worse," Peter interjected as he and Meghan walked into the kitchen.

"Let's get back to the business of the gingerbread hotel. I don't want to think of him having been at the inn right now. We're here to have fun. Okay?" Laurel asked.

The others agreed with her.

"Sure." Peter began fixing the after-dinner cocktails that tasted like Almond Joy.

"Ohmigod, this is good," Meghan said, sipping from her cocktail.

"Oh, yes," Ellie said. "You're officially our dessert-cocktail bartender."

Peter smiled, appreciating that everyone seemed to see him as part of the family already. "Frosty winter cocktails are great, as long as you like chocolate and coconut." He'd already checked with Brett and CJ to make sure all the ladies liked the ingredients he would use to make the drinks.

Laurel placed the paper templates for the house parts on the cooled gingerbread, and the sisters cut them out again, using sharp knives.

"Now is the fun part." Meghan mixed the icing made of egg whites, powdered sugar, and vanilla extract.

Laurel filled six pastry bags with icing, and each had different tips for the various jobs. They began decorating the piping on the cut-out pieces: doors, windows, roof line, and so on.

Once that was done, Brett made them more drinks, and they visited a while longer until the frosting had hardened sufficiently. Then they returned to the kitchen to finish decorating the gingerbread hotel.

Laurel began gluing the sides of the hotel together with frosting while Peter and Meghan held the pieces, and Brett and Ellie worked on another corner. CJ was gluing yet another, and then they finished up the last corner. They propped the house up and let the icing set up before they began to work on the roof. Once it was secure, they could finish decorating everything.

But CJ and Brett had their own ideas for decorating and kept trying to take over.

Laurel finally pulled out a clean mixing bowl and handed it to CJ. "Maybe you guys should make your own gingerbread house. You've seen us making our hotel. You know now how to do it. You could have fun saying you'd made your very own."

CJ and Brett both smiled, looking ready for the challenge. Peter wanted to help Meghan and her sisters, not rock the boat with them, but the guys both looked at him as though he had to be on their side.

"Why don't you go ahead and help the guys, Peter. We can have a mini competition," Meghan encouraged him as if she realized he was struggling with which side he should be on.

He was glad it was out of his hands and hurried to dive in to help the guys make their first gingerbread house.

Chapter 16

"WE CAN MAKE THE GINGERBREAD DOUGH FOR YOU," Meghan said, feeling bad for the guys. Laurel wasn't being mean, but she loved to challenge CJ and he loved taking up the challenge, which was why he'd made the Irish beef stew tonight.

"No, if we're going to do this right, we have to make this from scratch." CJ was mixing all the ingredients.

The sisters said they could use any leftover sugar glass they had.

Meghan thought they were going to let the guys do this all on their own, but Laurel supervised them so their gingerbread dough was correctly made and baked. Meghan was certain Laurel wouldn't help them with decorating tips. Meghan was going to assist them with their sugar mixture, but Brett said they had it.

After that, she continued to help decorate the hotel and landscape scene.

Meghan was filling the yard with sugar snow while her sisters were setting the candy cane fence posts, then topping them with the red candy balls. Then they created a snowman from rolled fondant. They also made green garland on the windows, a green wreath, and candles with yellow flames in each of the windows, all from fondant. After creating evergreen trees in the yard and decorating them with sugar snow and red-hot candy hearts, Meghan glanced at the guys to see how they were coming along. They were doing the final cutouts on their house, but it was small.

Then they were putting it together, and the sisters all paused to watch as the guys put too much frosting on it to hold it together. It was too runny, the drips running down the sides. Then they finally got the right consistency and started again.

Meghan saw the door with a crescent moon cut out. She laughed. "An outhouse!"

Her sisters laughed.

The guys just smiled and continued to work on their building.

The sisters created a gazebo of frosting-covered pretzels, a gingerbread roof, more pastel candy shingles, and frosting snow sprinkled on top. Snow frosting icicles hung from the roof.

Meghan fashioned a wolf weather vane from fondant to set on top.

Laurel and Ellie used some of the leftover fondant to create a little forest of trees. Then they topped them with snow icing. Meghan worked on three wolves.

Once they were all done, they stood back to admire the two buildings and the scenery.

"Now I guess we need to carry it to the inn," CJ said, motioning to the gingerbread hotel.

"And the outhouse?" Peter asked.

"We can display it either at the jailhouse or the newspaper office," Brett said.

"We'll toss a coin for it. Heads, it goes to the newspaper office," CJ said. He tossed a quarter, and it came up heads.

Brett smiled.

Peter and CJ shared looks, then Peter said, "Let's make another one."

The ladies laughed, but Meghan made a wolf for each of them to go with their outhouses.

It was late when they finished the second outhouse and everyone helped to clean up the kitchen.

When they got ready to carry the gingerbread hotel replica to the inn, CJ said, "You know we should have made this there."

"No way," Laurel said. "With all our laughing, we would have kept our wolf guests awake."

"Some of them probably would have joined in on the fun," Meghan said. "Maybe next year we can do it at the hotel, and if anyone wants to join us for drinks, they can."

"Good idea," Ellie said.

"I guess you'll be coming home with us, Meghan?" Laurel asked as they all began donning coats.

"Uh, yes, right." Meghan got the back door of the inn for Brett and Peter, who were carrying the gingerbread hotel. CJ carried the gingerbread outhouses to Brett's and his cars.

Bryce smiled to see them coming into the inn with the gingerbread creation. He quickly came around the check-in counter to help. "I didn't think I'd get to see it until tomorrow. That's a winner for sure."

"That would be nice," Laurel said, "but we just had fun doing it, and I'm sure our guests will get a kick out of it."

Once the gingerbread hotel was set up, Meghan and Ellie hung the tiny Christmas lights on the hotel, and Laurel turned them on. Brett took pictures of it for the newspaper. CJ joined them and wrapped his arm around Laurel. "Now *that* is perfect."

They all agreed. Then Laurel said, "Well, we have our pack's Christmas party tomorrow, so we should call it a night. Come on, mate of mine." She wrapped her arm around his waist and headed for the back door.

Brett took Ellie's hand and they hurried out after them.

Peter and Meghan paused at the back door. "This was a lot of fun."

"And you got an outhouse out of it." Meghan laughed. "Well, two."

"Thanks for the little wolves. They made the scene extra special." He lifted her face and kissed her mouth, wanting to return her to her house and strip and join her in bed again. Only this time, he wouldn't be leaving for the night.

When they came up for air, Meghan said, "They're waiting for me out in the cold."

Peter smiled. "Yeah, but they knew we had to say good night. Are you sure you don't want me to stay the night with you?"

She shook her head. "Let's get this other matter resolved first."

"All right. If we can get together earlier tomorrow, before the Christmas party, I'd love that."

"I would too," she agreed.

They walked outside to join the others. Brett and Ellie were waiting around and talking to CJ and Laurel until Meghan and Peter were ready to leave.

Peter opened the car door for Meghan, kissed her good-bye again, and then headed for his vehicle.

Laurel sighed. "I know you two are worried about Lena and the possibility of her ghost hanging around, but I don't think it should keep you and Peter apart."

"We're not apart," Meghan said. "We've had dinner three of the past four nights."

"You know what I mean. Peter looked like it was killing him to let you go tonight," Laurel said.

Meghan sighed. "I want to resolve this business with Lena first." Meghan could just imagine Lena sitting down to dinner with them and later joining them in bed.

Early the next morning, Laurel was making breakfast and Meghan hurried to join her. She'd been having nightmares about Rollins trying to murder the ex-girlfriend in the dark alley in St. Augustine again. She hadn't had them in a long time.

"Are you okay?" Laurel asked as she finished making blueberry pancakes for them.

"Yeah, just having the same old nightmares again."

"About Rollins. I checked on you when you cried out last night. Well, both CJ and I did, afraid Rollins had gotten into your guest room somehow."

Meghan rubbed her eyes and yawned. "That's why the little snowman nightlight was on?"

Laurel smiled. "Yeah. I hoped he'd chase away the dark."

"I don't remember that. I just was confused this morning and thought I'd turned it on before I went to sleep last night." Meghan's phone rang, and she saw it was Jessup. Maybe Clementine changed her mind and wanted to visit her son. "Good morning, Jessup."

"I'd like to visit my son again in the mine, if it wouldn't be a problem for you."

"And Clementine?" Meghan suspected she didn't want to go, or Jessup would have said so.

"No."

Meghan asked Laurel, "Can you take care of the inn without me for a little bit?"

"Yeah, sure."

"Okay. Can you pick me up at the inn? I can't go without an escort," Meghan told Jessup.

"Sure thing. In an hour?"

"Perfect." They ended the call.

"No Clementine, I gather from the disgruntled expression you're wearing," Laurel said.

"You're right."

The doorbell rang, and CJ ran down the stairs. "I've got it."

Then Meghan heard Peter's voice at the door. She smiled. They must have invited him over for breakfast, or he'd invited himself over to see her first thing. If he kept this up, she was going to have to give in, darn the consequences.

"Good morning," Laurel said cheerfully as CJ and Peter entered the kitchen.

"Morning," Peter said. Then he hugged and kissed Meghan.

No more hiding how he felt about her from family and friends, while in uniform or not. She loved this side of him.

"What are you doing today, Meghan?" Peter asked as they took seats and began eating their pancakes.

"I'll be manning the front desk for most of the day before the pack Christmas party gets started. But Jessup wants to see his son again at the mine. So I'll do that first thing." Meghan owed it to her sisters to get back on track doing her share of inn duties, though Laurel and Ellie both agreed she should help the spirits in need.

"Is Clementine going?" Peter asked.

"No."

"I'll ask Sam if he could meet you down at the mine. His tavern doesn't open until lunchtime, and he's been offering to help safeguard you ladies. I think Silva's been insisting he go too. You call me as soon as you leave the mine," Peter said.

"Thanks, that will be nice and I will call you afterward."

After that, they talked about the snowy weather coming, and then they finished eating and helped clean the kitchen before they all left for their respective jobs. Peter had gotten ahold of Sam, and he was eager to help.

"I'll pick you up at three at the inn for the party?" Peter asked Meghan.

"Um, at my house. I need to dress."

"All right. I'll see you then." Peter gave her a warm hug and kiss.

She could sure use these every morning before they went their separate ways to work. And cuddling with him at night when she was having nightmares? Much better than a snowman nightlight.

CJ and Peter drove their vehicles, following Meghan and Laurel to the inn, then waited while they parked and entered the building.

Meghan asked Laurel, "So whose idea was it for Peter to join us for breakfast?"

Laurel smiled at her, and they began pulling off their gloves, hats, and coats and hanging them up in the staff coat closet. "Let's say it was mutual. I thought it would be nice if we invited him and told CJ to call him, but Peter called first."

Meghan chuckled.

Ellie said from the check-in counter, "What did you expect? Peter is totally in love with you."

"I'll say," Laurel added.

"Where's our guard staff?" Meghan asked, not hearing any of the men around.

"Trevor and Tom are here. They're checking around outside. Bryce will come a little early this afternoon to man the check-in counter because we're going to the Christmas party, so I came in a little early to relieve him of his job."

"Thanks," both Meghan and Laurel said to her.

"It was going to be my turn at the front desk, but Jessup wants to see his son again in the mine," Meghan said.

Laurel brewed them cups of hot cider and made the guests some cinnamon buns.

"It's all yours when you get back," Ellie said, smiling, then moved around the counter to take charge of the reception desk.

When Jessup came to pick Meghan up at the inn, she wanted to ask about Oliver's mentioning he didn't want to mate the one woman to see if they could clear the air about that and maybe Oliver would then be free to go.

"I'm sorry. I should have called you before this, but Clementine stubbornly refuses to go to the mine."

"I totally understand. I had another thought. Sometimes spirits can't let go because they have unresolved issues. Maybe he feels guilty because he tried to stop Rollins and wasn't able to. Or"—she had to be so careful how she worded it—"well, he seemed really perturbed about the business with not wanting to mate a she-wolf. Had he been interested in someone else? I felt Oliver wanted to discuss something more with you, but he…was having a hard time doing so."

"You don't want to go there."

Meghan's lips parted in surprise. She really thought Jessup wanted his son to find peace. What *was* the issue with Oliver and his father? Meghan wanted to impress upon Jessup the importance of how discussing the matter with his son could help him leave, no matter what the issue was. That had been eons ago after all.

"Believe me," Jessup said, confirming he wasn't going to discuss it, "you don't want to know."

"All right. It was just an idea. Then we're back to square one with getting Clementine to agree to see him. Or if you can think of anything else that seems to be bothering Oliver that we might be able to talk to him about, then just let me know."

"I will. Thanks."

She figured whatever the matter was, the anger or hurt was still as raw as it must have been ages ago.

When they parked at the mine, Sam was waiting on them, eager to get this show on the road. They all went into the mine, but Oliver didn't appear for her. Maybe he was angry his mother wouldn't visit. Or maybe the issue with his father wasn't going away. Of course, she truly hoped Oliver had left, but she didn't feel that vibe down here. It was still eerily cold, and the feeling of oppression continued to permeate the tunnel.

"No sign of him," she said after they'd waited another half hour.

"Okay, we might as well go," Jessup said.

When they left the mine, Sam headed back to the tavern to do preparations to open for lunch.

"Uh, could you take me to another location before you drop me off at the inn?" she asked Jessup.

"I'm sorry we didn't connect with my son, but yeah, sure. I can take you wherever you need to go next."

She hoped Jessup didn't change his mind when she told him where she wanted to go. She needed to make headway with the Lena problem if she was thwarted with Oliver.

When they had climbed out of the mine, she asked, "Do you know where Peter's old homestead is?"

Jessup studied her for a moment, and she was afraid he'd tell her he couldn't take her there. She was certain from his expression he knew where it was. He finally nodded and drove her out to the old homestead. Meghan was glad he knew where it was. The small, one-story home had seen better days, the paint peeling off the exterior, moss covering the roof tiles, the trim rotting. Meghan felt sad to see it in such bad shape. Then her cell rang, and she saw the call was from Peter.

"Where are you?" Peter sounded anxious. "Sam said you were through at the mine already."

Uh-oh. She was supposed to call Peter as soon as she left the mine. She was so eager to see if Lena was hanging around the old house that she forgot to tell him she was out of the mine. And she hadn't headed straight to the inn.

"I'm... Wait, got to go. I'll talk to you in about half an hour." Meghan saw movement in the house. Part of the roof's shingles were gone, and the snow was hip deep. One of the porch poles was cracked, and the porch roof was tilting, looking like it could collapse at any moment. She got out of the SUV and began to trudge through the deep snow toward the house, glancing at all the *No Trespassing* signs posted around the place, including *Danger* signs nailed to the exterior of the house.

"Be careful," Jessup said. "Don't go inside."

But she'd seen a woman peering out. "Did you see someone in the house?"

"No."

Peter called again.

Oh brother. "Hello, Peter?" Meghan thought she sounded innocent and sweet, not frazzled and caught in the act.

Jessup looked at her as if he thought he might be in trouble for bringing her out here when Peter was trying to locate her.

"Where. Are. You." Now, Peter sounded highly vexed.

She couldn't fault him, given the trouble she could be in. "At your place. I'll be home shortly."

"My place? I'm at my place, and you're not here. You're not at the inn or your home either. Hell, Meghan, you're not at the old homestead, are you?"

"Wait, Peter, I see fresh tracks in the snow. A wolf's."

"Damn it, Meghan. Does Jessup have a gun on him?"

"Are you carrying?" Meghan asked Jessup.

"I just thought we'd be talking to my son."

"Okay, he said no," she said to Peter.

"I want you out of there now."

She knew he only wanted to keep her safe and wasn't just ordering her about for no good reason. Once she'd seen the single set of wolf tracks in the snow, she'd felt some urgency to leave too. Though she was torn about that and learning the truth about his mate. "All right, we're going." She ended the call and pocketed her phone. She carefully studied the windows again, not sure what she saw. A woman's face in the window, or just her vivid imagination? The glass was covered in ice and the windows were foggy too. Shadows and light could have caused the appearance of something shadowy in the window.

She let out her breath and trudged back to the SUV.

"Is the sheriff angry with me for bringing you out here?" Jessup asked.

"No. He's just worried the wolf tracks might belong to Rollins."

Jessup looked about at the snow. "I didn't smell his scent."

Meghan climbed into the SUV. "We found hunter's concealment spray at the mine where we think he was camping out."

"That explains it."

"The wolf tracks could have been made by a searcher," she said.

Jessup climbed into the SUV. "Everyone's supposed to be traveling in groups of two or more. No one should be searching for this guy alone. At first, we figured he wouldn't know the lay of the land and that would give us the advantage. But since he's one of us, he knows the territory as well as the rest of us who were born and raised here." Jessup started the SUV, but when he tried to back out, he couldn't get any traction. "Uh, I don't think we're getting out of here without using some muscle."

They climbed out of the SUV and tried to push the vehicle, but it was too heavy.

Meghan called Peter back, figuring he was on his way with an army to search for Rollins. "Hey, Peter, can you send a tow truck out here when you come? We're kind of stuck."

Chapter 17

THE NEWS ABOUT MEGHAN FINDING WOLF PAW PRINTS in the snow out by Peter's old house set his heart pounding even harder. That she was attempting to see if his wife's ghost was there was bad enough.

Peter should have known Meghan would ask someone to take her out to his old place at some time or other. Jessup was a good man but unarmed. Peter was certain he was unaware of the trouble she might find herself in if she tangled with his wife's ghost.

Nobody knew if Rollins had weapons stashed somewhere. They hadn't found any yet, but if he was running as a wolf and had them, Rollins would have had to hide them somewhere.

Peter assumed if Meghan had seen Lena, she would have told him, so that had to be good news at least. But what if Rollins had been using the old homestead as a hideaway? They needed to check out all the abandoned places everywhere.

Now Meghan was stuck there without any weapons to protect either of them, and Peter couldn't drive fast enough to reach her. Five other vehicles were headed their way to help in the search. But at least he and all the men were heavily armed.

As soon as they arrived twenty minutes later, Peter was glad that Meghan and Jessup were fine. He organized the search teams right away, and the tow truck drove up after that, hooking up to pull the SUV out of the snowbank.

Jessup looked guilty that he'd brought Meghan here, but Peter knew it had been all Meghan's idea and Jessup hadn't known Peter hadn't wanted her to come here.

He took her aside and asked, "Are you all right?"

"Cold, but yeah, I'm okay."

He didn't want to ask her about Lena when all the others could overhear them. If her ghost was roaming the place, he could imagine word getting out to the rest of the pack, and those who thought he shouldn't take a new mate would object to it even more.

He ran his hand over Meghan's arm, and she quickly said, "Don't touch me, Peter."

He pulled his hand away from her as if she'd scalded him, unable to mask the hurt of the rejection, but the notion Lena could be watching sent an icy chill through his body.

Meghan glanced back at the house.

"Lena's here?" he whispered, feeling like a dark cloud had settled over his soul.

"I don't know. But it isn't a good idea to show any affection toward me if she is," Meghan said softly.

Hell. Peter glanced at the SUV as it was pulled clear of the snowbank. "I'll see you later." He hated not being able to touch Meghan, to hug her, and to kiss her goodbye. Yet he hated that his late wife could be watching them and feeling bad that Peter was interested in a new she-wolf, as crazy as that sounded.

"I'll…see you tonight then." He hoped Meghan wouldn't cancel all their plans tonight because she was upset about this.

He should have been the one to open Meghan's car door for her, but Jessup took care of her instead. He was looking at Peter curiously, probably wondering why he didn't make a move to do it, why she had pulled away from him, and why he hadn't kissed her goodbye. Peter ached for the intimacy they shared, and he suspected Jessup believed they were having a fight about her being out here. *Hell.* He could just imagine the news spreading like wildfire through the pack, and every bachelor who was interested in her would be salivating at the chance to date her next.

He glanced back at the house. He didn't see anything but iced-up, dingy windows. Then he waved at Meghan and Jessup, but only Jessup waved back as they pulled out and left for the inn.

"Hey, Peter, are you all right?" CJ asked, joining him. Jake was right on his heels.

"Yeah." Peter frowned at CJ and Jake. "Do you see any sign of Lena's ghost?"

Jake shook his head.

"Not me. But we're outside. Maybe inside? Wolf tracks lead into the house. We need to go in to check the place out. We're waiting for you to okay it since it's your place, your call," CJ said.

"It's too dangerous. I'll go in and check it out. You just wait outside."

"Are you sure?"

"Yeah, it's my place, it's in bad shape, and it *is* my call." Peter didn't want anyone else getting hurt if the structure collapsed when he was inside. He trudged through the snow to reach the front door of the house. Men had already cleared the snow in front of the door so they could get to it.

His Glock readied, he opened the door. There was no lock. There hadn't been any need until that fateful day, and once Lena had been murdered, Peter hadn't bothered to put a lock on the house. He supposed he felt he deserved the same fate if anyone should try to attack him while he was living there, because he hadn't protected the love of his life.

Of course, no one had bothered him.

He glanced around at the Victorian furniture, the blue camelback sofa where he'd read the newspaper now covered in a thick coat of dust. He'd kissed Lena there once, but she was too much of a proper lady—at least with him—and she felt any intimacy should only be displayed in bed. Even then, she'd never remove her gown while they made love or slept together. He sighed, remembering how he'd worn a nightshirt in bed at all times to please her.

Peter recalled Meghan hugging him while he only wore a towel and watching him as he dressed that morning. He loved that they enjoyed seeing each other in such a way and weren't ashamed of their bodies.

Glancing around, he noticed the wolf paw prints in the dust covering the pine floors.

He heard movement behind him, his skin prickling with unease, and he turned with his gun aimed to shoot. "Hell, CJ. You weren't supposed to enter the house."

His own gun in his hand, CJ had moved into the living room and was looking at the wolf paw prints too. Peter also saw human footprints, bare footprints.

"Is it him?" CJ asked.

"You know I'm the sheriff and you're my deputy, right?"

CJ nodded, looking like he was fighting a smile.

"And that means you work for me and follow my orders, correct?"

CJ said, "Laurel would kill me if I didn't watch your back."

Peter scoffed. "This whole place could come down on top of the two of us." He glanced up at the ceiling to see the paint peeling off in chunks. Floral wallpaper was peeling off the walls, and the oil paintings of fields of flowers he'd bought for Lena were sagging in their frames. They were hers. All this was for her. He couldn't have taken any of it with him. They hadn't had a lot of money, so the furnishings were sparse. He'd given her the oil paintings for her birthday and as a wedding gift once she'd seen them and wanted them so badly, even though they could barely afford them.

"We think he came in the back way. The snow has covered up some of his tracks, but the porch back there was clearer," CJ said.

Peter nodded and looked at the coffee table covered in layers of dust. A plate had been set on top of it, leaving a circular mark. Had Rollins been here? Peter glanced back at the sofa. No imprints. But on the spoon-back armchair, the definite form of someone's imprint could be seen. "Someone's been sitting in my chair."

Lena always sat on the sofa, so that was his chair when she invited guests over. Which was rare. She had been a reserved wolf, not very social, except when it came to her old boyfriend.

"I see that. And the wolf ate something there." CJ pointed to a couple of beer bottles mostly hidden under the sofa. "Those are new. He didn't brush away the dust on the table, probably wanting to preserve the look if anyone peeked inside the house."

"Yeah." Peter followed the tracks to the only bedroom.

He and Lena had planned to expand the house when they had more money and when kids were on the way. The colonial bed sat against one wall, a tarnished brass mirror to one side. The quilt was something Lena's grandmother had made, blue and beige, faded, but not covered in dust as he would have expected.

"Someone's been sleeping in your bed," CJ remarked.

"Too bad we didn't catch him there." The mattress was a lumpy mess. Peter figured Rollins, if that was who it had been, would have had some time sleeping on that gawd-awful mattress. Served him right.

They moved into the kitchen and found a bowl and a spoon in the sink. The dishes were a hodgepodge of some of her mother's discards and some of his old bachelor plates and cups. Remnants of porridge were clinging to the bowl and spoon.

"Somebody's been eating your porridge," CJ said.

Peter smiled at CJ as he bagged up the evidence. They could now prove if Rollins had been here. "If he'd eaten anything left in the house, it probably would have killed him."

"Yeah. So he probably got fresh porridge from some-where else."

"Bertha was missing oatmeal and brown sugar from her place. Ask again if anyone's missing anything from their homes. This time, ask if anyone's missing bottles of beer." Peter opened a cupboard and found a stash of food—all new stuff, half hidden behind old canned and sacked goods. "We'll take the new cans of food with us."

"May be the cans the sisters were missing from their inn. He has to have a camp stove." CJ looked at the wood-burning stove. "Scratch that notion. He's been using the wood-burning stove. He'd have to get water from the stream, though. No running water in here."

"We'll check that next. I'll grab the beer bottles to see if we can get DNA samples off either of them."

CJ went to the front door and called out, "Anyone have a box or plastic bags?"

"Got a box, CJ. Be right there," Jake called out.

Peter found a lantern tucked away in a closet, all cleaned off. "He's been using this lantern for some light."

"And this old battered pot to cook." CJ pointed to the pot inside the kitchen cabinet.

"Yeah, an old hand-me-down that has seen better days."

Once they'd confiscated the food, empty beer bottles, cooking pot, and lantern, they loaded the items in one of the vehicles. Then Peter had everyone search down by the stream to see if the wolf had been using water from there.

"He broke through the ice here," one of the men hollered, about an eighth of a mile from the house.

They all hurried to the spot to see it. Peter studied the ground and found a couple of washcloths nearby. "Looks like he used them to clean stuff. I wonder why he didn't clean the porridge out of the bowl."

"Maybe he was just there," CJ said.

The idea that Rollins could have been there when Meghan was gave Peter heartburn. What if she thought she'd seen Lena at one of the windows when it had been Rollins all along? Peter was damn glad Jessup had been with her. Rollins wouldn't have known they were unarmed. Thankfully.

They heard a truck engine starting up, the vehicle parked with the others at the cabin. Everyone looked in that direction.

"That's my truck," Darien's brother Jake said.

"Did anyone stay to watch the vehicles?" Peter hadn't asked anyone to.

"I think we're all here," CJ said with some misgiving.

All of the men dashed through the snow as fast as they could manage, Jake leading the pack. But they wouldn't be able to stop the driver in time.

Was it Rollins who was stealing one of his pack member's vehicles? Well, hell, if he could evade all of them like he was doing, nobody had better fault Meghan for having ensured he was taken into custody the first time. She was the only one who had succeeded.

As soon as Peter and the rest of the men reached the parking area, Jake was swearing up a storm, all of them looking at the spot where his truck had been.

Yeah, that's how they all felt. Peter was sure Rollins was having a field day with besting them once again.

Peter glanced back at the cabin. He didn't see anything. Just a desolate house. And he hadn't seen or felt or heard anything that made him believe Lena was hanging around. Not this time. "Let's go, men, and try to track down the bastard who stole the truck."

Chapter 18

Sure Peter was going to be upset with her for going to the old homestead, Meghan manned the front desk at the inn for the rest of the day, trying not to think about it.

Then before three in the afternoon, Trevor walked her to her home and stayed there while she dressed for the pack party. He would be going too, but he would wait with her here until Peter arrived.

It wasn't long before she heard Trevor talking to Peter at the front door, and she hurried down to see him. This time, she was wearing a soft, kelly-green sweater, a MacTire plaid skirt, and boots. It was time to go to the pack party to eat, drink, play games, and dance. She grabbed the gift she'd made for the gift exchange and hugged and kissed Peter before they followed Trevor out.

"See you at the party," Trevor said, waving.

"See you there," Peter called out. He eyed the package she had in her hands. "For the gift exchange?"

"Yes." She saw his Santa Claus Christmas sack in the back seat of the car. "Yours?"

"Yeah. So what are *you* giving?"

She was giving a present to a woman, and he to a guy, so they didn't have to worry about revealing the contents to each other. "A wool scarf I made."

"That beige, rust, and white one I saw sitting on your living room side table a couple of weeks ago?"

"Yes, that's the one. I finally finished it a few days ago."

"Some lady's going to be lucky. I picked up an unbreak-able hatchet so someone has no excuse not to go out and chop wood for the fireplace this winter."

She laughed. "Sounds like a fun gift."

"I actually got one for myself after my hatchet handle broke while I was in the middle of cutting wood for the fire. It's come in real handy. You know stuff doesn't last as long as we do."

She chuckled. "You're right about that."

"I just wanted you to know Lelandi asked Darien if it would be all right to allow Bill a chance to come to the Christmas party."

Meghan frowned at Peter. "Why would she do that? Darien said no, right?"

"No, he agreed with Lelandi, but he talked to me first."

"And you agreed to it?" She couldn't help sounding annoyed about it. If Darien and the others hadn't come to her rescue, Bill could have gotten them both killed. From Peter's hesitation, Meghan knew he had agreed to it.

Talk about ruining the Christmas festivities with one fell swoop.

———————————

Peter knew this wasn't going to go over well with Meghan, and he'd talked extensively with Darien and Lelandi about the issue, discussing every scenario they could think of, and in the end, he'd agreed to his pack leaders' reasoning. The sooner they could catch this bastard, the better. And what better time than when Meghan was surrounded by people who would protect her? Bill would be the bait, since that's what he'd wanted in the first place, and he'd agreed whole-heartedly with the plan. Peter could understand Meghan's reluctance, though. He was certain that when their mates told them the plan, her sisters wouldn't like it any better than Meghan did.

They always had outdoor activities and indoor ones in the big building they used for pack parties during inclement weather, but both Meghan and Bill would be well guarded, no matter where they were. "All the pack members will be on high alert, playing and partying and watching and listen-ing for any sign of our former pack member. Bill isn't to go anywhere near you the whole time during the party."

"He's feeling all right?"

"Yeah, he's got a hard head. Trevor says he's got the bruises on his fist to prove it."

"He can't be handcuffed, or he won't be able to defend himself," Meghan said, sounding as though she was finally accepting the plan.

"No, he'll be free, but he'll be highly supervised. If he tries to leave the party or to take you away, we'll escort him to jail and let him stay there until we resolve this issue with Rollins. And we'll have a couple of men watching him there."

"Everyone gets to come to the party," she said, now sounding a bit morose.

"That's not why we're doing this. Lelandi said Rollins will be hanging around, watching for you. Maybe for Bill too. Rollins is going to be tempted to make a move. Even if he doesn't, we're going to have men searching the area, looking for him, in case he is out there. The damn guy is like a ghost. I swear I've never met anyone who is this elusive before."

"He keeps leaving clues, though. If he was that elusive, we wouldn't keep finding his stashes. He's real."

"True."

She glanced at Peter. "Did my sisters know Bill is coming to the party?"

"No."

She let her breath out in exasperation.

"It's hard to know what Rollins is going to do, but Lelandi is sure he'll be observing the party, whether Bill shows up or not. She feels it would be safer if he goes after Bill instead of you and we can take him out. I know you're still upset at what he pulled with you—"

"He scared the crap out of me!"

"I know. I've told him what I'll do to him if he even gets a few feet away from you. He said he wanted to apologize to you personally, and I told him he can call you, but he's not getting physically close to you, period."

"All right."

"I'm sorry. I hated to have to do this to you, but if we can eliminate Rollins tonight—"

"I would be thrilled." She took a deep breath and exhaled. "I hope you're ready to dance with me."

He lifted a brow.

"To every song." She smiled a little evilly.

He chuckled. "Then I'll have to make sure the band's only playing slow dances."

Smiling still, she seemed much more cheered at the prospect as she settled back against her car seat.

They were following behind Trevor, and CJ and Laurel's car was behind his as they made the drive out into the country to Darien and Lelandi's home.

When they finally arrived, Christmas lights were on all over the place—the house and barn, the trees and walkways. Brilliant outdoor security lights would come on at dusk so the outdoor activities could take place when it grew dark, mostly to keep everyone safe while participating in the outside fun, but for now, also to keep a look out for Rollins. Peter noticed even more lights had been set up much farther out from the activities to give them more security around a larger perimeter than they normally had.

"Are you sure you're up to this with Bill being here?" Peter asked, belatedly realizing he should have given her a choice. "I could take you home, and we could just spend a quiet evening there."

"No way. You're going to dance with me during *all* the songs. A deal's a deal."

He chuckled. He'd gotten himself into that one, but he wasn't reneging. He went to open her door for her and saw her sisters together, arms folded across their chests, frowning at him. He realized that's the way it would always be, the sisters sticking up for each other. They were wolves, and they were triplets. Just like he and his twin brother, Bjornolf, would be if he was living with the pack.

"Looks like your sisters are ready to eat me alive."

Meghan took his hand and exited the car. She smiled. "I'll tell them you're dancing the night away with me, and they'll be fine with it."

She led him over to where her sisters were standing and explained the deal.

Laurel was still frowning at Peter. "If Bill grabs her again, *I'll* kill him."

"I told him if he moves in Meghan's direction, he'll have

a whole pack on his back. He knows it. I don't think Meghan will have anything to worry about."

Christmas music was playing as several adults organized games for the kids and adults. First was a candy cane race, and Meghan dragged Peter over to run in it. He suspected she was going to wear him out tonight for agreeing to let Bill come to the party. As long as she had a good time, he would do whatever it took.

Meghan had been upset that Darien and Lelandi had decided Bill should be at the party as bait, but even more so when Peter hadn't talked them out of it. It wasn't just that she was worried Bill would go after her again, though she agreed there was probably little chance of that. Because he was her ex-boyfriend, she'd prefer everyone not see him for that reason alone.

When Peter agreed to dance with her, she figured that was the beginning of making up to her. Since the dancing hadn't begun yet, she thought she'd make him play a bunch of games. What better way to see if he could play along?

She knew he was a bit reluctant, the way she had to drag him, but she was certain it had to do with him being the pack's sheriff and a guy and not willing to let down his hair in front of everyone else.

"Are you sure?" he asked, looking at all the kids lined up.

"Yeah, it'll be fun." They each received a candy cane from Jake's mate, Alicia, and she smiled to see them lining up.

"We're the only adults doing this," Peter said, sounding a little intimidated by the idea. That was a new side of him she'd never seen. She thought he was cute.

"They don't know how to have fun," Meghan said.

But as soon as Meghan said that, Silva pulled Sam out to line up with them. Since they were the tavern owners, they often supervised the food and drinks at the big events, but Meghan knew everything was already set up inside. Everyone would just browse at the tables, not sit down for a dinner. That way, everyone could participate in the games and dance and eat whenever they wanted to.

Then Laurel dragged CJ to play the game. "We can't beat the kids," Laurel said to Meghan, "but you need the competition."

CJ said, "Peter's my boss."

Everyone laughed.

And then the jingle bells were rung, and everyone took off, each couple having to keep the crooks of their candy canes connected without breaking them as they ran to the finish line. The adults had to run a lot further, though no one had expected any adults to play in the game. Everyone was cheering the runners on.

CJ tripped in the snow and fell, breaking his candy-cane connection with Laurel. "You did that on purpose," she said, laughing.

Sam and Silva were neck and neck with Peter and Meghan, but Meghan wasn't quite as tall as Silva, so she wasn't running as fast. Peter reached around Meghan, lifting her against him, and ran the rest of the way as she wrapped her legs tight around his body, laughing.

She was gripping him around the shoulders with her free arm, keeping the connection with their candy canes as he sprinted across the finish line. Meghan swore Silva and Sam slowed down at the end on purpose, but the next thing she knew, Sam was carrying Silva, because Silva was always running around in high-heeled boots and had sprained her ankle in the snow.

"You should have won," Meghan said to Sam and Silva.

"No way," Silva said. "Any man who would carry his girlfriend across the finish line, while keeping their candy canes connected, deserves to win."

Meghan laughed, and when Peter put her down, she kissed him. "Thanks for being a good sport."

"That was fun."

"Good. Let's see what else we can do."

Peter looked like he had asked for that.

Jake's wife came over to give them a big bag of candy canes. "You're the winners of the adult contestants."

"Thanks, Alicia," Meghan said. "We can use them to make peppermint cocoa at the inn." To Peter she said, "Come on, this will be less vigorous. You need to save your strength for dancing." She pointed to where Lelandi was setting up bottles of colored water so anyone who wanted to could do snow art.

Peter groaned. "I'm not an artist."

"No problem. Neither am I. We can make crazy abstract art."

It didn't take them long to create a yellow sun, green grass, and blue flowers, which was totally a team effort. They'd decided abstract art wasn't for them. Before she could see what else they could do, Peter was glancing around. She immediately thought of Bill, which was too bad because she hadn't thought of him once while she was having fun with Peter. Instead, Peter pointed to a mini-snowman contest. "What about that? Want to give it a try?"

She grabbed his hand and ran for the mini-snowman

contest before they went in to eat. Unless there was something else fun to do first. She was having a ball, and she was glad she hadn't let Bill's being here ruin it for her. She was also glad Peter was beginning to loosen up and wanted to do more things with her.

Some of the kids were playing chase with the grown-ups in the snow, but the smaller ones soon wore out and the parents took them inside to warm up and feed them. Some of the bachelor males were wearing their wolf coats, and she knew that meant they weren't there to party, but to be on guard detail for any trouble. She hadn't even seen Bill, not that she was looking too hard. She wondered if he was inside while she was outside.

Because she and Peter had the candy canes from their win, they broke up some for the arms and broke off a small piece for the nose for their mini snowman. That made their snowman perfectly unique.

Dr. Weber won the adult contest when he used some of his bandages to create a snowman with a casted leg. The snowman was just too cute, and everyone took pictures of Doc's creation for posterity's sake. Brett was capturing it in a shot for the newspaper. Meghan wondered if he'd taken a picture of her and Peter crossing the finish line in the candy-cane race.

For another game, kids were making tracks in the snow, and other kids had to guess what animal made them. Most of the kids were good at guessing the animals that made them. As wolves, they were keen on tracking. On the other hand, it would have been a lot easier if they could have smelled the animal that would have made the tracks.

"Is there anything else you want to try?" Peter asked.

Beanbags, made in the shape of Christmas presents,

were being tossed into Santa's bag, a game of ring toss where kids were throwing the ring on a snowman's carrot nose was set up nearby, and a three-legged race had already started. Then Meghan saw a snowball relay race being organized. "Come on, let's do that, and then we'll go inside."

They hurried over to join opposite teams—she insisted. They had to grab a snowball from a stack and start a new stack of snowballs across the field. And then they had to race back to tag the next runner. The first team to move all their snowballs to the other side won.

Everyone was laughing so hard, and when Meghan's team won, Peter swore his team's side had extra snowballs to begin with. That brought on another round of laughter.

Meghan slipped her hands around his waist and smiled up at him. "Want to get warmed up and—"

"Yeah, I'll warm you up."

She laughed and pulled him toward the barn. "Let's go inside, and then we can eat. I hear the band starting up." And that meant dancing. She'd managed to get only a couple of dances out of Peter during the Victorian Days festivities in the fall because he and CJ were called on to break up a human fight at the ski lodge. This time, she hoped they wouldn't be interrupted.

The security lights suddenly went on, like they were supposed to do and did for every pack activity that they had here at night, but this time it seemed more ominous to her. As if they had come on to catch a rogue wolf.

As soon as the warm air in the building hit them, she started pulling off her gloves and hat. Peter had already removed his gloves and shoved them in his pockets, then helped her off with her coat. She did the same thing with her gloves and removed her wool scarf. He took off his coat, and they walked over to a long coatrack against one wall and he began hanging their things up together.

"Oh, we forgot our gifts," she said, noticing the gifts stacked up under the ten-foot-tall Christmas tree that had been decorated by the whole pack. One side had the women's gifts, the other, the men's.

"I'll get them. I'll take the package of candy canes out there and leave them too." Peter motioned to Jake, who was drinking cider with his mate.

Jake and Alicia crossed the floor to join them. "I need to run out to get the gifts for the exchange. Can you watch Meghan for me?"

"Sure thing," both said.

Alicia was a bounty hunter by trade and trained in all kinds of martial arts, so she really did mean what she said.

Meghan glanced around the big hall but didn't see any sign of Bill. She wondered if he had been inside and then ushered outside as soon as she headed in. She was just as glad. Then she saw Clementine drinking a glass of wine and talking to a couple of people. When she saw Meghan, she strode across the hall. Meghan didn't figure this was going to be a good talk, not as growly as the woman looked.

"Looks like Clementine's got a thorn in her paw," Alicia said. "Don't worry about her not liking you because of your ghostly sightings, Meghan. She doesn't like me because I'm more newly turned."

Meghan shook her head. The woman was intolerant of everything, it appeared.

"Do you want me to tell her to chill?" Jake asked.

"No, that's all right. I think I know why she wants to speak with me. I might as well get it over with." Meghan stiffened for the confrontation, though she was trying to relax. She noticed then Lelandi, as co-pack leader, was watching the whole situation too.

When Clementine drew close enough, she said, "Don't you dare send any more pack members to coerce me to go to the mine."

"I didn't send anyone. I don't have any idea what you're talking about."

"You're full of crap."

Meghan smiled, but then the smile slipped. "What you want to do about your son is up to you. Maybe you seeing him won't make any difference. Maybe it all has to do with the woman you tried to force him to mate."

Clementine's face turned red, her eyes widening. "For your own sake, you'd better drop that line of questioning." Then she glanced at Jake as if he knew something about it, turned, and stalked off.

Meghan frowned at Jake. "Do you know what she's talking about?"

"No. I don't have any idea why Clementine would think I'd know anything about their family affairs."

Jake sounded sincere, but Clementine sure seemed to think he knew about it. Alicia hadn't been in the pack long, so she wouldn't know what had happened that long ago. Maybe Brett would since he ran the newspaper. Meghan had probably been asking the wrong people. Surely someone in the pack would know and wouldn't be afraid to tell her. She still felt it might be the key to Oliver's release, since his mother wasn't keen about seeing him.

Chapter 19

WHEN PETER RETURNED TO THE PARTY HALL WITH THE packages, he noticed the tension in the air between Meghan and Jake and wondered what had happened.

The music began to play a waltz, and Meghan took his arm. "Let's dance."

Alicia took the presents from Peter. "I'll put these under the tree for the two of you."

Peter gave Jake one last look, and he shrugged his shoulders, but Peter would need to talk to him to learn what was wrong. Unless Meghan would tell him. But she seemed to want to dance nice and close across the floor, her head resting against his chest, her arms wrapped around his body. He realized they hadn't had anything to eat, and his stomach was already grumbling. Roast turkey, ham, and duck were set up on the tables, along with a number of other dishes that enticed him. But he wasn't moving in that direction unless Meghan wanted to eat, because he'd promised to dance every dance with her.

He suspected some of her need to dance with him was because he'd had to leave the dance early during Victorian Days. He loved being with her like this, though whenever he touched her this intimately, she worked him up. Already, his other head was rising to the occasion. "About tonight," he said.

"You want to come home with me after all this workout?" She rubbed her body against his erection.

"Hell, Meghan," he said, smiling down at the mischievous minx. "Yeah, that's what I mean."

"Hmm," she said and ran her hands over his back. "After we dance every dance?"

"Do you think we could get some eating in?"

"Is that why your stomach is rumbling so?"

He laughed. "I didn't have time for lunch, and I figured I'd get enough to eat at the party. Then here you are running me ragged in the snow and wanting to dance with me all night long and—"

"You need some energy food for what's next?"

He smiled down at her and kissed her head. "Yeah."

"Okay, two dances, and we'll get something to eat."

Four dances later, he finally peeled Meghan away from the dance floor to get something to eat. He was hot and sweaty and aroused and ready to take her home and finish this at her house. She was just as aroused but having too much fun to quit. Once she started eating, she seemed glad she did. The band quit for a break anyway, and Christmas music began to play overhead. In the middle of having wine and eating the food piled up on their plates, Lelandi announced they'd begin the gift exchange.

In years past, they would have the option of stealing a person's gift one time, but wolves are really possessive, and once they had a gift they wanted, they could get really growly if another wolf tried to take it away from them. Though some would think it was funny, others would hold grudges. So no more stealing gifts. Sometimes, wolves exchanged with others if they were agreeable. Sometimes, a gift that had been given in the past came back for each Christmas after, almost as a joke.

Even though the presents were initially put under the tree as a secret, once the new owner took hold of it, he or she would know who gave the gift because they'd smell their scent.

Alicia received Meghan's scarf, and she was thrilled. Meghan got a new cutting board, and she was delighted. When it came time for the men's gifts, Jessup got Peter's hatchet and thanked him from across the room. Several of the guys were offering their gifts in exchange for his, but he just smiled and wouldn't let go of it. Peter ended up with the men's Christmas sweater featuring a Santa with his hot abs bared that had been pawned off every year. But he had every intention of wearing it, as soft as the material was. And hopefully, Meghan would run her hands over his abs while he was wearing the sweater to feel just how hot they were.

"I dare you to wear it," Meghan said.

They were still handing out Christmas presents when Peter pulled off his sweater and several people who saw him laughed. A she-wolf across the room yelled out, "Take it off. Take it all off."

He smiled, felt his face flush a bit, and pulled on the Christmas sweater. Meghan was grinning at him. "Now feel those abs, why don't you," he said to her.

She quickly obliged, running her hands over his soft sweater. Everyone was watching them, most smiling, and he suspected some of the previous owners wished they had done the same thing with their she-wolves and not passed the sweater off during another Christmas round of gift exchanges. But *he* was the lucky one.

Some of the pack members clapped, and he realized they were clapping for him. He raised his fists in victory, and Meghan kissed his abs.

Then the gift-giving ended, and he and Meghan finished eating their meal. And they were back to dancing. Except for a bathroom break and one for a drink and dessert, they danced until the party ended.

Peter had never had this much fun at the pack Christmas party. Last year, he'd had to leave early. He was glad there weren't any interruptions this time. And thankfully, Bill hadn't created any issues.

"Ready to go home?" Peter asked Meghan, hoping she hadn't changed her mind about him staying the night with her.

"Yeah, you can chase my nightmares away."

He frowned down at her.

"I've been having them again since I heard Rollins was here."

"Oh, Meghan, honey, I'm so sorry. You should have told me. I would have stayed with you every night." He knew Laurel would have comforted her, but he would be right there in bed with Meghan, chasing the nightmares away.

Suddenly, they heard the sound of loud popping and crackling glass. Everyone was inside now, but Peter had told Darien once everyone was inside for the rest of the party, he wanted Bill to be incarcerated at the jailhouse. Some of their other deputized pack members would guard him. Peter was glad no one was outside right now except for some of the men serving as wolf guards.

"Stay here," Peter told Meghan, and he saw Jake and Tom coming to watch over her. Then Peter, CJ, and more men went outside to find that several of the outer perimeter lights had been shot out. The guard wolves had been searching for Rollins but came back, shaking their heads.

The only person who would do that was Rollins. They

examined the glass from the lights, and Peter realized explosives had been attached to the light units so Rollins had used a timer to blow them up. He truly had to have a death wish. But they weren't going to track him down tonight. That's what Rollins most likely wanted, and Peter didn't want any of the men to be led into a trap in the darkness. "Come on, men. Let's pack it up and go home." Inside, he told CJ, "I'll be staying with Meghan tonight."

"Do you want a guard on the house?"

"Yeah, I think it would be prudent."

Several cars full of pack members were heading in the same direction, so Peter knew Meghan would be safe on the trip home. They'd have additional backup outside if they needed it.

When they arrived at the house, Peter got a call while he was removing his gloves and Stetson.

"Hey, I'm at the jailhouse, safeguarding Bill, replacing one of our other guys so he could go to the party. I just got a call about the DNA findings on the stuff at your old homestead and at the mine. Rollins left fingerprints on all of it," Trevor said.

Peter tried to pull off his coat, and Meghan hurried to help him after hanging up her own. "Okay, so we know for sure Rollins was the one who had been at both places. It's good to get confirmation," Peter said.

"Uh, yeah, and the other thing is Bill wants to go home." Trevor sounded like he didn't want to bring up that bit of news.

Peter frowned. "To St. Augustine?"

Meghan pulled off her boots and set them under the side table resting against a wall. He realized now she often did that to keep anyone from tripping over them.

"Yeah, he said he doesn't want to be locked up any longer. He saw you and Meghan dancing, and he got the point. He realized he has no chance with her," Trevor said.

"Hell, if he'd had any chance at all, he screwed that up when he tried to take her hostage."

Meghan headed into the kitchen, and Peter followed her in there. She began making hot apple cider drinks for them. Peter sat on one of the kitchen table chairs, propped the phone between his shoulder and ear, and reached down and pulled off a boot.

Trevor cleared his throat. "He said it was because he wanted to prove he would have protected her this time from Rollins, to show he'd changed about how he viewed Meghan. Now he says she'd been right to do what she had done after he learned Rollins killed a bunch of our wolves."

"It's too late for that, but the thing is Bill could have gotten her killed! If he wanted to play hero, he could have gone after Rollins on his own and then told her he'd taken care of it, not involved her in a life-and-death situation." Peter pulled off his other boot and then rose from the chair and set his boots next to hers under the side table.

He turned to see her smiling at him. God, he loved her.

"I agree. But after seeing the two of you together, he says there's no chance he'll ever change her mind about him. He knows we'll catch the bastard, and he wants to go home," Trevor said.

Peter didn't trust the guy entirely, but he often asked his deputies' opinions about an important matter, then made the final decision. In this case, he'd run it by Lelandi too. With all her psychology training, she often knew the inner workings of a person's mind better than any of them.

"What do you think, Trevor?" Peter asked him first because Trevor had spoken to Bill personally about it.

Meghan carried the red-and-green Christmas-tree decorated mugs into the living room and set them down on the coffee table. Peter was glad she wanted to take a moment to relax with him, even though he'd had it in mind that they'd head up to bed right away.

"Truthfully, I'd say there's a fifty-fifty chance he'd return home," Trevor said. "I think he's still got it in mind to take Rollins down, whether he gets Meghan back or not. If he wants to risk it—on his own, not by involving Meghan—I say let's go for it. As long as she's protected at all times, I don't see a problem with it."

"Okay, let me ask Meghan, Lelandi, and CJ, and I'll get back to you." Peter sat down with Meghan on the couch.

"All right. I'll be here," Trevor said and ended the call.

"Okay, now what?" Meghan asked Peter when he set his phone on the coffee table next to hers.

"Bill wants us to release him so he can go home."

Meghan scoffed.

"I'll ask CJ and Lelandi what they think, but since it mostly affects you, it's your call."

She chuckled, then sipped from her cider. "You are trying to get on my good side after all of you let Bill go to the party and didn't clue me in first."

Peter sighed. "Is it working?"

She laughed. "Listen, if he's a problem, and the others agree he shouldn't be released, then that's what should happen. For his own good. So ask them first."

"Are you sure?"

She leaned over and kissed him. "Yes."

"All right." Peter called Lelandi next, as their expert psychologist. "Trevor is down at the jailhouse with Bill and says Bill wants to be released and he'll return home. Do you think he will? Or that he could still be a menace to Meghan?"

"Well, I believe he's still hung up on Meghan, for whatever reason. Maybe because she's found someone new to replace him? I don't know. Will he return home? I'd say he might, or he might go after Rollins himself, but I really don't think he'll make the mistake of trying to take Meghan hostage again. I believe after Trevor knocked him out, he doesn't want to try that again. I think enough people told him if he tried it again, he'd be considered a rogue wolf and would be on everyone's terminal list. I believe you were one of the ones who told him that."

"You're damn right I did."

"Well, I think he took it to heart. I went to see him after Trevor knocked him out and Bill had come to, which is why I thought Bill should attend the party. To prove he couldn't get near Meghan again. But also to try to draw Rollins out, and Bill was eager to do it. I believe it worked out well that he saw the two of you together, confirming that he's not renewing their relationship."

"I never saw him. How did he see Meghan and me in all the activities? Bill was supposed to be out of her sight the whole time."

"He was watching out the windows of the barn when you were outside with Meghan, and when you were inside, he was peeking in through the windows from the outside. I swear he's like a lovesick puppy, but from what Meghan's told me there wasn't the connection between them that she and you have."

"So you're of the opinion we should release him?"

"Yes. I don't believe he'll go after Meghan. If he wants to be released, it'll be on him to do what's right. I wouldn't recommend having anyone shadow him or protect him. He's on his own. Just make sure someone's keeping a close eye on Meghan."

"Okay, thanks, Lelandi. Trevor thinks there's a fifty-fifty chance he'll go home or try to take Rollins down."

"I'd say he was right."

"All right, I'll ask CJ's opinion and then Meghan's again. She said she wanted to know what you all thought first."

"Give her a hug for me. Night, Peter."

"Night, Lelandi." Peter rubbed Meghan's thigh and then drank some of his cider. "Lelandi says she thinks you'll be all right if we release him."

"But *he* might not be if he's not being protected and he tries to go after Rollins," Meghan said.

"It's his choice."

Meghan nodded.

Peter called CJ next, but he wanted to take Meghan to bed. They were caroling tomorrow night, and they had a busy day tomorrow. He really wanted to make love to her and then get some sleep. "Hey, CJ, I hope I didn't wake you."

"What's up?"

"Bill wants to be released from jail."

CJ groaned.

When they ended the call, Peter finished his cider and rose from the couch, taking Meghan's hand, and headed for the stairs. "Everyone was in agreement. Release Bill, and let him be on his own. But we'll do it tomorrow during the day."

"Okay, that works for me."

Peter called Trevor back and gave him the news. "See you in the morning."

Glad to get that business done, all Peter wanted to do now was immerse himself in everything that was Meghan—her scent, the taste and feel of her, the way she reacted to his scent, his taste, the feel of him.

He and Meghan soon reached her bedroom, and he scooped her up and set her on the bed so he could pull off her socks.

She reached forward and ran her hand over the front of his jeans in a seductive caress. Her touch on his arousal amplified his desire for her. He breathed in her seductive scent, her pheromones that he swore were designed to compel him to meet her needs.

He pulled off her sweater next and tossed it aside, throwing his own on top of it a moment later.

And then he pushed her against the bed, her red hair spilling over the green sheets like a Christmas present, and he spread her legs apart. He moved on top of her, centering himself against her. He rubbed his jeans-covered body against hers, the friction between them making his cock rock hard.

She moaned softly, slipping her fingers around his belt loops and pulling him harder against her.

His mouth devoured hers as she reciprocated in kind, each eager to ravish the other, their breathing ragged, their hearts beating hard. *You are mine*, he wanted to say in every way possible.

His cock was eager to penetrate her slick, wet sheath, to fulfill a need to make her his mate for all eternity.

She wrapped her legs around his waist and bowed up

toward him, encouraging his contact. They still had too many clothes on, and he rested his elbows on her bed, then unfastened her bra and removed it. He kneaded one breast, feeling the nipple extend to the palm of his hand, and he licked and kissed the other with a tender touch. She was writhing beneath him, pressing herself against his swollen cock, the need to take her filling him with urgency.

He moved off her and unfastened her jeans, then pulled them off. He did the same with his own and took a moment to gaze at her beauty, her nipples dusky pink and hard, her skin soft, her blue panties wet. He smiled.

Then he pulled his boxer briefs and socks off. And slowly removed her panties, her red curly hairs dewy with moisture. He knew, if she'd consented to a mating, she'd be ready for him to take it all the way. Damn that they had to wait.

He climbed into bed with her and skimmed his hand up her inner thigh. She was running her hand over his arm, tense with anticipation, as he drew closer to her intimate spot. "You are a tease," she murmured huskily.

He smiled and nibbled her neck, and she scraped her nails against his shoulder. And then he began to stroke her in earnest, wanting to watch her come, to see what she needed from him to make it happen. Her hand grasped his and pressured him to press harder, rougher, faster. He kissed her on the mouth and tangled his tongue with hers, his cock itching to join her.

He felt the urge to take this further, to consummate their relationship, to tell all other wolves paws off because he and she had declared their love for each other. He groaned when she reached down and brushed her hand against his cock, and then she slowly began stroking him.

He plunged two fingers between her feminine folds, like he'd wanted to do with his erection, his whole body aching for release. She was killing him kindly, but he was doing the same to her.

He kept rubbing her clit, and her hand stilled on his cock. He knew she was ready to climax, her body tense, and then she cried out in rapture. "Oh," she said in a half groan, half sigh.

He continued to stroke her gently while she got back to the business of stroking him firmly, pressing kisses against his chest, licking his nipples, and softly nibbling on them.

He couldn't last, but rather than making a mess in the bed again, he pulled away from her, and she looked surprised, then disappointed. Offering his hand to her, he smiled, his cock stretching out to her. "Let's finish this in the shower."

"Oh, yes! No changing sheets, and yes!"

Smiling, he pulled her from the bed, and they hurried into the bathroom where he turned on the hot water in the shower, and she pressed her body against his cock, rubbing vigorously to keep him erect. She didn't have to worry about that. With her head cupped in his hands, and his mouth pressed warmly against hers, his cock was ready for the finale. Then he pulled her into the shower and under the hot water, kissing her mouth, her cheeks, her lips again, while she stroked him until he exploded.

She continued to stroke him until he was spent, and then she rubbed her body against his before they began soaping up and rinsing off. He bundled her up in a towel and pulled out her hair dryer to dry her hair. She raised her brows, smiling at him.

"It's cold, though I aim to keep you warm the rest of the night." And then he dried her hair, running his fingers through the strands and against her scalp, and he swore he heard her purring. When her hair was dry, he scooped her up and headed to bed.

Once they were in bed, he pulled the curtains closed, making the bed like a royal hideaway, and they joined each other under the covers. He tucked her against his sated body and again thought he couldn't last at this if they didn't mate soon. They didn't say anything further, their fingers softly caressing each other's skin, saying *I want to make you mine.*

The next morning, Meghan and Peter enjoyed having breakfast together before leaving for work.

Peter finished his omelet. "I'm going to release Bill from jail first thing and then run out to look again at those lights Rollins destroyed to see if I can find any clues to his whereabouts anyone else might have missed."

"Okay. I'll be helping my sisters at the inn in the meantime."

They bundled up in their winter garments, and then he walked her over to the inn and kissed her before he drove off to the office. "See you as soon as I can."

"See you." She couldn't believe the incredible night—and morning—she'd had with Peter.

She took a deep breath of the sweet scents coming from the inn's kitchen. Her sisters were making all kinds of treats for the celebration they were holding at the inn while Meghan and Ellie were caroling. The carolers would come here for refreshments on one of their stops and sing at the inn.

Ellie was wearing her Victorian gown already, an emerald-green one to set off her pretty red hair, and brought in a tray of treats to set on the counter for guests, visitors, and Meghan. Laurel was wearing a gold gown, both of them looking beautiful.

"Tempt me, why don't you?" Meghan teased, then took one of the chocolate petit fours and ate it.

Ellie smiled. "You need to keep up your strength." Then she frowned. "Why aren't you dressed? You didn't forget, did you? Oh…you're not going to skip out on the caroling, are you?" She sounded so disappointed.

"No. I thought I'd run back and dress a little later," Meghan said. "Oh, and if CJ didn't tell you last night, Laurel, Peter's releasing Bill from jail and I agreed to it."

"He's not allowed to come anywhere near you, is he?" Ellie leaned against the counter while Meghan manned the desk.

"No. We figure he'll either go home like he's supposed to, or he'll try to locate Rollins."

"That's not a good idea," Laurel said.

"I agree. But it's Bill's decision." Meghan sighed and grabbed a lilac-frosted petit four.

"Yeah, it needs to be done," Laurel said.

Suddenly, the front door of the inn opened, and Trevor walked in and greeted Meghan. He'd already greeted her sisters earlier, Meghan suspected.

The phone rang, and Meghan answered it. "Silver Town Inn, this is Meghan. How may I help you?"

"You think you're so clever, don't you? Finding all my

stashes. But how? That's what I can't figure out. You think being in prison was easy? For a wolf? Hell, you don't know how many times I wanted to shift and kill someone. The only thing that kept me from doing it was thinking about what I'd do to you when I got out. But I couldn't wait any longer."

"Rollins?" Meghan felt a shiver steal up her back. "I should have killed you when I had the chance, for all those women you've abused and for the miners who died in the Silver Town Mine. Now everyone in your pack knows the kind of evil bastard you are."

"That was an...*accident.*"

"That's not what Oliver said."

"Oliver?" Rollins sounded shocked to the core that she might know what Oliver had said. "Hell, he died with the rest of them. All but the two they saved."

Trevor got on his phone and was texting someone.

"But you saved yourself first, didn't you? Set off the explosion and sealed the other miners' fates. That's why you left, disappearing for good, letting the pack believe you were dead. Until now," Meghan said.

"I can't believe you're here of all places."

"Everyone is after your blood, Rollins. You don't stand a chance." Meghan wished now that the inn phone had been tapped and they would know where he was.

The phone line went dead.

Ellie was frowning at Meghan. "That was him? The bastard himself?"

Meghan was so shaken, she couldn't think straight for a moment. Rollins had to be her main priority. Not Lena or the ghost in the mine, though she couldn't help wanting to aid them.

"Peter's on his way here," Trevor said. "We'll have your phone tapped in case Rollins calls again."

Meghan knew now Rollins really had planned to come for her, not just Bill. She picked up her cell phone, ignoring that she had an incoming call on the reservation line, which Ellie hurried to pick up.

Laurel hurried to join them and came around the counter to give Meghan a quick hug.

"Peter," Meghan said, hugging Laurel back, loving that her sisters were always there for her.

"I'm on my way over there, honey. I'll be there in a second."

She knew Peter would be as upset as she was to hear what Rollins had said.

Chapter 20

AFTER RELEASING BILL FROM JAIL, PETER AND HIS MEN were searching for any sign of where Rollins had gone when Peter got the text from Trevor and then the call from Meghan. She sounded so shook up that he dropped everything, put CJ in charge of the search, and headed back to town to see her at the inn.

Peter stayed on the phone with her while Ellie took over the reservation desk. "Listen, Meghan, we'll get him. I promise you that. I can't believe the bastard hasn't left the area and is still trying to get to you."

"I think that's why he called. He isn't able to reach me. Not with Trevor and Jake or Tom at the inn during the day, or with you watching over me. He just can't catch a break."

"And he's not going to." Peter was sick with fear that the bastard would kill her. "Hell, Meghan, I'm so sorry."

"It's my fault. I should have handled things differently the first time around."

"Like hell it is. We should have taken care of one of our own centuries ago. No one else should have ever had to deal with him."

"Peter?"

He knew what she was going to ask. Yet he didn't want to talk about it right now. "Yeah, honey?"

"I want to see if Lena is at your old residence. I have to know for sure one way or the other."

"I know. It's in your blood to help others in need." Though Peter suspected it wasn't all about that but also the need to put Lena to rest. "I know. We'll…we'll do something."

"The sooner the better. If this maniac wasn't out there…"

"Don't you dare go over to the site." He needed to let everyone in the pack know they weren't to escort Meghan or her sisters over there while Rollins was still in the area. Beyond that, Peter didn't want to risk that Meghan would anger Lena's ghost, if she was there, and suffer the consequences. He assumed Meghan would want to go inside the house, and that could be dangerous.

Peter came into the inn looking like a wolf ready to hunt some prey. Everyone stepped aside, respectful of the way he looked so concerned. He quickly joined Meghan and pulled her into his arms. "Are you all right?"

"Yes. He can't get to me. That's why he resorted to calling me."

"The bastard," Peter said. "Bill's been released, and several pack members watched him leave town. I heard a few even followed him for several miles."

Meghan smiled. "I love your pack."

"Ours. They're as much yours now as they are mine. I'm having someone put a tap on your inn phone and the one at your home."

"Thank you. Though I suppose Rollins will assume that and not call again."

"True. I never thought he'd be that bold, or I would already have placed them on the phones. I'm making sure we have a guard force watching our backs the whole time we're caroling."

"I wouldn't think Rollins would try to go after me when we're going to be with such a large chorus of carolers," she said.

"We'll be busy and not on the lookout for him."

He let his breath out in exasperation, wishing this business with Rollins were over.

After that, Peter hung around and pulled guard duty over the sisters too, just in case, and had lunch with them. Then before it was time to leave, he escorted Meghan home to get dressed.

"Are you ready for caroling this evening?" Peter asked as they entered Meghan's home. He couldn't imagine how she'd feel after having to deal with Bill and Rollins and the issues with the ghosts. When he had to work a murder case, that's all he thought of for days, even after the case was resolved. It was hard to let go of things like that.

"Oh, absolutely." She reached over and ran her hand over his arm, smiling. "I'm sorry if I seem a bit preoccupied. I just keep wondering how we can resolve the business with Oliver. But I'm really looking forward to caroling with you. When we're through caroling and nibbling on all the sugary treats everyone's preparing for us, we'll have a nice dinner."

"I'm already hungry." But he was thinking more of what he was planning for after the caroling. He knew Meghan wanted to resolve the situation with Lena's ghost, if she was hanging around, but he wanted to move forward with Meghan. He didn't want to wait, which was why he hadn't canceled the next phase of his plan.

He smelled the delightful aroma of the pot roast she'd

started earlier in the day and was looking forward to having dinner with her. He wrapped his arms around her and kissed her generously on the mouth, parting her lips with his tongue, invading her, luxuriating in the feel of her sweet, silky softness. "I wish we could spend all our time like this."

"You see why I say we need to resolve the situation with Lena soon?" Meghan rubbed her soft body against his.

"Yeah, and I agree." He didn't want to think about that right now. "I still need to change into my Victorian attire. You do, too, or otherwise I'd say we could make time for some...loving." But he knew they needed to leave soon. Later tonight, they would have all the time in the world. He hoped.

Peter took hold of her hand and escorted her upstairs, checking all the rooms before she entered her bedroom and began to strip off her jeans and sweater.

"Do you need any help?"

She chuckled. "No, I've got it. You can help with the corset, though."

"I can sure do that." Peter unfastened and removed her bra for her, too, and ran his hands over her bare breasts. He groaned, wanting to skip the caroling all together. But they had too much at stake tonight. He tied up her corset for her, then kissed her breasts. "Gotta keep our minds on business, or we'll be late."

"And you are *never* late." Meghan pulled on her petticoats while Peter called CJ about what was going on now.

"The wiretaps are on the phones," CJ said. "But I doubt he'll call either of the landlines now. Guards are in place at the square and will follow the group of carolers throughout the festivities."

"Good."

"Is everything all right between you and Meghan?"

"Yeah, we're good."

Meghan flashed Peter a smile.

"What are you going to do about Lena? Laurel's been asking me as if to remind you the situation needs to be resolved."

"We'll have to figure that out later."

"Okay. We haven't found Jake's truck, and he's about ready to blow a gasket. One of his cameras was in the truck. He'd been taking pictures of the snow scenery for a new Colorado art gallery," CJ said.

"Well, hell. I'm sure we'll get it back." At least Peter hoped.

"Yeah, I hope so. He said he'd been called to help out and hadn't taken the camera out of his truck like he normally would have."

"Hell, I'm sorry to hear that." Peter knew how much photography meant to Jake. That was Jake's whole life. Well, and of course Alicia and the kids. Though Jake had been talking about the two of them starting a bounty-hunter business, since that's what she'd been doing before he met her and mated her. The kids were getting bigger, and pack members would take care of them when he and Alicia took off after bail-bond jumpers.

Peter realized Meghan had already pulled on her boots. She grabbed his belt loop and headed for the stairs.

"Hey, we're running to my place so I can get dressed," Peter said to CJ.

"Okay, and we're all set for the finale."

"Great." Peter was thankful there hadn't been a hitch with that. "See you soon."

As soon as they were downstairs and he slid Meghan's woolen cloak over her shoulders, she took Peter's arm. "Ready?"

"Absolutely."

After Peter dressed at his home, he and Meghan met at the square where everyone else had gathered.

All the carolers were decked out in Victorian clothing, and Jake was there taking pictures of everyone with one of the spare cameras he had, partly for his own exhibits, but also for the newspaper because Brett was caroling with Ellie too. Meghan and Peter joined the group of twenty others who would do their caroling down the main part of town, into the tavern, and back outside where people from all over were gathered—human and wolf visitors alike and pack members enjoying the festivities. The carolers had practiced for months on their songs and the route they'd take. It was the first time Peter and Meghan had taken part in the caroling. He'd done it because she'd wanted to, and he'd wanted to do it with her. Ellie and Brett were singing beside Meghan and Peter at every stop they made, while Laurel and CJ had prepared a sweet feast for anyone who wanted to drop in at the inn.

Meghan had bought Peter a red wool scarf and red-and-green-plaid vest, early Christmas presents to wear with his top hat, long winter coat, white shirt with turnover collar, wide red tie, dark tailcoat, trousers, and black leather gloves. He loved them. He'd ordered a white fur muff and hat to keep her warm as her early Christmas presents, and she seemed just as pleased to wear them. She was wearing a forest-green velvet gown and a heavy wool cloak. She'd opted for a full petticoat, not one of those whalebone hoopskirts. He couldn't imagine wearing one either, but she looked great.

Midway through their program, the carolers stopped at the MacTires' inn for refreshments—hot cider or eggnog, and petit fours and pecan pie. Then they sang several songs to the guests and visitors before they made their way outside into the snow and cold and began caroling again at Silva's tea shop. The shop was normally only open for lunches, but Silva had opened it that night for the special occasion. They also dropped by Bertha's bed-and-breakfast. Then they went to the Silver Town Tavern where the local wolves hung out to make them sing along.

Peter hadn't thought he could have this much fun singing, but it was all because of the she-wolf who was bumping his side, trying to snuggle up to him to keep warm. He finally wrapped his arm around her and hugged her tight, carrying the caroling candle and loving being with her like this. He kissed her cold nose and was glad the caroling was about done so he could take her home and they'd have a hot dinner and warm up. But first he had a special treat in store for her.

Their final stop was a trip out to the ski lodge where night skiers were getting in a last-minute trip down the slopes. Beside a warm fire blazing at the hearth, and the obligatory Saint Bernard sleeping by the fire, they sang their final songs as skiers hurried in to hear the music and lodge guests stood around with hot toddies cupped in their hands.

Afterward, the carolers were given hot drinks of their choice and more sweet treats to eat, though Peter and Meghan were saving room for their late dinner after the sleigh ride home. He'd thought of a lot of different scenarios that would make for the most special way to pop the mating question. This topped his list, and Laurel had told him none of the sisters had been on a sleigh ride before. They had lived in the warmer regions of the States, for the most part.

Of course, when he'd originally planned this, he'd thought he and Meghan would be alone. He'd never considered his ghostly mate could be hanging around or that Rollins would be an issue. Or Bill. Instead, they had to have their very own guard force on the sleigh ride. Everyone who was asked to be part of the sleighing guard force was thrilled to take part in the memorable occasion.

CJ bowed low before them and made the announcement, "Your sleigh awaits, my lady."

Meghan's expression was one of surprise and then delight. She threw her arms around Peter and kissed him lavishly. He kissed her back hungrily. He couldn't have been happier with the way she had reacted to the announcement.

He'd decided he wanted to mate Meghan, and he wasn't getting talked out of it this time.

Whether Lena's ghost was haunting the old homestead or not, he had decided he had to move on, and he wanted to spend the rest of his life with Meghan. He just hoped she felt the same way. But he wasn't naive enough to think she would agree before they discussed matters further. What a special way to do it, though! At least he hoped that would help convince her how important she was to him.

When they went out into the snowy night, lanterns were lighted on the three sleighs. One had green leather seats, another blue, and the last one red. One had a burgundy exterior, and the other two black, each with gold trim, and they all had miniature, battery-operated strings of lights draped along the sides. Drivers were dressed in Victorian attire, and two horses were pulling each of the sleighs. Peter's other deputy, Trevor, was driving their sleigh. Though everyone was dressed in Victorian clothes, the men were all armed with modern guns. Brett and Ellie were in one of the sleighs, and CJ and Laurel in another.

"We would have taken the sleigh ride alone if the issue of Rollins hadn't come up," Peter said, wishing they had more privacy like he'd planned all along.

"Oh, Peter, it's just beautiful. And this makes it even more special for me." Meghan smiled at her sisters and brothers-in-law.

They smiled back at her, delighted to take part.

"I'm so glad you're happy." Peter helped her into the sleigh, and everyone gathered around to take pictures of them sitting in it.

Jake was busily snapping shots, and Brett was taking some for the newspaper, though if his didn't turn out, Jake would give him whatever photos he needed.

Peter just hoped Meghan would say yes to a mating and wouldn't want to wait to consummate the relationship. He couldn't imagine anything worse than all the fanfare and then Meghan turning him down over the ghost business. Which was why he told both Jake and Brett to hold off publishing any of the pictures of the sleigh ride until after he knew for sure she would say yes. They both agreed to wait. Brett wasn't a reporter who reported the highs and lows of pack issues. He was careful to post only what wouldn't hurt any of their people.

After all the picture taking, Peter told Trevor to take them for their ride.

Settled under a red-and-green-plaid wool blanket, Peter

and Meghan snuggled together as the sleigh slid over the snow.

"I wanted to tell you that you are the only one for me. If we wore jewelry, I'd be giving you a ring." He leaned over and kissed her, and she kissed him right back, her lips clinging to his. "But I know we still need to talk." His voice was husky with emotion. He wanted her for his own in the worst way.

A full moon spilled light all over the snowscape, and Meghan said, "I agree. If it's all right with you, I'd love to stop the sleighs before we go all the way to the house and run as wolves."

"We talked about it beforehand, and everyone said they'd love to after they'd eaten so many sweet treats tonight. We'll stop by Bernard's old barn and run from there down to the river and back. That's a three-mile trek, so the men guarding the horses and sleighs don't have to sit in the cold for too long. The food you have cooking in the Crock-Pot will be fine, right?"

"I'd love that. And yes, it can cook for another couple of hours or so and be fine. I put the Crock-Pot on low." She let out her breath. "I don't want to ruin this nice surprise and what you want to ask me, but if you don't mind me asking, why didn't you tear down the old house, Peter? Did you sense Lena's presence there? Did you see or hear Lena while you were still living at the house?"

Peter really didn't want to talk about this and have Meghan think less of him, but they did need to discuss it *before* they were mated.

"After Lena died, I was drinking a lot, not eating enough, and I imagined...seeing her a couple of times. Hallucinations. Nothing more. I thought I heard her sometimes, but it was just the creaking house, or the wind stirring the trees nearby, or the rattling of the shutters on the windows."

"But you thought the sounds and sightings might have been her. That's why you kept the house and property."

"I…I don't know. Maybe. Did you see her?" Peter asked.

"Peering out the window at us, maybe."

As sensitive as Meghan was to seeing ghosts, he was afraid of that. "Unless it was Rollins."

"True. Then the face was gone and I wondered if it was my mind playing tricks on me. I need to go inside to verify if she's there or not."

"You can't go inside the house. It's not safe."

"Is that where you had always seen her? Inside the house?" Meghan asked.

"I *imagined* seeing her. But yes, it was always inside. Once in the kitchen, once in the parlor, and once in our bedroom. I slept on the sofa that night."

Meghan smiled at him. "I don't blame you. Did she have a favorite season?"

"Summer. She loved the flowers. She was from New York City."

"Okay. Was she a real homebody? And didn't get out much?"

"Yes."

"No garden or other interests?"

"She had a vegetable and flower garden. She'd never had one when she was in New York City."

"I wonder if she ever goes outside as a ghost. If I really did see her."

"You're saying you think she's really there."

"Maybe. What I'm wondering is if she's attached to the

house. She might never leave it. If it's torn down, she might roam the area where it had been. Did she like to run as a wolf?"

"No, she didn't like that wild side of her. Her parents were proper Victorians from New York City. They came here to start a millinery shop because they had too much competition in the big city. Plus, they wanted to be with a pack. They blamed me for Lena's death because I hadn't protected her, but I'd had a job to do, and I never thought anything like that would happen in our territory. They closed down their shop and moved back east. But they felt the same about running as wolves as she did. I'm sure it was because they'd all been raised in the city."

"Okay, so she probably won't be running as a ghost wolf then."

"I doubt it." Peter wondered what Meghan was getting at, and he hoped this wasn't a sign of her continued reluctance to mate until they resolved the issue with Lena.

Chapter 21

MEGHAN WONDERED: IF SHE WENT INSIDE THE HOUSE, Lena's territory, would Lena be angry? What if the roles were reversed, and the house and Peter had belonged to Meghan while Lena was a rival wolf trying to steal her mate from her? Meghan would be mighty territorial, she figured. Even if she was a ghost. Though Peter had said Lena was sweet—sure, toward him, but toward another she-wolf who wanted her mate? She suspected that would be another story.

"What if we run to the old home as wolves?" Meghan was trying to come up with any scenario she could think of that might work to get Lena to move on if she was hanging around.

"Couldn't she still attach herself to you?" Peter asked.

"Maybe."

"Can your ghost-hunter cousin, Yolan Wernicke, see if Lena's there? Maybe exorcise her himself so you wouldn't have to be there? I know we talked about her maybe attaching herself to him and then him showing up in Silver Town for whatever reason, but maybe he'd just see her. And maybe he could help her find her way to the other side."

She shook her head. "I've been thinking more about the possibility, but I really don't believe it would work. The brothers are likely to ask to do a ghost-hunter show for their help in the matter. They see every ghost situation as a moneymaking opportunity."

"Hell no."

"That's what I'd assumed you'd say, and I feel the same way. I'm glad they haven't heard about what we're doing in the mine." If her loved one had died, she wouldn't want the ghost hunters to feature him in a story to profit from his death. She'd only want to help him pass over.

"You don't happen to know any other...people who can see them, do you?" Peter asked.

"Just a few people who have seen Chrissy." Meghan thought about Chrissy and realized she was gone. That just hit Meghan all at once. She'd so wanted to help Chrissy find resolution in death, but it hadn't sunk in that she was gone forever. "Have you seen Lena recently?"

"I didn't see her when I was in the house looking for clues Rollins had been there."

"Spirits don't always appear for us. They can still be there, lurking about."

He looked so serious. "Meghan, I would do anything for you. I'm not giving you up. I want you in my life, today, tomorrow, the next day, and every day after that. I've been trying to do this for a long time, afraid of telling you about my past when here you were afraid to share yours with me. I've never felt surer of anything in my life."

"But your mate..."

"She's gone. She's been gone for a very long time. I loved her. I still do. But it's time for *me* to move on. Will you mate me?"

"I love you, Peter. I've seen the way you've looked at the other bachelor males since we've been dating when they've been trying to catch my eye. It's our way, a wolf's way, of proving to a prospective mate he or she is the center of your life. Bill had no competition in that regard. He had nothing to prove. I don't know how he would have reacted if he'd had to show other wolves I wasn't available."

"He wouldn't have done a good job of it."

She chuckled.

Peter pulled her closer and began kissing her. "I love you, and I'm so glad you moved to Silver Town to be mine."

She wrapped her arms around his neck and smiled up at him. "So *that's* why I moved to Silver Town."

He smiled, dimples appearing on his cheeks. "You know once you saw me in my uniform, you couldn't resist me."

"Oh, you better believe it."

Peter smiled again.

Smiling, she shook her head. "But…"

"But…?"

"I want you to play with me not just as a human, but as a wolf too."

Peter smiled. "I was afraid I might be too rough with you. I'd never played with a she-wolf until you tackled me. Just with my brother, Bjornolf, and other male wolves. But I'm ready and willing."

"I'll let you know if you're too rough, believe me. So yes, I'll mate you! I love you, Peter. I worry about you and your late mate, but…"

"We'll be fine. I know we will."

Whether they would be or not, she didn't want to wait either. "My house or yours?"

"Yours. I told Trevor to take us there first."

"And you'll move into my home and sell your place?" Meghan didn't want to give up the house behind the inn. The two properties needed to stay together.

"If that's what you want. I figured if we mated, I'd be selling my place. I'll be even closer to my job this way. And closer to you." Peter kissed her nose. "Loving you is going to be so easy."

"I guess my sisters weren't surprised about all this."

"Oh, believe me, they were. Once we had to change plans at the last minute and have a guard detail, we wanted to have them come along for the ride. They were ecstatic that we'd come this far and thrilled to take part."

"I think they figured we would take a lot longer to get to this point."

"Not when we'd both made up our minds—a long time before this."

Trevor pulled the sleigh next to the old barn, and the others followed suit.

"We're going for a short wolf run," Peter said. Then he smiled. "She said yes!" Though everyone knew it wasn't a done deal until they actually had consummated sex.

Everyone cheered them with heartfelt congratulations, and then the men helped the women down from the sleighs. The sisters hugged Meghan while the guys shook Peter's hand and slapped him on the back.

Meghan's eyes teared up. She never believed she'd be the last one to have a mate, but this felt so right with Peter.

"We're going to run about three miles to the river and back," Peter said, "if you think the horses and the drivers will be okay."

Trevor nodded. "We'll be warm as toast." He jerked his thumb at Michael, the Army Ranger who had volunteered to be a driver, since he was also sniper-qualified. "Michael tells us he can handle any weather. The horses are fine. Go have your run. As *lupus garous*, it's all part of the deal."

Which it truly was. Their wolf halves were an integral part of who they were.

They all agreed to run and then climbed into their sleighs to strip out of their clothes, which was a monumental task with all the Victorian garments they were wearing. Everyone was laughing as the men helped their mates strip out of their cumbersome clothes so the women could shift faster. And then the men hurried to remove their clothes and shift. Wolf after wolf leaped out of the sleighs and into the snow. They gathered together, greeting each other as wolves do, nuzzling and licking, and then they tore off.

Meghan knew Peter wanted to make this quick for the horses and drivers, and so he was pushing the limit on their ability to run through the snow. They stayed on top of it for the most part and continued to yip and bump into one another affectionately as they ran to the river.

Even though she had told Peter she wanted him to play with her, this wasn't the time. She loved running with him and the others in the cold night. The moon cast a white light on the snow and trees, the shadows of the tree branches stretching out like ghostly figures against the pristine snow.

Playing meant stopping and tackling, and they didn't have the time, so instead she nipped at his tail and he yipped with joyful glee. They soon reached the river and circled around. In a mad dash, the six of them raced back to the sleighs as if in a race for their lives. Meghan and her sisters were just as fast as the men, but Meghan had sunk into deeper snow and that had slowed her down. She leaped out of it and followed behind Laurel and CJ to stay on the earlier path they'd made through the snow. And she nipped at Peter's flank. He bumped her back, his tongue hanging out, his eyes glinting with interest. So much for not playing with him, but she couldn't help it. She was eager to be everything with him—his lover, his playmate, his wolf mate. And she wanted desperately to show him just how much she loved him.

She considered not shifting when they returned to the sleigh and instead just riding the rest of the way back as a wolf. It would be much easier than dressing in the Victorian clothes in the cold. Her fur coat would keep her warm. Best of all, when she arrived home, she'd be ready for what came next.

Wait, dinner came next. Well, they could throw on robes for that. Or eat dinner afterward!

A shot rang out in the vicinity of the sleighs, and the wolves ran faster than Meghan thought they ever could. She knew everyone was afraid for the drivers' safety. She was ready to use her teeth on Rollins this time if he was there.

When she and the others ran into the area where the sleighs were, Trevor quickly said, "We didn't find Rollins, but it looks like he was camping out here in the barn. I fired the warning shot so you'd return, afraid you might run into him out there. I've alerted more of our men to join us in a search of the area."

Peter jumped into the sleigh.

Damn. Meghan had wanted this time with Peter. Now she was afraid he'd have to be with the search team.

She leaped into the sleigh, but she didn't shift. Peter did and hurried to dress. She realized he had to give orders concerning what they were going to do about Rollins.

"Okay, we'll head back to the houses, and you and our other drivers can take the horses in while we have men search the woods for Rollins," Peter said, pulling on his coat.

CJ had also shifted and dressed, but no one else had. "You and Meghan have the night off," he told Peter.

Peter smiled. "You still work for me."

Smiling, CJ gave him a thumbs-up.

Meghan loved how the wolves were all there for each other.

They waited until men arrived to search the area, and then they continued their sleigh ride home. Meghan hoped Peter didn't feel like he was abandoning his men while enjoying his time with her. But wolves understood that matings and children were at the center of their being. Without both, their kind couldn't carry on.

They finally reached her home, and this time, Trevor went to the door of Meghan's house and guarded it, rifle at the ready. Peter carried Meghan's clothes inside and set them on a chair. Then with his gun readied and Meghan still wearing her wolf coat, they checked everything—the upstairs: the bedrooms and bathrooms; the downstairs: sitting area, office, and kitchen—making sure Rollins wasn't hiding anywhere in the house. The aroma of the pot roast cooking in a Crock-Pot permeated the air, and Peter's stomach rumbled.

Meghan smiled when she heard it. She shifted and grabbed her cloak off the couch and wrapped it around her naked body.

"Dinner smells good," Peter said, kissing her cheek, then giving the all clear to Trevor and locking the door.

"What should we do first? Mate or eat?" she asked.

He smiled at her as if he was surprised she'd have to ask. "Are you kidding? Mate first. Not just because I want to do this before anything else happens that would delay us from making the commitment, but because it will kill me to wait any longer. Besides, you're dressed right for it."

She chuckled, and he swept her up into his arms and headed for the stairs to the bedroom. She loved it when he was decisive. And when he had his priorities straight.

Once he reached the bedroom, he set her next to the bed. He slid the cloak off her shoulders and set it on a chair. He began kissing her cheeks, her neck, her breasts, her tummy, and then he pulled her close and hugged her tight. "God, I've wanted this for so long," he murmured against her hair.

Meghan knew this was where she wanted to be—in Peter's arms, loving him, no matter what other situations they had to face. They'd do it together. "I feel the same way about wanting you." She'd just been too much of a coward to tell him everything when she feared losing him.

She began helping him out of his clothes, pulling his jacket off first, then making him sit down on the bed. She pulled off his boots and socks, and when she rose, she moved his legs apart so she could step in between them. He cupped her buttocks and pulled her even closer, smiling up at her.

"I thought it was going to be too much of a hassle taking off all these clothes, but I like this. You naked against me, stripping me."

She chuckled and moved one of his hands to her breast. He began to massage her breast, and she felt the familiar achy need pushing her to hurry so he could finally plunge his cock deep inside her, giving all of himself to her, like she was opening herself up and giving all of herself to him. As she hurried to unbutton his shirt, he leaned over and nuzzled her cheek, his mouth kissing her neck. She was bending over now to pull his shirt from his pants when he moved her hair aside and kissed her shoulder, licking and nipping at it.

Every action of his spurred her to strip his clothes off him as fast as she could. She wanted them bared to each other, rubbing, and licking, and kissing, and touching. Their pheromones were already surrounding them, urging them on as she pulled off his shirt. Then she pushed him back against the bed and looked at the bulge in his pants. The *prominent* bulge. It had to be killing him to still be so dressed.

She ran her hand over his crotch, and he groaned.

She unfastened his belt and unzipped his pants, then pulled them off. Then she went to his boxer briefs and molded her hand to his erection through the fabric. But that was enough. From the strain on Peter's face, she didn't think he could hold off any longer, any more than she could, and she stripped his boxer briefs off. His erection sprang free, which was a sight to behold. Not to mention his gorgeous abs that she leaned over and caressed.

Meghan was on top at first, resting between his legs, his hands caressing her buttocks with abandon, their lips melded in a fierce kiss. This was it. The beginning of the beginning for them as mated wolves.

She rubbed her mons against his erection, his hands pressing against her ass to keep her close. And then he was rolling her over on her back and moving her legs apart so he could center himself on her.

She thought he was going to plunge his cock deep inside her, but he turned so he could stroke her first, her nub already swollen and thrumming with rampant need, her curls wet with the same urgency. She was so ready for him, he needn't have done anything further.

At least she didn't think so. But then he was stroking her into the next world, sending her colliding with the stars, and she felt the wonder of release, right before he centered his cock between her feminine lips and pushed in, pulled out, and then plunged in deeper.

She cried out with climax as he took her to another plane of existence, and then she centered every conscious moment on feeling the power of his thrusts as her orgasm surrounded him. In, nearly out, in, the bed moving with his powerful lunges, and then he held himself still for a moment. He began working it again until he groaned loudly, his face strained, then at peace. When he settled on top of her, she wrapped her arms around him.

"Now, you're mine." She just hoped that nothing or no one would come between them. "I love you."

He didn't say anything for a moment, then he kissed her mouth. "I was afraid this time would never come. I can't love you any more than I do."

She had felt the same way, that it might never have happened, and yet it was the best thing that had ever happened. For both of them. She hoped.

Chapter 22

AFTER MAKING LOVE, PETER CUDDLED WITH MEGHAN, wanting to hold her like this always, but he knew they still had issues to deal with.

Meghan ran her finger over his abdomen. "Are you hungry?"

The aroma of the pot roast lingered in the air, and yeah, he was hungry. Peter ran his hand over her breast. "For more of this." He was serious too.

She kissed his shoulder. "We either have to eat the roast, or I need to put it in the fridge for tomorrow."

He chuckled. "Okay. Let's eat. We'll need our strength for later."

They both got out of bed. She slipped on a nightie and a robe, and he pulled on his boxer briefs. He realized he didn't have a change of clothes that would be more comfortable than the Victorian outfit he'd worn today.

She pulled an oversize sweatshirt and sweatpants out of her closet and tossed it to him. "We'll have to bring your clothes over here."

"Yeah, though when I'm home with you, I don't plan on wearing them." He realized he was going to need to take some time off to move all his clothes and whatever else he might need over to her place. He was really glad to be doing that.

When they went downstairs for dinner, Meghan set the platter of pot roast, carrots, and potatoes on the table while Peter poured glasses of cabernet for them. The meal smelled delightful, and he was glad they'd left the bed to eat. Then he began carving up the tender meat.

He handed her the fork so she could serve some of the roast for herself first.

Afterward, Peter forked up some meat and set it on his plate, then spooned out some carrots and potatoes like she had done.

"Okay, even though I'm trying to set this business aside, you know you have to do something about the old homestead," Meghan said.

Peter let out his breath. He was afraid this would continue to haunt him.

"I don't mean about Lena, but about the house itself." Meghan sliced some of her meat. "Like you said, the place is dangerous. You don't want someone being seriously injured or dying there. Even though you have the *No Trespassing* and *Danger* signs posted, what if kids found their way there? Or anybody, really. It would just take one calamity, and you'd never be able to forgive yourself for it. Not to mention the insurance risk."

Peter knew Meghan was right. As much as the place had deteriorated, he needed to do something about it. Repairing it wasn't an option. Tearing it down and carting off the debris was the only solution. He didn't believe in burning it down—too much air pollution. And some of the scrap lumber and items in the house might still be salvageable. It was amazing what crafters could do with old timber.

"You're right."

Meghan ran her hand over Peter's in a consoling way. "Which leads us right back to the issue of Lena."

And the point Meghan had made about Lena not liking to be out of doors. "You think she would roam the land aimlessly?"

"Yes. Even if the house is gone, if she's there," she said.

"All right. What if your sisters and their mates, someone posing as your mate, like Tom, you, and I all go to the homestead to confuse the issue. If she's there, she won't know we're mated."

"Okay. When?"

"With the way this snow is falling, that roof won't last for long. If we can get everyone and everything together and find someone to man the front desk of your inn, we'll do it tomorrow, as soon as we can."

"You have to remember not to acknowledge me in any way. Try not to look at me, no touching, and if whoever we have accompanying me as my mate holds my hand or wraps his arm around my waist, you don't growl," she warned.

Peter chuckled, though he wouldn't know how he'd react if Tom put on too much of a show. Their territorial behavior was purely instinctual.

"If I begin talking to Lena, you can glance at me, like most would who wonder who I'm talking to. In other words, don't make it obvious that you're trying to avoid me," she added.

"All right. This might be more difficult to do than I suspected." He hoped he didn't screw things up.

"We'll tell her the house is coming down because it's no longer safe and ask her what she needs so she can move on. We'll convey messages from her to you."

"Okay, if she's there." He didn't know how he'd feel if he could hear what she had to say to him. It was not the same when others were speaking to their loved ones through

Meghan. "Dinner is wonderful by the way." He took second helpings of everything, and she smiled. "Energy for the rest of the night."

She laughed. "All right. I'd better have a little more too."

He didn't want to rush through dinner, but he was looking forward to loving on his beautiful mate some more. He still couldn't believe they were mated wolves.

After they finished eating, they put the leftovers away, cleaned up the dishes and Crock-Pot, and returned to bed.

Wrapped up in each other's arms, their legs tangled, Peter caressed Meghan's arm. "I love that your name means 'wolf' in Irish. Will you keep your maiden name?" There were so many things they still hadn't talked about, he realized.

"I will keep mine as my middle name, like my sisters have."

"All right. We'd better tell CJ and Laurel if something comes up that I need to deal with, I'll drop you off over there so he can watch over you."

"I'm sure they figure that, but it's always good to clarify things." She dreamily traced Peter's nipple.

"I could stay with you like this forever." Then his phone rang. "Great." He untangled himself from her and got out of bed to search for his phone in his dress trousers. Phone in hand, he saw it was CJ and hoped he was only concerned they were safe. "Hey, CJ."

Meghan smiled and closed her eyes.

"Laurel's been bugging me to check on the two of you. She wants to go to bed, but she wanted to make sure Meghan was staying with you. I asked her how she expected the two of you to become mated wolves if you didn't have some private time together."

Peter laughed. "Well, tell her we became..." He glanced at Meghan.

Without opening her eyes, she nodded.

"Mated wolves."

CJ said, "Okay, I thought you'd do it tonight, except that there's the issue of Lena."

"We'll deal with that when we can. Meghan and I weren't waiting any longer."

"Well, congratulations are in order. Have you told anyone else?"

Peter sighed. "It's late, so no. I was going to call you to tell you she's staying here at her place with me tonight. But if I get called up to investigate something, I'll drop her by the house so you can safeguard both the sisters."

Laurel took the phone from CJ. "You'd better tell Ellie that you're officially mated, or she'll be miffed."

"All right."

"Oh, and congratulations, you two," Laurel said, sounding overjoyed.

"Thanks. We couldn't be happier. I'll call Ellie so you two can get some sleep."

"We'll be celebrating this tomorrow night. Just be prepared."

He chuckled. "All right. Night, Laurel. Tell CJ good night for me." Peter glanced down at Meghan. She was sound asleep. He called Ellie and Brett next. "Hey, Brett, tell Ellie her sister is a mated wolf."

"Hell, that's good news. Wait, who's the lucky guy?"

"Wiseass. We're staying at Meghan's place, selling mine, and Laurel said we'll be having a celebration tomorrow night."

"Sounds good to me. Are you telling Darien and Lelandi that you're mated wolves?"

"Yeah, I guess I better. Just wanted to let you all know. Night, Brett."

"I'll tell Ellie. She's sound asleep."

"All right, talk later." Peter called the pack leaders next to let them know. Everyone would know by morning, and Brett would be sure to make an announcement in the paper.

Peter set his phone on the bedside table and climbed into bed, then pulled Meghan into his arms.

That night they'd made love again, and Peter was glad Meghan had agreed to mate him despite still needing to deal with the issue of his deceased wife.

Maybe they could take a nap midday. Though he doubted they'd get a lot of shut-eye that way either. Not when all he'd want to do was make love to his sexy mate.

Chapter 23

THAT MORNING, AFTER A WONDERFUL NIGHT OF LOVE-making and *no* nightmares about Rollins, Meghan and Peter didn't want to get up. They enjoyed being together in bed like this, sharing mated bliss. But she knew Peter had made arrangements with everyone to do something about Lena and his former home, and they would be waiting to hear when they were to meet out there.

"Let's have breakfast, and we'll need to run by my place to get some clothes. I don't want to wear my Victorian duds out to the old homestead. In fact, if you don't mind, you can drive us there and I'll go as a wolf, and then I'll just get dressed there."

"Sure, that sounds like a good idea." Meghan fixed French toast for them before they headed over to his place.

When they arrived at his house, she unlocked his door and waited until he checked the whole place out. He ran up the stairs as a wolf, shifted, and called out, "All clear."

Meghan joined him while he was pulling on a pair of boxer briefs, jeans, and a sweater. Meghan looked in his closet, trying to figure how they were going to fit everything into her place. It would work.

"CJ and Trevor are holding down the fort for now, though CJ will be out there with us this morning at the old homestead until I can take care of some business," Peter said, throwing some things in a bag. "I need to move some of my things to your place—clothes, food, anything else I might need or that we can use. Later, we can put the place on the market. But for now, I just want to grab some essentials to take to your house after we take care of this other business."

She hoped they could. She was unusually quiet, working over in her mind how she was going to do this. Peter was unusually talkative, which she thought was his way of dealing with this issue.

When he finished packing the bag, he threw it in her car. He called CJ and told him they were ready. Tom, who was taking Peter's place as Meghan's mate, arrived at Peter's house a few minutes later.

"Are you ready to go?" Tom asked Meghan.

She gave Peter one last hug and kiss. "Remember, you are *not* my mate."

"Hell, I finally have you for my own, and now I have to pretend you're not my mate." Peter sighed, shook Tom's hand, and thanked him for taking care of Meghan.

"We'll resolve it soon, Peter." Then Meghan climbed into Tom's vehicle, hoping they really could settle this today. "Thanks, Tom, for helping out with this. And thank Elizabeth for me for giving you up for the morning."

Tom chuckled. "She loves games, and this is the ultimate game."

Meghan hoped Lena had already moved on and they didn't have to "play" at being mated wolves any further.

They drove out to the old homestead while Peter followed in his sheriff's car, keeping some distance. When they reached the place, they were the first ones to arrive.

Meghan shivered, feeling dread wash over her.

Tom reached over and ran his hand over her back. She knew he was just comforting her and putting a show on for Lena if she was there, but Meghan hoped Peter wouldn't be perturbed by it when he arrived.

She waited for Tom to open her car door, though she intended to get out on her own. Wolves tended to be old-fashioned, as many years as they'd lived—unless they were newer wolves—and still liked the tradition of getting the door for their mate. If she had jumped out of the car first, how would that have looked? Like Tom wasn't her mate.

She just wished all the others had gotten here already. She felt super-exposed being here all by herself. Well, with Tom—and then Peter drove up, looking official in his sheriff's car. But Meghan would probably be the only one who could see Lena if she was here until Meghan's sisters showed up.

She studied the windows but didn't see any sign of anyone. The sun was slowly rising, and the sunrise was beautiful, painting a wash of pink and purple against the white snow.

Then she saw a woman peering out, her dark hair swept up in a chignon.

"She's here," Meghan said softly to Tom and Peter, both of whom were watching the house. "At the right window."

The woman was watching all three of them, not moving away from the window.

"Can you see her, Peter?" she asked quietly.

"No."

Meghan began to move toward the house.

"Shouldn't we wait for your sisters?" Peter quickly asked, his head turning sharply to look at her.

"I'm just getting a little closer. I'm not going into the house." She refused to look at Peter.

Tom took her hand and walked her slowly toward the house.

"Do you see her, Tom?" she asked.

"No, honey."

She smiled at him and slipped her arm around his waist. She was cold, but this was more for show than anything. He looked down at her and kissed her nose.

The woman stayed at the window. Meghan was dying to talk to her. It really was in Meghan's blood to help displaced spirits find their way home.

Peter was walking beside them, and she hoped he was fine with the small display of affection Tom had shown her.

"She's still there," she told them.

Then the cars began to pull up behind theirs. CJ's and Brett's. Everyone climbed out of their cars, but the woman in the window vanished.

Meghan pulled Tom toward the house. "She disappeared." She worried Lena was afraid to see that many people. Maybe she'd only speak with her and not with all three of the sisters.

"Wait," Laurel called out to Meghan.

Meghan sighed and stopped in the deep snow.

Laurel and Ellie ran to catch up to all of them, their mates running behind them.

When they were all a few feet away from the house, Meghan said, "I saw her. She waited at that window until you drove up."

"From everything everyone's said, she's shy," Laurel said. "She's made first contact of sorts with you. You've seen her twice now. You may be the only one she'll appear to. But I'll look inside the house and see if she'll make an appearance for me."

CJ was frowning at the prospect.

"I won't go inside. The house looks like it's seen better days." Laurel moved toward the front porch, and Peter hurried to open the door for her. CJ was close to her, in case he had to protect her if the house began to collapse.

Meghan shoved her hands in her pockets and watched her sister, as Ellie and Brett stood next to her and Tom.

"Lena? Peter is a friend of ours, and the house is in such bad shape that he needs to tear it down before someone is injured."

Meghan listened for anything but didn't hear any response.

"If you're still living here, we—my sisters and I—want to help you find a way to leave. The house will be torn down, and we don't want you to have to roam the property when you could find peace." Laurel waited a long time before she spoke again. "Maybe you'd like to speak to one of my other sisters." Laurel motioned for Ellie to take her place, and then Laurel moved away from the house.

CJ and Peter continued to stand on the porch, watching over Ellie now. Frowning, Brett folded his arms.

"Hi, Lena? My sisters and I have a gift of being able to help people move on. Would you like to talk to Peter? I can convey your words to him." Ellie waited, then shook her head at her sisters and the others. "Laurel's right in saying Peter needs to tear down this building before some kids come in here to play and hurt themselves, or worse." Again, she paused, but then she stepped off the porch. "She's not willing to see me either. Maybe there are too many of us offering to help her. She could be feeling overwhelmed."

"I'll try." Meghan ignored Peter's stricken look. She wanted to tell him to chill because right now he was looking like much more than the sheriff of Silver Town and Lena's mate. He was looking a hell of a lot like Meghan's protective mate.

When Meghan stood in the doorway and peered in, she felt the melancholy pervading her soul. She felt the isolation, the hopelessness, and the pain cloaking the house. "Lena," she said, not seeing her, but feeling the woman's presence filling the place.

"He's mine," a voice whispered. A woman's stern voice. Not belonging to a shy, frail ghost. This was a she-wolf who wasn't about to part with her wolf mate.

Meghan shivered involuntarily. She couldn't believe the woman was finally speaking to her. "Yes." At least when Lena was alive, he was. "Do you want to say anything to him?"

Lena snorted. "Who are you?"

"Meghan MacTire."

Looking bothered by the fact that Meghan was talking to his wife's ghost, Peter moved closer to Meghan. She wanted to move away from him, but she'd run into CJ.

Then the woman appeared before her, startling her. She was just inches away, and Meghan fought stepping back. Lena was telling her by her posture that the home was hers and Meghan hadn't been invited in. Not that Meghan was going inside anyway.

"You won't have him," Lena said, her blue eyes sharp.

Meghan was afraid the woman might try to possess her. Laurel had done that with spirits, to allow them to talk through her, but Meghan hadn't done that before, and no way did she want to do so with this ghost.

"Peter, why don't you tell Lena how you feel about her," Meghan said.

Peter looked a bit pale. She suspected he'd really hoped his wife's ghost had been a figment of his imagination when he'd been drinking too hard.

"Lena, you don't know how much I've missed you. I love you," he said.

Meghan didn't think this was going well at all. Peter's sentiments didn't sound like he meant them, maybe because he'd just professed his love to Meghan and he didn't want to let on how much he'd cared about his former mate. She felt bad for him because she knew just how much he'd loved Lena. That's what made him so special to Meghan. He'd loved and lost but was willing to try again.

Lena didn't look at Peter. She only cast Meghan an evil smile as though she knew Peter was courting her. Would Lena lose the smile if she knew Peter and Meghan were mated wolves?

"Do you want to say anything to Peter?"

"Like how much I hated him for not protecting me when I had to face a murderer? Did they ever catch him, by the way? Or is he running around, continuing to kill the innocent?"

"Peter killed him."

Lena frowned at her. "You keep calling him Peter. Why?"

"We all call each other by first names. All the pack members. Except, maybe, Dr. Weber. A lot of us call him Doc. Same with the vet, Dr. Mitchell. We aren't as formal in this day and age." That was the truth, but Meghan wasn't sure a woman who was brought up on certain kinds of etiquette during another era could understand how it was today.

"I…I can't believe he's the sheriff of Silver Town," Lena finally said.

"He's a good sheriff. Honest, law-abiding."

"But he didn't protect his mate, *me*," Lena said.

Meghan could understand how she felt, probably wishing her mate had arrived to save her.

"I'm sorry. You shouldn't have died."

"You're right." Lena folded her arms. "What do you propose to do about it?"

"Help you to move on, if you'll let me."

"Why would I do that? Peter comes to see me regularly. That's how I know he misses me and loves me. Even if his words don't sound like it now. I wonder why that could be?" Lena tilted her head, frowning at Meghan.

Meghan glanced at Peter.

He looked at her in question.

"She knows you love her." Meghan wasn't about to mention the rest. Lena might be lying about Peter coming to see her regularly, or she might be confused. Or maybe she was being truthful. Maybe Peter *had* wanted to return to be with Lena for all these years because of the connection he'd felt with her and the sorrow he hadn't protected her.

Meghan didn't mention anything else.

"Why aren't you telling him everything?" Lena asked, narrowing her eyes at Meghan.

Meghan had to be careful how she responded, or Peter might suspect she was trying to protect him.

Ellie and Laurel were close enough to hear what was

being said, if they could hear her. They wouldn't tell Peter anything either. Not if it would make him feel bad.

"Tell him to join me, and then we can move on... together." Lena gave her an evil smile.

Okay, so this really wasn't going how Meghan had planned it. She wanted to tell the ghost that she must not love Peter that much if she wanted him to die too, but she held her tongue. If he hadn't been standing there, Meghan would have spoken her mind. She wanted to speak with Lena again, but not with Peter hearing everything Meghan said to the woman.

Meghan told Peter, "She said she would move on if you removed the house so that no one else would die in it. Then she vanished. It's cold out here. I've got to get to work."

Her sisters and the ghost gaped at her. Okay, so her sisters had heard everything Lena said too. So they had to know Meghan was totally fed up with the woman for wishing Peter were dead. Still, knowing how much Laurel was into ghost etiquette, Meghan knew her sister would lecture her about it later.

Meghan took Tom's hand and headed back to his vehicle when nobody else made a move to leave. Fine. Maybe Laurel or Ellie could deal with the ghost in more of the "proper" way.

Sometimes Meghan had to get stern with uppity ghosts and then they'd settle down.

When she climbed into the car, she saw Lena was gone. Her sisters shook their heads at her, then headed back to their vehicles with their mates. Peter was still standing there, looking at the house.

Did he really return to the homestead all the time? She

knew she should have resolved this before they mated. Meghan frowned as she watched the house while Tom backed the car down the drive. She felt suddenly uneasy, her skin felt all prickly, and though she turned up the heat in the car, she was chilled to the bone.

Tom pulled off his parka as if the heat was too much for him.

She thought she heard a whisper, but unearthly, not all there.

Oh. My. God. Meghan didn't even want to think what that could mean. She glanced into the back seat of the car, but no one was there. That didn't mean Lena hadn't tagged along for the ride.

"I need to drop you—" Tom started to say.

"Off at the inn," Meghan quickly said. She was certain Tom had planned to drop her by Peter's place to pick up her car, and she really felt seriously spooked right now.

Meghan felt uneasy, as if she had a ghostly hitchhiker with her. She couldn't see her, but she just felt…as though someone was lurking nearby. Wolves were sensitive to their surroundings. They had to be to survive. She always wondered if wolves who could sense spirits had a more attuned ability.

If Lena was now with her… Meghan shook her head. Somehow, she had to know if Lena had attached herself, and she had to let everyone know she suspected that's what had happened. That meant she and Peter couldn't act like mated wolves until this was resolved.

Her cell rang, and she saw it was Laurel.

"Hey, is everything all right with you?" Laurel asked. "Ellie and I are worried."

"Yeah, you have every right to be. I…really can't discuss it right now."

Looking worried, Tom cast a glance at her. She hoped he didn't believe *he* was the reason she couldn't discuss this with her sisters, but she'd never had a ghost attached to her, and she had no idea what to do.

"Uh, okay. Tell Tom to take you to your house. We'll meet you there. We still have babysitters for the inn. We'll get this resolved, Meghan. I'll let, um, you know who know what's going on," Laurel said. "See you in a few minutes."

"Okay." Meghan loved her sisters, and she was glad they all had these abilities. She just hated to have to tell Peter what had happened. "Tom, scratch that. Just park behind the inn. I'm going home and meeting my sisters."

"Sure thing. Who's going to be watching over you?"

"CJ and Brett, I imagine."

"All right. I'll just make sure."

Meghan was glad Tom didn't ask about Peter.

Then he pulled into the parking area by Meghan's home. She waited for Tom to open her car door. She immediately took his hand and walked him toward her house, and he looked down at her. She hoped he'd figured out what could be wrong.

"Uh, hey, honey, I'll be home after I help the others look for Rollins."

"Okay, thanks, Tom." She opened the door to the house, and her sisters and CJ and Brett greeted them.

She thought they all looked a little worried. Meghan imagined *she* looked worried.

"Hey, will all of you be okay, or do you need me to hang around?" Tom asked.

"We'll be fine, Tom," CJ said.

"All right. See you all later." Tom pulled Meghan into a hug and kissed her on the mouth.

She was trying hard to make it seem real. She really didn't want to upset his mate. Or her own. But she was in a real pickle now. If she didn't figure out a way to make peace with the ghost and send her on her way, Meghan could be stuck with her forever.

Chapter 24

PETER PACED ACROSS HIS SHERIFF'S OFFICE. HE COULDN'T believe Lena had actually attached herself to Meghan.

Jake watched him for a few minutes, then said, "The sisters are all good at what they do. They'll sort it out."

No way in hell did Peter want Meghan to go through this because of him. He wanted to be by her side through this ordeal and any other she might have to face in the future.

"I want to be there for her."

"I know. I would feel the same way. I suspect she believes things will be worse if you show up. Which is why Tom told me to see you so that you don't barge into her house in the middle of whatever the sisters are planning to do."

"I should be there. Hell, Tom's pretending to be her mate! What if Lena wonders why he doesn't stay the night with her?"

"Meghan will spend the night at CJ and Laurel's place with the ruse that Tom's chasing down Rollins."

Peter ran his hands through his hair. "I can't believe this. Maybe Meghan shouldn't have told her I was tearing down the house."

"Darien and everybody else have said it's the only way. I thought you made arrangements to have it torn down in the morning."

"Yeah. But then Lena wouldn't have a place to return to, and she could be stuck to Meghan. Even though Meghan said Lena wanted to protect others and have me tear it down." Peter could just imagine trying to sleep with his mate and having to share his bed with two of them. Though only Meghan would truly be aware of it. Still, talk about a wet blanket.

Ellie called Peter, and he immediately answered, hoping it was good news, though he suspected if Meghan wasn't calling him, it wasn't.

"Hey, Peter. Brett and I are home now, so I wanted to call you right away. Meghan's staying with Laurel and CJ tonight. Jake probably told you she might, but it's for certain. From what we could gather, Lena has decided to follow Meghan wherever she goes. None of us could see her, but Meghan told us, in a cryptic way the three of us would understand, that she senses Lena's presence and can't shake her. Lena talked to her too, so Meghan knows for sure she's hanging around her. Meghan plans to meet Jessup in the mine to see his son again tomorrow first thing. You could meet them there as additional protection so you can see her."

"I'm having the old homestead demolished first thing in the morning." Peter had decided to once Meghan had talked to him about it. Mostly, he wanted to tear it down before someone was hurt or killed in it. He hadn't been there in eons and hadn't realized how bad a shape his house was in.

"Okay, well, Meghan could go *there* first, and then maybe Lena would return to the property. Maybe if Lena sees the house being torn down, she'll want to leave our world. There's never any way of telling with spirits. Meghan will pretend to call Tom tonight, but she'll be calling you and saying whatever she wants to you," Ellie said. "She hopes she can convince Lena to move on without her learning the two of you are together. She's afraid if Lena learns the truth, she might stick with her for good."

"All right. What can I do to help?"

"Until she says differently, stay away from Meghan, except in a sheriff's capacity. We'll figure something out. Ghosts are all individuals, so there's no telling what would work on one and not on another. They're totally unpredictable."

He didn't want to ask Ellie how many times they'd failed to exorcise a ghost who didn't want to leave. "I guess you tried calling Lena or whatever you do to try to send a spirit on its way."

"We did. We tried several different techniques. Laurel is usually in charge of them, so she went first, but when that didn't work, Meghan did. We didn't think it would make any difference, but I tried. Even CJ tried."

Peter smiled. He couldn't imagine CJ trying to call on a spirit in whatever rituals they might have performed.

"Okay, Brett and I are headed for bed. Just wait for Meghan's call, all right?"

"Yeah, thanks, Ellie." They ended the call, and Peter told Jake what Ellie had said. "You might as well go home to your mate. I'm headed home too. Though I sure would have preferred being with Meghan tonight."

"I can't imagine what that would be like."

"Yeah, tell me about it. And the worst of it is," Peter said, grabbing his hat and leaving the office with Jake, "Meghan would be the only one having to deal with it."

When Peter arrived home, Meghan called. He quickly answered the phone.

"Hey, Tom, I sure will miss all your kissing and hugging and loving tonight."

Peter grimaced and began stripping off his clothes. "Me more than anything, honey. I'm so sorry about all this."

"Don't be. We'll get it worked out. I just wanted to tell you Jessup said his wife still doesn't want to see their son in the mine. But Jessup wants to speak with him again. Maybe we can find another means to help him find his way to his final resting place. Maybe you could meet me there?" Meghan asked.

Peter loved hearing her beautiful Irish lilt. He wished he was hearing it in his ear while they were snuggling in bed. "Ellie was telling me about it. I have a wrecking crew tearing down the old house first thing in the morning. Do you want to meet me there first? I could ask Tom to take you or meet up with us to continue the charade." As much as Peter hated to see Tom still pretending to be Meghan's mate, he'd do it a while longer. "And then I can be one of the ones protecting you at the mine after that."

"Sure. I'll call Jessup and see if he can meet me in the afternoon instead. I'll try to get ahold of him right now, and then I'll call you back."

"All right. Love you, honey."

"Love you right back," Meghan said, and Peter again wished they were sharing another night of mated bliss.

He hoped that this business with his former mate wouldn't cause trouble for them much longer. He didn't think he could hold out for very long.

Meghan was about to call Jessup when Lena suddenly appeared and sat down on the end of the bed. Annoyed with her for not having shown herself earlier, Meghan ignored her while she phoned Jessup. "Hi, Jessup, I hope this won't be too inconvenient for you, but I have to go to another site first thing in the morning. I'm not sure how long it's going to take. Did you want to see Oliver—"

"Oliver?" Lena asked, her eyes rounding.

Meghan stared at her, surprised Lena knew him. Though they had all lived in Silver Town at the same time, and he had been around her age.

"Um, did you want to see your son in the afternoon?" Meghan asked Jessup. "I can call you as soon as I'm done with the other matter."

Lena was staring hard at Meghan, probably not liking that Meghan hadn't answered her. But Lena had been rude to ignore the sisters' entreaties to appear before them and tell them what she wanted. Lena was being a total pain in the butt.

"Yeah, sure. We can do that. I'll be looking forward to hearing from you, and maybe I can convince Clementine to go with me by then. I'll see you tomorrow," Jessup said to Meghan.

"All right. Good night."

"Night, Meghan."

She wanted to call Peter right back, but instead she decided she'd better learn what she could from Lena if the woman was going to open up with her more. At least Meghan hoped she would. "You knew Oliver?"

Lena looked down at her lap and brushed off her long skirt as if she had a piece of lint on it. "Is he mated?"

"Oliver?" Meghan sat down on the bed, surprised to hear the question. Lena still wasn't looking at her, but when Meghan didn't answer, she looked up.

"No. He died two years after you did," Meghan said.

Lena's eyes grew big again.

Hmm, now *this* was interesting. Maybe Peter wasn't the only one Lena had cared for. But how could Meghan ask Peter about Oliver as it related to Lena without saying it in front of her?

"He's stuck in the mine because Clementine won't go to see him. At least we think that's the reason," Meghan said.

Lena snorted.

Meghan looked at her in surprise. Lena wasn't anything like the way Peter had described her. Then again, if Meghan had lived through what Lena had, she probably would have been an entirely different woman too. Even she had changed after she'd had to deal with Rollins. She'd never walked to the grocery store at night again, for one thing. And she'd always carried a Taser to the store after that, even when she walked during the daytime.

"Do you believe there's another way to help him move on? I was able to help a couple of others, but Oliver still can't leave. He wanted to see his mother first. At least that's what we assume is keeping him from leaving."

"His mother," Lena said derisively.

"Right. She doesn't like me. Which is part of the reason she won't go to the mine. I'm too Irish for her liking."

"I have a New York accent she didn't like."

Meghan stared at Lena. Ohmigod, had Lena and Oliver been an item before she hooked up with Peter? And Clementine was the reason Oliver and Lena never had a chance? *She* was the woman Oliver loved?

"Uh, yeah. And that you're not from Silver Town, born and bred? That's what she doesn't like about me and my sisters," Meghan quickly said, hoping to make more of a connection.

"Oh yes, same with my parents and me. We were foreigners, as far as Clementine felt. Not as foreign as *you*, though," Lena quickly added, twisting a loose, dark curl dangling by her cheek.

"Right. We have the added issue of seeing ghosts. And she really doesn't like that." Meghan wasn't sure how Lena would respond to that, but she thought she'd throw that in.

Lena studied her for a long moment. "That would make you odd."

"It does. Some folks appreciate what we do for their loved ones, though."

Lena scoffed. "You're trying to send me away when I want to be with Peter, just like he said we'd be—together forever."

"But you're *not* with him. You're with *me*."

"Well, he can't see or hear me, now can he? I can talk until I'm blue in the face to him and he ignores me, so what good does that do me?"

"You didn't talk to him when you had the chance." Meghan didn't know why Lena would hitch a ride with her unless she suspected Meghan and Peter were courting and she wanted to interfere.

Lena shrugged. "There were too many people at the house. I can't handle that many people."

So what Peter had said about Lena not being very sociable must still be true. Meghan hated to ask, but if it helped her move on, she had to. "What if I arrange to have Peter meet us? I'll pass along anything you want to tell him. It'll be just the three of us."

Lena raised her brows. "You have a mate."

"Yeah?" Meghan realized what Lena was getting at. "In this day and age, women aren't chaperoned. No one believes a woman might be having an affair just because she's alone with a man who isn't her mate."

Lena tsked.

Meghan considered telling Lena about the plans to tear down her home tomorrow. Wouldn't it be better to forewarn Lena rather than spring it all at once on her when Meghan went to the site and they began ripping Lena's beloved home to shreds in front of her?

Meghan thought so. "Tomorrow, I'll be meeting with others who will be demolishing the old house and carrying off the debris."

"Mine and Peter's?" Lena asked.

"Yes. It's just too dangerous to leave standing. It won't be standing for long in any event. Another heavy snowstorm and the roof will collapse."

Lena rubbed her arms as if she'd taken a chill.

Meghan decided not to mention Lena wanting Peter to join her in death. Lena might have just spouted off because of feeling so isolated from him and not meaning it at all. And then she might clam up again.

"Anyway, then I'll be seeing Jessup and Oliver at the mine that afternoon. You can come with me to both places, if you'd like." Meghan had to try to appear at least helpful to the ghost if she was going to convince her to leave.

"As if you're going anywhere without me."

Meghan didn't know if Lena was being so contrary because she couldn't help herself at this point or not. "I still don't know why you attached yourself to me."

"I have no idea. One minute you were telling Peter all those lies about me wanting my house torn down, and the next, I was"—Lena shrugged—"stuck to you."

"Because you were angry with me," Meghan said.

Lena looked at her long skirt and brushed off more imaginary lint.

"It's okay. I'm sorry I didn't tell Peter all the things you said. I didn't want to say anything to hurt him. He loved you, and he still does. He felt terrible about not being there to protect you. He went after the killer and ended his miserable life, but that wouldn't bring you back. Did you hear him howling for you?"

Lena brushed away tears and nodded. "I was afraid he was going to die. He wasn't eating. Just drinking alcohol. It killed me to see him that way. And then he left, and I thought maybe he had died. The next time I saw him, he came to the house as a wolf. He would run out there daily, then he began to let me go. I watched out the window for him every day, just standing there like an idiot, hoping to catch sight of my beautiful gray wolf. Then he stopped coming all the time. Maybe a month would pass? I don't know."

"It's been a long time since he came to see you, hasn't it?" Meghan asked.

"Maybe. I don't know. Time runs together for me. It seemed like only yesterday I died." Lena rose to her feet and walked over to Meghan's guest-room window and peered out through the curtains. "I saw the way you and Peter looked at each other. The way he touched your arm with protectiveness. You pulled away as if you didn't want him to do anything so scandalous. Not when you're mated to Tom Silver." She glanced back at Meghan as if wanting to know the truth.

Ghosts might not be able to tell time, but as wolves, they sure were as perceptive as ever. "He worried about me. He'd asked me to see if you were there and try to learn what we needed to do to help you move on. Everyone has been after him to tear down the old house. You might have noticed all the danger signs posted on the property. Anyway, I said I would see if you were there and try to help him talk to you. I just did that with one of the miners. He'd been trapped down there nearly as long as you have been trapped at your home."

"But you couldn't free Oliver."

"He wants to see his mother."

"The old bag," Lena said with disgust.

"I can't imagine anything worse than…" Meghan quit speaking. She was thinking that being entombed in the cave was really bad, but Lena had suffered just as much. "Well, than being stuck in a place you want to be freed from so badly and have no way out unless someone can help you."

"Like you want to help me?" Lena turned to face Meghan. "You're the reason Peter's destroying the house! You thought you could get rid of me, didn't you? So you told him I'm the one who wanted him to tear it down! You thought I was stuck to the house, and then when it was gone, I'd have to leave. Didn't you?"

"No. It has to be done, whether you're living there or not. What do you want anyway? If others died in the house because it collapsed on them, would you think you'd have people to visit with? You'd no longer be alone?" Meghan wasn't sure what was going through the woman's head.

Lena's face was scrunched up in annoyance.

"What if you didn't like your new houseguests?" Meghan figured Lena would be territorial and not like them invading her privacy. It was one thing to see people wandering through her house, another for ghosts to actually move in with her.

Lena lifted her chin. "Maybe they wouldn't have any stake in staying there and just move on."

"You still would be the one responsible for their deaths. And they could make your...um, life a living hell. Would you want that?" Meghan wasn't sure Lena would care. Unless the ghosts disturbed her "peace." Who knew who she'd end up with as permanent houseguests. "Peter needs to do this for the safety of the pack and anyone who chances to come upon the place in their travels." It's not just about *you*, Meghan wanted to say.

Her phone rang, and she grabbed it up, glanced at the caller ID, and sighed. *Peter*. He must have been worried about her when she didn't call him back right away. "Hi, Tom, love you, honey. I'm fine. I wish I could crawl into bed with you right this very moment." She tried to ignore the way Lena was staring at her, as if she shouldn't be mentioning such a thing when other people were present. But Meghan was in the privacy of her guest room, and Lena wasn't an invited roommate.

"Hey, honey, are you sure you're okay?" Peter sounded concerned.

"Yeah, I was just talking to Lena." Meghan wasn't sure why she mentioned the business with Oliver with Peter next. Maybe because Lena was going to be a real nuisance in their lives if Meghan couldn't find a way to make her leave. "Hey, did you know that she was friends with Oliver?"

There was complete silence on the other end.

Meghan raised a brow. "So...you *knew*." And it sounded

like a bone of contention between Lena and Peter. Not that Oliver had been courting Lena before she began seeing Peter. Meghan should have questioned Peter about Oliver and the woman he loved! But then, oh, God, poor Peter. She was certain it was something Peter wouldn't want anyone else in the pack to know. That his mate had loved another wolf.

"Yes, Tom knew about it. Everybody did," Lena said, sounding exasperated with her.

"She says everyone knew she was seeing Oliver. So what was that all about? Seems I'm the only one who doesn't know about this." And maybe it was significant. Meghan never knew when a bit of history could play an important role in a ghost's moving on.

"No one knew Lena was seeing Oliver after we mated each other but me. She's talking about *before* we mated. And yes, he'd been courting her before I started courting her. She didn't get along with Clementine. She thought Lena was too snooty, too educated. Her family had the shop in town. They were wealthy merchants. The Frasers were poor miners."

"Ah, okay. So her parents wouldn't have liked it either."

Lena snorted. Meghan took that as a confirmation.

"But they wouldn't have been happy with..." Meghan almost said *you*. She cleared her throat. "Um, with Peter either, since he was a poor hunter."

"They weren't," Peter said. "She finally stood up to them and said no one in the pack would be good enough for her parents."

Lena said, "I wasn't about to become an old maid because my parents didn't think that anyone in the pack was good enough for me. Boy, did I make a mistake."

Meghan assumed Lena meant she'd made a mistake in mating Peter when Oliver could have been her mate and protected her better. Meghan practically bit her tongue before she said anything she regretted. Oliver was probably working in the mine at the time.

Meghan frowned at Lena. She was staring out the window again. Meghan sensed something more hadn't been right between Lena and Peter. That the animosity Lena felt for Peter was for more than him not having been there to protect her. What if they'd had words before he left? Meghan had found that couples who had fought each other before one of them had died would often regret their final parting words, and the spirit of the dead partner could linger.

"Did you and Peter have a fight when he left that day to go out and hunt?"

Lena didn't answer her, and Peter was just as silent. *Jeez, folks!* Stuff like that could mean the difference between a spirit moving on and one who was stuck there permanently. But Meghan realized she couldn't ask Peter about it because she was supposed to be talking to Tom, and he probably wouldn't have known. Unless Peter *had* talked to him about it later. "Did Peter ever mention to you that he and Lena had fought before he left her that fateful day, Tom?"

"What difference does it make?" Lena asked angrily.

It could make all the difference in the world.

"Did they?" Meghan asked Peter again when he didn't answer her the first time.

"Yeah." His voice was rough with emotion.

"Okay, about what?"

"She wanted all the finery her parents had. They could afford it. I couldn't. I was doing everything I could to earn the money to get her what she wanted, but she always wanted more. She was always perusing the catalogs, looking to buy all kinds of unnecessary stuff. We needed the essentials back then. Food to sustain us, money to pay the taxes on the place, and building materials to maintain the house. But it was never enough. That morning, she told me either to bring in enough money so she could buy some nice things, or to never come back."

"You were mated wolves," Meghan said softly.

"What?" Lena asked.

"Um, you and Peter," Meghan said to Lena. "You were mated wolves." Meghan quickly had to correct her mistake. Trying to pretend she was talking to Tom and not Peter was a bigger problem than she had thought it would be.

"So the light just came on? What have we been talking about all along?" Lena sniped.

"I stayed away that night and went farther than I had ever gone to hunt. I sold the meat to families and furs to anyone who could use them to make coats back then. But I wasn't finding much to hunt closer to our land. I always tried to get home by a decent hour so she wouldn't be home alone at night. She was used to the city life and was afraid to be alone out in the country. I was determined to bring in more money this time, even if it meant leaving her there by herself overnight," Peter finally said.

"And that's why you…Peter was so disconsolate about losing Lena. If…he hadn't traveled farther and had come home that night, he could have killed the man before he hurt her."

Lena looked gloomy and sat down on a high-backed chair in the guest room.

"Yes," Peter said.

So Peter had felt it was his fault for listening to an unreasonable wife and not having been there for her when he should have just set his foot down and he would have been there that night. But that showed how much he had tried to please her, even though Meghan suspected he would never have made enough money to make Lena happy.

"Okay, so Peter didn't return that night, and you were scared?" Meghan asked Lena.

"Of course not." Lena was haughty when she answered.

"Not until the man broke into the house?" Meghan asked her.

Lena looked away.

Peter cleared his throat. "I don't know if she'll tell you the truth or not. I hadn't planned to tell a living soul because both people who were involved are now dead, so what difference does it make now? But Oliver had been at the house while I was gone."

Oh. My. God. That is huge, Meghan wanted to tell Peter.

"Oliver came to visit you while Peter was away," Meghan said to Lena.

Lena's eyes widened, and she looked ready to faint. "Whoever said that lies. I am a married woman. I can't believe you'd accuse me of something like that."

"Peter told Tom about it. Peter smelled Oliver had been there."

"Multiple times," Peter said. "And yes, we fought about it."

"Multiple times," Meghan said for Lena's benefit. She guessed at the next part. "Oliver was a frequent visitor at your home while Peter was away trying to earn enough money to support you. Your home was out in the woods, isolated from the pack, and it gave Oliver the perfect place to see you. You should have realized Peter would know what was going on between the two of you. Unless you didn't care." Meghan realized the very prim and proper, very Victorian she-wolf wasn't as goody-two-shoes as she was trying to let on. Peter had to have been upset about what was going on. Meghan hated that she'd had to bring it up now. She couldn't help looking at Oliver in a different light either.

"Okay, so Lena was having an affair with Oliver," Meghan said to Peter, watching Lena's face turn red.

"That's not true! We were just friends. Yes, he came out and visited me when he wasn't working in the mine. I would have mated him first. But I didn't. My dad would have cut me off from my inheritance if I had. He didn't say he would if I mated Peter. I guess Dad knew that before long I was going to do what I wanted if he kept saying no to my choice of mate."

"You kept seeing Oliver because he was your one true love, but you want to punish Peter for not being there for you when the attack occurred. Why didn't Oliver save you?" He should have been the one to do so if that's how Lena felt about the two men!

"I was mated to Peter, and Oliver only came by for some tea and then he left. If he'd stayed, he would have protected me like my mate should have."

"But Oliver didn't stay because he thought Peter was coming home that night, right?" Meghan asked Lena.

Lena looked sulky but didn't respond.

"All right. Fine." Meghan said to Peter, "Tom, can you ask Peter to come over to CJ and Laurel's house to speak with me? I'll be waiting in the living room." Whether

Lena would appear to her there or talk at all didn't matter. Meghan needed to speak with Peter about this, person to person. And she suspected Lena wouldn't be able to resist being there.

"What do you think you're going to do?" Peter asked.

"The two of…um, *them* need to forgive each other and themselves. And *mean* it." Meghan knew that wouldn't be easy, maybe impossible. She wouldn't blame Peter for having regrets. No one wanted to be second best.

"All right. I'll be there in a few minutes." Peter ended the call.

"Okay, I'm talking to Peter downstairs. You can come, or you can just…disappear. But if you want to speak to him, I'll help you to say whatever you want to tell him." Meghan hoped Lena would give this a chance.

"Everything? You didn't last time. You didn't want to 'hurt' him."

"I think we're beyond that at this point. Say what you will, and he can respond." Meghan truly felt if they could clear the air, maybe this would finish this business between them, and Lena could leave here in peace. And Peter could finally give up the ghost.

Meghan headed downstairs and waited for Peter to arrive, turning on the Christmas tree lights for a bit of cheer. Lena didn't follow her.

When Meghan heard a soft knock on the door, she hurried to look out the peephole. Peter was standing on the doorstep, looking as tired as she felt.

She opened the door and heard a creaking on the stairs and turned to look. CJ was peering at the two of them from the stairs. "Just checking to make sure everything is okay."

"Yeah, thanks, CJ. Peter and I were just going to have a little talk."

"Okay. See you in the morning." CJ tromped back up the stairs.

Peter looked like he wanted to pull Meghan into his arms and hug her, just as much as she wanted to do that with him.

Lena appeared next to Meghan, folded her arms, and said, "All right, let's begin."

Chapter 25

PETER COULDN'T BELIEVE ALL THIS CRAP WITH OLIVER was being dredged up now. It had hurt back then, but Peter had kept it secret from everyone, telling Lena he never wanted her to see Oliver again. But when Peter left to do his work, Oliver managed to see her whenever he could. A year of marriage, and she hadn't even had the decency to stay away from Oliver during that first year. Yet Peter had loved her and had hoped she'd give Oliver up. He'd even fought with Oliver twice about it, still trying to keep the affair secret from the pack. He sure hadn't wanted Meghan to learn of it. It was the past, and he thought he'd buried it with Lena. But now it was coming back to haunt him.

He'd so wanted to hug Meghan and kiss her and let her know that things would be different between them. He knew it with all his heart. He'd wanted to remember Lena as sweet and innocent, like when he'd first met her. She'd soon shattered the image when he learned she was seeing Oliver on the sly. Were they having sex? Not in their lumpy bed at least. And Peter hadn't wanted to know for sure.

Now, he watched Meghan sit on a chair in the living room. She motioned for him to take a seat on the sofa so he was near her, but not as close as if they'd been sitting together on the sofa. He was annoyed with himself that he had to put on this charade about not being Meghan's mate, but he did worry about her well-being.

"Lena's standing beside my chair," Meghan said.

"Okay, I guess I'll start this. Yes, Lena and I had a fight first thing that morning. I was angry. I knew Oliver had been at the house again the day before, drinking and eating at the place. Who knew what else."

Meghan glanced in the direction Lena was supposed to be standing, as if giving her the opportunity to rebut what Peter had accused her of.

Meghan again looked at Peter and nodded. So Lena wasn't going to deny it.

"We fought about having kids. I told her point-blank I didn't want to have any while she was seeing Oliver. I didn't want to be second-guessing if they were mine or his."

Meghan glanced at Lena and then said, "She said it wasn't an issue. You were just angry she was seeing Oliver. She hadn't wanted kids either."

"All right, fair enough. We fought about the issue of money again. She wanted all brand-new furniture. Some places were offering credit. I said no. We always paid as we went. We didn't need the furniture. And we sure as hell didn't need to be in debt."

"We did too need the furniture," Meghan said to Peter, relaying Lena's words. "You knew I couldn't entertain my parents or any friends I made because of how shabby everything looked. That's why I didn't socialize."

"You were shy, unsociable. You didn't attend many pack functions unless I dragged you to them. Your parents were the opposite. They went to everything as a way to promote their business. I didn't realize you were so"— moneygrubbing, Peter wanted to say—"fashion-conscious when I asked you to mate me."

He'd been blinded by her simple beauty and soft-spoken ways and the way she had seemed to adore him. But her sweetness had been something her mother had taught her to show when trying to catch a mate. Even in bed, she'd been unwilling to remove their clothes, and she'd acted like the sex was just an obligation she had to get over with quickly. Had she and Oliver been together naked when he had sex with her? Was it wild and passionate like Peter had hoped for with her?

"Okay, so I'm curious. Did you sleep with Oliver naked? You wouldn't with me."

Meghan's eyebrows shot up. Then she frowned at Lena. "All right, she said we're here to discuss your behavior, not hers."

"Like hell we are. It goes both ways."

"Oliver would have put the furniture on credit."

"The two of you were discussing what a lousy provider I was? Oliver wasn't making as much money as I was. He was just telling you what you wanted to hear. You would have always wanted more." Peter sighed. "Listen, I'm sorry for not being there for you."

"You wanted me dead," Meghan said softly.

"No, never. I wanted things to be right between us." Peter had known they never would be. Even if Oliver had died first, she would always have wanted him. He just knew he'd made a mistake and hoped she would grow out of her obsession with Oliver and make the most of what they had.

Meghan glanced in Lena's direction. Then she grimaced and repeated what Lena had said: "I wish you had died on one of your trips and never come back."

"I'm sorry, Lena. You deserved to be happy. So did I."

Meghan was listening to Lena and looked mortified. Frowning, she said to Peter, "Sheridan sent the man to kill me."

"What?" Peter couldn't have been more shocked to learn the news.

"Sheridan told Lena, through the killer he'd sent, that he couldn't have a woman cheating on her husband in Silver Town. It wasn't right, and he sent the man to take care of the problem. Lena thought maybe you learned later that the sheriff was behind it. You must have killed Sheridan, then became sheriff," Meghan said. Then she added, "Why wouldn't Sheridan have killed Oliver too?"

"Hell, I didn't know any of this. Sheridan was a bastard. He played by his own set of rules. Maybe he thought it was all the woman's fault for doing what she did. And the man wasn't to blame. Oliver was a bachelor," Peter said. "Damn, maybe that's why Sheridan made me his deputy sheriff, out of a sense of guilt. Though I never really knew him to feel guilty about anything. When Sheridan murdered Darien's first mate, who had been cheating on him, Sheridan felt completely justified." Hell, the sheriff had cheated on his *own* mate.

"Lena wondered if you got the job because you arranged through Sheridan to have her killed."

"Oh God, no. I hated that she loved Oliver, but I still was totally hung up on her. I was devastated when she died."

"She thought that was because you were ultimately responsible and felt bad for what you'd done. And that's why you stayed away for so long—all through the day, that night, and the next day—to give yourself an alibi."

So all along, Lena had thought Peter orchestrated her death? He hated that she'd felt that way. Maybe that's why she couldn't leave. "I was gone for longer that time so I could bring home more money, knowing full well the longer I stayed away, the more likely Oliver would be visiting my mate. I had the damnable notion if I brought in more money this time, and Lena could have what she wanted, she would finally realize I was the one for her. Not Oliver, but me. I can't believe, and yet I can, that Sheridan was the one behind all this. Hell, if I hadn't killed the murderer, he could have told on Sheridan, if anyone had tried to take him to trial. No wonder Sheridan was glad I killed Lena's murderer."

"I'm sorry... I thought you might have killed me."

"I wouldn't have harmed you, honey. I was beside myself with grief when I lost you. What can I do to help you now?"

"Let me go."

He thought he had. He thought he'd given her up a long time ago. He thought falling in love with Meghan and mating her had been proof of that.

"Find someone to love...I'm ready to go."

"I love you, Lena. Despite Oliver coming between us"— and the issue of money—"I always loved you."

"I'm sorry for what I did to you. It wasn't right. I should have known you would never have hurt me. Goodbye, Peter."

Meghan rose, looking a little shaky, glassy-eyed, her soft lips parted as if she had something to say but couldn't.

Peter, forgetting to keep his distance, immediately went to her. As soon as he held Meghan in his arms, he didn't want to let her go. She didn't pull away, melting against him, but her eyes were filled with tears. Then she began to kiss him.

"She's...she's gone?" Peter was hoping, but also hesitant to take this too far.

"Yes. She's gone. She didn't want to see her house in ruins. I thought maybe she'd want to go to the mine tomorrow to meet with Oliver, but I think she realized she had wronged you. Even in death, she must not have wanted to renew her friendship with him. I'm so sorry about all of this. I...I guess it wasn't anything you'd wanted to share with anyone."

"I shouldn't have any secrets from you, Meghan. I love you."

They heard the stairs creaking and turned to see Laurel watching them. "Is everything all right?"

Laurel had to know Lena was gone for good, or Peter wouldn't have been hugging Meghan.

"She's gone," Meghan said. "Permanently."

"Oh, thank God!"

"We're heading home to my place," Meghan said. "Thanks for putting me up here. We'll go to the old homestead to watch the men tear it down, and then we'll visit the mine tomorrow. I guess I won't be working at the inn until the next day."

"Don't worry about it," Laurel said. "We've got it covered. You and Peter need some time alone together, after all that's happened."

"Thanks, Laurel. We'll see you soon." Meghan and Peter said good night, and then they headed out to his vehicle.

"You know, your car is still at my place with my bag of stuff."

Meghan chuckled. "Do you want to get it?"

"Sure, let's make a detour that way, and then we can return to your place for the night." He'd been so shaken up about Lena attaching herself to Meghan that he hadn't had time to make any arrangements to take Meghan's car back to her place.

It was already really late, though.

"Are you going to tell anyone that Sheridan was behind your wife's death?" Meghan asked.

"Only if it comes up. I won't lie about it, but since he was CJ, Brett, Sarandon, and Eric's father, I'd rather not bring it up if I don't have to. They've been through enough with what they've learned he'd pulled." Peter opened the car door for Meghan. "As to my mate's affair with Oliver, the same thing. His parents don't need to know what was going on between their son and my mate, and no one else needs to know either. Unless something comes up that makes it imperative that I tell all. Otherwise, there's no good reason to."

"I agree. Your secrets are safe with me. But I think Clementine and Jessup knew something."

"Would any of this have changed how you felt about me before we mated?" he asked.

Meghan shook her head. "I completely understand why you wouldn't want the pack to know about your mate having an affair with Oliver. I felt so bad for you and wanted to hug you when you were telling your story."

"It was pretty weird talking to you as if you were Lena."

"I know."

"I worried that she might have taken over your body or something. Do you think she suspected about us?" Peter hadn't wanted to upset Lena. He didn't know if she could have taken it out on Meghan or not. He supposed in a way she had because he and Meghan couldn't be together. He was damn glad the business with her was over.

"Maybe, maybe not. It was impossible to tell. I think we kept up the charade pretty well." Meghan sighed. "I'm just so glad we're fine now."

"Hell, yeah." He pulled into his driveway, and then she drove her car back to her place while he followed her. He called Tom, despite how late it was, and said, "Hey, Tom, you're off the hook. Meghan's mine again."

Tom laughed. "Hallelujah. Elizabeth will be thrilled."

"Thanks, bud, for helping out. And thanks to Elizabeth for being such a good sport."

"No problem. You would have done the same for me. I'm glad it all worked out. Is Lena gone now? For good?"

"Yes. I'm following Meghan back to her house. See you at my old homestead tomorrow."

"See you there."

Peter finally pulled into the parking lot next to Meghan's car, got a call, and answered it. "Yeah, Trevor?"

"One of the pack members in Green Valley called to say he found Jake's truck at one of the twenty-four-hour quick stops."

"What shape is it in?"

"Pristine, except that some of those fruit gum wrappers were on the front seat."

"What about Jake's camera?"

"It was under a blanket on the floor of the back seat. It was perfectly fine."

"I'm glad about the camera and the truck, and thanks. I'll let Jake know. Did they impound the vehicle?"

"Pack leader's got it at his house, taking care of it."

"Okay, good." Peter and Trevor ended the call, and Peter called Jake. "Hey, listen. Trevor just got a call that your truck was found in Green Valley."

"In what shape?" Jake asked warily as Peter grabbed his bag out of Meghan's car.

"Good shape." Peter told him the rest, and they ended the call. "God, it's good to be home again," he told Meghan. He felt so lighthearted, the first time he'd felt this good since she'd told him she would mate him.

Once they were inside the house, Peter dropped his bag on the floor and did his usual routine of making sure the place was safe. "All clear." Then he grabbed Meghan up in his arms and rushed her to the stairs. "This is long overdue."

She laughed. "I so agree."

Then they were in the bedroom and stripping off their clothes as fast as they could.

They paused only to kiss each other, her breasts pressed against his chest. She rubbed herself against him as if she couldn't get close enough to hit the sweet spot. His lips fell hungrily on hers, passion stirring between them as he felt her nipples bud against his chest. She was demanding more, parting her lips for his deeper touch, and he quickly pushed his tongue between her lips. She sucked on his tongue, her fingers tracing down his back and lower to his buttocks before she edged them to the bed.

She was only in her bra and panties now, he in his boxer briefs. But he was unfastening her bra and then pulling her panties down before she could get him on the bed.

Then she pulled his boxer briefs down. She loved to see his iron-hard arousal spring free, standing at attention, the tip weeping just a little, begging for release. Just as much as she was already wet for him and needing release.

He cupped her face and kissed her deeply as if he had to draw her in, and she felt the tension in him begin to melt away. He pulled away from the kiss and rested his head against hers, his eyes closed, as if to reassure himself she was his again, and all was right with the world.

She guessed this had been really hard on him, not being able to do anything about his late wife. But none of that mattered now. "It's in the past," she whispered and drew him in for another searing and fiercely raw kiss.

That seemed to draw him back into the here and now, and he immediately took charge of the pleasure at hand, lifting her onto his hips and then crawling into bed with her.

She admired his strength and ran her hands over his biceps. He leaned over her, his darkened eyes filled with lust, and kissed her mouth with tenderness. Then he worked his body between her legs, and she felt the rampant need to have him filling her with his cock. But he began to stroke her inside, wanting her to come first. She reached up and caressed the hard line of his jaw, seeing the determination in his expression, the love for her there, the relief they were together again as mated wolves, and feeling the heat and desperation in his touch.

He was so intense that she wondered if he felt he was reclaiming her as his wolf, and she loved him for it, for wanting to make the connection all over again, to banish all other thoughts that could tear them apart.

His mouth took one of her nipples in and suckled. The shock of it leaped straight to her groin, and she combed her fingers through his hair, relishing the sensations that were rocketing her into space as his other fingers continued to stroke her sensitive nub. She must have clung to his hair for a minute as the tidal wave of a climax crashed over her, and she moaned in absolute ecstasy.

Peter knew he was screwing things up by having a time letting go of what Meghan had gone through—for him—over his late mate. He couldn't begin to say how much he loved her for it and everything else she meant to him. But then the orgasm hit her, and he was glad he'd finally centered all his loving on her and had not been stuck in the past. Now, he was ready to renew their mated vows, and he entered her, gently at first, and then began to thrust. He'd been afraid they would have had to put this off a lot longer, worried that they might not ever resolve things, and now they were free to love each other like they deserved to be loved.

He didn't hold back, wanting to love her all night, realizing just how much he had to lose. He wasn't taking her for granted ever.

She was scraping her nails softly against his legs as he continued to plunge his cock into her, deepening his thrusts as she arched to accommodate him. *Oh yeah, like that*, and then he was coming, every muscle straining. She smiled at him with wicked knowing that he couldn't last much longer. But that wasn't all he had. He'd be back for more.

And the notion he could made his heart soar, right before he came. He finally finished pumping into her and pulled out. Then he rolled off her and onto his back, both of them looking at the ceiling of the canopy, hands linked.

"I think we are truly mated wolves." Meghan patted his sweaty belly.

He turned to look at her and smiled, and then he frowned. "You said you and your sisters wanted to wait."

She raised her brows in question.

"To have babies."

Meghan sighed and placed her hands behind her back and looked up at the canopy again. "I think...it's too late for that."

He chuckled darkly, then settled her in his arms. "That's fine with me."

"Shows your prowess, right?" she asked, smiling at him.

"Hell, yeah. Teach the other guys to be so slow."

She laughed. "Don't you dare start a competition with my brothers-in-law."

He kissed her again and sighed, wishing he didn't have to witness his old homestead being demolished, and that Meghan didn't have to either, but he needed closure, and he suspected she felt the same way.

Chapter 26

IT WAS TWO DAYS BEFORE CHRISTMAS WHEN MEGHAN
and Peter went together to see his house being demolished.
Meghan felt sad for what had gone on there before he had
lost his mate, and then everything that had happened afterward. No matter what, she'd wanted to be with him while he
found closure. But then Peter wrapped his arm around her,
and she knew he was ready to move forward with her, and
everything would be fine between them.

Even though Meghan was certain Lena was gone, she
couldn't help watching the windows for any sign of her
while workers hauled everything salvageable out of the
house. She felt bad that the house had to be torn down—
which was probably due to her need to repair old buildings
and restore them to their former glory. She could see the
beauty in old buildings when others couldn't. But it was a
relief that the dangerous structure would be removed from
the property.

A track-hoe excavator tore at the walls and the roof of
the house, and the onlookers all stood back while the roof
and walls began to collapse in a plume of smoke and dust.

Darien came by to speak with them, and he seemed as
somber as everyone else, considering the reason Peter had
let the property run down. "Thanks for donating the land
to the pack for all the wolves to use. We'll enjoy running
through the forested land once it's safe."

Meghan appreciated that Peter had asked her if it was all right to give the wooded acreage to the pack. He needn't have, but she loved him for being so thoughtful to ask. The pack would pay the taxes on the property and maintain it.

"It'll be put to good use finally after all these years," Peter said, sounding upbeat despite the circumstances.

Darien patted Peter on the back. "It was time to put all of this to rest." Then he smiled at Meghan. "Congratulations to both of you on your mated status."

"I was afraid that was going to be awfully short-lived," Peter said.

"No way," Meghan said. "We would have figured out something if what we did hadn't worked."

About twenty minutes later, the demolished house was stacked on the ground in a pile of debris. A man used a loader to carry the debris to waiting dump trucks that would take the materials to another place to sort through.

Meghan thought about seeing Oliver after lunch and how different she would view him this time. He'd hurt Peter by continuing to have an affair with Lena. Oliver was no longer just someone she knew very little about, but a real person who had foibles like anyone else. If it wasn't for Jessup and Peter being with her when she talked to Oliver, she would have told him she knew all about it and hoped he was sorry for what he had done.

Then she wondered if that was what Oliver needed to do: come clean about it with Peter. That it had nothing to do with Clementine seeing him one last time. Ugh. If that was the case, she didn't want Jessup hearing what had happened. Unless he already knew or suspected what his son had been up to. And she thought he might.

She would see if Peter wanted to go down to the mine with her first and then meet up with Jessup after that.

"I'm headed off to watch the kids so Lelandi can have some of her regular sessions with folks. If the two of you need anything else, just let me know." Darien said goodbye to them and left.

Meghan wasn't sure how long Peter wanted to hang around the old homestead, but she was willing to wait as long as he needed. Though she was ready to go.

She shoved her gloved hands in her pockets. "When we're done here, let's have breakfast at my place. I want to go a little early to the mine to speak with Oliver."

"Before Jessup arrives at the mine?" Peter asked.

"Yeah, we can let him know to come afterward."

"You want to talk to Oliver regarding Lena and me, don't you?" Peter asked.

"Yeah."

Peter frowned. "It's the past—"

"Right, but he might be holding on to the past like Lena was. What if he can't move on because of the business with Lena?"

Peter let out his breath. "Okay, you could be right. Then I'll have some closure too."

Unless Oliver wouldn't admit he was wrong in what he did. Meghan imagined that was the only way he could get closure.

"Come on. The house is demolished, and it'll probably take a day or so to finish the cleanup," Peter said. "Let's eat and resolve the rest of this business, if we can."

Peter and Meghan returned to her home—now their home—and they fixed ham-and-cheese omelets and hot apple cider, then took off for the mine, wanting to arrive before Jessup did.

Peter absolutely dreaded seeing Oliver. Or not really seeing him, but hearing Meghan ask him about Peter's late wife and Oliver's conduct. He didn't know what Oliver would say to her, and he really didn't want her to have to hear it. But at this point, Peter was ready to get this business over with.

When they reached the mine, they were surprised to see Jessup's car already there.

"Well, so much for us getting here earlier than the dad," Meghan said.

"It's got to be said, no matter what," Peter said.

Meghan agreed, and they climbed down into the mine and headed for where Oliver seemed to be hanging out.

Peter couldn't believe it when he heard Clementine's voice deep in the tunnel where they were headed. He glanced at Meghan, and she seemed just as surprised but took his hand as they made their way to Oliver's location.

"I scratched Rollins's face! Okay? He came to tell me Oliver deserved to die for what he wanted to do to him. If you hadn't come out with your shotgun, I don't know what he would have done. But he didn't say he'd murdered Oliver and the other miners. I swear it."

Peter frowned at Meghan. He couldn't believe Clementine, or Jessup, for that matter, hadn't told anyone that they'd seen Rollins before the alert went out.

"How could I know there'd be a manhunt for him later? We were told about all that after he left, including that he'd been in prison. And had escaped from prison!"

Before Peter and Meghan walked much farther, Clementine shut up. Peter figured they'd heard him and Meghan approaching. When they reached them, Jessup was looking ashamed and Clementine had her arms folded across her chest, her chin tilted up in a haughty way.

Meghan greeted both of them and said, "Oliver is here."

Before she could say anything further, Peter needed to get everything off his chest, and maybe it would be the key to helping Oliver leave here. "I know you still loved Lena."

Meghan jerked her head around to stare at Peter, and he guessed he should have given her a heads-up first. But he'd only decided to do this once he was down here. "I don't care if you were sleeping with her."

"How could you accuse him of such a thing?" Clementine said, horrified.

But she sounded like she was horrified he was bringing it up, not that she hadn't known about it all along.

"Oliver's listening," Meghan said, encouraging Peter to continue. She gave Clementine an annoyed look, though.

Glad Oliver and Meghan seemed to think he was handling this well enough, Peter continued. "After Lena and I talked everything over, she went in peace. There's no reason why you and I can't bury the hatchet. You need to make your peace with me so you can move on. Hell, I forgive your transgressions. If our roles had been reversed, I know I wouldn't have been seeing her behind your back, but in my heart, I wouldn't be able to let her go. I understand that. I've moved on and mated Meghan, whom I truly love with all my heart, and the past is the past."

With tears in her eyes, Meghan reached over and took hold of Peter's hand. She nodded at him.

"Don't go," Clementine said in the direction of her son.

Peter frowned at her. So did Meghan.

"Oliver says he's sorry for what he did," Meghan said. "That he was wrong to see Lena. But her parents keeping them apart had been wrong too."

"If it's any consolation to you, she told me she only mated me because her dad had threatened to disinherit her if she'd married you," Peter said to Oliver.

Meghan relayed to Peter, "No, she didn't tell me that. Hell, I must not have been worthy enough either, or she would have kissed her inheritance goodbye."

"We told you she was leading you down a path of ruination!" Clementine said to him. "But you wouldn't listen! She wasn't good enough for you! She—"

"Oliver's leaving now. Thanking you, Peter, for forgiving him. He's gone."

"What did you do that for?" Clementine asked, highly agitated. "I hadn't said my piece with him."

"You said enough. More than enough. You always have," Jessup said, then turned to Peter and Meghan. "Thanks to both of you."

Peter nodded, and Meghan turned and pulled Peter out of the tunnel toward the ladder.

Clementine was still spouting off to Jessup behind them as they followed them out.

"You had your say. Be glad you're still alive," Jessup said to Clementine.

Clementine continued her tirade, her loud voice echoing off the tunnel walls. "I can't believe he was still seeing her. As much as we told him to quit it before he ruined our good family name."

Once they were out of the mine, they said their goodbyes, Jessup shaking Peter's hand and thanking him for forgiving his son. "I'm not sure I could have been man enough
to do it, had I been in your shoes."

"You're not going to say a word about this to anyone, are
you?" Clementine asked, as if she realized her son couldn't
cause them any more grief over Lena, but Peter could.
Meghan too.

"Not that I ever plan to discuss it with anyone. I wouldn't
have now if I hadn't thought it might help Oliver move on.
But if it has any important bearing on anything with the
pack, I won't keep it buried any longer."

Clementine glowered at him, but he said it like it was.
He wasn't going to hide from the past any longer.

Then Jessup nodded. "We understand. Come on, dear."
He led Clementine to their car, and Peter and Meghan
climbed into his and headed back to his place to move
things over to her home.

"I take it Clementine could see and speak to Oliver,"
Peter said.

"Yeah, what a shock. I guess when we first heard her
talking in the tunnel before we reached him, she was rebuk-
ing her son, not Jessup," Meghan said, finally settling back
against the seat. "Oliver appeared grateful we had arrived,
because it stopped her from berating him any further. For
a few minutes anyway. Peter, I so love you. You are such a
good person to have forgiven him. I'm not sure I could have
done so easily if I'd been in your shoes."

"I had my own selfish reasons."

"Oh?"

"Yeah, I didn't want you to have to return to the mine,

and if it helped send Oliver on his way, I was willing to forgive him."

She smiled. "You are the only one for me."

He reached over and squeezed her hand. "Listen, I've been thinking. If I have a murder case—"

"You want me to see if a ghost can tell me what happened?"

"If it wouldn't be too upsetting for you. Maybe he or she could give you a description of the assailant, if the ghost didn't already know who it was, and I could draw a sketch of the perp."

"What a brilliant idea. Here's hoping you never have another murder case to investigate, but if you do, I'll help you out in any way that I can."

"Thanks, Meghan, for everything." And Peter sincerely meant it. She was everything to him.

"Hey, do you want to get some help to move what you need over to my house?"

"I believe we can do it ourselves."

"Nah, it would take too long."

He chuckled. "Sounds like you have some other ideas in mind."

"Yeah, plus I want to see the Christmas lights all over town. I want to know who wins this year's lighting competition."

"You've got a deal."

Then Meghan got a call. "Yeah, Laurel? Woo-hoo! Yes! Talk later. We're going to Peter's house now. Both the miners have found peace." She smiled. "Yes, right before Christmas." Then they ended the call and Meghan told Peter, "Our gingerbread hotel came in first place!

Your outhouses got honorable mention for cleverness. Apparently, several of the judges remembered the old outhouses they had used when they were younger and loved the gingerbread memory. Oh, and Laurel said she's sending some guys over to help us move your things. Apparently, a ton of guys have been waiting to help you move, but they also wanted to harass you about not giving me up."

Peter laughed. He was ready for anything.

Chapter 27

PETER AND MEGHAN SPENT THE REST OF THE MORNING and afternoon moving stuff from Peter's house to her place. The rest he planned to sell or give away the week after Christmas. The bachelor males were all haranguing him in a good-natured way for mating her. She got a kick out of them and was glad they made short work of the move.

Ellie was fixing roast-beef sandwiches for everyone, while Laurel was storing Peter's food items in Meghan's pantry. Meghan was making those fun white Christmas coconut drinks for everyone. When she brought out a tray of the cocktails and sandwiches to the guys, she saw Peter hanging up his Christmas stocking next to hers on the fireplace mantel. She smiled, realizing they truly were a couple for Christmas, and she couldn't have been happier.

Jake chuckled. "He's been looking for his Christmas stocking for over an hour. Someone tossed it into one of the boxes and buried it."

Peter smiled. "If I didn't find it before Christmas Eve, Santa couldn't slip any presents into it."

Everyone gathered in the living room laughed.

Once everyone was done with anything that they could do, they decided to take a drive around town and see all the lights since it was already dark by five. Her sisters and their mates would follow Peter's car, just as extra protection.

Meghan would have loved to do it with her sisters and

their mates anyway, but she hated that she always had to have the protection.

The Silver Town wolf pack loved contests, so they had to have one for Christmas lighting, too, and everyone voted for the most extravagantly, beautifully lit home and business, with runners-up and honorable mentions for each category. They also had categories for most creative and most humorous.

Darien and Lelandi's place won first place for their decorations for the Christmas party. Their house and barn and yard truly looked like a winter wonderland. Silva won the most creative for her tea shop after she created 3-D cups and saucers on top of her roof, teapots decorated in lights and pouring tea.

And the band they always used for activities had the funniest one where they coordinated lights and did their own vocals in a cancan Christmas song fashion.

After looking at the beautiful displays of Christmas lights for about an hour, the sisters and their mates stopped at the tavern for dinner and drinks before they went home to belatedly celebrate Meghan and Peter's mating.

Laurel reminded them, "You know we still have to build our snow wolves. It's our last contest to enter."

The contest had traditionally been for snowmen, but last year, Laurel and CJ had created a snow wolf. It was such a big hit that they won first place, and the contest was now for snowmen or snow sculptures.

"We can't have just one snow wolf this time. It wouldn't be enough," Meghan said. "It's still early." But what she was about to propose would be a lot of work, and she was thinking if they only created a couple of wolves, that wouldn't take too long for all of them to make.

"All six of us," Peter said, smiling. "Has to be. The three sisters and their mates. The six of us."

She loved Peter for being willing to create that many wolves.

"Hey, let's get to it," CJ said.

The ladies all agreed, and so did Brett. "Six wolves," Brett said. "We have to win this time."

They headed across the street to the inn, parked their cars in back, and then went through the inn to the front yard. Bryce looked up from the horror story he was writing at the check-in counter and smiled. "Looks like you're up to something."

"Snowmen competition." Meghan smiled.

"Wolf sculpture," Bryce said, nodding. "Can't wait to see it."

Soon, each couple was working on the first of their wolves.

Laurel and CJ were to the left of them, Meghan and Peter in the center, because she was the middle triplet, and Ellie and Brett on their right nearer to the walkway that led to the inn.

"Our wolves will be facing toward your wolves," Laurel said. "Ours will be howling."

"Ours too," Ellie said, excited about the prospect. "They'll be howling about Meghan and Peter's mating."

"And we'll be nuzzling each other," Meghan said, "cheeks against each other, looking like two happy wolves."

"That's it," Peter said, smiling.

Brett reiterated, "I told you we'd make the winning sculpture this time."

CJ agreed.

They worked for about three hours on the wolves

and then added the finishing touches, securing the scarf Meghan had given Peter around the nuzzling wolves to show they were sharing the warmth. The others each used their own scarves to wrap around their wolves' necks—the ladies' MacTire wool plaid scarves and Christmas scarves the ladies had given their mates last Christmas.

They stood back and looked at the four wolves howling, telling the pack of the mating, and the two wolves in the center, looking happy to be mated.

They heard someone walking on the snow-covered walkway and saw it was Jake with his camera in hand. "I've got to take some pictures of this for the newspaper and for an art gallery."

They all smiled at him.

But once he'd taken several pictures with all the Christmas lights casting sparkles of light onto the sculptures, he had each of the couples stand behind their creations to show not only who had made the snow wolves, but which couples they represented in their snow wolf forms. In playful mode for one of the pictures, Laurel pressed a kiss against CJ's cheek and he was all smiles, Peter and Meghan embraced, lips pressed together in a kiss, and Brett kissed Ellie's cheek while she offered a brilliant smile.

"How did you know we were doing this, Jake?" Meghan asked, surprised to see him here.

"Bryce called me to tell me what you were doing. I've been sitting in the tavern across the street with a number of wolves drinking, eating, and watching you the whole time. One reason we were watching was because we have to keep an eye out for trouble with Rollins, but we were having a blast guessing what you were doing this year. At least everyone in the tavern said they were voting for your wolf snow sculpture."

The MacTire sisters and their mates gave shouts of excitement, all hugged each other, and then hugged Jake too.

"Hey, since we're done here, I think it's time for me to take Meghan to bed…um, home," Peter said.

Meghan felt her face heat and gave him a kiss.

"Yeah, we know what you mean, Boss." CJ slapped him on the back, and then they thanked Jake. The sisters and their mates headed through the inn to reach their cars.

Meghan gave Bryce a thumbs-up.

"Hey, I had to let Jake know about the artwork you were creating, in case the winds messed some of it up, but he said he was already watching the whole thing."

"Thanks, Bryce," Laurel said.

"It's got my vote!" Bryce said.

Meghan hoped the pack wouldn't get tired of them winning. Then again, everyone loved wolves.

Once they all said good night to Bryce, and Meghan's sisters and the Silver brothers walked out to their cars, Peter and Meghan entered her home. He did his usual thing of pulling out his gun and checking over the house to ensure Rollins hadn't broken in.

Then he went outside and motioned to the brothers that everything was all clear as they idled their cars, warming them up, and waited for word. They waved back, and Peter shut and locked the door and pulled off his coat, then hung it in the closet beside hers. He was thrilled to think he was now living with her, sharing the space with her, and was not just an invited guest. He pulled off his scarf and hung it on a scarf holder above hers, then closed the closet door.

"Ohmigod," Meghan said upstairs in the bedroom.

Worried something was wrong and his heart thundering, he raced for the stairs, taking them two at a time until he reached the landing. She'd sounded surprised, not scared, though. He hadn't seen anything that looked bad when he checked for Rollins. Peter reached the bedroom and hurried in to see Meghan looking up at the mistletoe hanging around their curtained bed, over the doorway, and over the bathroom doorway. He glanced in the bathroom and saw one hanging from the shower stall.

He laughed. "I was so busy looking for any sign of Rollins, I never noticed it. The pack never ceases to amaze me."

"Everyone who did this was so cute. Did you know the Druids thought mistletoe chased away evil spirits, but in Norse mythology, it was used as a sign of love and friendship, and that's where the kissing comes from?" She wrapped her arms around his neck and kissed him.

"We don't need any incentive."

"Oh, I so agree. But it is a cute touch."

They pulled aside the curtains. Several sprigs of mistletoe hung from the canopy. They both laughed.

"Are you as cold as I am?" he asked.

"Freezing! After making the snow sculptures for all that time, I can't get warmed up. I would have been undressed for bed already if I hadn't been so cold."

He kissed her nose. "Your nose is cold."

She kissed his and licked his lips. "So is yours."

"How about we take a nice hot bath?"

"Oh, I like that idea."

He went into the bathroom to start the hot water and turned on the overhead heater to keep the room toasty warm. She went into the bathroom and lit little evergreen-and-cinnamon-scented candles. Peter closed the bathroom door to keep the heat in, and then they began to strip out of their clothes, the room getting hot and steamy.

"Perfect," Meghan said, running her hands up his bare chest.

He cupped her breasts and leaned down to kiss her mouth. "*You* are perfect."

While the bathtub filled up with water, they finished stripping and he climbed in first, and then she joined him. He pulled her against his back, loving being in the heated water with her. "Are you warming up now?" He pulled her hair aside and kissed her neck.

"Oh, yeah, this is just the way to do it."

The heat of the water wasn't all that was warming them up. He began to kiss her back and shoulders and then pulled her tighter against his rigid cock. He couldn't help it. When he even thought about making love to his mate, he became aroused.

"Oh my, Peter, I'm not sure I made that wolf anatomically correct at the town square."

He chuckled darkly, cupped her breasts covered in the warm water, and ran his fingers over her rigid nipples. She arched back against him, but he leaned his head over her shoulder and nuzzled her face, moving one of his hands down to stroke her clit.

"Ohmigod," she said, barely breathing out the words.

"Good, huh?" He knew it was, the way she was spreading her legs and trying to lift off. He kept the strokes up, wanting her to climax in the heated tub. They could make love in bed afterward, but this was getting them both nice and warmed up after being out in the cold all that time. And it was something new and different for both of them. He realized he was rather a traditionalist, a little bit of a stick-in-the-mud, so to speak, but with Meghan, he was willing to experiment a bit as long as she got as much pleasure from the experience as he did.

She was holding on to his thighs with a death grip now, so tense he felt she'd snap. He inserted a finger between her folds and stroked inside, releasing her breast with his other hand, and continued to stroke her outside.

"Oh," she cried out, and he felt her shuddering inside with release.

She turned her head, and he kissed her mouth. "That was so good."

"I thought you enjoyed that," he said huskily, needing to finish this before the water cooled down too much and they were cold again. Though the hot shower would work.

He helped her move around so she was facing him, her legs spread over his hips to receive his cock, and he inserted it between her feminine folds and began to thrust upward, making waves in the bathtub. He hoped he didn't make the water spill over the sides.

He continued to thrust into her while she wrapped her arms around his neck and kissed and licked his mouth, tonguing him and then nibbling his ears and his neck. Her teeth and tongue tickled and teased. He was hot, and she was making his blood even hotter. He lowered his face and kissed her lips again, feeling the passion erupt between them as he felt the end coming. His whole body shuddered with release, and he groaned her name out loud.

She smiled at him and held him between her legs for a bit longer, then he pulled out.

"Let's get dry before we get cold, and we'll warm up more in bed." Peter had every intention of making love to her again in a little while.

The next day was Christmas Eve, and Meghan and Peter planned to organize things better after Peter had moved his stuff into the house, but that went out the window when they stayed in bed until early afternoon, getting up only to get to meals, shower, make love again, and then climb back into bed.

After their last bout of lovemaking, Meghan kissed Peter's cheek and said, "We have the Christmas Eve family dinner with the Silver brothers, cousins, and their families starting at three. You know if we don't arrive at Laurel's place on time, they're going to worry something bad has happened." She hated that Rollins was still a dark cloud hanging over their heads. Normally, everyone would have just figured they were being a newly mated couple. Not now.

She could see half the pack arriving within the hour and banging down their door to make sure they were all right.

Peter hugged her tight. "You're right. Let's go have some family fun, and then we'll be back to this."

"We have a deal."

They both hurried to dress and gather the presents they

were giving all the families. Meghan would have bought chocolates from her aunt Clarinda's candy store in Green Valley for everyone, but she knew her aunt would be bringing everyone candy too. So Meghan had started early in the year, making everyone wool scarves. To her amusement, Peter had bought unbreakable hatchets for all the men in each of the families. And for the women, he'd ordered beautiful vases so their mates could fill them with flowers. She'd thought that was cute.

They soon arrived at Laurel and CJ's house, and everyone ushered them in with greetings and good cheer. The party had started without them. Laurel was a wonderful hostess, and Meghan released Peter's hand to help her out in the kitchen, but she wasn't there. Ellie quickly grabbed Meghan's hand and headed her up the stairs.

"What?" Meghan asked, worried, but Ellie looked so happy, Meghan couldn't figure out what was going on.

Ellie hurried her into the master bedroom where Laurel was coming out of the bathroom, looking ashen.

"Oh, no, Laurel, are you sick?" Meghan asked.

Laurel held her stomach and gave her a small smile. "I'm pregnant."

"Ohmigod, Laurel. That's wonderful! Who all knows?" Meghan asked, giving her a warm hug.

"CJ and the two of you."

"You've been having cocktails," Meghan said, worried.

Ellie laughed. "That's the first thing I said."

"CJ's been drinking them, in case it turned out I was pregnant."

"Why, you sneaky guys," Meghan said, giving her another hug. "I'm so excited for the two of you. How did CJ take it?"

"He's over the moon. He's champing at the bit to tell everyone, but he's been waiting until I could tell the two of you."

"Well, I'm over the moon for you both too," Meghan said, just thrilled for her.

"Me too," Ellie said. "Here I thought we'd just be planning Meghan's wedding. But next year, we'll be planning a baby shower too. Jake will be the official wedding and baby photographer."

"Oh, gosh, I forgot about Peter's brother and sister-in-law. We have to let them know we're mated," Meghan said.

"You've had a lot on your mind," Laurel said.

That was an understatement. "Are you feeling well enough to join the party?" Meghan would stay with her sister if she didn't. Ellie and she could swap off.

"Oh, absolutely. Come on, before CJ just dies from not being able to share the good news."

Meghan and Ellie laughed and went downstairs with Laurel.

Everyone who had come to the family gathering heard firsthand from one proud father as CJ wrapped his arm around Laurel and announced their good news.

To the sisters' amusement, everyone took over Laurel's hostess duties and made her play all the Christmas games while she sat on the couch and rested. Even Ellie and Meghan made a nuisance of themselves, checking to see if Laurel had plenty of water to stay hydrated and got enough to eat at the prime rib meal, because, as they told her, she could be feeding a whole bunch of little wolves since her mate was a quadruplet, and she was a triplet. Laurel reminded Ellie and Meghan they could be next. But Peter only had a twin brother, and Meghan wasn't worried. Ellie was in the same boat as Laurel since she'd married one of the four brothers.

Then the doorbell rang, and Peter answered it. Meghan was surprised to see Jessup carrying a big box wrapped in gold-and-silver Christmas paper.

"For Meghan," Jessup said, "for helping us."

"Come on in," Peter said, and CJ brought him a beer.

Ellie brought him a tray of treats while everyone waited for Meghan to open the Christmas box. She couldn't imagine what it could be. When she opened it, she saw it was filled with a whole bunch of angels, one from each family who had lost a family member in the mine, with a little note on them thanking her for learning the truth and sharing it with the pack about how their men had died so that justice could prevail once Rollins met his end.

She quickly brushed away tears. "Thank you. They're beautiful."

"I can't take credit. Clementine actually was the one who organized this at the last minute with all the families still living. And everyone chipped in to pay for the angels for the miners who had perished who had no families left."

Meghan smiled. She assumed the reason Clementine had been so vocal about Meghan and her sisters being ghost-seer frauds was because she was denying her own ability, but she had finally come out. Even Silva had mentioned Clementine bragging about it to a group of ladies at her table at Silva's tea shop.

To Jessup, Meghan said, "Tell her and the others thank you. They're beautiful, and I'll put them on the tree in the inn's lobby to remember each of the miners lost in the Silver

Town Mine." It seemed fitting to give them a place of honor, each and every Christmas.

"I will. But thank you."

Then more Christmas treats were passed around, including some of Aunt Clarinda's peppermint bark candy that Meghan ate too much of. She would have loved to run as a wolf tonight after the party, a special Christmas Eve run with her mate, but with Rollins still out there, she couldn't—and she hated him all the more for it.

She must have looked a little bummed because Peter joined her and rubbed her back. "What's wrong?"

"I'm having a ball, but you know, this is our first Christmas Eve as mates."

He nodded, looking serious but not getting what the matter was.

"I want to run as a wolf with you on Christmas Eve, our first one as mated wolves."

Darien overheard her talking and said, "I don't know why we can't run tonight. A beautiful finale to a beautiful family Christmas celebration."

Jessup looked like he was getting ready to leave, but Lelandi grabbed his arm. "Let's all run, whoever wants to."

Everyone glanced at Laurel.

"I'm running. For heaven's sake, I'm not injured, just pregnant."

Jessup smiled. That was the first he'd heard of it.

After that, everyone was stripping out of their clothes and shifting. Then they began bounding out the wolf door. Once they had gathered outside, CJ and Laurel took the lead, Darien and Lelandi following the group to the park and the woods leading out of town. The snow was lightly falling, and Meghan thought this was the best Christmas Eve ever. Not just because she was mated to Peter and had such a beautiful family, but because the first of her sisters was going to have little wolf pups, and she couldn't wait to be an auntie.

Chapter 28

AFTER MAKING LOVE A COUPLE OF TIMES THAT NIGHT, Peter and Meghan slept in a little the next morning. They snuggled, enjoying the moment, though she was eager to open presents. She couldn't wait to enjoy the aroma of the turkey roasting in the oven, the Christmas tree lights twinkling, while she drank her breakfast tea. On the other hand, she thought Peter could sleep the rest of the day away, happily snuggling with her. No way could she wait any longer, and she kissed his cheek. "I'm going to unwrap presents." With or without him, preferably with him.

He chuckled, rubbed his whiskery chin, and smiled at her. "All right, but we're returning to bed afterward."

"Tired old wolf."

He waggled his brows. "I'll be raring to go."

"I'll be ready." She threw on a pair of red pajamas and her robe.

He tugged on a wolf T-shirt and a pair of shorts, followed her downstairs, and turned on the Christmas tree lights. She made them white chocolate peppermint lattes served in Santa Claus mugs—forget breakfast tea—and added candy canes from their win at the Christmas party.

He started a fire in the fireplace, but she noticed they were running out of wood.

"After opening the presents, I need to cut some wood so we'll have enough for the rest of the day," he said.

She set their mugs on coasters on the table. "Okay." One of his Christmas presents would be perfect for the job.

She couldn't wait to open her first present. She tore off the gold foil paper and pulled a sexy, red baby-doll pajama set out of a box. "I know what you were thinking of when you got this."

"You better believe it." He opened his gift and ran his hand over the soft, blue sweater. "I know what you intend to do to this."

"Run my hands all over you. You bet." The sweaters were for her as much as for him.

He chuckled. "Yeah, just like I intend to do with that." He pointed to her nightwear.

Her next gift was a pink-footed sleeper with wolves all over it.

"To keep the wolves at bay if I ever have to leave you for a night or more. And…to keep you warm in my absence."

She laughed and opened her next present. This one was a short nightie, blue, silky, and with lace trim. "Boy, do I know what you had your mind on when you were Christmas shopping." She knew she wouldn't be wearing any of her nightwear for long when she went to bed with him.

He laughed and opened two more packages of soft sweaters, a green and a dark brown. "For you to hug on me. You must have seen how shabby some of my sweaters were getting. I love my gifts."

"I love mine too. Thank you." She opened a pen and said how lovely it was, but he showed her how it was a tactical pen, with a small knife inside, in case she ever needed protection. "Hopefully, I won't ever have to use it for anything more than a pen, but what a great idea."

Then he opened his next package and laughed. She'd gotten him a new 9mm semiautomatic to use for his own protection, or to protect her. "Thanks. How did you know that was just what I wanted?"

"CJ told me you'd been talking about wanting one."

"That's just great. Thanks." His next gift was an automatic log splitter, and he chuckled. "So much for my new unbreakable hatchet."

"You have the hatchet in case this one breaks down."

"I agree. CJ told me now I can also cut the wood for the inn's fireplace. But he said he and Brett would pitch in whenever I needed them to. He must have known you bought me the log splitter." Peter had gotten her a snow blower and smiled when she removed the wrapping paper. "That's for both of us. It'll be perfect for clearing the walkway between your house and the inn and out to our cars. I can take it out front to clear the walkway from the inn to the sidewalk. Now that I'm actually living on the property, I can help with some of the chores others have been doing for you."

"That'll be great. I never even considered mating you would mean I'd have a live-in snow blower and wood chopper."

He smiled and pulled her in for a kiss. "And lots more."

"Hmm, the lots more is what I can't wait to get back to. But after we have breakfast and watch a movie." She was thinking they'd probably get into the mood right then and there.

The next present she gave him was a shoe rack for their closet, so he could organize his boots and find the matching pairs. He laughed and pointed to a present for her in a box the same size and shape.

"Don't tell me." She opened it and chuckled. He'd gotten

her one, too, for when they came in out of the snow. They could set their shoes on it in the alcove by the front door and coatrack. "I love it. What a great idea." She loved that he knew how she liked to have things organized.

She opened another package and found two new Christmas stockings—both with embroidered wolves. "These are beautiful." Then she smiled when she realized they were filled with something. "All ready for Christmas, I see."

"I commissioned them earlier this year, hoping you'd agree to a mating."

"Whenever you finally got around to asking," she said, smiling.

He smiled back and opened his present and laughed. "Cast-iron wolf Christmas stocking holders, each with our names engraved on them. These are great."

"I had them commissioned at Thanksgiving time with the same thought in mind. Speaking of Christmas stockings, we haven't checked to see what's in our old ones either." She pulled them off the fireplace and handed his to him, then sat down on the couch with him. She poured the little wrapped gifts out of her new Christmas stocking and smiled. "Peppermint candy and mint chocolate candy from Aunt Clarinda's shop."

"Yeah, I figured I could fill the new stockings with our favorite chocolates because they weren't hanging by the fireplace." He poured out his peanut-butter brickle and peanut-butter chocolate cups.

Then they tackled their old Christmas stockings. He laughed at the recipe she'd given him for the MacTire Irish stew. "I guess I'll have to learn how to cook that next." He loved the MacTire plaid scarf she'd made for him. Then he pulled out a cocktail recipe book. "Ha! I guess I am the official family cocktail maker."

"You are." She emptied her stocking and found a black lace garter belt, new stockings, socks with wolves on them, and black lace panties. She laughed again. "I guess you liked the red ones that went with the red dress."

"Yeah, I was thinking you needed a black dress like the red one. I can take you shopping for one when we have the time."

She smiled. "I love all my gifts. This has been the perfect Christmas for me."

"I love my gifts, too, and I feel the same way. Before you were here, I'd just get together with some of the single guys, and we'd watch sports or something. But this is a hundred times better."

"I'd get together with my sisters, and then last year with CJ and my sisters. This has been the best with you. Why don't we start the turkey, and I was thinking about starting breakfast, but..."

Peter pulled her up from the couch and gave her a kiss. "You want to model your lingerie for me?"

She smiled and ran her hands over his T-shirt. "Yeah, I do."

"Good. That's why I got them for you."

"The wolf one first, right?"

"That one you wear when I'm *not* around."

She chuckled, took his hand, and led him into the kitchen. He pulled the turkey out of the fridge while she readied a turkey pan. After they rinsed the turkey and removed the neck and giblets, they put the turkey in a roasting bag and then placed it in the oven and set the timer.

Meghan grabbed up their clothes and carried them

upstairs while he put the shoe racks under the side table to assemble later. She had just placed the new clothes on a chair when she heard him jogging up the stairs to join her.

"Which do you want me to put on?" She held up the red baby-doll pajamas and the blue nightie.

Peter's smile was totally wolfish as he rested his hands on her shoulders and stroked them through the red silky pajamas she was wearing. "This."

She laughed. "You didn't even have to get these for me."

"Oh, yeah, for later." He took them from her hands and set them on top of his sweaters on the chair.

He wasn't waiting for a style show. And she was glad about that.

"This is just as sexy on you. Anything you wear, or *don't* wear, is sexy." He pressed his leg between hers and began to rub. "*You* are sexy."

"So"—she kissed his stubbly chin—"are"—she licked his mouth, her arms wrapping around his neck, feeling her blood heat as he pressed his thigh so wickedly between her legs—"*you*. Every delectable part of you."

He kissed her mouth and his lips lingered there, hot and soft and greedy. She licked the seam between his lips and poked her tongue into his mouth, tasting the peppermint candy and white chocolate latte he'd had earlier. He smiled a little before sucking on her tongue. An erotic shot of electricity went straight to her groin, and she moaned against his mouth. Now she knew how it felt when she did that to him.

He slid his tongue into her mouth and she quickly reciprocated, sucking on his tongue with vigor. He groaned and wrapped his arms around her tighter, his steel-hard cock bumping against her tummy. She ran her fingers underneath his T-shirt, feeling his smooth skin and hard abs all the way to his pebbled nipples. She rubbed them with the heel of the palms of her hands, eliciting a low growl. His wolfish pheromones let her know just how keen he was to have her, how much she was turning him on, her own pheromones eagerly responding.

He slowly moved his hands to her breasts and caressed them through the satiny pajama top, then gently tweaked her budded nipples. She pressed her breasts into his hands, and he cupped them, then leaned down to lick one of the protruding nipples.

Oh God, she was about to come unglued. She pulled his T-shirt up and nuzzled her mouth against one of his nipples, and he jerked his T-shirt off and tossed it. Then he began unbuttoning her pajama top. Slowly at first, making her feel sexy, but then he started working faster. She figured, though he thought the pajamas looked sexy on her, he'd probably prefer one of the new ones he got her. Easier to pull off and toss.

But this was fun, too, as he came to the last button, unfastened it, pulled her top open, and then molded his hands around each breast again. Then he licked and kissed each of them in turn as she slid her hands over his back, loving the muscular feel of him.

She hadn't known what she was missing before Peter. She slid her hands down the back of his shorts and cupped his naked buttocks and pressed him harder against her. She was already slippery and wet for his cock, her body thrumming with need.

He slid her top off her shoulders, and it slipped to the floor. Then he pulled her pajama bottoms down, and she stepped out of them. Eager to free his cock, she slid his shorts down his legs, and he kicked them off. She climbed into bed and he followed her, covering her with his body, lifting her legs around his, and pressing his penis into her.

He was so big, and hard, and perfect for her. He began to thrust, easy at first, then pressing his hand between them to stroke her already swollen clit. She felt her world tilting on end as he continued to stroke her, slowly pushing into her, the feeling more erotic than she'd ever experienced.

She was practically holding her breath as she tensed. The feelings washed over her in a cascade of sensation, the end coming, the exquisite release, and she finally relaxed against the bed, feeling at one with the world, loving her mate with all her heart.

Loving that they could take their relationship to this level on Christmas Day, the first of many to come, Peter began thrusting harder as she propelled her hips upward to take his thrusts. God, how he loved her. He continued to rock into her, harder, easing off, and kissing her breasts, then pumping into her again, no longer able to hold back. He felt the release coming and let go, plunging into her until the very end, and then he held her tight, moving onto his back and pulling her with him so they were still tied together. Then they cuddled, and they slept for a while before she started to stir.

"I'm hungry. Want some breakfast?"

"And more of this," he said, running his hand over her naked thigh. "I'll help clean up the living room, and then I'll get wood for a fire and we can watch a Christmas movie."

"I'd love that. I'll just make us breakfast, and we can sit and eat it in the living room. How do cinnamon buns sound? Or monkey bread? I didn't want to fix anything too heavy for breakfast because we're going to have such a feast for a late lunch."

"Yeah, monkey bread sounds good. And mugs of hot chocolate?"

"You got it. We can run before lunch, if my sisters and their mates are up to it."

"That sounds like a good plan."

They both dressed in jeans, sweaters, and boots, then Meghan cleaned up all the wrapping paper and boxes in the living room while Peter hauled the snow blower outside and returned for the log splitter. She gave him a kiss and headed for the kitchen. Peter put on his coat and went out back to set up the snow blower and try out the new log splitter.

Meghan pulled out the Bundt pan and then brought out two tubes of biscuit dough, a stick of butter, cinnamon, and sugar. She tied on her Merry Christmas apron and was about to preheat the second oven when she heard the doorbell ring. Thinking one of her family members had dropped by with some goodies, she headed for the door and peeked out through the peephole.

A four-foot-tall Christmas angel—the kind that was wired with lights—was sitting on the porch, wearing a big, red bow. She smiled, wondering who had given it to them. When she opened the door, she knew she'd made an awful mistake as soon as Rollins jumped out from behind a snow-covered holly shrub and punched her in the head. Her world instantly turned to night.

Chapter 29

WHEN MEGHAN CAME TO, SHE WAS LYING ON A ROCKY floor shivering. She realized with horror that she was down in one of the tunnels of the Silver Town Mine. Two lanterns were lit nearby.

She smelled Bill's scent, surprising her, and looked over to see him lying on the floor nearby, unconscious, his leg bleeding from what she thought looked like a gunshot wound. His hands were tied together with a plastic tie. She tried to sit up, but her head shrieked with pain and she nearly passed out. She heard someone, most likely Rollins, muttering off in the tunnel out of view. She forced herself to get on her hands and knees, her head swimming, and crawled over to where Bill was. Pulling off her apron, she wrapped it around his wound and wished she had something to cut the plastic tie off his wrists.

"Bill," she whispered. He didn't stir. She didn't think he would be much help fighting Rollins, but maybe the two of them could do something. She needed to shift into her wolf. Maybe she could bite through Bill's plastic tie.

She pulled off her boots and socks and shivered again in the cold. At least Bill was wearing his coat, ski hat, and gloves, which were all black. She suspected he'd been trying to find Rollins. But in the snow? He probably would have blended in better in all white. She hoped he'd be all right. His heart rate was normal, his face pale, but he was breathing steadily.

She heard someone coming and lay down as if she had moved and blacked out again. She wished it was Peter with half the pack coming to rescue her, but she was certain it was Rollins. Peter and the others would have been calling her name.

Rollins drew close to her. "I know you're awake. I can smell your fear, and your heartbeat is racing too fast for someone who is unconscious."

Had he made a study of women he'd beaten to see the effect he'd had on them? The bastard.

She recognized his voice, but he was still wearing hunter's concealment spray. She opened her eyes to see the brown-bearded man staring down at her, his blue eyes hard. He had a few more creases around his mouth now. Scowl lines, not from smiling. And he was wearing a white snowsuit like Bill should have been, seamlessly blending in with the snow.

"I've been waiting for the perfect opportunity to grab you. Bill was easy. He practically gave himself up to me. You were always protected. Except today. The sheriff was out chopping wood, and Jessup left a present on your porch. Perfect timing. He left it as a surprise, probably not wanting to disturb your Christmas, but it made the situation ideal for me. As soon as he left, I hurried to ring your doorbell and hid, hoping your mate wouldn't return to the house and protect you before I could carry you off. I almost feel sorry for Peter. First he lost Lena, now you. He ought to cut his losses and forget mating again."

Meghan couldn't think in terms of Peter losing her and going through the grief all over again. She had to think in terms of winning against the rogue wolf.

"Why are you risking your neck to kill us?" Meghan asked Rollins. "You had your freedom. The Silver Town wolves would never have gone after you if you'd left us alone." Which wasn't true. Once they learned Rollins had killed the miners, they would have tracked him down or sent Anna and Bjornolf to take Rollins down if he was no longer in their territory.

"All I've wanted since I was imprisoned was to kill the two of you. Bill for threatening to kill me, and you for having me imprisoned." Rollins shrugged. "How could I know his warning was just that? He's too weak to do anything more than verbally threaten me. But no one ever bullies me and lives to tell about it. Ask any of the inmates I was incarcerated with. I was so ready to kill you for putting me in that hellhole. You don't know how many times I fought the urge to shift and tear into someone. It took all my strength not to give in to my wolf. And I vowed I'd kill you both for all the trouble you caused me. That's all that kept me sane in there. To learn you were back in my own stomping grounds could cause problems, sure. Everyone knows the old me. My scent. Hunter's spray worked for the most part. But then you kept running into my stashes. How the hell did you manage to do that? You were like a noose around my neck."

"What are you going to do?" Meghan hoped if she could keep him talking, Peter would have time to gather some men and search for her and find her before Rollins could kill her. She imagined no one knew Bill had returned to the area, trying to track Rollins down.

She wanted to strip out of her clothes and shift, then tear into Rollins as a wolf—it was the only weapon she had—but that could take too long and he might shoot her to slow her down. He had a gun holstered at his belt, and she probably wouldn't be able to reach him in time. This was so reminiscent of the last time when she had fought with herself to make the right call. If Rollins shot her, he might not kill her, but she could bleed out before help arrived. It might be better to wait and hope the pack members discovered she and Bill were entombed down here.

"You wanna know what I'm going to do to the two of you? Trap you down here like I was trapped in prison. They'll never get you out before the two of you suffocate. You were right. I killed the other miners, though how the hell you knew that is beyond me. They planned on killing me first."

"For abusing your mother."

"She got what was coming to her. My stepdad was great, and she murdered him. After I do what I gotta do here, I'm outta here for good. No one will ever find me. But I always take care of those who side against me.

"You might want to move back a way so the blast and falling stones don't kill you right off. But, hell, it's your choice. Maybe you'd prefer getting it over with quicker." He moved away from her, and then she saw a wire she hadn't noticed before. He brought out a lighter and moved toward the wire.

Screw it. She wasn't just going to let him dictate the way he wanted this to go. She had to take a chance, even if it was the wrong one. She began stripping out of her clothes as fast as humanly possible.

Rollins glanced over his shoulder and smiled darkly at her as soon as she was naked. "You'll never reach me before I set off the explosion, and you'll be caught up in the blast. Like I said, it's completely your choice."

Her head and heart pounding, she shifted and raced toward him, but she realized as soon as he set the flame to the wire on the dynamite, he could be right. But if he was going to bury them in here, he wasn't leaving either. When his back was turned, she bit into his leg and he cried out. He whipped his gun out. She let go of his leg and grabbed the gun in her mouth before he could point it at her. She pulled it out of his grasp and tossed it back toward Bill like a dog bone. She turned to go after Rollins, but he'd hurried as fast as he could go with his bloodied leg away from her and the blast. She knew she couldn't go after him again before the blast went off and stones fell and killed her. She whipped around and ran back toward Bill's unconscious form. She had to agree with the bastard that Bill would never have managed to kill Rollins. The wolf was too crafty.

The explosion was deafening and shook the walls, roof, and floor of the tunnel. The impact knocked her off her feet, and she fell near Bill, light rock debris and dust raining down all over them.

Coughing as a wolf from all the rock dust, she glanced back at the entryway that was filled with boulders, loose rocks, and debris. Rollins's headlamp light cast a soft glow through the murky dust, poking through a hole big enough she could slip her hand through. She felt a bit of relief that she and Bill were still alive, they weren't cut off from air, but she knew it could be short-lived if Rollins set off another blast and blocked their air supply. Though it appeared they were buried in here anyway.

She worried Rollins was now preparing more dynamite to make sure she and Bill were truly trapped. The only way to fight Rollins was as a wolf. If she could take him out for good this time, then she could get help for Bill. She raced toward the boulders, her head throbbing. She couldn't pass out now. Not when she had to stop Rollins from sealing them in all the way.

She slowed her pace when she reached all the debris and picked her way over the rocks littering the floor, finally reaching the bigger rocks blocking the entrance. The headlamp hadn't moved. With any luck, the explosion had knocked Rollins out. She prayed it was so and that he didn't kill her when she tried to remove the debris that she could and make her way out. Though she realized he might have set his headlamp down on the ground and was still trying to set up another explosion.

She climbed carefully up the angular rocks, then heard groaning on the other side. Maybe the blast had knocked Rollins out initially, but now he was reviving. Hopeful that Rollins was incapacitated for the moment, she had to make a hole big enough to crawl out of and take him out before he could do anything else to harm them.

She reached the hole and had to crawl on her belly to peek through the small opening. Dust particles floated around the headlamp on the rocky floor, the light angled upward. But then she heard Rollins groan again. The sound was coming from the base of the cave-in. She glanced to her left and saw a hand poking out of the rubble. Ohmigod, he had been buried underneath large rocks. Karma came to mind. If he'd left them alone, he could have lived for a long time without any trouble from the wolves. But she suspected she was the one who'd caused him to be pinned under the rocks when she'd bitten him and slowed him down.

She prayed he'd buried himself well enough that he

couldn't move the debris that pinned him down as she shifted and began to pull away smaller rocks from the hole. She felt the ones below her suddenly falling away.

Peter carried logs into the living room and realized Meghan wasn't in the kitchen making the monkey bread. He'd expected to smell the sugary, cinnamon bread cooking. He set the logs on the rack near the fireplace and then called out to her, figuring she was in their bedroom or the bathroom. She didn't respond, and he immediately was concerned. He tore up the stairs, and in a panic, he looked through all the rooms. There was no sign of her.

Heart racing, he called CJ and Trevor on his way down-stairs. He rushed out the front door. "CJ, call the alert roster. Meghan's gone missing. Trevor, gather whoever you can get hold of to start a search." Peter stared at the angel on the porch and saw the card that said it was from the Frasers.

"Rollins," CJ said, his voice dark.

"I'm sure of it." Peter observed footprints by the shrub and along the walk. He saw her car was missing. "Put out an APB on her car. Fresh tire tracks were left in the snow. I'm tracking the car now."

"All right. Tell me where it leads. Talk to you in a minute." CJ hung up.

Peter got in his car and followed the car's tire tracks down the back road. One good thing worked in his favor. It was early Christmas morning. Everyone was probably still at home unwrapping Christmas presents, and all the shops were closed, so no other tire tracks could be seen that morning. After the snowfall they'd had during the night, it couldn't have been more perfect. He just prayed he'd catch up with Meghan before Rollins killed her.

The further he drove, the more he realized what their destination was. He called CJ back. "They're headed for the mine."

"We've got a dozen men ready for search and rescue."

"Send them to the mine."

"Will do." CJ ended the call.

Peter tried to drive faster, but his tires lost traction twice, and if he was going to get there without wrecking his car first, he had to slow down, as much as he hated to. "Meghan, honey, I'm coming. Just hold on," he said out loud in the car, wishing she could hear him and praying he got there before it was too late.

Chapter 30

MEGHAN SLID WITH THE PILE OF ROCKS AS THEY SUD-denly loosened, and more rocks and dust tumbled down. She suffered new bruises and cuts, but she realized she needed to get dressed and work at this further, since Rollins didn't appear to be in any shape to do anything to her. And in truth, she had his gun on this side of the cave-in.

She returned to her clothes and dressed, feeling some-what warmer, then pulled Bill's gloves off, as much as she hated to. She needed to dig at the stones, and the gloves could help protect her from cutting her fingers to shreds.

With willful determination, she climbed back up to the hole that was no longer there, and disheartened, she began pulling the rocks away, seeking the small hole again. She wanted to have any size hole, just to make her feel con-nected to the outside world and continue to have breath-able air. God, she hoped Peter would find them here soon.

Coughing on the dust, she finally managed to create a new hole, smaller than the other one, but she worked on it until it was big enough to poke her hand through. Still, there was a wall of stones between them and the other half of the tunnel that led out of the mine. All they needed to do was make enough of a hole to work their way through.

She kept working at it, making a little progress, finally able to see farther into the other side of the tunnel, but she couldn't make the hole any bigger. Rollins was buried from his shoulders down, only one hand and his head visible, both covered in dust and blood. The large boulders appeared to pin him sufficiently so he couldn't dig himself out without the aid of heavy-duty moving equipment. Good. He wasn't going anywhere. He had tried to bury her and Bill alive like he had the miners so long ago, only this time, he got caught up in his own dastardliness.

His breathing was labored, and when he saw her, he croaked out, "*Hell.*"

But she couldn't leave the mine any more than he could. She needed a pickax to create a bigger hole.

She was relieved he was pinned down and couldn't hurt anyone else. Yet she needed to get Bill help pronto. If Rollins died, would his ghost attach to her? He had unfinished business with her, so it very well could.

Wearily, she tried to dig at rocks farther away, hoping she could maybe break through another part of the wall. She wasn't giving up, no matter what.

"Meghan!" Peter shouted from somewhere far away.

"Here!" she screamed, relief washing over her to hear his beautiful, very concerned voice. "Peter, we're here!" She cupped her mouth, tilted her head back, and howled as a human, able to make just about as perfect a howl as she would as a wolf. She knew he could smell her scent and was able to track her and even Bill down here.

"Meghan!" he shouted, getting closer.

"Here, Peter. We're here! Trapped! Bill's wounded. Gunshot to the leg."

"We're coming! Just hold on. We're almost there."

She thought he was calling from a ladder some distance off. And then she heard running footfalls and the clanking of equipment. She so hoped the pickaxes would suffice and she and Bill wouldn't be stuck down here for too long because the boulders were too big.

She saw Peter heading the pack, running to rescue her. She so loved him. "Peter," she choked out, tears running down her cheeks.

He reached the rubble and climbed up it to stretch his arm into the hole to clasp her hand. She pulled off Bill's glove and took his hand. "We'll get you out, honey. I need you to step far away from the cave-in. We'll start digging at it. Half the pack is here to help."

She smiled to know they would be here at a moment's notice to rescue them. "I'm so sorry they had to do this on Christmas."

"Hell, Rollins was the reason for it. Not you. I love you. We'll get you out soon."

"I love you too." She hated to let go of Peter's hand, but the sooner she moved out of the way, the sooner they could get them out of here. She scrambled down the rock pile and returned to where Bill was finally conscious.

"Sorry," Bill said to her as she pulled his gloves back on his hands. She still couldn't do anything about his plastic tie.

Peter was thankful Meghan was alive. Bruised, scratched, and dusty, but alive.

Rollins's head and hand were the only parts of his body visible from beneath part of the cave-in. The rocks covering him would weigh too much for the men to lift. Rollins had killed himself as surely as if he'd thrown himself down a shaft.

"Looks like you have yourself in a bind," Peter said to Rollins, his tone of voice dark. He was glad Rollins wasn't going anywhere.

"What about him?" CJ asked Peter, pointing at Rollins.

Peter had seen men who had suffered injuries from being crushed, and he knew Rollins wouldn't live, no matter how much their wolf genetics helped heal them faster than humans. It would just mean it would take him longer to die. "He's made his bed."

As much as Bill annoyed him, Peter was worried about his fate. They needed to reach him as quickly as they possibly could.

Peter didn't like the look of the boulders and rocks blocking the entrance to the tunnel, but after talking to the men who had worked in the mine and knew what they were doing, they advised Peter and the other men where to take out the rocks.

Then Peter leveled his pickax at the debris, and other men began to pick away at the rocks and debris while others moved them aside.

The miners had pointed out that boulders blocked much of the rest of the entrance, and they'd have to get heavy-duty power equipment down here to break through the rock if they couldn't manage with the pickaxes in the one area.

But Peter thought the rocks were beginning to give away, and several more fell back inside the tunnel where his beloved mate was.

"Hurry, Peter," Meghan pleaded with them as the pickaxes clanged against the rocks.

He knew she was worried about Bill and the bad shape

he was in. The blamed fool should have left their territory for good like he said he was going to do.

More rocks broke away, and after an hour, Peter was finally able to poke his head through the hole. He saw Bill lying on the other side of the tunnel against a wall, conscious, his leg wrapped in her Christmas apron, and his arm around her, trying to keep her warm. He could see she was shivering.

"Bill's here, bleeding but conscious," Peter said, relaying the information to the other men. "Hey, Bill, we're here to get you out. Rollins is dying, and you won't have to worry about him further." He hoped the news would help Bill hang on until they could get him out.

He turned to the men waiting to help with something. "Did any of you bring bottled water and blankets?" He shrugged out of his coat and pushed it through the hole. "Here, Meghan. Take my coat."

A couple of the men handed him blankets, and another gave him a couple bottles of water and four chocolate candy bars.

Peter took them and shoved the blankets through the hole, one at a time.

Meghan climbed the rocks and reached for the bottles of water and candy bars. She was shivering hard and dropped the candy bars.

"Put my coat on, honey. Get warm."

"Thanks."

She pulled his coat on, then stuck the candy bars and water bottles in the pockets. But before she climbed back down the mountain of rocks, she leaned in to give him a kiss.

"We'll get you out soon." Peter wanted to pull her into

his arms and hug the breath from her. He would, as soon as he could reach her.

She carried the blankets back to Bill, then gave him a bottle of water and a couple of candy bars. Peter began working on the wall of rocks again. Though others relieved the men who were picking at the walls, Peter wouldn't stop until they had broken through enough for him to reach Meghan.

Then a sizable rock broke free and Peter was able to squirm and claw his way through. He ran through the debris on the other side and reached Meghan and Bill while the pickaxes began slamming into the wall to widen it more to make it easier to get Meghan and Bill through.

"Nurse Matthew is here," someone called out.

"Good. Let's get you out of here," Peter said, wanting Meghan out before Rollins died, in case his ghost showed up.

"Bill…"

"We'll stabilize him first, and then we'll move him. Please, Meghan, I want you out of here and safely above." Peter knew she didn't want to leave him, not that she wanted to stay with Bill.

"All right."

Peter patted Bill's shoulder as two men climbed through to aid Bill. "We'll get you out of here in no time." Then Peter carried Meghan to the widened hole and helped her through while CJ took her the rest of the way down the mountain of debris. "Can you take her out of the mine?" Peter asked CJ.

"Yeah, you got it."

CJ lifted Meghan off her feet and carried her back toward the ladder leading out of the mine.

"What happened?" Peter asked Bill as Matthew hooked an IV to him and began a drip line.

"Rollins shot me because, though he said I was too beta to attack him, he wanted to make sure I wouldn't. Bastard. I'm glad he can't hurt anyone else."

"We'll get you doctored up and on your way." And Peter meant out of their territory for good, as soon as Doc Weber said Bill was well enough to travel.

"Hey, man, thanks," Bill said, looking the worse for wear. He was as dust-covered as Meghan, and he was sporting a couple of bruises on his forehead where it looked like Rollins had hit him.

"We'll get you out of here now."

Two of the men brought in a carrier to take Bill to the hole, but they were going to have to pull him through by his shoulders and out the other side, then use the carrier to haul him to the first of the ladders. The guy groaned with every jar of his body and finally passed out from the pain.

As soon as Peter and the rest of the men had climbed through the hole, he saw that Rollins was fading fast, his eyes barely open, his heart rate slowing, and his breathing raspy. Then the man took his last breath.

Trevor checked his pulse. "He's dead."

Two of the men had gone out ahead of the rest to help pull Bill up and out of the mine. Two more hurried to get him up the next ladder. Some had followed behind them. CJ and Meghan were waiting at the last ladder for Peter.

"Thanks, CJ," Peter said. "You can go, and we'll be right behind you. Trevor's going to wait until they can excavate Rollins's body and take it to the morgue."

"I'll stay with him," CJ said and headed back to the cave-in.

Peter gave Meghan a hug. "Come on. Let's get you out of

here." Peter frowned and touched the area beside a bruised place on her forehead. "He hit you."

"Yes, but he didn't shoot me, thankfully."

He pulled her gently in for a hug and kiss, his eyes growing as misty as hers. He cradled her tenderly, their warm embrace comforting him as much as it seemed to comfort her.

Peter wanted to get her home where it was warm and safe.

"How did you figure out where we were?" Meghan asked.

"Because of the snow we had last night, your car's tire tracks led me right to the mine," Peter said. "And then it was easy to follow your scent, Rollins's, and Bill's."

"I was foolish to have opened the front door like that. I just thought the angel was from someone in our pack."

"It was. The Frasers had given it as a gift, I guess wanting to do something more for you."

Then Peter waited for her to reach the opening to the mine. Once she was out, Peter followed her. Some men had already taken Bill to the hospital. That was one thing about the wolf pack; everyone knew what to do, and Peter didn't have to give orders and organize to the last detail.

Then they saw Jessup hurrying to reach them before Peter took her home.

"I'm so sorry I left the present on the doorstep like I did. I didn't want to disturb you, and Clementine and I wanted it to be a surprise. She said the small angel was for the tree, but the big one was to show our profound gratitude for all you have done for us," Jessup said.

"Thank you for the gift. It's lovely. We'll set it up as soon as we get home. I'll cherish it always. It's"—Meghan took a deep breath and shivered—"finally over."

Darien met up with them, and Peter explained what had happened. "We no longer need guard details for the sisters," Peter said. "CJ and Trevor are down at the cave-in where Rollins is entombed."

Darien shook his head. "I'll release them from their duty. It's time for everyone to be with their families for Christmas. It won't hurt for Rollins to stay where he is in the cold cave until we can get a crew down there to excavate him."

Peter was certainly ready for that. "I'll contact the authorities who are looking for Rollins to let them know he's dead."

"Good show."

Peter was glad they no longer had to deal with that concern. He climbed into the car and took Meghan home while Trevor drove her car home for her. Jessup would take Trevor back to his own car after that.

"Are you sure you don't want to see Doc about your head injury or cuts or bruises?" Peter asked Meghan.

"No. I feel fine. We were far enough back from the explosion that we weren't injured when the rocks caved in. Bill was in bad shape because of his gunshot wound and loss of blood. All I need is a warm fire, our new angel lit up outside, um, I guess our monkey bread, turkey dinner, Christmas movies, and most of all—you."

With the fire crackling at the hearth, Christmas lights sparkling on the tree, and the turkey roasting in the oven, Peter wasn't thinking of romancing his little wolf the rest of the day. Instead, he was taking care of her, showing her how much he needed her in his life, and making all her hurts feel better.

But when they arrived home, he saw Brett's car at the house. Brett, Laurel, and Ellie hurried out of the house to greet them. Peter should have known they would be here for Meghan as soon as he brought her home safe and sound.

They all gave Meghan hugs and then moved into the house.

"We'll wait for you downstairs," Laurel said, and Peter took Meghan upstairs to shower and check out all her scratches and bruises.

"They'll heal," Meghan said. "Quickly. It was a good thing I used Bill's gloves, or my hands would have been shredded."

Peter still put several bandages on her worst scrapes, then dried her hair and helped her dress.

Then they hugged and kissed, and he didn't want to ever let her go.

"I think Laurel and Ellie might want to help us make the monkey bread," she said softly.

"And we have a large enough turkey that they should stay for dinner." Peter knew after the worry of nearly losing Meghan for good, everyone would want to be with her longer.

Meghan smiled up at him, and he kissed her mouth again.

"All right. Let's do this," he said.

Delighted that Meghan and Peter wanted them to stay, Laurel took charge and began making the monkey bread. Everyone pitched in, and Peter couldn't have been gladder about taking Meghan as his mate. Not only did he have the joy of being hers for all time, but he had inherited her whole family.

They all began to tear off bits of dough and rolled them into balls and placed them on a plate. They dipped each ball in melted butter, then again in a bowl of cinnamon and sugar, and finally set the balls in the Bundt pan.

Meghan drizzled the rest of the butter on top of the dough, then Laurel sprinkled the remaining cinnamon and sugar on top. Ellie set the pan in the second oven.

"Hot cocoa, everyone?" Peter asked.

Everyone said yes.

"And you'll stay for turkey dinner?" Meghan asked, making sure.

"Absolutely," Laurel said. "We were going to eat leftovers from the party last night, but turkey appeals, if you're feeling up to it."

"We'll take care of it," CJ and Brett said at the same time.

Peter figured if they could show him the ropes, he'd help them.

Ellie smiled. "Brett and I hadn't started cooking anything. We got up really late this morning."

Meghan smiled. "Then it's all settled." She gave Peter a big hug and kiss. "Thanks for helping to make the dinner and coming to my rescue."

"I would do anything for you." He kissed her cheek and led her into the living room. "You need to sit down and rest, and we'll take care of everything else."

He got a call from Dr. Weber and took it. "Hey, Bill came through surgery just fine. The bullet passed through and didn't do much damage. He's receiving blood, and I'll let you know when he's released from my care and on his way out of our territory."

"Thanks, Doc. I appreciate it." Peter knew he and

Meghan would be in bed after visiting with the family for Christmas the rest of the day—with turkey snacks to give them energy, taking it easy until Meghan said she was ready for more, but this was really nice, the family gathering together after what Meghan had been through.

He finished making mugs of cocoa for everyone and topped it with whipped cream. Laurel pulled the monkey bread out of the oven and set it on a platter, then placed it on the coffee table. Ellie set reindeer napkins next to the platter.

They all kicked off their shoes to sit down and watch Christmas movies, share monkey bread, and drink their cocoa, but Peter began gathering the shoes and setting them under the side table, which had Meghan smiling and telling him she loved him.

He loved her right back, more than anything else in the world.

Meghan still had a mild headache after Rollins had knocked her out. She took a couple of pills to help alleviate it, trying not to let anyone notice, but Ellie did. Meghan gave her a look that said not to mention it to anyone. Ellie sighed and nodded.

Meghan felt so much love for Peter and her family for being here for her after what she'd gone through with Rollins. Everyone being here made this Christmas extra special, and she was glad Peter seemed just as pleased to have everyone here. She had really wanted to make the monkey bread for them, but having everyone help made it all the better.

"Next Christmas, we have to do this at Laurel's house," Ellie said, "because of all those cute little wolf pups she's going to have."

Everyone laughed. And Meghan knew this was the beginning of a new family tradition, all of the sisters mated, and wolf pups on the way, monkey bread for breakfast and turkey for dinner, and the rest of the time, playtime with their mates.

She nestled against Peter on the couch as everyone else snuggled with their respective mates, and they smiled as the Christmas movie began. Being mated to Peter made this *the* best Christmas ever.

Epilogue

"MY BROTHER, BJORNOLF, AND HIS WIFE, ANNA, ARE coming to see us to ring in the New Year," Peter said, getting off the phone with his brother and smiling at Meghan. He couldn't have been happier to share the news with his twin brother and his wife that he and Meghan were now mated and they wanted to celebrate it with them. "And they said they'd return for our St. Patrick's Day wedding."

"Oh, that's wonderful!" Meghan was frowning when she saw a large, padded envelope and a medium-size box from the postal service. "What are these for?"

"Just open them," Peter said, hoping she'd be happy with the new Christmas apron and angel and not see either of them as something that brought back bad memories.

She opened the envelope and pulled out the apron that said *Member of the Wolf Pack*, with a picture of everyone with their snow wolves.

"Ohmigod, I love this." She gave Peter a big hug and kiss, her arms wrapped around his neck. "To replace the apron I used on Bill's wound, right?"

"Yeah. Nurse Matthew tried to get the bloodstains out of it at the clinic, but he said they wouldn't come out. I hoped this one would give you better memories."

"Of us finishing the snow wolves that won first place in the snow-sculpture competition? You bet!" She eyed the other box.

He was glad she loved the apron, but he still wasn't sure how she'd regard the angel.

When she opened the box and found a cherub-like angel sitting on a star, she smiled. "For helping Lena move on."

"I hoped you would like it and that it wouldn't bring bad memories."

She hugged him to her breast. "I love it, and I love you. Why didn't I mate you a long time ago?"

He chuckled and kissed her again. "That's what I keep asking myself." He glanced at the clock. "It's time for you to speak to the pack about Rollins. Are you ready?"

She sighed. "Laurel said she's been having bouts of nausea, and Ellie's running things at the inn. So I guess I'm on my own."

"Not at all. I'll be there with you every step of the way."

She slipped the little angel into her coat pocket before he helped her into her coat. "What would I do without you?"

He kissed her, then pulled on his own coat. "I would have convinced you I was the only one for you before long if we hadn't already settled this. I can't even imagine not waking up next to you in the morning, or playing with you in the snow as wolves or as humans. You make my world complete."

He took her hand and led her out to the car. He couldn't be prouder of her.

Meghan felt the same way about Peter making her world complete. She'd worried when her sisters had mated and left her that she might just be feeling the need to have someone around, like her sisters had been all her life. But with Peter, every moment was special. Just the gifts he'd gotten her to bring her better memories of the issues she'd had to deal with showed how special he was to her. She loved him, and when she stood up before who knew how many wolves to talk to them about Rollins, he would be right there beside her.

But she wasn't expecting to walk into the barn to find a whole display of angels as the backdrop for her session. Before she could begin her talk, everyone there gave her a standing ovation for having discovered the truth of what had happened to their men in the mine and helping to take the murderer down. One thing was for certain: she never intended to return to the mine—just in case Rollins's ghost was now haunting the tunnel. She brushed away tears, loving the pack she now truly belonged to, and Peter most of all, standing at her side as her sisters and their mates applauded her.

She turned and kissed Peter, to show the pack he was the reason she was here today.

And the pack cheered even louder as photos were snapped and Peter kissed her back with abandon.

*Read on for a look at Book 1 in the
new Wolff Brother series by Terry Spear*

CO-OWNER OF THE WOLFF TIMBERLINE SKI LODGE,
Blake Wolff had to hurry to get Rosco ready for his canine
avalanche training. He entered the lodge and saw his older
quadruplet brother, Landon, feeding the dog.

"Hey," Landon said, grinning at Blake. "Hell, if I'd
known all the trouble you would have with the snowblower,
I would have come out and helped you."

"You watched."

"Of course. You were really entertaining this morning."

"I hadn't dreamed I'd have that much trouble with it."

Landon laughed. "You won't be so eager to volunteer
when our hired help calls in sick again. I told you it wasn't
a piece of cake."

"Next time, I'll be a pro." Luckily, no one else had seemed to notice, except for one pretty skier in pink and white, who'd made him smile when he'd heard her laughing when he fell on his ass.

He'd had a rough morning of it when the family Saint Bernard, Rosco, had shot off after a rabbit on a walk. Blake had barely been able to stay on his feet on the icy snow while trying to get the dog under control. He swore Rosco had pulled him for half a mile before finally giving up on the chase and doing his business. Rosco was usually well behaved and mild-mannered, until it came to rabbits and squirrels on a walk. The dog had never caught up with one, and Blake wondered what would happen if he ever did.

"Hey, Rosco, are you ready to train to locate avalanche victims?" Blake asked, petting the dog's head.

The Saint Bernard stood and wagged his tail.

"Okay then. When I return, we can take turns skiing?" Blake asked Landon.

"Yeah, you can go first."

"See you in a bit." Blake grabbed the equipment he'd need, then took Rosco out to where several volunteers were being buried in ice caves just out of sight so the avalanche rescue dogs could practice searching and finding them once they were given the signal.

The avalanche "victims" were wrapped in thermal blankets and had hooded, insulated cloaks. Thermal-insulated pads were used to line the snow inside the ice caves, which were dug large enough to give the volunteers plenty of air while the dogs searched for them.

Rosco had to take training every year, and this was a

perfect situation where he could work with *lupus garous*. The Saint Bernard had saved two men's lives after an avalanche at the family's ski resort in Killington, Vermont, so the family was proud of their dog.

"Hey, Blake," Jake Silver said, coming over to shake his hand. He was one of the subleaders of the Silver Town wolf pack and glad they had another rescue dog in the pack. "Is Rosco ready?"

"Hopefully. This will be the first time he'll be looking for our kind buried alive."

"He'll do great."

"Thanks, Jake."

The dogs and their handlers were kept away from the victims' positions so they wouldn't see where the men were being buried. In only thirty minutes, a rescue dog could search two-and-a-half acres of avalanche terrain, unlike humans who would take four hours to cover the same area. Of course, as *lupus garous*, the wolves also had the advantage of being able to smell the scent of humans up to fourteen feet underground, and running as a wolf helped to speed up the equation.

Then the alert whistle called for the dogs' searches to begin.

And the hunt was on. Ten dogs ranging from German shepherds to Labradors and golden retrievers, plus one Saint Bernard, raced off to search for the buried victims. All their handlers ran after them with shovels, probes, and first aid kits.

Nicole was watching her suspects coming off the slope when they turned in the direction of the avalanche dog training. Her suspects and several other skiers had started to watch the trials so Nicole did too. Observing the rescue dogs in motion was fascinating. They ran one way, then another, noses to the ground, and were as excited to find their victims as she was watching them. Then she saw Rosco and his handler, and she smiled. Now she had a handler/dog team she really wanted to cheer on. Not that she didn't want the other dogs to find victims. That was the whole point, and everyone wanted them to work as quickly as they could. But she already had a soft spot for the wolf and his dog. After the business with him trying to get the dog under control on his walk, she really hoped they'd come out on top.

One of the German shepherds had already found a victim and was digging at the snow like crazy, his handler and rescuers ready with shovels to help dig out the volunteer. Rosco was still turning one way and then another, stopping, smelling, wagging his tail like crazy. And then Rosco barked and began digging at another location, snow flying.

Adrenaline was flowing through Nicole's blood, and she hoped Rosco had found his victim. Considering how many people were gathered around him as he started to dig, she figured he had succeeded.

The handler was encouraging Rosco, and then the dog was deep in the hole with only his backside hanging out, his tail wagging. The handler pulled the volunteer out of the ice cave, and the victim gave Rosco a treat as part of the game. It was a way of reinforcing the behavior of finding.

The wolf made sure the victim didn't have any ill effects from being in the ice cave, then slapped the victim on the back and turned his attention to the other handlers' dogs, who also had found victims. The one that had found the first victim was already done. It had taken fifteen minutes for Rosco to find and dig out the victim.

He had done a good job. New dogs could be confused by all the different people who had passed through the area. When all the victims were rescued and checked over, the handlers and dogs took off for their vehicles, all except Rosco and his handler. He gave Rosco a treat and praised him generously. The dog adored him. Suddenly, as if the wolf knew somebody was observing him, he glanced in her direction and looked surprised to see her watching him. He smiled a cocky, little smile and winked.

Nicole felt her whole body flush with heat, which never happened. Of course, she didn't often ogle guys, especially ones who were wolves, and get caught at it.

He led the dog on a leash to the lodge, and Nicole switched her focus to her suspects.

Then she saw Rhys and his cousin headed in her direction, returning to the ski lodge. They were smiling, talking to each other. Before they noticed her, she walked in ahead of them, thinking that this would be a really good time to have her partner to hug. She began looking for a male who appeared to have no female companion at the moment and that she could turn into her boyfriend for just a few minutes as her cover. Of course, it could all backfire if the man made a scene and the cousins witnessed it.

Then she saw the cute guy who had been trying to get the Saint Bernard and the snowblower under control. If anyone deserved a hug, it was him. As long as the wolf didn't have a mate or girlfriend and ruin her Good Samaritan deed.

Besides, it was his fault he'd winked at her after the dog avalanche training.

"How'd Rosco do?" Landon asked Blake. "I wanted to come out and watch, but I got stuck on guest issues."

"Nothing bad, I hope." Blake unhooked Rosco's leash.

"No, typical stuff. Somebody had their TV playing loudly all night. I wish their neighbors had told us last night and we could have dealt with it. One person said he couldn't figure out the coffeemaker."

"We provide the easiest ones to operate to alleviate trouble," Blake said.

"Right. He still couldn't figure it out. Too simple, I guess. He had an aha moment when I showed him how it was done. Then a woman was having trouble with her alarm going off so she finally unplugged it—but she wanted to use it. I had to show her how to reset the times. We probably should have gotten a simpler model."

Blake smiled. "Kayla insisted we have the ones with the automatic change for daylight saving time so we wouldn't have to change all the clocks in the rooms twice a year. I'm glad you were here to take care of the issues. As to Rosco, he did great. He found an avalanche victim in record time."

"I'm glad to hear it. Saint Bernards suit the lodge, and I'm glad he's knuckled down to do his duty during avalanche rescues."

"I agree. We really thought he'd be an avalanche rescue dog dropout when he was a puppy. Have you heard from either of our sisters about the closing?"

Roxie and Kayla planned to join them in Silver Town after closing the deal on the sale of the family's ski lodge in Vermont, but they still had to correct some issues with the lodge before the sale went through.

"I got a call from Kayla. She said she and Roxie accomplished everything needed to satisfy the buyers, so the closing took place and our sisters are on their way here. I should have told you earlier, but you were so busy, and I forgot."

"That's great." Knowing the Vermont lodge had sold was a real relief. Blake was glad his sisters had been able to manage that while he and Landon opened the ski lodge here. "Did they need one of us to pick them up at the airport?"

"No. Kayla said Lelandi was eager to pick them up and welcome them to the pack."

Blake was glad she would do that for them. "Since Lelandi's the coleader and psychologist for the pack, I wonder if she intends to warn them about all the bachelor males who are looking for mates and are anxious to meet with them." That's all he and Landon had heard when they first arrived. Where were their sisters?

"Could be. And she wants to make sure they feel welcome. Which is one of the reasons we all wanted to be part of a pack." Landon glanced around at the hubbub in the lobby: skiers and other visitors were entering or coming out of the restaurant, others leaving the lodge to ski or coming in from skiing, some sitting around the double-sided fireplace. A couple of kids were sitting on the floor petting their sleepy Saint Bernard. "I'm glad our sisters are arriving soon. Kayla needs to help us with our marketing, and Roxie does wonders with the staff. We'll be a lot better organized when they're here. I bet they can't wait to try out the new slopes here too. Powder snow in Colorado instead of ice skiing in Vermont—they'll love it."

"Yeah, they're excited about it." There wasn't anything the family loved more than being part of the ski community. They were also looking forward to having visitors interested in hiking and other sports in the region. They loved being here with a wolf pack, which was why the family had solicited Darien and Lelandi Silver to allow them to open a ski lodge here, once they learned Silver Town was actually run by wolves. Not everyone in the pack had been happy about them opening the business at first. "I think most of the wolves in the pack accept us now," Blake said.

"Yeah. We knew we'd have to work at it a bit. I suspect when our sisters show up, some of the bachelor males will be even more agreeable to us being here."

Blake shook his head. "Roxie and Kayla won't be prepared for the onslaught of dating offers, I bet."

"They might not admit it, but I think they're looking forward to it. Little did we know there were so many males looking for she-wolf mates."

The brothers had worked super hard at trying not to take business from the bed-and-breakfast and the Silver Town Inn in town, doing everything they could to help advertise the other wolves' businesses too. It was good wolf-pack public relations. Most of the wolves were warming up to them being here. They'd finally opened the Hungry Wolff's Bar and Grill at the lodge, and that had also concerned some of the business owners in town.

The Silver Town Tavern, which boasted the best drinks and lunches and dinners around, was open exclusively to wolves, courtesy of a high-dollar membership that the wolves didn't really pay, so human visitors needed some-place else to go for dinner. Even so, the tavern's owner, Sam, and his mate, Silva, had worried the Wolff restaurant might take more of the wolf population's business. Silva ran the Victorian Tea Shop, which was open for lunches, but not everyone wanted to leave the slopes to eat lunch in town.

The ski lodge featured a large deck, offering dining for skiers who wanted to grab an appetizer, a drink, or a meal before they hit the slopes, and they had indoor dining too. A lot of folks came there on dates, not just to ski.

The Wolff brothers had downplayed their competitive nature, so this past Christmas, they hadn't participated in any of the competitions—snowmen or snow sculptures, gingerbread houses, even Christmas lighting. They'd dec-orated the whole lodge in lights, of course, but they hadn't entered their place in the competitions. Except for getting their business off the ground and making it a profitable ven-ture, they hadn't had time for a whole lot of anything else.

"Looks like I've got some business to take care of." Landon frowned, his gaze focused on someone behind Blake who he could hear was fast approaching. From the sound of the ski boots on the tile floor, he thought the person was female. "You go ski, and when you're done, I'll take a few runs down the slope."

Blake glanced back and saw the pretty blond he'd noticed observing him and Rosco during the avalanche training. She was headed straight for them, her expression intense, brows furrowed, her gaze shifting from Landon to Blake. He smelled a whiff of her scent—fresh air and she-wolf. No wonder his brother was eager to assist her. At the same time, Blake was a little embarrassed that the woman approaching had witnessed him struggling with the snowblower. Good thing she hadn't seen him with an out-of-control Saint Bernard even earlier.

Blake smiled. "I can hang around for a moment and take care of whatever issues she's having."

"No, that's okay, Blake. The sooner you ski, the sooner I get to."

Blake knew that wasn't the only reason his brother wanted to take care of the woman's concerns. Landon had recognized she was a wolf too.

When she drew closer to them, she targeted Blake, and he was eager to be the one to handle whatever was upsetting her. *Happily.* Conflict didn't bother him or his brother. It was a chance to prove they could resolve any issues that arose at the lodge with the least amount of fuss. When he caught another whiff of her wolfish scent, that made him even more eager to help her. Though he reminded himself she could have a mate or a potential one.

She smiled brightly at Blake, her cheeks and the tip of her nose rosy from the cold. She was wearing a white parka, the furry hood down; a light-pink-and-white ski hat, dickey, and gloves; and light-pink formfitting ski pants and white ski boots, looking as if she'd just came off the slopes. She reminded him of cotton candy and snow bunnies, innocent and sweet.

When she reached Blake, she threw her arms around him in a hug, startling him. He smiled down at her, amused at where this was going. Since he was single, he didn't have to worry about a mate throwing a fit. If he had, all she'd have to do was smell this woman all over him, and he would have been in the doghouse. As long as the woman hugging him didn't have a mate either. Then again, wolves mated for life, so she probably wouldn't act this way if she were mated or courting another wolf. She could smell that he didn't have a she-wolf's scent on him either. Not until now.

He was surprised at her action. Did she think he was someone else? But she would recognize his scent, which quashed that theory. The only other thought that flashed through his mind was that she was trying to pretend she had a relationship with him because some guy was hassling her. Whatever the reason, he was all too willing to play along and take care of whoever was giving her trouble.

She kissed him, startling him even more, and his brother laughed. "It appears your day is looking up, and I think you have a handle on this." Still chuckling, Landon walked off.

Blake was enraptured with the woman. Her lips were soft and malleable as she pressed them gently against his, but she began building up the steam, licking his mouth and then nipping and melding hers with his.

Relishing the scent of the she-wolf and the crisp, cold out-of-doors that she carried with her, Blake wrapped his arms around her waist and pulled her tighter against his body, enjoying her soft curves and warmth, building a slow fire deep inside him. They were kissing like they needed a room, he realized, not family fare in the lobby of their lodge. He *very* reluctantly pulled his mouth from hers and smiled. "Do I know you?"

"Took you long enough to ask." She smiled up at him, and he wondered what he was getting himself into.

Hell, he was game.

"I'm Nicole Grayson, and you're my fiancé. For the moment. My life depends on it."

Blake frowned, worrying she was really in trouble, though she didn't seem overly anxious—not in her facial expression, and certainly not in the way she'd been so easily intimate with him. "Do we need to call the sheriff?" He should have already had his phone out, but he didn't want to let go of her if there wasn't any need. This was just too damn nice.

"No, I've got a handle on this."

He wanted to laugh at her choice of words since Landon had said the same thing about Blake. "All right, good show. By the way, I'm Blake Wolff."

"Wolf? I'll say."

He smiled. He liked her easy banter and didn't think she could be in any real danger. He would have smelled her anxiety for one thing, instead of her enticing arousal that was fueling his own. "I'd shake your hand, but I think we're beyond that."

"For this to be believable, yes." She smiled up at him as if she truly adored him. "I saw all the trouble you were having with the snowblower earlier."

"Uh, yeah." That kind of blew his macho image, he was afraid. He had hoped she wouldn't bring it up. "I've never used that kind before."

"I kind of figured that. I haven't either, or I would have tried to help."

He smiled. "You watched instead."

Her cheeks pinkened. "You were entertaining."

"You saw everything?"

"You mean the spill you took too? Yeah, you should have seen me hit a patch of ice on the slope this morning. I was sprawled every which way."

He chuckled, not feeling as bad now. He liked how she could make him feel better about it. "I was just going to ski. Did you want to come with me?" He thought that would be fun, if it was in line with the ruse she was playing and because they would both be dressed for it once he put on some ski boots. Besides, he hadn't been this interested in a she-wolf since he and Susie Northrop ended things between them. She'd been so pissed off that he and his brother and sisters were moving to the "wilds" of Colorado, the Wild West, she said, that she broke it off with him a year before he left. Good thing for that.

"I just came in from out-of-doors. Take me to your room instead," Nicole said.

He raised a brow. He hadn't quite expected that. Then again, he hadn't expected any of this—the hug, the kiss, now this. He wasn't letting go of her though. "Because your life depends on it."

"It would seem more realistic. If we're lovers. And we can talk."

None of this seemed real to Blake. Well, the kiss sure did, but the rest? No.

He rubbed her arm, his other arm still keeping her locked against his body. His was hot and aroused, to be sure. He couldn't believe how much he didn't want to let her go. Then again, she was the one who had tackled him first.

He glanced around the lobby, looking to see if anyone was eyeing them with speculation. Their guests all seemed to be enjoying visiting with friends or were on their way somewhere—to the restaurant, restrooms, seating by the big center fireplace, out-of-doors to ski, or to their rooms. "Okay, we have a little problem with going to 'my' room."

"Don't tell me your roommate won't go along with it."
She sighed.

"I'm not staying here."

"Okay, you can come to my room. But my partner has high-altitude sickness and might be sleeping."

"Partner. Male?" As in a *real* boyfriend? That could be awkward. Then again, he couldn't be, since Blake didn't smell a male's scent on her except his own. Blake hadn't met her before, but he was definitely showing any other eligible wolf bachelors here that he had a real interest in her. Was she was part of the Silver Town pack, and he just hadn't met her yet? He didn't think so, or she wouldn't be staying at the lodge.

"Yes, he's a he. So you live in Silver Town? And are just up here for the day skiing?"

"I'm part owner of the ski lodge and restaurant, along with my brother and two sisters." He normally wouldn't have mentioned that to a she-wolf he'd just met who wasn't a member of the pack, feeling like it was bragging a little.

Her brows rose this time. "Oh, *Wolff* as in two *f*'s. Okay, this won't do. I need to find somebody else." She started to pull away from him.

He held on tight. "No. Wait."

She smiled up at him again. Then she frowned. "I shouldn't involve you. You seem like a nice guy."

"I'm already involved. And I can be a not-so-nice guy if you need me to. Ask my brother and sisters."

She chuckled, but then she grew serious again. "Okay, here the two men come. Make this look good. You can be my lover, and Larry is my brother."

"Larry, as in your partner?"

"Yes." She didn't give Blake a chance to ask any more questions as she kissed him again.

She didn't smell like she'd been around another male, so he didn't think the guy was really her partner as in mated. Instead, Nicole was wearing Blake's scent and he was cloaked in her sweet fragrance, making it seem, to other wolves, that *they* were together.

Blake had every intention of making it look real, but he wanted to see who she was worried about. He wanted to ask her who she was, who her "partner" was.

For now, he concentrated on the workout they were having, his mouth pressed hungrily against hers, and that was not faked in the least. She kissed him back just as greedily, her olive-green eyes feral as she gazed up at him, and then closed them again to concentrate on the kiss.

He could feel her pulling her mouth away finally, and he reluctantly went along with the plan. Her cheeks were flushed with heat, her gaze still on his mouth, as if she was thinking of kissing him again.

He smiled. She was hot and interesting, and he could have kissed her all day long.

She sighed. "Let's go."

Blake glanced back to see if his brother was busy working. Landon was standing near the fireplace, arms folded across his chest, watching them, smiling. Which was normal for a family member and a wolf who was curious how this would play out.

"Wow, we leave you guys alone for a couple of months, and what do we come home to?" Blake's sister Roxie asked. He turned to see her and their sister Kayla openmouthed and staring at him in surprise.

Acknowledgments

Thanks so much to Donna Fournier, Dottie Jones, and Darla Taylor for beta reading this book! All their comments were so helpful and much appreciated. And thanks to Bonnie Gill and Cheryl Amer for Christmas present ideas. Thanks to Deb Werksman for all her wisdom and loving the books! And to the wonderful cover designs that readers want to take to bed with them.

About the Author

Bestselling and award-winning author Terry Spear has written over sixty paranormal romance novels and four medieval Highland historical romances. Her first werewolf romance, *Heart of the Wolf*, was named a 2008 *Publishers Weekly*'s Best Book of the Year, and her subsequent titles have garnered high praise and hit the *USA Today* bestseller list. A retired officer of the U.S. Army Reserves, Terry lives in Spring, Texas, where she is working on her next wolf, jaguar, cougar, and bear shifter romances, continuing with her Highland medieval romances, and having fun with her young adult novels. When she's not writing, she's photographing everything that catches her eye, making teddy bears, and playing with her Havanese puppies and grandbaby. For more information, please visit terryspear.com or follow her on Twitter @TerrySpear. She is also on Facebook at facebook.com/terry.spear. And Terry Spear's Shifters on Wordpress at terryspear.wordpress.com.

Also by Terry Spear

SEAL Wolf

A SEAL in Wolf's Clothing

A SEAL Wolf Christmas

SEAL Wolf Hunting

SEAL Wolf in Too Deep

SEAL Wolf Undercover

SEAL Wolf Surrender

Heart of the Shifter

You Had Me at Jaguar

Billionaire Wolf

Billionaire in Wolf's Clothing

*A Billionaire Wolf for
Christmas*

Silver Town Wolf

Destiny of the Wolf

Wolf Fever

Dreaming of the Wolf

Silence of the Wolf

A Silver Wolf Christmas

Alpha Wolf Need Not Apply

*Between a Wolf
and a Hard Place*

All's Fair in Love and Wolf

Heart of the Jaguar

Savage Hunger

Jaguar Fever

Jaguar Hunt

Jaguar Pride

A Very Jaguar Christmas

Highland Wolf

Heart of the Highland Wolf

A Howl for a Highlander

*A Highland
Werewolf Wedding*

Hero of a Highland Wolf

A Highland Wolf Christmas

White Wolf

*Dreaming of a
White Wolf Christmas*

Flight of the White Wolf

Heart of the Wolf

Heart of the Wolf

To Tempt the Wolf

Legend of the White Wolf

Seduced by the Wolf